P9-DNC-211

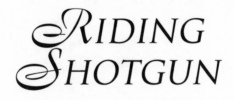

RIDING SHOTGUN

BOOKS BY RITA MAE BROWN

The Hand That Cradles the Rock

Songs to a Handsome Woman

The Plain Brown Rapper

Rubyfruit Jungle

In Her Day

Six of One

Southern Discomfort

Sudden Death

High Hearts

Starting from Scratch:
A Different Kind of Writers' Manual

Bingo

Venus Envy

Dolley:
A Novel of Dolley Madison in Love and War

And the Mrs. Murphy Mysteries with Sneaky Pie Brown
Wish You Were Here

Rest in Pieces

Murder at Monticello

Pay Dirt

RIDING SHOTGUN

RITA MAE BROWN

BANTAM BOOKS
New York   Toronto   London   Sydney   Auckland

RIDING SHOTGUN
A Bantam Book / April 1996

All rights reserved.
Copyright © 1996 by American Artists, Ltd.

Book design by Donna Sinisgalli

No part of this book may be reproduced or transmitted in any
form or by any means, electronic or mechanical, including
photocopying, recording, or by any information storage and
retrieval system, without permission in writing from the publisher.
For information address: Bantam Books.

Library of Congress Cataloging-in-Publication Data

Brown, Rita Mae.
Riding shotgun / Rita Mae Brown.
p.   cm.
ISBN 0-553-09605-2
I. Title
PS3552.R698R53   1996
813'.54—dc20   95-36103
CIP

Published simultaneously in the United States and Canada

Bantam Books are published by Bantam Books, a division of Bantam Doubleday Dell
Publishing Group, Inc. Its trademark, consisting of the words "Bantam Books" and the
portrayal of a rooster, is Registered in U.S. Patent and Trademark Office and in other
countries. Marca Registrada. Bantam Books, 1540 Broadway, New York, New York
10036.

PRINTED IN THE UNITED STATES OF AMERICA

BVG   10 9 8 7 6 5 4 3 2 1

With love

to

Herbert Claiborne Jones, Dr. Foxhunting

AUTHOR'S NOTE

Flopping on my butt and sliding over an entire acre, the ice six inches thick, caused my mind to speed along as fast as my body. During the winter of 1993, the power died: no heat, no hot food, no hot water . . . and no light except for candles during those long, dark nights.

As I searched my shelves for something to read, I passed on my Greek and Latin books. After all, I was struggling enough trying to keep the farm going during the hammering storms. Did I really want to conjugate irregular verbs?

Then I thought about improving my German. That might require a miracle beyond study.

I pulled out *Das Kapital,* put it right back with a big "ugh."

The worn spines of *Tom Jones, War and Peace,* all of Jane Austen, and all of Turgenev greeted me, but I'd read them many times. I wanted something new, something to take me away.

It wasn't just the ice storms battering me, I'd lost a chunk of my timber crop to the pine beetle; acres and acres of fine, healthy trees quickly devastated; and not a hint of relief from Washington. Between that and the Tax Reform Act of 1986, I was feeling like the tail end of bad luck.

I tried to look on the bright side. None of my horses or cattle had died in the storms. No tractors or trucks had been smashed. No one had broken any bones, and the fences were still standing, despite the battering.

Still, I wanted something to read to escape my troubles, small when compared to some of the truly awful things that can happen, but troubles nonetheless.

Travel was impossible for a week during the worst storm. I couldn't cruise into town and pick up a new novel. So I wrote one.

Riding Shotgun was started with a pen and yellow tablet while I sat in front of the fireplace surrounded by cats, dogs, and one abandoned puppy. The winds howled, rattling the windows, the snow swirled with each gust.

Whenever and wherever you pick up this novel, I hope the weather will be kinder, and whatever troubles you may have will vanish for an hour or two.

Rita Mae Brown, M.F.H.
Afton, Virginia

PART I

1

Cig Blackwood was stuck the entire day with a middle-aged couple from L.A. who were bent on fleeing that unstable basin. It wasn't just the earthquakes they wanted to put behind them, it was everyone else in the Los Angeles basin, all three million of them squeezed into a crescent once paradisial and now parasitic.

The husband, Troy Benedict—though that could hardly be his real name—wore a burgundy silk shirt buttoned so high up on his neck Cig wondered if his Adam's apple might not be pressed into a cherry. A dark, swirling-patterned tie, a pair of perfectly pressed khaki pants, and crocodile Gucci loafers completed what he perceived as his country outfit. His Schaffhausen watch cost more than the car in which she was carrying them. The wife, Lizbeth, must have been on her second facelift because her eyebrows were poised midway between her eyes and her hairline. The hair itself had been crimped so that it exactly resembled a Hereford's tail. And it was about the same color, too.

Lizbeth, Versace all the way, wished to share her innermost feelings with Cig as they drove through the emerald rolling hills of central Virginia. Each time they stopped to inspect an elegant estate, nothing under a million and a half, Lizbeth would discover some resonance of her childhood or her first marriage or the three films she'd acted in during the late 1970s—"B.T." as she said. "Before Troy." These confidences, registered in a lowered, breathy voice, must have been a form of big-city female bonding, Cig thought. To her a bond was what the dentist stuck on your teeth, or if you were a little kinky, something you did in bed with black leather.

During these intimate exchanges, Lizbeth probed Cig's own psyche while Troy inspected the heating system or put his hands—no callouses—on the basement walls searching for dampness, unaware that dampness and central Virginia were synonymous. If you want dry, she longed to tell him, go to the Sahara.

Lizbeth, when not wrenching treasures from her deepest self, breathed Troy's name every third sentence. This cast a spell on him as though his name were a mantra that belonged on the lips of his wife and, Cig suspected, on other women's lips as well.

Cig, trapped in her aging Wagoneer, which guzzled gas like rednecks guzzle beer, heard how Troy, president of Mecca Studios for fifteen years, a miracle of survival in that business, had been forced out in a conglomerate takeover.

Lizbeth embellished her story. "Troy, poor darling, used to drag home from meetings with ungrateful producers and egotistical directors—they were the absolute worst—and he'd say, 'When I grow up I'm going to be a farmer.' And here we are. The takeover by those dreadful people was a blessing in disguise."

Cig thought to herself, Yes, indeed, farming in a two-thousand-dollar Versace scarf.

At three in the afternoon she dropped the Benedicts at Keswick Hall, just east of Charlottesville. It was the only hotel that approached their comfort zone, a phrase Lizbeth repeatedly used.

They waved merrily, and Cig waved back good-bye, a smile frozen on her face like dried glacé. Her shoulders sagged as soon as they crossed the threshold.

Troy had used her car phone every five minutes. The bill would be more than her mortgage. He assured her he'd pay, he'd simply forgotten his cellular phone. Cig believed such promises when the check cleared the bank. Her experience was that often people with the most money were the most insensitive to others' need for it—on time.

She headed back to the office, turned on the radio and listened to twenty ads in the half hour it took to get back to the Boar's Head complex. As she clicked off the radio she knew she wasn't a true American because she didn't buy Chevrolet, America's truck; she'd never be beautiful because she didn't use the antiaging compound touted by Princess Marcella Borghese; and she didn't really know how to have a good time because she rarely drank an ice-cold Bud. Funny that women's voices never sold beer on the radio. Would men switch brands if they heard a woman's voice pitching the sudsy brew? She gladly would have grabbed a beer at that moment despite the antifemale bias of brewers, anything to wind down, but the day was far from over.

An avalanche of pink message slips spilled out of her office mailbox. Tiffany, the receptionist at Cartwell and McShane, known lovingly among the women realtors as Slutbunny, never folded message slips for anyone—they were just stuffed into the wooden cubicle—except the messages for Max Cartwell, the head broker and company owner. His messages were delivered personally. Why anyone would want to name her child after a Yankee jewelry store mystified Cig, but then why anyone would keep Tiffany as a receptionist also mystified her. If she'd been the girl's mother she would have wrapped her lunch in a road map.

As she picked up her messages—two already from Troy and Lizbeth—Tiffany flounced by.

"Roger Davis called. I've been so busy I just didn't have time to write it down."

No, but she'd had time to do her nails. Plum today. Went nicely with the magenta silk blouse and the black skirt clinging just above the dimpled knees.

"Thanks."

"Oh, Mrs. Blackwood, I have a video of my cousin singing at the Foxfield Races. She was the entertainer for the Mobile Phone Company's annual picnic. Do you think Mr. Benedict would look at it?" Her impulse was to flirt, but since that rarely worked with women, Tiffany's approach had an uneven quality to it.

"No. He ran a film company. You need to send the video to a record company."

"What about the music in movies?" Tiffany was either very loyal to her family or getting a percentage of the action.

"The producer selects the composer. It's a closed circle, Tiffany. You need a record producer." Cig, while not an expert on media responsibilities, knew the basics.

She eyed the mountain of paper on her desk as an annoyed Tiffany sashayed off. On top of the pile was an article cut from the tabloid paper that Jane Fogleman insisted on bringing to work every morning to read aloud over everyone's second cup of coffee. Jane should have been on *Entertainment Tonight* because her rendition of aliens turning Granny into a sex-crazed rap goddess filled the office with screams of laughter.

The attached note read,

"Cig, you were out with the mogul at the crack of dawn, so I saved this clipping for you. P.S.: Do you need me to whip in or should I just whip Roger instead?"

Being Master of the Jefferson Hunt, a full-time job, unpaid, was a labor of love for Cig. There were too many times recently when it provided the only happiness she enjoyed. As the Master of Foxhounds, she assigned the task of assisting the Huntsman to keep the hounds moving in the right direction. Called whippers-in, these wild riders were the unsung heroes of foxhunting. Actually, fox chasing was the more accurate term. Jefferson Hunt did not want to kill foxes.

The clipping saved for her benefit was about a twenty-five-year-old woman living in Milwaukee who claimed to have the Bible tattooed on her eyelids. This way she would never close her eyes on the Word of God. She also had the Bible tattooed on her other parts; there was something spiritually uplifting about seeing the Lord's Prayer disappear into considerable cleavage only to reappear on the sumptuous right bosom. One would have to part the protuberances to fully read the prayer. Then again, that may have been a sacrament of the good woman's form of worship.

Cig held up the clipping just as Jane popped her head in the door. "Her temple is a body open twenty-four hours a day for worship."

"Three points." Jane made an imaginary basketball toss at Cig. "Sell any property?"

"They like Hardtack Manor. But then again, Lizbeth feels a deep emotional pull toward Cloverfields. The walls speak to her."

"And what do they say?"

Cig dropped her voice to a hollow whisper. " *'Spend money . . .'* Course it's been vacant for five years," she continued. "Today I heard about Lizbeth's struggle for self-esteem. She snorted too much white powder and her breasts were too small, past tense, I assure you. Her search for meaning encompassed everything from channeling to a macrobiotic diet to Prozac followed by week-long fasts. And let's not forget Freudian analysis five days a week. I think I would have liked her better if she'd gotten drunk and rolled in the gutter with those sex-crazed Martians. I don't know, Jane, either it's too late to force-feed people manners or I'm a callous bitch. I don't want to hear this shit."

"M-m-m. You have your moments but I don't believe confession substitutes for conversation. It's different for us. We're connected over time, our families knew one another. Out there no one is connected to anything. Maybe they think if they vomit up these intimacies they'll feel close to one another."

"No. They'll just have a mess to clean up."

"You've got a mess to clean up no matter what you do," Jane said matter-of-factly.

"Would be super if the Benedicts would buy Hardtack Manor and restore it. Remember the barn dances old Miz Amorous used to give when we were in high school? She'd tell us about her seven husbands, or was it eight?"

"I think some were unofficial, which was why Andy's mom kept her away from the sauce. She thought it would fry our innocent ears. Andy, to his credit, is the male version of his grandma. He never met a woman he didn't like."

Jane clapped her hands together. "Harleyetta West is reported to have had lunch with Andy yesterday. Now that is a truly fascinating prospect."

"Who did the reporting?" Cig, prepared to dismiss the gossip, challenged.

"A reliable source."

"There is no reliable source in Charlottesville."

"Your sister, Grace."

"Oh." Cig's voice dropped. "Well, just who was she having lunch with?"

"I forgot to ask her that." Jane leaned against the doorway. "How long are the Benedicts in town?"

"I don't know." Cig sighed. "We must all seem like repressed snobs to them because they sure seem like three-dollar bills to us."

"We are repressed snobs, Cig. And if we're not snobs we're still insular. That's part of our charm, we're so parochial."

"Call for you on line six, Miz Fogleman." Tiffany yelled when she could have easily buzzed. Except that she had never completely mastered the switchboard.

"Hell. Want me to whip?" she called over her shoulder.

"Yes."

That welcome intrusion over, Cig again stared at the pile of papers. She heard the beep of the fax machine down the hall in the office machine room. After the beep came the odd grinding noise the fax made as the page slowly appeared, the machine sticking out its paper tongue. Her colleagues said they didn't know how they had lived before the fax. She did. She had liked it just fine.

The beeper, the fax, the Xerox, the computer, the cellular phone, and whatever interactive media would be invented and merchandised soon—these technologies supposedly simplified life but all they did to Cig was add more pressure, especially the fax's implicit demand for instant replies. If Cig acted in haste she wasn't as concise or precise as if she'd had time to collect her thoughts. Lately, she wasn't sure she had any thoughts to collect.

She checked her watch. Four thirty. She gathered up brochures, messages, notes, and standardized forms, shoving them into her tote bag.

Her younger child, Laura, aged fifteen, was waiting to be picked up from field hockey.

Laura, dark, intense, and athletic, looked a great deal like Cig's younger sister, Grace, a stunning beauty with jet black hair and electrifying cobalt blue eyes. People who didn't know the family often mistook Laura for Grace's daughter.

As Cig dashed through the office foyer, the senior partner in Cartwell and McShane, a University of Virginia graduate in 1969 who never got over it, strode out of his office.

"How'd it go?" Max Cartwell gave her a hearty slap on the back.

"Good. They love the area."

"Well, close that sale, Cig. A big commission in this one." The shine of profit glowed on his reddish skin.

"Evermost on my mind," Cig truthfully replied, although she lacked that ruthless instinct that makes a successful realtor close a sale even when knowing the property is dead wrong for the buyer.

"Oh, we changed the in-house meeting to Tuesday at four."

"Okay. As long as you don't ask me to be in charge of training the new recruits, I'll be there."

His face wrinkled. "But you're so good at it."

"Max, it's fall. The Jefferson Hunt is one of the things that makes this area so attractive. I'll train recruits in the spring."

"Forgot. Forgot. You're right." Max, a golfer himself, appreciated the sporting attractions of Albemarle County. "Say, you think this Benedict guy could get us a high-definition television? Wasn't his company bought out by Sony?"

"No, that was Columbia Pictures."

Max snapped his fingers. "Damn."

"The right deal will come your way, Max." And you'll milk everyone you know in the process, she thought to herself.

In the car she remembered she hadn't called Roger Davis. She picked up her cellular phone. It was heavy and too fat for her hands. She punched in his number, the digits making beeping sounds of different pitches.

"Roger, it's Cig. Sorry I missed your call. I'm picking up Laura. I'll leave the car phone on. I'll be at the barn in forty-five minutes. It's now almost five." She pressed the "End" button but not the "Off." Roger was punctual about picking up his messages.

The high school parking lot, still filled with cars, hove into view in ten minutes. Without traffic it would have taken five but Charlottesville, like so many small attractive cities, had outgrown its road system, a fact that was painfully obvious at rush hour, especially with the weekend starting.

Laura, fuming because her mom was a few minutes late, waited at the side of the field, her best friend, curly haired, adorable Parry Tetrick at her side.

"Hi, Parry."

"Hello, Mrs. Blackwood." Parry smiled, which only enhanced her sweet demeanor.

"Mom, you're always late," Laura groused.

"Next year you can drive. Let's see how on time you are."

"Parry, need a ride home?"

"Uh—"

"She does." Laura threw her gear in the back of the Wagoneer, as did Parry. Their hockey sticks clattered together as they both climbed into the back seat.

Cig smiled—a limo service. She handed the cellular phone to Parry. "Do you need to call your mom and tell her you're on the way?"

"No." Parry handed the phone back up front. "Mom's cool."

The two girls fell into a conversation about school, about their coach shifting people into different positions and that old standby of gossip: who was dating whom. Cig pulled into the Tetrick driveway.

"Thank you, Mrs. Blackwood."

"You're quite welcome, Parry. Come out and visit us real soon." Cig liked Parry. She was a level-headed kid.

Parry stared a moment at Laura then hurried to the front door.

"Are you moving up front or am I that boring?"

"Huh?"

"Laura, are you to the left of Pluto or what?"

"Sorry, Mom." Laura hopped out. "Shotgun." She slid into the passenger seat closing the heavy door behind her. "The only time I get this seat is when Hunter's not in the car." Laura gazed out the window as they left the manicured grounds of the Tetrick residence.

"Not true."

"Is so."

"Unh-uh." Cig shook her head.

"It is, Mom. Hunter's a real pig about riding shotgun."

"Hunter's driving that ancient truck so he's hardly ever in this car."

"Ah," Laura pounced on this, "but for the first fourteen years of my life he always took the shotgun seat. I'm damaged forever. I think I'll go on talk shows, Mom. It's child abuse."

"Tragic."

A long silence ensued. "Made an A on my pop quiz in English."

"Goody."

"And Donny Forbush asked me to the Harvest Dance."

"And?"

"I said no." Laura turned her beautiful blue eyes to search her mother's face. "I like him, but—I don't know."

"He's a nice fellow, Donny Forbush, and very popular, but if you aren't wild about going to the dance with him, okay by me."

"Uncle Will won't like it."

"Uncle Will doesn't run this family."

"Well, he's trying to since Dad died."

"You leave Uncle Will to me." Cig smiled.

"Mom—he's so concerned about social stuff, like Donny's father being our state representative. Uncle Will wants me to brownnose the Forbushes."

"Like I said, leave Uncle Will to me."

"Harleyetta gave me the color test. I'm a winter complexion." Laura jumped to another subject, a habit of hers, disconcerting, like her father's.

"Harleyetta should stick to nursing."

"But Mom, it's true. I borrowed Hunter's dark green shirt and everyone told me I looked great."

"Hunter know you borrowed his shirt?"

"No, I ran home and washed and ironed it before he even knew it was missing." A smug smile crossed her full lips. "Guys don't care about clothes."

"Your father cared more than I do. No more borrowing your brother's shirts unless you ask. Hear?"

"I hear."

"Yes, but are you listening?"

"Oh, Mom." Laura slumped in her seat as they turned off Route 250 onto the narrow paved road that would lead to the long gravel of the driveway.

"You need to work Mosby and Go To. Oh, and Roberta's coming for a lesson. Which reminds me, how did Reebok go yesterday?" Cig asked about the saintly horse responsible for Roberta Ericson's welfare.

"Push-button."

They drove down the dusty driveway to the barn. Peachpaws, the golden retriever, rushed out to greet them as did Woodrow, the huge, long-haired tiger cat who leaped on the hood of the car to pat the windshield, his form of "Hello."

"Hey, big fella." Cig got out and scooped up the cat in her arms, which inflamed Peachpaw's jealousy. Laura called the dog to her and fussed over him. It generally took five to ten minutes for the animals to settle down.

Hunter, seventeen, tall and bearing a strong resemblance to his mother, was riding Kodiak, his Aunt Grace's horse, in the ring. He waved when he saw his mother and sister.

"Aunt Grace isn't coming out today?" Laura sounded disappointed.

"Later. She's afraid she won't have time to ride so Hunter's working Kodiak. We don't want him too fresh for tomorrow. You know we always get good foxes at Muster Meadow."

Cig walked into the tackroom, Woodrow still in her arms, placed him on a saddle, and quickly changed her clothes while Laura pulled on her paddock boots.

"Laura, don't wear your good shirt to ride."

"I won't, Mom. I've got my sweater."

The phone rang. Inwardly Cig groaned and picked it up. "Hello, After All Farm. Oh, hi, Lizbeth. Yes, I just got to the barn, and you're the first on my list to call as soon as I zip up my pants."

"Is there any way we could see Maplewood on Sunday? I've been going over the brochure and the vibes are just fabulous from that place."

"I'll call the owner and see if it's convenient."

"We've scratched Hardtack off our list for a second visit. I thought the living room was wonderful but Troy says the heating system is too old, and he doesn't want to replace it. He wants a turnkey operation."

"I can certainly understand that." Which she could.

"And we're going to bring along our video camera and shoot everything. That will help us. I don't know why we didn't think about it today. Too fuzzy, I guess."

"That's fine, Lizbeth, just don't shoot me."

Lizbeth giggled, then hung up.

"Mom?"

"Yo."

"No one's going to talk me into going to the Harvest Dance with Donny."

"No one's trying to." Cig grunted as she pulled on her left boot. Woodrow watched but declined comment.

"Well, someone will."

"Don't pay any attention."

"I won't."

Cig tapped a little baby powder into the right boot. She'd forgotten to do it to the left. It slid on like butter. "Hey, child unit."

"Oh, Mom, you're so corny."

"You call me 'parental unit.' "

"It's different when I do it."

"I see." Cig walked out into the center aisle of the old, airy barn, Peachpaws at her heels. "Why don't you want to go to the dance with Donny though? He's the most popular boy in the senior class. Not that I'm trying to force you. I just want you to be well-armed when Uncle Will starts his motor."

"He's kind of arrogant." Laura fumbled.

She clapped her daughter on the back, then opened Reebok's stall door. "Good for you. I never could stand men like that."

The 15.2-hand foxhunter nickered. He was one of those golden horses, not pretty, not wildly talented, won't win ribbons at the big shows, but totally bombproof. He'd get you through trappy ground, over a stone fence, through a narrow gate. If you made a mistake, he covered up for you. The better the rider the more she learned to appreciate the Reeboks of the world.

Cig brushed him off, threw on his everyday blue saddle pad, floppy and worn, then slipped on his bridle as he ducked his head for her. Just as she put the saddle on his back Roberta Ericson bustled into the barn.

"Yoo hoo."

"In Reebok's stall, Roberta."

"Well, aren't you nice. That's my job."

"I figured you were running late and we'll run out of daylight."

"That's the only thing I hate about fall. Once we get on the other side of September twenty-first we lose a minute of light a day."

"Actually, Miss Ericson, we lose a minute a day after June twenty-first. The equinox in autumn means we now have less light than darkness." Laura picked Go To's hooves as he stood in the crossties in the aisle.

"You're right." Roberta smiled. A tiny woman with tight curls on her head, she'd never had children of her own. She adored Cig's kids.

Cig quietly said, "Since when do you correct your elders, Miss Priss?"

"Mom, I wasn't correcting."

Roberta jumped in, "She was illuminating, not correcting."

"You two are thick as thieves." Cig grinned as she led Reebok out of the stall.

"Hello, Miss Ericson." Hunter smiled when she rode into the arena.

"Hello, Hunter."

"Mom, you want me to ride Full Throttle?" Hunter loved to ride his mother's horse.

She looked at the sun dipping closer to the mountains. "You'd better. Just keep a light leg, Hunter. You know he hates a strong leg."

"I know. Hey, Mom, did you hear that Jessie Wells is pregnant?"

"If I didn't come out here for riding lessons I'd never know what was going on in this town." Roberta shook her head.

"No, I didn't know. It's your turn to feed the dog and cat tonight. Remind Laura she's on salad duty."

"Okay." He rode Kodiak back to the barn.

"Jessie Wells." A flutter of Roberta's eyelashes accompanied the shake of her head. "Ever since her parents divorced that girl's been crying for attention."

"Well, she got it," Cig said forthrightly.

"Only ten minutes without stirrups," Roberta pleaded as Cig prepared to work her on the longe line. "My legs will be jelly tomorrow if we do any more."

"Cross your stirrups. Ten minutes." Cig fed out the longe line and clucked to Reebok who obediently picked up a nice even trot. "Okay, toes down. Toes up. Toes out. Toes in. Good. Hands over your head. Now out from your sides. Make little circles with your arms. Okay, right arm only. Left arm only. Toes down. Toes up. Toes out. Toes in."

"I hate the toe part."

"It's worse for ballerinas."

This made Roberta laugh. Cig longed her for five minutes in one direction and then five in the other. After that she unsnapped the longe line and set a figure-eight course for Roberta. The jumps weren't over two and a half feet but the size wasn't important. Getting Roberta to stay in a nice even canter with soft hands was what was important.

"Eyes up," Cig barked at her when Roberta dropped her eyes over a jump.

"Oh, I know." Roberta pursed her lips together.

She finished the rest of the course in good order.

"You look good. How do you feel?"

"Good. Except I still tense up before the jump. I wish I'd stop that."

"You will. Look how far you've come."

"Really?"

"Well, two years ago you swore you'd never foxhunt because you'd never take those jumps and look at you now."

After Roberta's lesson was finished, Laura and Hunter picked out the remaining stalls, and Cig fed those horses on field board out of the rubber buckets hanging on the fence posts. Field boarders didn't come into stalls at night but stayed in the fields, a situation that pleased them immensely, since many horses got bored in a stall.

If Cig could keep the twelve-stall barn full and keep another ten to twelve horses as field boarders she could pay her mortgage. Whatever she made selling real estate, never a sure thing, took care of food and other necessities. If she could sell a big farm to the Benedicts she'd be able to pay off some outstanding debts and put a little away for the kids' college fees. She prayed but never spent the money before she'd made it.

Very often buyers would come back year after year until they found just the right place. Cig had worn out so many sets of tires for the Wagoneer she'd lost count. Some years were good. Some years were bad. The last four years business had taken a nosedive. Even though interest rates were relatively low, taxes shot up, and people were scared. Sooner or later the Federal Reserve would hike the interest rate again with the immediate damaging effect on real estate. People also didn't trust that they'd make enough money over the long haul to purchase the house of their dreams. This mood of fear infected everyone and everything. Cig often thought to herself that if businesspeople—farmers and people who had to make a payroll—ran the government, things would be dramatically different. But the age of the citizen politician passed with the tricorn hat. Public service had devolved to professionals whose first order of business was their own job security. She'd soured on most of them.

And she'd soured on real estate. Many people regarded realtors as a lower life form, right down there with used-car salesmen. She didn't want to sell property, she wanted to sell homes. She liked finding the right property for a person. Max used to kid her that this approach was due to raging estrogen. She never refuted him. She didn't find that an insult even though he'd meant it to be. More of an insult was the constant pressure to sell, sell, sell, no matter how shabby the methods.

"Mom, I'm done," Laura called out.

"Go start the salad then. I'll be there in a few—"

Laura interrupted, "What's Hunter doing?"

"He has to feed Woodrow and Peachpaws."

Mollified that her brother didn't have an easier time of it than herself, Laura trudged up to the house. The sun was setting, an autumn chill descending with it.

The phone rang in the tackroom. Cig hurried in to pick it up. "After All Farm."

"Where do you want to cast tomorrow?" Roger's tenor voice rang out.

"Back side of Muster Meadow."

"Well," he hedged, "I'm taking the full complement tomorrow. I think the young hounds really have blossomed of late, and I don't know if they'll slow us down, but I think not. I don't want to walk them through the woods, I can't count on the puppies' discipline. How about if I cast off the dirt road? Or I can cast down by the river."

"Cast off the road. You can lift them if it doesn't work out. Bet we wind up by the river anyway."

Hounds were "cast" just like a net. Cig found hunting language poetic.

"Jezebel bit Delilah. Got her on antibiotics."

"She's a hateful bitch but such a good hunting hound." Cig was sympathetic.

"It's her drive."

"I need some of Jezzie's drive myself. I'll see you tomorrow, Rog."

A thin blade of light blue wedged between the dark sky and the mountains. A wisp of pink still hovered on the rim of the tallest mountain.

Cig checked each stall for water and hay. Checked the tack. Checked the truck and trailer. She took ten minutes to fill the hay nets and hang them inside the trailer. One less chore to do in the morning. She loathed leaving in a rush because she always forgot something when she did.

Laura's job was to put their whips, hunt caps, and a spare bridle in the trailer. Cig opened the door to the trailer tackroom. Laura had done her job without any haranguing from her mother. With a small smile, Cig shut the door. Before she could walk up to the house the phone rang.

"After All Farm."

"I'm not selling my land for three hundred and forty thousand dollars, goddammit!"

"Now Harmon, you just do what you want." Cig's heart sank.

Harmon Nestle owned a nice patch of land way out Garth Road. When his mother died five years back the land was divided between the two brothers, Harmon and Mason. Mason sold his one hundred acres for three hundred and sixty thousand dollars last year but his land had a small lake on it. Harmon's did not.

"Why you bothering me with this?"

"Because I am bound as a realtor to bring you every offer in writing. That's why I left the contract in your screen door when you weren't home. Even if they offered two thousand dollars I would have to bring you the contract. Otherwise you could accuse me of holding out for more money and a higher commission."

"You'd never do that."

"Well, thank you."

"Don't be doing business with people you don't know and trust."

"Good point." But she was resigned to spending the rest of her life carting around strangers to properties. How could you trust them? As for getting listings, that was usually a matter of friendship as well as the ability to get results.

"I got to get as much as Mason. Hear?"

"I hear you. We'll get there." She had no idea whether or not they would but Harmon sure didn't make it any easier.

Gruffly he said, "I'm tired of waiting."

"I understand. It is frustrating but if you counter at three hundred and sixty thousand I'll take the contract back to these folks. They are really interested. We might can work something out."

"I'll think on it. Good-bye." He slammed down the phone.

Most people couldn't see farther than the nose on their face. Harmon was one of them. Cig hung up the phone, paused a moment, and hoped she'd never be that narrow a person, circumscribed by the tiny circle of family and friends. Harmon was ready to blow a good deal because he wanted to equal or best his brother. The reality of the lake meant nothing to him. His only reality was lifelong competition with Mason—and Mason was usually the winner.

Cig sprinted up to the house, the cold nipping at her heels.

She opened the mud room door, wiped her boots on the bristly hedgehog on the stoop, and then stepped inside. She checked the soles of her boots. Clean. She hung up her barn jacket on a peg, then opened the door into the kitchen. Laura was twirling the salad greens in the crisper while Hunter set the table.

They really are good kids, she thought to herself. Whatever else I've done in this world at least I produced two good people.

She overlooked the conspicuous silence.

2

In the background the television showed mangled corpses from an unexplained explosion in a midwestern granary.

"Hunter, turn off the news. I can't face that stuff tonight."

He clicked off the set just as Grace came through the back door. Woodrow and Peachpaws rushed to greet her. The cat hopped up on his hind legs and then rubbed against her leg. She bent down to scratch him behind the ears. Peachpaws wanted to shake hands.

"Just in time for supper."

"What are you having?" Grace walked over to inspect Laura's salad. "Umm."

"Beggars can't be choosers," Cig replied.

"Ain't that the truth." Grace agreed, and joined Cig at the stove. "I'll do the veggies, if you do the pork chops. You're better at meat than I am." Grace tossed her luxurious vicuña shawl on the church pew along the wall.

"How come you don't have some ball or ameliorative social function to attend?"

Grace slit open a pouch of baby limas and grabbed a microwave-proof dish out of the cupboard. "Will's staying late at the hospital, and there aren't any balls tonight. If there were I'd make you go with me so I could relish your misery."

Cig stabbed at the pork chops in the big iron skillet. "I'd sooner bleed from the throat than go to one of those balls."

"I'll go." Laura spoke up. "I need experience."

"Are you sure this isn't your child?" Cig pretended to stab at Laura with the meat fork.

"We look alike," Grace said.

"Think alike," Laura chimed in.

"You think?" Hunter appeared surprised.

"Ha, ha." Laura ignored him.

"What's the scoop, Grace? Harleyetta West had lunch with Andy Trowbridge and you saw them. So who were you having lunch with—hmmm?"

Grace opened the microwave to pull out the lima beans and remembered she'd forgotten a hotpad, which Hunter threw at her. "Thanks." She caught it and fetched the lima beans. "Cig, how far along are you with the pork chops?"

"Far enough. You can put those in a bowl *while* you tell me about your lunch. I'm more interested in that than in Harleyetta and Andy Trowbridge, although I'd never blame her if she had an affair."

"Imagine being married to Binky West." Laura shuddered.

"He looks like a manatee in drag." Cig laughed.

"He wouldn't be so bad if you could get the shot glass out of his mouth." Hunter put ice cubes in each of the glasses, poured water, and surveyed his handiwork. He decided something was missing and disappeared from the kitchen.

"Hunter, we're about to eat," Cig called after him.

"I know." The voice receded.

"Who were you having lunch with?" Cig's voice became more insistent.

"What are you, my keeper?"

"I am my sister's keeper."

"Yeah, well—" Grace pinched Laura as she carried the big salad bowl to the table. "Walt Manceron. He's on the committee for the Cancer Ball."

"He's also drop-dead gorgeous." Cig commented on the owner of the BMW dealership.

"That fact has not escaped me." Grace smiled, revealing perfect teeth. "Nor the fact that maybe he'll even give me a discount on that 7 series BMW I'm lusting after."

"Lust for more than a 750i and he'll give you the car," Cig said wryly.

"Aunt Grace, all you have to do is wink at them. Men fall at your feet." Laura stood behind her chair as the adults put the rest of the food on the table.

Hunter reappeared with a handful of golden mums. He plopped them in a low crystal vase and put them on the table.

"A centerpiece." Grace beamed.

"We needed something." He held the chair for his aunt as she sat down and then did the same for his mother. "I took them out of the back garden."

"Good idea. The season will soon be over and we should enjoy them." Cig was happy to get off her feet. She felt suddenly exhausted.

"What about me?" Laura, hands on hips, stood before her chair.

"What if I pull it out from under you?" He nonetheless seated his sister.

"Let's say grace." Cig reached for her sister's hand, and they all held hands around the table.

"Heavenly Father, thank you for the food we are about to receive into our bodies and the love which we receive into our souls. Amen."

"Amen," they said in unison, each squeezing hands.

Hunter filled his plate, while the women watched in awe. Conversation could wait a moment. He was starved.

"Laura, what do you have to tell me?"

"Nothing, Aunt Grace."

"Donny Forbush asked her to the Harvest Dance." Hunter filled in the blanks. "She spurned him," he continued in mock horror.

Laura glared at her brother. "So what!"

Grace cut into her pork chop. "Let's not tell my husband, shall we?"

"Uncle Will will find out sooner or later," Laura said.

"Later." Grace's voice had an edge to it. "Listen, he's so busy at the hospital he probably won't hear about it until after the dance so let's not push it."

"He's in tight with the Forbushes. He will notice," Laura declared.

Cig shot her a reproving look, although she agreed with her. Laura ducked her head and concentrated on her food.

Grace said, "Dr. William Von Hugel saves lives, he genuinely helps people, but let's just say that he has his peculiarities, as do we all. He feels there are right people and 'unright' people."

Hunter and Laura looked quickly at one another and then back at Grace, whom they loved and adored. But then everyone adored Grace.

"Will's not the only one." Cig sighed. "Laura, your salad is very good. Tossing in the sunflower seeds was inspired."

The phone rang. Cig groaned.

Laura jumped out of her chair. "I'll get it!"

They heard a polite murmur, signifying that the call must not be for Laura. "For you, Mom."

Cig, her mouth full of delicious pork chop, wiped her lips with her napkin and excused herself from the table. While answering the phone during supper was uncivilized she couldn't afford to lose business. The battery acid churned in her stomach.

"Hello."

"Hello," Lizbeth said. "Listen, we've decided to fly out tomorrow. Troy wants to look for property around Bozeman, Montana. We'll compare and then let you know if we'll be coming back."

Cig's stomach knotted. "It's supposed to be unbelievably beautiful out there in Montana. I hope you find what you're looking for there—or here."

"Thanks. Ciao." Lizbeth hung up the phone.

Cig returned to the table and sat down heavily.

The kids said nothing.

"More Looky Lous?" That's what Grace called people who ran a realtor's legs off then decided they weren't ready to buy, didn't have the money, or didn't like the area. Realtors, unofficial tour guides, got the shaft more often than they got the sale.

"Yep."

Hunter and Laura finished eating, then patiently waited for the adults to finish. Cig noticed.

"Go on. I'll do the dishes."

"Thanks, Mom." They both scooted from the table.

Grace and Cig cleared the table. While Grace stacked the dishwasher, Cig built a fire in the big living room fireplace. She poured out two glasses of vintage port.

Grace joined her, kicked off her shoes and flopped on the comfortable old sofa. Woodrow stretched out on the back of it, while Peachpaws collapsed in front of the fire screen.

"Sorry about the buyers, Cig. Jane told me they'd been looking at really expensive stuff. That commission would have been a godsend."

"If I really thought about it I could be incontinent in my hostility." Cig felt morose.

A loud blare from upstairs could have shattered the windows. Cig lurched up and trotted upstairs. What good would it do to yell? They couldn't hear her.

"They'll all be deaf by the time they're thirty." Cig reached for her glass again as soon as she returned, the music turned down. "I'm beat, and tomorrow is a five thirty wake-up."

"I still operate on the three-alarm system. One by the bed, one halfway to the bathroom, and one in the bathroom. Will sleeps in the other room on hunting nights."

Cig's mind switched back to business. "I'll probably never see the Benedicts again, and much as I need the commission, I'm relieved. The wife comes out with the damnedest things. The first day I became well-acquainted with her physical person. Most especially her high-fiber, no-fat diet. But each day she yakked more and more about how she felt when she turned thirty. She hasn't admitted to turning forty yet and my guess is she's on the near side of fifty. Jesus, but it was one thing after another. By the third day she was discussing the relative strength of orgasms according to the position."

Grace laughed. "I'd have paid good money for that one."

"And the husband would occasionally open his mouth to insert some important fact into the conversation, well, monologue was closer to it, and she'd shut up and look at him as though he were Albert Einstein. Believe me, that's a woman who's earned every Cartier bauble dangling from her starved body."

"Was he smart?"

"Hell no. Dumb as a sack of hammers. He didn't even know that sandy loam perks differently than clay, nor did he care."

"He has to be smart about something if he's looking at properties going for a million dollars."

Cig thought about that. "I guess in his business he is, but haven't you ever noticed how a man or a woman can be just terrific at one thing and completely oblivious to everything else—and they expect to have their asses kissed at regular intervals anyway?"

"I'm married to one." Grace held out her glass for more port.

"Will isn't that bad." Cig poured.

"He's not that good."

They sat in one another's company, staring into the fire.

"Isn't it queer to be alive today?" Grace broke the silence. "I feel like we're living through the end of something but I'm not sure what it is. Oh, here I am getting morose, and the reason I stopped by was that I thought you might need cheering up tonight."

"Me?"

Grace knew her sister too well to be surprised that Cig was slow to admit the significance of the day. "Tomorrow Blackie will have been dead a year."

"He did fall off his perch on October twenty-second, didn't he?" Cig tried to make light of the day that had changed her life forever, plunging her into grief and debt simultaneously.

"Cig, you don't have to be tough for me."

"I'm much more worried about money right now than my emotions. If I can keep my boarders and pick up some more lessons, I can make the mortgage, the electric bill, and food—barely. Some months I'm slow on paying—if only the Benedicts had bought something! And I can't keep taking money from you."

"You're not taking money from me," Grace said, smiling, "you're taking it from Will."

"Same difference, and I feel guilty as hell. Besides, Grace, I've got to make it on my own."

Grace inhaled, her perfectly shaped nostrils flaring slightly. "It took almost a year just to untangle Blackie's deals."

"I don't think we'll ever know it all. He kept a lot under his hat. And he was in so much debt. If only I'd taken an interest in the way things ran while he was alive . . . but you know me, I never cared. It took all my meager brain cells to learn the real estate business, and I'm no whiz at it even now. Crass as Max is, he doesn't have the heart to throw out his best friend's widow."

"Max isn't that generous. You're a good agent."

"Not recently. I feel like I can't get arrested." Cig put the glass of port against her cheek. "But I mean it. I can't keep taking money from you."

"I told you, it's not my money—then again, I helped him earn it."

"In your own way, Grace, you earn it as much as Will does."

"Doesn't every woman?" The startling blue eyes clouded over.

"I don't know." Cig placed the glass on the coffee table. Tonight she felt genuinely old and beat up. "I'll take the kids out of private school during the semester break. Western Albemarle is a good school."

"Cig, all their friends are—"

Cig held up her hand. "Hunter needs a paper route, they pay pretty good, and I don't know what Laura can do; but the kids have to pitch in."

"Let me get them through high school."

"Grace, you are generous to a fault. But a year is long enough to get my feet under me. Now I've got to stand up, corny though it sounds."

"I can't let you do this to yourself. I know how you feel about the kids' education." The full lips became a compressed line.

"And I can't live off your charity."

"It's not charity! Think of it as recompense. You've gotten me out of one jam after another."

"Grace, we're talking about money, not your little side trips." It was what Cig called Grace's affairs.

"Oh God, Cig, you've been rescuing me from the consequences of my rashness since grade school. I leap before I look. You'd think I'd learn, but I don't." She folded her hands in her lap, giving her a schoolgirl air.

"You're talking about impetuousness, love, I'm talking about money."

"It doesn't matter. We're sisters. We stick together. The Deyhles always stick together."

"Damn the Benedicts." Tears filled Cig's brown eyes, as soft as her sister's were electrifyingly blue. "And damn Blackie. I thought only the good died young." She smiled ruefully.

"M-m-m," Grace murmured.

"I miss him. There were plenty of times while he was alive when I wished I'd never see him again, but now . . ."

"Things will work out, Ciggie, really they will."

"I hope so. Sometimes I'm so scared I can't sleep. Or I wake up in the middle of the night and my heart feels like a jackhammer. I can't breathe and I think, how am I going to make it? How?"

"You will."

"I wouldn't have gotten this far without you."

"You'd do the same for me." Grace put her feet up on the coffee table. "Many's the time I've wished it was Will who had died, not Blackie."

"Grace!"

"Oh, it's not like I wish him dead but he's such a grind. Blackie was full of life."

"He certainly shared himself."

"He just liked women. Sleeping with them was how he paid the compliment."

"Easy for you to say!"

"Yes, it is. Will is faithful, hardworking, and too dull to have been born. Be honest. Would you rather be married to an unfaithful Blackie or a faithful Will?"

"I don't know."

"The hell you don't."

"Life with Blackie could be very painful. I loved him but I learned not to trust him." She paused. "I wonder if I should go up there and lash them on with their homework? The deal is, if they do all their homework Friday night then they can go out Saturday and Sunday. Remember how frantic we'd get Sunday night because we'd left it to the last minute?"

"Don't get up. We're comfortable. They're quiet enough."

"Laura whispers on the phone. It makes whatever she's saying sound more important. She got that from you. I don't do it."

"Works, doesn't it?"

"Yeah, I guess it does."

"Mother used to say if you want someone to pay attention, whisper. Never shout."

"G-mom used to say it, too. And I bet her mother said it and her mother before that." Cig spoke of their Great-Aunt Pryor, called G-mom, who had died last year at ninety-nine. Cig was Pryor's namesake, her maiden name being Pryor Chesterfield Deyhle.

"Sometimes I take out the old family Bibles and look at birth and death dates and all those names. Pryor, Charles, Margaret, Solon. I love the way they recur. It's a way for the new generations to remember the old. Our family lived through hell and high water," Grace said. "They've been around so long we've gone through four huge Bibles."

"Why do you think Mother left me the papers after the War Between the States and you, the papers before? Why did she divide it that way? If she told me I forgot, but lately I'm forgetting lots of stuff."

"Mom figured the seventeenth-century papers were safer in my library than yours because I don't have children—and the reason you're forgetful is because you do."

"I miss Mom." Cig turned away from Grace to stare into the fire.

"Me, too."

"People say it's better if someone dies fast, better than watching them linger, but at least if they take their time about dying you have the opportunity to make peace with them. Both Mom and Blackie died so suddenly. Sometimes I'm knocked flat by guilt. I don't remember telling Mother that I loved her, but I sure couldn't wait to tell her how much smarter I was than she was."

Grace reached up and patted Cig's shoulder. "She didn't even think about it. Do you think about the crap your kids dump on you?"

"Not really. I count to ten."

"Mom did the same thing."

"She liked you better than me."

"Cig, you make me so mad when you say that. She did not. I was a little more—tractable."

"Devious. You told her what she wanted to hear."

A silence followed. Grace finally said, "Most times I was diplomatic. I don't care about being right. You have to be right. You always want to analyze everything, as if life were a big test we were all going to be graded on. I don't care about intellectual arguments. I don't see that they've advanced the human race one inch. So I just smile and roll on—wouldn't hurt you to try it."

Cig rested her chin on her hand. "I always intend to do that, then I forget." She changed the subject. "See Dad today?"

"For a minute. He wants to go to Nag's Head to hang glide."

"Lord." Cig shook her head. "Mamie is probably urging him to do it so she can collect the insurance once he crashes into the Atlantic."

"Cynic. You don't like her."

"She's thirty years younger than he is! No, I don't like her. She's a black widow. All she's missing is the red hourglass on her abdomen."

"Men can't live without women. We do fine without them."

"He could have waited longer to remarry, you know."

"Well, he didn't. He's our father. We'd better make the best of it—and his drinking has slowed down, so be grateful."

"What is this, Grace? Wisdom 101?"

"No. I just think these are hard times for you. Grappling with emotional hot wires has always been hard for you, just like being sensible and thinking about the future is hard for me."

"I certainly never expected Blackie to drop dead of a heart attack at fifty-four. I know he was fifteen years older than I am but he never seemed like it—because he never grew up, I guess."

"Never looked old, either. I'm starting to believe that when your number's up, it's up."

Cig squinted into the fire. "I'm sorry he died in your living room. If he hadn't been dropping off those contracts for Will. . . ."

Grace reached for Cig's hand. "If Blackie didn't teach me anything else he sure taught me to grab life while you can."

"What shocks me is that I was twenty-two when I married him. What will I do if Hunter or Laura marry at twenty-two?"

"Celebrate!"

Cig blinked. "Celebrate? I ought to have them committed."

"Oh, Cig, remember the feeling?"

Cig recalled the first time she saw Blackie. Maybe she had been enchanted, but the years, the infidelities, had burned away the sensation. "No, I don't. Whatever I felt then I've forgotten, and I've lost the capacity to feel it, period."

Grace's luminous eyes clouded. "Don't say that, Cig."

"Why not? It's true."

"If you feel that way, you've given up on life."

"I've got Hunter and Laura. I'm not giving up on life."

"Your life. Their lives are separate from yours."

"Their lives are separate from mine once they're out of college, earning their own keep."

"Stop being obtuse," Grace said sharply, her lips pursed together, a disapproving rosebud.

"You're telling me I've given up on life because I'm not driven by raging hormones. That's what I'm getting out of the conversation. Yes, I miss Blackie . . . but I couldn't rely on him. And I couldn't stand the smell of other women on his skin. Stolen flowers."

"Huh?"

"Stolen flowers seem to smell sweeter than the ones you've grown in your own garden. Those women were stolen flowers."

"You could have stolen a few of your own. What's good for the goose is good for the gander. Vice versa in your case."

Cig shrugged. "When would I have had the time? Someone had to keep life stable for the kids."

"You were too busy being a martyr."

"I was not. I didn't want my kids packing suitcases for their weekend with Dad. I figured maybe I would divorce him once Laura was in college and that would have been four years down the road. What's four years?"

"Could be the difference between life and death."

"In Blackie's case it was."

"It's not sinful to be happy. He was happy, but I agree he was irresponsible in some ways. He made a vow and he couldn't keep it, he couldn't stay faithful. But he fulfilled the rest of the marriage bargain."

"I fulfilled all of it!" Cig snapped.

"You would never have divorced him."

"You started this. You said what was good for the gander is good for the goose."

Grace twisted some shiny hair around her forefinger. "Did I say that?"

"Yes. You just did."

"Yeah . . . well, playing devil's advocate. I'm not sure it matters if your husband is faithful to you. It only matters that you love him."

"Of course you say that. You've been unfaithful to Will since year one of your marriage." She leaned toward her sister slightly, like the Leaning Tower of Pisa.

Grace took her stockinged feet off the coffee table and pushed Cig backward. She flopped back on a pillow.

"So . . . ?" Grace said.

"You don't know what I feel!"

"Well, feel something! Say something. Do something." Grace's cheeks flushed. "I hate to see you suffer."

Cig sat up and twirled around, tucking her legs under her so she faced her beautiful sister. "Sometimes I hear the clock ticking. Sometimes I hear my heartbeat. I hear myself breathing. That's my life that's ticking away. I've never seen Paris. I've never been to Munich or St. Petersburg or Buenos Aires or Santiago or the fjords of Norway—you name it. Blackie took me to Ireland—once. I'd like to go back. I want to go places that are magnets for energy, for culture, for whatever the human race has thought and done over the centuries. I want to feel that crazy sweat running between my breasts when I see a man who excites me. But it seems out of reach . . . what I want. I can't even pay my bills. I can't imagine falling in love again. My one solace is foxhunting. I'll still have that when the kids leave."

Grace grew solemn. "You know what I want? I want to go to the airport and hop on the first plane that has an open seat. I don't want a plan, I don't even want to know anyone wherever the destination may be—Istanbul, whatever. I just want to go. Maybe I want to forget myself. Maybe if I don't hear English spoken I will forget myself."

"What's keeping you?"

"I don't know." Grace wistfully pushed a lock of hair off her forehead.

"Will?"

"God no."

"Dad?"

"No."

"Me?"

"I want to make sure you're all right. I want to see you laugh again, really laugh. Then I'll go."

Touched, yet somewhat disbelieving, Cig shook her head. "You are not your sister's keeper."

"We all are. You said it yourself. You and I have unfinished business. Maybe when that's done I can go."

This startled Cig. "What are you talking about?"

Grace blinked. "I don't know, really. It's in the back of my head. When it comes to the front I'll let you know."

Cig, long accustomed to Grace's ways, didn't press. Instead she asked, "Are you really that bored?"

"Sometimes." Grace shifted her position. "Aren't you?"

"The kids . . ." She smiled at Grace. "I think I want less than you do."

Grace started to speak then seemed to think better of it. "I don't even know what I want."

Cig reached out to pat her sister's hand. "I think the anniversary of Blackie's death is hitting you harder than it's hitting me."

Grace thought a bit, then said, "I miss him. He could be a bad boy but he was so much fun. Sheer irrepressible fun."

They sat a while longer before Cig observed, "You know how I know that Laura's blabbing on the phone? It hasn't rung once. She doesn't quite get that the phone is business."

"You need another line."

"The noise! It'd be off the hook. Anyway, I can't afford another line. I think I'll go up there and yank the damn cord out of the wall."

"Later. Don't you remember what it was like at that age—you had so much to say and it was the first time you'd ever said it? The first time you exchanged a confidence over a crush or talked about a book you loved and actually understood? I hear myself now and it's like an old tape."

"Maybe you do need to go to Istanbul."

"You could come with me when Laura gets into college."

"Can you wait that long?"

"I don't know." Grace became serious, then suddenly stretched out her arms and wiggled her fingers under Cig's nose. "Snakes!"

"Snakes." Cig repeated the gesture, and they fell on one another laughing.

Their mother used to do that whenever she wanted to hex somebody, usually at the card table, but she was known to do it at social gatherings very discreetly so that only her family could see. She said she had learned it from her husband's mother. Dad wouldn't do it because he thought it was undignified. Blackie loved to do it after he picked it up from the Deyhle family. There has to be an oddball in the family, and their mother often played that part.

"I miss Mom." Cig laughed again, remembering the delight in Amy Deyhle's eyes when she'd pull one of her snakes.

"Is this what getting old is about?" Grace innocently asked. "Do we just say good-bye all the time?"

"I guess it is, but we get to say hello, too. Hello to grandchildren. Hello to the new generations."

"What if I don't like the next generation? I certainly didn't want to produce any of them. I left that to you. Will still harps on it though."

"Some people are meant to be mothers and some aren't. You aren't."

"I don't think I'd be a good mother." Grace sounded unconvincing.

"Probably because you're still a child." Cig laughed. "I'm hungry again. Can you believe it?"

They repaired to the kitchen where Cig served up a delicious carrot cake she'd bought on the way home, and Grace declared she was not a child and if she really wanted to she'd be a superior mother or a mother superior, take your pick. After devouring the cake and washing it down with a good cup of tea, Grace glanced at the big wall clock. "Time to boogie."

"Stay here if you want. We've got to get up so early."

"Will pitches a fit if I'm not home when he's had a late night at the hospital. I don't know why. I'm usually sound asleep."

"He loves you in his own way."

"No—he's dependent in his own way."

"All men are dependent, Grace. Big deal."

Grace pushed down her fork to mash the crumbs on her plate. She ate them, too. "Why? If I just knew why. You start out as their siren and wind up as their mother."

Cig shrugged. "Who knows?" Then she added, "I'm glad you came over tonight."

"Me, too." Grace scooped up the vicuña then hugged her square-shouldered sister, who walked her to the back door. As they entered the mud room, Grace said, "October has to be the very best time of year. The leaves changing, the first frosts, those clear, crisp nights that cut into your soul."

"Yeah." Cig agreed and wished she could be as glib, as descriptive, as Grace.

Grace turned to face her. "Cig, I have this premonition. It's—well, last night I came home after my tennis committee meeting for the country club and the moon was huge—huge like a bursting melon."

"Saw it." Cig smiled.

"Well, I had this feeling, like a chill crawling down my spine. Even my hair tingled. And I just looked at the moon and a thin cloud passed over it like a Prussian blue knife blade and I thought, 'Something's coming down. Something's coming down and we'll never ever be the same,' and I don't know if it's good or bad but—I'm scared."

"Blackie's death. You're so sensitive, Grace. The anniversary's working on you."

"No. This is about the future, not the past." Grace reached up and kissed her sister then opened the mud room door and walked to her car as Cig switched on the light for her. "Hey," Cig called, "maybe the past is in the future."

She stopped on the worn brick walk. "Wouldn't it be perfect if there were no time, or at least if we had no sense of it?" She threw her hands in the air, undone by the philosophizing, and changed the subject. "Has Laura talked to you about the dance?"

"Yes."

"I mean, really talked to you?"

"She said she's not going with Donny Forbush. And she's worried about Will." Cig suppressed a flash of impatience. "We talked about this at supper. Are you suffering from early Alzheimer's?"

Grace gulped in the sparkling air. "No." She started to say something then continued walking. She reached the car and then called out, "I love you."

"I love you, too." Cig waved. She closed the door once Grace had started the car. A whiff of clear, cold air snuck into the room.

3

∞

From the mud room window, Cig watched the silvery curlicue of exhaust from Grace's tailpipe as she cruised down the driveway. She crossed her arms over her chest, not realizing how tightly she was hugging herself until she couldn't breathe. She shook her head and walked back into the kitchen. Hunter was eating a huge piece of carrot cake.

"This is great, Mom."

"I slaved hours over the stove to make that cake."

He winked at her. She returned the wink and walked into the library where she picked up the family books and papers stacked on a wide shelf next to the dictionaries. She opened the massive maroon leather book, gilt edged, and studied the cursive handwriting that cataloged births and deaths since 1860. Like so many Americans, she was indifferent to her family's history as well as history in general. She wasn't a total fool, she knew the past was prologue, but somehow she never got around to studying the part that the Deyhles, the Buckinghams, the Charters, the Burkes, the deVries, the Chesterfields, the Merritts, and who knows who else had played in creating Virginia, the nation, and her own self, genetically anyway.

Hunter entered the room and read over her shoulder. "How did they do that?"

"Years of practice, plus india ink and pens with gold tips."

"When did we stop using quills?"

"Do you really think I know the answer to that?" She laughed at him.

"You might. You know some incredible stuff, Mom."

"Like what?"

"Like you remember Richard Nixon."

"You remember what you lived through. I was about your age then."

"Well, I bet quills were fun to use."

"As long as you weren't the goose." Cig traced a big C with her finger. "Not that they killed them for their feathers."

"Mom, feathers fall out—kind of like Uncle Will's hair."

"I swear, he's hitting the dye pots or using Grecian Formula 44. He was grayer, I know he was." She glanced at her own hair in the mirror. Not much gray. "Did you finish your homework?"

"I've got two problems left in physics."

"Knock 'em out."

"Okay." He didn't budge.

She put her hands on her hips. "Yes?"

"Can I borrow twenty dollars?"

"Twenty dollars?" Cig's voice rose.

"I know it's a lot, but I want to take Beryl Smith to the dance and I'm short."

"Hunter, I'm not made out of money."

"Mom, it's only twenty bucks."

"Twenty here and twenty there—it adds up. You've got to get it through your head that we don't have money like we did when Dad was alive."

"What if I put in extra hours at the barn?"

"I've heard that before."

"I'll do it. I'll clean out the cobwebs, change the light bulbs under the eaves, fix the broken washer in the wash stall. I promise . . . please."

"What's so hot about Beryl Smith?"

His eyebrows knitted together. "She's, uh, she's . . ."

"A space cadet," Cig blurted out. "I take that back." She sighed. "Hunter, I hate crabbing about money, I hate denying you anything, but every penny counts."

"Mom, I swear I will keep my promise. I'll do those chores. I'll even wash and wax the car."

"And the next question is, can you borrow it for the dance? Hunter, you're transparent." She paused, then held out her hand. "Oh, all right. Deal."

"Deal." He shook her hand.

"Is your sister bagging the dance altogether?"

His face blanked. Hunter's ignorance had an artful air. "I don't know."

"Oh yes, you do."

"You always tell us to be direct. You should ask Laura, not me."

She stared at him. "You're absolutely right."

He bounded out of the library, happy to have twenty dollars, leaving Cig to wonder just what was going on. She heard his door close. She climbed the stairs, passed his room and heard Laura hang up the phone. She thought she heard her say, "I love you." Cig blinked. She'd never thought of her daughter as falling in love and hoped she'd misheard. She tried to recall how she had felt at fifteen, but it was too far back or she had pushed it too far back.

"Laura?"

"Hi, Mom." She sat at her desk.

"May I come in?"

"Sure." Laura's nonchalance was forced.

"Finished?"

"Mostly."

"What's left?"

"Have to read the last part of *Macbeth* for English."

Cig sat down on Laura's bed. "There's pussyfooting going on."

"Uh—"

"Your Aunt Grace wanted to know if we'd talked about the dance and your brother says he knows nothing, which means he knows everything. What am I missing? Is there more between you and Donny than I know or want to know?" She half-laughed.

"I don't like Donny."

"Are you going to the dance with someone else?"

"I'm thinking about it."

"Who?"

Laura flipped through the last two acts of *Macbeth* as though it were a card deck, then quietly she said, "Parry."

"That's fine. There will be lots of boys who go without dates, too. In fact, it will probably be a lot more fun." Cig brightened.

Laura drummed her fingertips on the top of the desk. "Yeah—well."

"Honey, I think that's a marvelous idea and I'll drive you all there if Hunter won't give you a ride. He's taking Beryl Smith. Guess you know."

"Yes," Laura said, her eyes now firmly on her mother's. "I want to take Parry as my date."

"What do you mean, your date?"

"My date."

"You mean you're going to dance with her?" Cig's shoulders rose then lowered. "Well, I suppose you can but I promise you there will be boys there who—"

"I don't care about the boys." Laura's voice grew more firm with each exchange.

"I'm missing something."

"Mom, I'm going to the dance with Parry. I like her more than anybody."

Cig held up her hands. "Wait a minute. You like her or you *like* her?"

"I *like* her."

"Ah." Cig gripped the edges of the bed with both hands. "Like her like you want to kiss her?"

"Mom," Laura implored, "I don't want to go into details."

"You have a crush on Parry. Now, have I got that right?"

"Yes."

Cig waited a moment. "At your age I guess that's par for the course but really, you don't have to date the girls you have crushes on, honey. I never did."

"But you're straight. I'm not."

"How do you know that?" Cig challenged Laura without meaning to do it. It had just popped out of her mouth.

"Mom, that's something you . . . know."

"You're a perfectly normal child!"

"Mother!" Laura slammed her book shut and the dust flew off the pages.

"Now I didn't mean that the way it sounded, it's just that this is sudden and you're so young and—"

"It's not sudden. I've been thinking about it for a long time."

Cig didn't ask what a long time was. "Why didn't you come to me?"

"I talked to Aunt Grace." Laura's voice lowered.

"What in the hell does Grace know about a thing like that?"

"She said that I should follow my heart. She didn't think it was such a big deal."

"I didn't say it was a big deal, and furthermore, Aunt Grace has followed her heart too many times."

"You're upset. I knew you'd be upset."

"I'm not upset," Cig lied. "It's a little, uh, surprising, that's all, and I think you might not want to act in haste."

"I'm not acting in haste. I have a right to go to the dance with whomever I wish!"

Cig held up her hands for peace. "I know, but the world is hardly the liberal, wonderful place we wish it would be and you're asking for trouble."

"How come when gay people want to be happy they're asking for trouble?" Laura yelled.

"Because the world is fucking unfair, that's why! All I'm doing is telling you what to expect. I'm not saying that it's right."

"Well, I can take it. I'd rather be happy with Parry than accepted with somebody I don't love."

"Laura, you're fifteen. Let's not get too carried away here. Who knows what will come of you and Parry?"

"Whatever becomes of me and Parry isn't going to change the fact that I'm gay."

"I hate labels. It makes people sound like cans of tuna."

"I am gay, Mom. That's that." Laura stopped, exasperated.

"You're my daughter and I love you." Cig abruptly stood up. "I'm a little confused. Let's sort this out later."

"There's nothing to sort out."

"About the dance, there is."

"I'm going!" Laura's jaw jutted out.

"I know. I'm not forbidding you but perhaps I'd better go along. I don't want any trouble."

"Hunter will be there. No one's going to beat us up."

"I don't know that. It's a crazy world." Cig leaned against the doorway for a moment. "Laura, go slow. Take lots of time."

"Mother, I know who I am. Inside."

"Well, I'm glad one of us does." Cig smiled at her. "I'll take a little time to get used to this."

Laura wanted instant acceptance but was smart enough to know this wasn't a bad beginning. "Okay."

"Just let me think about the dance, okay? I'm not saying you can't go. Just let me think about the repercussions."

"Okay."

Cig left her daughter's room, nearly tripping over Peachpaws who was lying over the threshold. She alternated between wanting to go to sleep and wanting to rip Grace's face off for usurping her maternal role. How easy to be glorious Aunt Grace who counsels that you follow your heart, indulge in a sapphic rapture. She wouldn't have to pay the price. Then Cig caught herself.

Damn the Benedicts! If they'd bought Hardtack Manor, she could rub money on her troubles.

4

∞

Closing her bedroom door behind her, Cig flopped on her bed, covered by a faded Black Watch down comforter. Woodrow flopped down beside her. He was all set for serious interspecies kissing when he saw Cig pick up the telephone. He decided to wash himself instead.

"Hi, Will, how are you?"

"Can't complain," said the man who usually did. "Want to speak to Grace?"

"Sure."

"Oh, before I buzz her—she's in her office—I wanted to ask you why Laura turned down Donny Forbush's invitation to the dance."

Cig knew Will's "can't complain" was bull. "Will, I was a teenaged girl once, and all I can say is it's a wildly irrational time." Cig scrambled to think of something more original to say but originality wasn't her strong suit.

Will chuckled. "Teenaged boys are worse but you might want to have a talk with her. Apparently, Donny is trashed, I believe that's the word he used with his father."

"It's probably the first time any girl has ever turned him down."

"I wouldn't know about that, but the Forbushes are valuable friends. One can't have enough friends in elected office, you know."

"Will, these are kids. Surely Gene Forbush knows that."

"Gene Forbush has a big ego for himself and for his son." Will attempted to keep a genial tone.

"Come on, don't pressure Laura. She doesn't want to go out with the boy. Anyway, at that age they're in love one day and at each other's throats the next."

"Umm, well, let me buzz Grace." Will tired of the subject. "But Cig, if there's anything you can do to change her mind I do believe it would be beneficial to all of us."

She heard a click and then Grace picked up. "Hello."

"Grace, what are you doing telling my daughter to be a lesbian?"

A sharp intake of breath preceded her reply. "I did not!"

"She thinks you did."

"What I said," Grace patiently, even patronizingly, began, "was that the leopard can't change its spots."

"We're talking about my daughter, not a leopard."

"You know what I mean." Grace sounded flat-out superior now.

"No, I don't."

"You can't force Laura into anything."

"I'm not. I wouldn't. But this is the first I've heard of it."

"She was nervous."

"She wasn't nervous tonight."

"Good."

"What's good about it? You're encouraging my child to embark on a life of social rejection, economic hardship, and no security whatsoever."

"There is no security on this earth, only opportunity."

"Gag me, Sister. You are sitting in a shitload of security even if you are bored out of your skull."

Grace flashed back. "Listen, if you resist Laura on this she'll turn into a motorcycle dyke just to spite you. If you try a little patience, don't make a fuss, what you'll get is a very beautiful girl who likes other girls. It could be a whole lot worse."

"How can she possibly know who she is or what she wants at fifteen?"

"Don't be an ass, Cig. People are born that way. If homosexuals were made then we could unmake them. Obviously, we can't."

Cig, furious now, demanded, "Why didn't you come to me the instant she talked to you?"

"I'm not going to betray a trust."

"You don't mind betraying your husband." Cig aimed a low blow, very low.

"That's different! Sex is not about ethics."

"And you're a Republican, speaking about ethics and family values?" Cig steamed, then thought a second. "Actually, of course you are. God-damned hypocrite."

"Being a Republican has nothing to do with it and we will bring the party back to the center so just shut up. You don't know your ass from your elbow when it comes to politics and you don't know your ass from your elbow when it comes to your daughter. This is a trying time for her."

"Me, too. A big fat help you are."

"What do you want me to do? Tell her she has to screw boys?"

"Don't be crude," Cig snapped. "And that little hint when you left, 'Has Laura talked to you?' " Cig mimicked her sister's voice. "You could have told me then. I hate innuendo."

"You hate subtlety. You want it all plain in black and white. You should have been an engineer or an accountant. They always have clear answers."

"I don't like futzing around. That's not wanting the world to be in black and white."

Grace tacked to a new breeze. "What are you going to do?"

"Wring your neck."

"After that."

A long pause. "I don't know."

"Scared?"

"No—yes."

"Of what? What people will say?"

Cig reached over and scratched Woodrow. "I'd like to say I'm im-mune to public opinion but I'm not. I mean, it isn't going to send me over the edge if they dog me or my child, but Jesus, life is easier if people like you."

"They'll still like you but some will pity you, some will blame you, others will blame it on Blackie's death at an impressionable age for Laura, and others won't care as long as she's happy. That about sums it up."

"Actually, I'm much more worried for her. I mean, you asked me about other people so I answered but it's Laura I care about. My life is over in a way."

"Don't say that!"

"All right. But Grace, people are so hateful. Strangers will despise Laura without knowing her and she's a great kid. She could get fired from jobs—if they'll even hire her. She has no legal protection of any kind. If she ever settles down, I mean. I don't want to think about this . . ."

"That's pretty far in the future. My advice is, don't make a big deal out of it. If she really is gay she'll have plenty of time to adjust and so will you. Right now she's feeling the first flush of puppy love—and look on the bright side: no unwanted pregnancies."

Cig laughed despite herself. "There is that."

"Are you done yelling at me?"

"For now."

"Good. Go to bed. We've both got to get up early tomorrow."

"Yeah, yeah." Cig sighed. "Night, Gracie."

"Night, Ciggie."

The phone clicked. Cig hung up the receiver, gave Woodrow a pat then walked into the bathroom to brush her teeth. She read the cutout she had taped on her mirror. In Old English typography it read "Shit Happens."

She mumbled with the toothbrush in her mouth, "Oh, shit."

5

∽

Two green eyes stared into her own when Cig awoke at 5:30 A.M. Woodrow, in his sphinx pose, paws under Cig's chin, stretched over her chest.
His purrs rumbled throughout her body.

Cig thought the Sphinx had been a Maine coon cat—the Egyptians
just didn't get it right. Snuggling was his second favorite activity. Eating
was his first, and he trilled when she opened her eyes. His tail swished like
a windshield wiper in high gear. He was blissfully unaware of the cause of
last night's tensions, nor did he set store by anniversaries. For Woodrow,
today was all that mattered.

"Morning, Woodrow."

He meowed his greetings as Cig swung her legs over the edge of the
bed, her bare feet touching the smooth heart pine floor. Peachpaws woke
up, yawning.

Cig found her worn slippers and hurried into the bathroom.

Old houses exude a charm, a gathering of all the energies poured
into them. They're also cold as a witch's tit. The bathroom, added to the
house in the 1920s, had some insulation, which Cig and Blackie had
augmented in the 1980s. Dashing into the bathroom provided relief since
it was warmer than the bedroom. As she washed her face, brushed her
teeth, and quickly twisted her hair into a braid, Woodrow purred, rub-
bing against her legs.

"Come on, pussycat. Tuna treat this morning? What about you, pooch? Lamb stew on crunchies?" She threw on her red robe, and they hurried down the narrow curving back stairway leading directly into the kitchen with its large fireplace. Woodrow managed to purr even as he ate. Peachpaws inhaled his food. Cig put up coffee, set three bowls on the table and checked the thermometer. Thirty-eight degrees Fahrenheit. As she looked out the tall windows toward the stable she could see that ground fog hung over the pastures like old cigar smoke, a leftover perhaps from a stag party for the gods.

She walked through the kitchen, out to the center hall of the federal home and to the foot of the big staircase. She thought about yelling and then decided against it. So she climbed the stairs, the banister railing worn shiny through generations of use, and entered her son's bedroom.

"Hunter, get moving, honey." She shook him awake. He blinked at her with deep brown eyes like her own.

"Good day for scent, Mom?"

"I think so. Breakfast in fifteen minutes."

"Okay."

She headed down the hall and opened the door to Laura's room, plastered with posters of Anne Kursinski, Katie Monahan Prudent, and Charlie Weaver. A small photo of Parry Tetrick had been placed on the wall last night. Cig sighed and touched Laura on the shoulder. "Up and at 'em."

"Uh." Laura was loath to leave her warm bed.

"Come on, hotshot, breakfast will be ready in fifteen minutes and we've got worms to turn and eggs to lay."

"Uh-huh." Laura emerged from under the down comforter and groped her way to the bathroom.

Woodrow enjoyed presiding over breakfast or any other meal. He sat in Blackie's chair and gravely watched each forkful of egg as it made its way into the various mouths.

Hunter gave a piece of egg to the cat.

"Hunter, don't feed Woodrow at the table," Cig chided.

"You do."

She thought a moment. "Well—only when you're not looking."

They laughed. They had been laughing more recently. The weight of numbness having passed, intense grief had set in. But during the last few weeks they'd begun to awaken. Blackie's death had blindsided his family. It took a year to accept that he was gone. Cig, Hunter, and Laura had gone over and over his last day as though grasping every minute would keep him closer longer. Blackie had stopped at Grace's house to drop off contracts for Will concerning a small downtown rental property Will wanted to buy. Blackie was Will's lawyer. Such an ordinary visit, a drink offered and a drink accepted. He died when Grace returned to the kitchen for more ice. No one could believe he'd slip away that quietly or quickly. There was nothing quiet about Blackie.

Grace and Cig, known as Beauty and Brains when they were children, both possessed cool heads. Grace called 911, administered all the first aid revival techniques she knew, and then had the painful duty of driving out to the farm to tell Cig that she was a widow. She didn't want to tell her over the phone.

Cig shut the door on that memory this morning, cracking the whip over Hunter's and Laura's heads to hurry them up.

Grace pulled up at the stable, and shortly after, the phone rang.

"I'm on my way," Cig told her sister, who called from the tackroom. "Let's just table all significant topics, all right?"

"All right," Grace agreed.

"Hunter, Laura, come on!" They shoved extra doughnuts into their mouths as they washed their cereal bowls.

Cig stepped into her L.L. Bean duck boots and opened the back door. Woodrow and Peachpaws shot out, both pausing to inhale the crisp October dawn, which promised a beautiful sunrise, the odor of turning leaves rich yet melancholy, a perfect day for a foxhunt.

"Great day," Grace hollered at Cig as she strode into the stable. "Passed Harleyetta on the road. I expect she'll be the first one at the meet. And I should have spent the night here. Will came home last night in a foul mood, apart from everything else."

"Sorry. Was Binky with Harleyetta?"

"No, her consort was missing."

"I don't suppose he'll miss the hunt. He'll throw another drink down his throat and get to the fixture somehow." Cig smiled as she took Full

Throttle out of his stall, put him on the crossties, and grabbed a soft grooming brush. He was a 16.1 handsome bay with good bone, a fabulous equine athlete.

"By this time you'd think those two would be pickled given the amount of alcohol they've gargled." Grace turned as Hunter, soon followed by Laura, padded into the barn. "If Will keeps being such a crab, I may turn to it myself."

"Hi, Aunt Grace." Hunter waved.

Woodrow raced into Full Throttle's empty stall, the attraction being a family of mice that lived behind the wall boards. Peachpaws stole a galloping-boot then dropped in the tackroom for more sleep, his booty by his long nose.

"Morning." Laura skidded into the tackroom and deftly removed yet another extra bridle, which she carried out to the horse trailer.

"Aunt Grace, do you know what Jeffrey Dahmer said to Lorena Bobbitt?" Hunter said.

"I have no idea." Grace's dark eyes sparkled.

"Are you going to eat that?"

"Hunter!" Cig reached out to punch him.

"That's really gross," Grace replied. "I'm so glad you didn't tell me that last night at dinner."

Cig peeped over Full Throttle's neck as Grace blithely gave Hunter and Laura, spinning through their chores, a blow-by-blow description of Will's silent sulk last night.

"Don't look at me like that, Cig. These two are old enough to figure things out."

"Mom, how long were you married to Dad?" Laura piped up.

"Laura, sometimes it amazes me how you forget these things."

"I don't forget exactly it's just it's—"

"Out of the Dark Ages—I know. Like, why remember the dates of Vietnam?" Grace filled in for her beloved niece.

"Yeah."

"Grace, you spoil her." Cig's voice had an edge.

"Someone has to," came the saucy reply.

This made them all laugh. Even Cig.

"I was not quite twenty-two when I married your father. So—nearly eighteen years."

"And Hunter was born ten months after the wedding. Thank God because everyone in central Virginia is an expert at math," Grace added.

"Dad was old, wasn't he?"

"Ancient, Laura," came the acid reply. "He was thirty-six going on thirty-seven."

"I didn't mean old, Mom, I meant older. Don't get weird."

"Everyone gets weird when they hit forty," Grace, thirty-eight, added.

Hunter brought Tabasco into the aisle. Laura picked out Go To's hooves. "About ready here."

"They don't look brushed to me." Cig cast a careful eye over the horses.

"Mom, that takes two minutes. They're really clean 'cause I washed everyone yesterday afternoon," Hunter replied. "You just didn't notice."

"Okay, okay. We've got Mosby and Reebok to load up for Bill and Roberta."

"Chill out, Mom. We haven't been late yet." Hunter tried to pacify his mother. For whatever reason, it was easier for Hunter to communicate with Cig than it was for Laura who was always ready to come back with a full-scale defense about how she was on time, she was always prepared, she would always be on time and prepared. Hunter deftly headed off his sister while calming his mother.

As the kids loaded the horses, Cig and Grace repaired to the tackroom to throw off their duck boots and pull on their good boots. Grace's had black patent leather tops while Cig's had brown leather tops. Then they tied each other's stock ties, careful to stick the pin through the knot horizontally, although Cig was tempted to stab Grace in the throat. They put on their canary vests and rummaged around for their deerskin gloves. Grace brushed off her coat with the plum colors piped in gold on the collar. Cig wore scarlet, bold for a woman in this part of the world, but she was the Master of the Foxhounds and she knew from her own experience that it was a lot easier to find the MFH in the field if she was wearing scarlet. This also entitled her to wear the brown tops on her boots, normally a flourish reserved for men. Male masters always wore scarlet.

Cig put her hands on her knees, ready to stand up and wiggle her toes in her boots. "If I could only figure out how to keep my feet warm without extra heavy socks."

"Tried those space-age insoles?"

"I've tried everything. My toes ache from the cold."

"Scorn pain. Either it goes away or you do." Grace quoted Seneca. "Laura seems fine."

"Yeah." Cig was noncommittal.

"This isn't the end of the world."

"Am I acting as though it is?"

"Don't get dramatic."

"Just because I raised my voice a hair doesn't mean I'm getting dramatic."

"Don't pull one of your turtle numbers either—close up your shell. I can't stand it when you get like that."

Cig tapped the horn handle of her hunting whip against her boot. "I'm not shutting down, I'm not in a huff, I'm not going to suffer the vapors," she sarcastically replied. "But I am going to get to the meet on time and things will work out however they work out. So shut up and come on." She paused. "You're always fishing."

"I am not," came the stout defense. "I don't want you to be laid low by some emotional boomerang."

"Come on, Grace. Nothing's going to lay me low." Cig gave Grace a light whap.

"Shotgun," Grace called to Hunter and Laura as they opened the truck door. Riding shotgun was Grace's favorite place, and she had precedence over her niece and nephew who also wanted the passenger seat.

As the two sisters walked to the rig, a casual observer would be struck by how similar yet dissimilar they were. Cig was an imposing woman of Junoesque proportions. Her clean features, strong body, and lustrous eyes would mark her out as stunning in a European country, but American men liked their women less powerful and majestic. Grace, more to their taste, markedly resembled her older sister facially: even features, great teeth, beautiful eyes. Smaller of stature, Grace was more huggable. Grace derived her sense of importance from male attention so she carefully rehearsed those tricks so obvious to other women, so beguiling to men. When Grace spoke to a man she dropped one of her shoulders just a tad so he would appear even larger, she smaller. She turned her face up toward his, light shining in her eyes, all rapt attention. Her eyebrows danced up and down with his every intonation. She leaned forward toward him in a posture of invitation and supplication. Her voice lilted upwards as though each sentence ended in an unconscious question that only he, that repository of all strength and wisdom, could answer. They fell for it hook, line, and sinker.

Cig loathed choreographed femininity. She said she didn't want a man in her life if she had to lie to him no matter how silent the lie. So she spoke directly to a man, gaze level into his own. No inflections upward. She stood square and spoke her mind, usually diplomatically. The results were predictable. Men respected Cig. They liked her even if they were sometimes half-afraid of her. They lusted after Grace.

People who had not known the sisters as girls often wondered aloud, out of hearing range, of course, how Cig Deyhle had captivated handsome John Blackwood with the adorable Grace around. Those who had grown up with them or watched them grow up eagerly told the tale.

Cig, a junior at the College of William and Mary, met John Blackwood when he moved to the area to join the law firm of Marker, Gunderson and Shay . . . and to escape a vituperative ex-wife still raging in Baltimore. Cig came home for Thanksgiving, and everyone agreed it was love at first sight for her. Grace, a freshman at William and Mary, was visiting a friend's house that Thanksgiving. By the time she did meet Blackie, at Christmas, he was intrigued by Cig, and for whatever reason the seventeen years between them seemed a far greater gap than the fifteen years between Blackie and Cig. Even so, everyone was sure that if Blackie had met Grace first everything would have come out differently.

As it was, Grace met William Von Hugel, an intern at Columbia Presbyterian in New York City, after she graduated from college and moved to the big city. A far more judicious choice as it turned out than Grace's sister's handsome husband, Will found a job in central Virginia so he and his bride could move back to her home. Grace found she liked New York in smaller doses than 365 days a year.

The worry over Blackie's infidelities, plus the hard physical labor took their toll on Cig. Lines creased her face. A bit of gray appeared around her temples, making her look more imposing than she felt. Grace, on the other hand, took full advantage of her husband's profession, going to doctor friends for a nip and a tuck whenever she felt she wasn't perfect enough. She looked pretty perfect all right.

"Okay now. Let's rehearse how to keep Harleyetta from murder and mayhem." Cig watched the road as she crawled around a curve, careful not to suddenly shift the weight of the horses in the trailer. She liked to create an agenda on the drive to the fixture, as the meeting place for each hunt was called.

"Keep Binky in the back of the field," Laura suggested sensibly.

"Harleyetta will run over anyone and everyone, so you might as well let her up front." Riding near the Master was an honor that should be earned, but Grace believed harmony in the field was more important than protocol.

"If Binky's sober he'll stay in the back," Cig commented.

"Mom, Binky is never sober. And I'm beginning to wonder about Harley," Hunter said.

"She was sober in grade school." Grace supplied this information. "That was when she decided to paint the arching eyebrows. She thought if she plucked her eyebrows she'd look better and older. They never grew back."

"If she'd sober up she'd draw better ones," Laura noted.

"Binky doesn't mind." Hunter shifted his weight.

"Too drunk to notice." Cig eased down on the clutch and carefully slipped into third. "If sex were banned as a topic of conversation Binky would be struck mute."

"Is every hunt club as weird as ours?" Laura asked.

"Hunt club? Laura, every group of people in every country around the world *and* in every century has been weird. People are crazy as hell. You might as well learn that lesson now. Just wing nuts."

"Aunt Grace, where'd you pick up 'wing nuts'?"

"From you, Laura."

"Oh."

"I like 'doesn't have both oars in the water' myself," Cig chimed in.

"Elevator doesn't go to the top," Hunter said.

"Somebody shot the dots off his dice." Grace sang the phrase.

"A quart low," Hunter added.

"Fruitcake." Grace again. "Or how about lost his marbles?"

"Looney Toons." Cig slowed for a stop then swung wide as she turned right out of the dirt road and onto the blessed macadam. "Listen, you aren't getting me off the track no matter how hard you try. Hunter, you ride in front of Harleyetta."

"She'll run me over, Mom."

"No, she won't. You're bigger and smarter but she will run over people like Roberta on Reebok. She scares the hell out of people."

"Should have stuck to Harleys." Grace reached in her vest pocket for a hair net.

"She's got that burnt metallic orange one," Laura said. "Same color as her eyebrows."

"If I had a motorcycle I could cut gas costs." Hunter tried to lean forward but couldn't so he flopped back.

"You will drive that '81 Toyota truck until it dies."

"It's already got over a hundred sixty thousand miles on the speed-ometer. The day of doom fast approaches." He sounded like a TV preacher.

"Yeah, well, you'd just better pray that truck lasts until you get to college because there's no money for another one."

"What about selling the tractor?"

"Hunter, how do you propose to run a farm without a tractor?"

"The way our illustrious ancestors did it."

"Our illustrious ancestors didn't have to pay minimum wage, smart guy," Cig replied. "Now, just get your butt in front of Harleyetta and *don't* let her pass you."

"What about Binky?" Laura elbowed her brother. "He won't stay in the back, I bet."

"Binky will fall in next to Roberta and that will keep him happy."

"Say, you don't think—?"

"Grace, get a grip. Roberta wouldn't take up with Binky if he were the last man on earth."

"Well, to hear Roberta tell it she's been without male companionship for a long, long time."

"So have you—to hear you tell it." Cig smiled too sweetly at Grace who held up her fingers to indicate two points.

Before they could bicker, Muster Meadow came into view and sure enough, Harleyetta was there, along with Roger Davis, scowling by the hound trailer. Must have been a bad night because her eyebrows wiggled and waved, burnt orange, of course.

6

Harleyetta was her real name. Her father, a Hog devotee and general wild man, christened her himself. At thirty-two, a nurse, she had "bettered herself," as people say, with her marriage to Binky West. She'd also chunked up; not that she was fat, more square than fat. Good-hearted and impulsive, Harleyetta was not afflicted with tact, but if you told her a secret she made heroic efforts to keep it, since so few people ever confided in her.

Not especially bright, she could be quick on her feet. No one would ever let Harley forget the time in Sunday school—she was ten—when the teacher asked the name of Noah's wife and she replied, "Joan of Ark."

Often her wrong answers were more interesting than people's right ones, and it was that tilted creativity combined with a bubbling energy that had attracted the wealthy, lost Binky West. Marrying Harleyetta, one of his many acts of defiance, could have saved him, except he never let her forget where she came from—he ruined it for both of them.

Cig and Grace waved as Cig pulled the rig around, truck nose outwards. The dirt road into Muster Meadow, an old farm along the upper James River, was packed hard as brick and was just as red. A pouring rain would eventually soften it up, but they'd had no rain in nearly four weeks.

"Hunter, go help Harleyetta unload. She never can back out Gypsy." Cig cut the engine.

"Mom, I don't mind helping her unload but do I really, truly have to ride in front of her?"

"Yes. Come on, honey, a lot of our business comes from the club so when people hunt we need to keep everyone happy."

"All right," he grumbled and slid out as soon as Grace vacated her seat.

Foxhunting clubs, being nonprofit, could charge dues and day rates, known as capping fees, to offset the costs of the sport. Jefferson Hunt kept those costs low through efficiency, but many clubs had elegant club-houses, huge kennels filled with hungry hounds, a paid huntsman, and even paid whippers-in—those special outriders selected for skill, sense of direction, and obedience to the Huntsman. Some clubs had annual oper-ating budgets of hundreds of thousands of dollars, even providing mounts for the staff.

People in the club came to Cig for lessons, often bought horses from her, and referred other people, so in a sense the club augmented her business. She scrupulously followed the regulations of the national associ-ation, The Master of Foxhounds Association of America, to make certain she didn't step over the line from nonprofit to profit.

As Hunter performed his good deed, Laura and Grace deftly un-loaded the horses, which they had tacked up before loading back at the barn.

Cig walked over to Roger. "Hey, Rog."

"If we can start at seven thirty on the dot, might be a good day."

This October had been unusually warm. Cig and Roger liked to start early because when the temperatures rose so did the scent until it wafted over the hounds' heads. They could no longer smell it, hence no more hunting. Once frosts came, the departure time could be pushed to nine or even ten in the morning as the frost held the odor close to the ground.

One by one the horse trailers and fancy Imperatore horse boxes rumbled down the farm road. Roberta chugged along in her sturdy Subaru, pulling in next to Cig's trailer. Dr. Bill Dominquez, hopping a ride with David Wheeler, soon arrived, too. Binky drove up in his brand new tricked-out Dodge Ram half-ton truck, parked next to his wife's trailer and was bitching before he shut the truck door. Harleyetta ignored him.

The start of a hunt was full of promise and forgotten stock pins; happy greetings between people madly rushing from trailer to trailer to see if anyone had an extra pair of stirrup leathers, pins, gloves, socks, hunt caps. Each beginning was different yet somehow the same. All the scurrying and shouting eventually settled into everyone being tacked up, jackets on, boots clean, tails brushed out, flasks filled, and girths checked and double-checked. Finally the last, the slowest, would be mounted—usually Florence Moeser, two years older than God—then the group would gather around the Master.

Today the heel came off Roberta's right boot. Boarders can be a pain in the ass, and Roberta, a nice enough lady, was no exception. She never could quite pull herself together without assistance.

"I'll never be able to keep my foot from going through the stirrup. What'll I do?" she wailed.

"Don't worry, Miss Ericson, I can fix it." Hunter reached into the trailer tackroom, yanked out the toolbox, found a hammer and nailed the heel back on. "There. Guess you'll have to get them resoled."

"I'm sure not going to buy a new pair." Roberta gratefully took her boot from Hunter's outstretched hand. "Binky gets a new pair every two years. Can you imagine being that rich?"

"No, ma'am," Hunter truthfully replied.

"Helps to be born to the right person, I guess." Roberta wiggled her foot into the boot.

"I was," Hunter stated matter-of-factly.

Roberta stopped a moment. "Well, of course you were, Hunter. I didn't mean that, I just meant that inherited wealth surely solves a lot of life's problems." She paused a moment. "Then again, I never did know any of them that were truly happy. There."

"Ought to last the hunt anyway." Hunter handed her Reebok's reins. "If you hold him for a minute I'll go get the mounting block."

"Hunter Blackwood, you're a perfect gentleman, just like your father."

"Thanks, Miss Ericson." He carefully placed the mounting block, painted with Jefferson Hunt's colors, on Reebok's left side, placed the reins over the gelding's neck and walked to the right side where he put his left hand in the right stirrup iron to make certain the saddle would be rock steady for Roberta. He kept his right hand on the reins behind the bit until she was up and settled.

Reebok whinnied.

"He's ready to hunt this morning." Roberta loved the little fellow. Most foxhunters love their horses. In many cases they love the animals more than their spouses, the horses proving more reliable.

Hunter turned to make sure Bill Dominquez and Mosby were getting along. Laura had them ready to go.

"Wish we could whip today." Hunter enviously sighed.

Laura lowered her voice. "We've got to baby-sit."

His voice brightened as his sister came up next to him. "Miss Ericson is better than Harleyetta. Oh, well, Mom always makes us work in the field on Saturdays. Weekdays we can whip."

"You can. I've got algebra class at nine in the morning this year and they couldn't change it."

"I forgot about that. You could tell Mom you don't want to work on Saturdays."

"Nah." Laura glanced around to make certain everything was done and they could mount up.

"Sometimes I wonder what Mom's going to do when we're gone. She can't make it alone." He grabbed a rag and wiped the dust off his boots then wiped off his sister's once she swung onto Go To. "I think about it a lot, you know. Like maybe I should bag college and stay here and work."

"You can't do that. You're going to be a veterinarian and then you'll make good money."

"I don't know."

"Hunter, come on. You've got to go next year. Besides, Mom would kill us if we didn't go to William and Mary. Deyhles always go to William and Mary."

"Yeah. Yeah." He squeezed her toe.

Harleyetta astride Gypsy, a 16.2-hand mare, walked in circles since the mare wouldn't stand still. Binky clambered aboard Whiskey, the perfect name for his horse. Even though Harley was mad at him, she'd cleaned his horse and loaded it on the trailer. The two humans didn't speak to one another. The horses did, neighing away and nosing each other.

Before convening the group, Cig checked her pockets. In the left pocket of her heavy melton jacket she carried a tiny flashlight, Kleenex, and a small folding toothbrush in a square plastic case. In her right pocket she carried fifty dollars, some change, and a small sharp pocketknife. Inside she had a small red moroccon-bound notebook made by Smythe of England with a tiny pencil inserted in a loop at the spine.

In her canary vest she carried her driver's license and her Virginia hunting license. She also carried Motrin.

Usually she carried a pistol loaded with ratshot but today she'd absentmindedly left it back at the barn.

Nothing she could do about it. She stood up in her stirrups. Everyone was just about ready.

"Gather 'round," Cig called out.

Binky warned Harleyetta through clenched teeth, "You keep your trap shut. All you do is stir up trouble."

"I feel guilty."

"You had nothing to do with Blackie's death," he whispered fiercely. "You kept your mouth shut for a year. Keep it shut forever. It's October twenty-second. You're having a flashback."

"I know that, idiot, but I feel guilty. This secret is making me sick."

"You're sick with or without secrets." He rolled his eyes.

"Why even talk to you? You don't have any feelings. What if I was the one who died?"

Binky squinted. The light hurt his eyes. "I wouldn't want to know."

"That I died?" Harleyetta peevishly replied.

"How you died. I wouldn't want to know." He may have been hungover but Binky was crystal clear about what he felt.

"Binky," she whispered, "I feel like a liar."

"Come on, Harley. It's time to move off. You're massaging your emotions. That's one thing about women I really can't stand."

"Then live without them."

"I could live just fine without women. Don't flatter yourself. It's none of your business."

"But it is. I was in the E.R. that night," Harleyetta whimpered.

"You'll be in it this morning if you don't shut up because I'll knock you clean off Gypsy. Now come on."

With wounded eyes she followed him to Cig.

"Come on, gang," Cig called again, standing up in her stirrups.

The group of thirty trotted over to Cig. Roger stayed in the back with the hounds, their eyes upturned to him as he sat on Sidekick, his huge chestnut. Carol Easter, Agnes Clark, and Jane Fogleman stayed with the hounds, too, as they were whipping in today. This was Carol's first time as a whipper-in, and she nervously coiled and uncoiled the sturdy leather thong on the whip. Not that mild-mannered Carol would actually whip a hound. She wouldn't, nor would most whippers-in. The hunting whips had a thin colorful nylon cracker at the end of the braided leather thong, which when expertly snapped out in the air emitted a rifle-shot noise. That usually did the trick. Of course, you had to practice or the cracker ended up in your face, on the horse, or worse, entangled in the branch of a tree. That had happened to Florence Moeser back in 1952, yanked her right off her horse. Said something about hunt clubs that no one ever forgot, and the story was passed along to each new member of the Jefferson Hunt—usually by Florence herself. In her eighties, she had lost none of her sense of humor even if she was a little stiff in the saddle.

Cig's alto voice carried well. "Roger's going to cast along the farm road first. We'll probably wind up down by the James. Archie Griswald just plowed under his riverside cornfield so stay to the side of it. He left the other corn standing, which was good of him, so if you run into him at the feed store or in town do thank him for his kindness. Roger, did I forget anything?"

"New coop, in-and-out, when we cross over into George Lawrence's, right there on the other side of Tinker's Creek."

"Oh, right. Now don't fret," Cig consoled them. "New coops always look bigger than they are. It's a two stride in-and-out. Every horse and rider can do it. This means you, Roberta."

Roberta blushed, but the attention from Cig gave her some courage.

Laura and Hunter, being young, never could fathom why middle-aged people who came to riding as adults feared jumping in-and-outs, two jumps placed with only one or two strides between them. Usually this configuration occurred between two fence lines as it did on George Lawrence's property. All you had to do was stay in your jumping position—eyes up, hands down—and let the horse do the work. Now if you had a horse that wanted to run out or refuse the jump, well, then you had to do the work.

When Go To was four, green and full of himself, Laura had to hold like mad on the side to which he wanted to run out—hold with all her might with her lower leg and check, release, and check again on the opposing rein. Finally, after one hairy hunt season, Go To decided it was easier to obey Laura than to exercise his own will. Then again, Laura had talent to spare, so Go To came along much faster than if someone else had been working with him.

"All right then. Let's escape the twentieth century."

The group laughed as Roger blew a few clear, piercing blasts on his horn. He stayed at the front of his pack. Carol was ahead on the left, Jane on the right, Agnes at the rear.

Fifty sterns, up in the air, wagged. Eyes bright, bodies sleek and in perfect condition, the Jefferson's pack of American hounds displayed the attention, affection, and discipline poured into them by Roger and Cig. Roger, a quiet Huntsman and bullheaded like them all, rode out on the farm road to the big meadow near the James River. There he cast his hounds, blowing a staccato signal on the horn, doubling the notes. With an encouraging tone of voice Roger called to them, "Yit try rouse 'im!" Within minutes they hit a scorching scent.

Madonna, the fast bitch strike hound, picked up the line first. She was quickly followed by Caruso and Pavarotti, two hounds with voices so beautiful they could bring tears even to the eyes of the uninitiated. Cig, at the front of her field, kept one eye on the Huntsman and the other on the territory. Grace, riding right in her sister's pocket, laughed, a laugh of fierce physical joy and of freedom. Cig let her reins out and Full Throttle, a born foxhunter, eased into a ground-eating gallop, his big, smooth reach making every stride a comfort.

Harleyetta's wiggly eyebrows shot upwards, she forgot her worries and plunged into the group of riders, Hunter adroitly keeping her from bumping into anyone but him.

As Cig predicted, once his wife was up front and running, Binky sidled up next to Roberta.

"You and Reebok look great today." Binky liked to think he still had an effect on women.

"Thank you." She gulped since she was moving so fast the air was rushing into her mouth. Within seconds the pace accelerated, and Roberta's eyes blurred from the speed.

Charlie, the generic name given a fox until the hunters knew exactly which fox they were chasing, needed his exercise this brilliant October morning so he led the pack through the in-and-out on George Lawrence's land. The coops, painted black, loomed like pyramids before the fearful. Cig and Full Throttle glided over. "A jump is just an interruption in your flat work," Cig told her students. And so they were. The fox, a sleek red, flew across the open pasture, giving the field the thrill of viewing him. Usually hunters don't see Charlie, but today he felt like tormenting them to the fullest. They were running flat-out so no one even had time to stop, point the horse's nose in the direction of the fox and hold out his or her cap, derby, or top hat at arm's length in the fox's direction, which was correct form for a sighting.

Then Charlie zigged to the right, plunging into a stand of hardwoods leading down to the river. The mists were rising off the water. He melted into them. The scent was good though and the hounds gave tongue. This particular fox, Old Charlie as he was known, an old hand at being chased, ran straight then zigzagged left up through the woods and out onto the plowed cornfield for they had long ago left George Lawrence's land. Then he dove into the standing corn. This was one of his favorite ruses since his den was on the far side of the cornfield. Once he was certain the hounds were crashing about in the corn he simply strolled out and walked casually to his den.

However, today proved a little different for, unknown to Old Charlie, Fattail happened to be in the same cornfield, on his way home from ravaging a chicken coop. The two had not time to dispute territory claims or rights of passage because Old Charlie, slick boy, kept to his original plan of action and the hounds found themselves with two fresh scents.

Roger didn't want his pack to split but since they were in the cornfield he could only go by what his ears were telling him. Cig pulled up on a rise at the edge of the field. The group enjoyed the check since no one had expected such a hard run so early. But then nothing in foxhunting could ever be expected, which was part of its appeal.

Roger trotted around the edge of the field. Old Charlie, well-known to him, would go to ground once he tired of so much strenuous exercise. Roger gathered his hounds, who obediently left the tantalizing scent.

Grace, her flushed cheeks only adding to her incredible beauty, stood next to her sister. "Hot damn!"

"This is going to be a great one—I feel it in my bones."

"Makes me forget everything silly. I'm starting to think that if I'm unhappy it's my own fault. This is how I want to feel every minute of my life."

Cig laughed. "Well, if you could hunt every day you would."

Grace tilted her head back, sucking in air. "Blackie knew how to feel. Maybe he's with us today."

Cig shrugged. "Maybe, but now he knows what it's all about, doesn't he?"

Grace turned. "What?"

"Life . . . and death."

Cig quieted as Roger swung the pack close to them. Talking might distract the hounds.

Roger hoped Fattail would have exited in that direction. No such luck. Then he moved to the east side of the field. Before he could turn the corner, little k.d., her first year out with the pack, struck. Her young voice, still high, rang true though, and the older hounds came to her. Within seconds they honored, or validated, k.d.'s call. That fast they tore over the meadows.

"Let's rodeo!" Cig smiled at Grace as Full Throttle surged forward.

The footing, padded with still green grass, cushioned the pounding hooves. The little ribbon on the back of Cig's hunt cap fluttered for a second in a ferocious crosswind, which died down as quickly as it came up. Kodiak used the occasion for some airs above the ground. Grace, a good rider, quickly put an end to that nonsense. She knew Kodiak felt unfulfilled if he didn't pull at least one stunt per hunt. He had a right to find out if she was asleep at the wheel.

The sound of thundering hooves sent a bevy of quail up into the air. As the hunters neared the woods from which they had so recently emerged, a huge buck and three does charged out right in front of them. Full Throttle never blinked or shied as Cig turned and hollered, "Ware deer!"

Deep music filled the air as the hounds sang to them with one voice on this shining day.

At the edge of the wide meadow the ground dipped into a swale. Coming out of the swale a post-and-rail fence line separated the grazing land from the woods. Since the land fell away, wherever they jumped would be a drop jump.

Cig never minded if her field took their own line over an obstacle like this. That meant the riders could jump the fence line anywhere they wanted. The one forbidden thing was for you to pass the Master. This is akin to peeing on the President.

At coops or on narrow trails Cig wanted the field to queue before the jumps. Otherwise she liked giving her people the opportunity to exercise their own judgment.

She picked a spot she figured had good footing and felt Full Throttle lift up, a mighty jet. She put her hands forward as he stretched out his dark bay neck. Landing on the other side, she searched for a decent trail through the woods, which also had many rock outcrops. Billygoat land.

Roberta, stuck on the other side of the post and rail, shivered with terror. Laura jumped back over the fence as soon as she realized Roberta hadn't cleared it. Binky, too thrilled by the pace, never looked back so he lost his chance to "attend" to Roberta.

"Miss Ericson, I'll give you a lead. Reebok can do it."

"I know Reebok can," Roberta wailed. "It's me I'm worried about."

Laura heard the hounds' voices moving farther and farther away. Finding the field while picking one's way through heavy woods was a Kit Carson job and Laura didn't want to be separated from them. Also, she knew that on a flaming scent like this her mother would fly like a bat out of hell. Ask no questions, take no prisoners.

"Miss Ericson, climb the fence and hold my horse. I'll get Reebok over. This is the only really hard jump we've got in this territory so there's nothing to worry about after this."

"No," came the quavering voice. "You give me a lead. I've got to learn."

"Reebok's push-button." Laura plucked her up, jumping back over the fence. "Just point him at the fence, keep your hands low, grab mane—I always do—and squeeze."

"You do not grab mane, Laura. Don't lie to make me feel better."

"I do. Hunter does. Mom does. Sometimes you just have to. Ready?"

"Yes." The pale voice was now almost colorless.

Laura took Go To in a slow circle. "Fall in."

Roberta did. As Laura approached the post and rail, she deliberately kept Go To from speeding up because that would scare Roberta half to death, and Reebok would do whatever he saw Go To do. Up and over the Laura/Go To team sailed, two creatures, one mind. Reebok cleared it with Roberta, stiff-armed, clutching mane, her knuckles white. Her eyes widened, her toes pointed down but she hung on.

"You okay, Miss Ericson?"

"Yes, thanks to you."

"You did it. Take a deep breath and drop your weight into your heels."

"Oh dear, did my leg come up?"

"Hey, that's what jockeys do. Flap your arms like a chicken for a second. Okay, we'd better boogie."

Laura squeezed the gray flanks and plunged into the sweet-smelling woods, sunlight dropping through the leaves like powdered gold through gauze.

"I can't hear the hounds, Laura."

"I think they'll head down to the river. If not, we'll pick up tracks once we get to the old canal road."

As the two hurried along, Cig was indeed on the old canal road, which needed to be cleared each summer by the club lest it become a tangled mess. The James wasn't the easiest river to cross even this far north in Nelson County, Buckingham County being on the other side of the water. As the James rolled on, growing and widening down through other hunt territories, it became a huge river, enriching the very land it cleft in two. The whole United States could be viewed as not only an aggregate of states but as a patchwork of hunting territories carved out over the centuries with rivers, mountains, and deserts as natural boundaries.

The canal road, a little slippery, proved trickier than Cig had anticipated. For one thing, the mist that usually lifted off the river hung thick and moist. A silver fog enshrouded the riders as they followed the hounds, their voices ghostly and muffled. Cig slowed to a trot.

She motioned for Grace to come alongside her. "What do you think?"

"He can't get across the river at this point but if he makes it back to Tinker's Creek he'll go right up the middle of the creek and run upland—if it's the fox I think it is. Fattail."

"Yeah, he's smarter than the rest of them put together. I'm going to cut up on the other side of the creek. Let's see if we can stay clear of his line but still get out of here fast."

"Okay."

At Tinker's Creek, Cig held up her arm for the field to halt. She strained to hear the hounds. She heard hoofbeats. Laura and Roberta pulled up at the rear of the field. Hunter turned and winked at his sister, put his fingers to his lips. They all strained to hear a twig snap, a hound call, anything.

Cig turned to Grace and shrugged. The fox must have leaped the creek and continued on. They picked their way over the creek and just when the entire field was on the other side, Caruso burst out of the woods, followed within minutes by the rest of the pack.

"Staff!" Cig yelled.

Everyone crowded to the side of the road, horses' tails turned away from the oncoming hounds as the pack splashed into the creek, which fed the James, then scrambled up the opposing bank. Roger and Sidekick cleared it in one huge arc. Carol, Jane, and Agnes were nowhere to be seen.

"Reverse field," Laura called from the back just as her mother soared over the creek.

They turned around in the order in which they had been moving and blasted out of there. At least they hadn't lost the hounds. The pace accelerated. By now they'd been running, with the exception of the cornfield check, for a solid forty-five minutes.

Harleyetta, next to Hunter, was gasping. "If this keeps up we'll be in Richmond for lunch."

A tree blocked their path looming dangerously in the mist. It must have come down in the previous week's high winds. Cig reacted instantly. She slowed up, warned the field, then adroitly picked her way around the outstretched branches and continued on.

Finally they curved to the left, away from the river, out of the fog and back through the woods into a very small clearing. Not a sound could be heard other than people and horses trying to catch their breath. Cig halted in the clearing.

"We're over to Jace Goodling's place," she said to Grace.

"Damn. I didn't think we'd gone that far."

They sat quietly for a bit. A red-tailed hawk, gazing down at them, decided they weren't worth squat and flew on.

As they strained for an echo, a reverberation, the mist from the river crept into the clearing. Cig rode to the edge and, scarcely breathing, sat still. She glanced back to look at the field. Roberta, worn out, pulled on her flask filled with a concoction of orange juice, bourbon, and many tablespoons of sugar. Binky sidled up to her, checking to see where the dreaded Harleyetta was, and gratefully knocked back a swig when it was offered to him. Grace, face flushed, chatted with Bill, a colleague of her husband's, an OB/GYN man. As it was a small hospital, everyone knew everybody.

For an instant Cig felt as though time were frozen. She was in a tableau painted by Sir Alfred Munnings, George Stubbs, or Ben Marshall. Here at the close of the twentieth century, the most murderous era of all human history, here for this brief moment, she and this intrepid band belonged to something ancient, something Homer wrote about, something great Elizabeth I enjoyed, something so deep in human bones that no amount of technology or "progress" could change it: the chase.

The horses, nostrils flaring, large kind eyes looking about, pink tongues playing with bits, could be horses that Achilles would have admired, or Balzac, that passionate foxhunter. Century after century, the bond between human and horse held them together in a ballet of use and love, a negotiation between need and service. The horse submitted to domestication, the human to providing food and training, until a time came when one couldn't quite live without the other. Not even the advent of the automobile could dissolve this bargain of friendship.

The scarlet coats of the gentlemen answering the flaming red of the turning maples, the shining black patent leather boot tops of the ladies who had earned their colors, the white saddle pads and the rich Havana brown of the well-oiled tack, the vibrancy of the scene filled her with a sense of fragile holiness.

And for a flash, a fleeting screech of time, she could see how truly beautiful her sister was. The high peach shine in Grace's cheeks, the dancing eyes, the hard-won and bought perfection of her body, the light touch of her hands, the perfect pitch of her voice. Yes, her sister was Aphrodite and for that split second she forgot decades of suppressed jealousy, the pain of not being the beautiful one, and she just drank in her sister's beauty as though Grace had stepped, laughing, from a sensuous canvas by John Singer Sargent.

Hunter, tall, the black shadow of his shaved whiskers barely visible beneath his square jaw, his curly black hair peeking out from under his old hunt cap, so worn the black was now faded to brown, could have stepped off a canvas as well. His lips glistened red. His teeth were as straight and white as the orthodontist could make them. Hunter didn't realize he was irresistible. For that his mother thanked God.

Laura was a template of Grace, her beauty unripened whereas Grace's was in full flower. In a culture that worshiped surfaces, Cig knew beauty would help her daughter survive. Laura, without ever consciously knowing it, had learned a woman's watchfulness. Her brother was far more trusting and innocent. Laura listened, weighed, and then acted. As for last night's declaration, Cig couldn't make head or tail of it. She stared at Laura, straining to remember how it felt to teeter on the edge of womanhood.

And she thought of Blackie. How he would have loved today's hunt. No fence was too high. No run too hard. He delighted in putting the pedal to the metal. His rider's ego was out of proportion to his accomplishment, but no one had much seemed to mind.

The funny thing was, even though he was never a true partner, a mature man, she had loved him longer than was reasonable because he was all she knew. His sheer physical intensity overwhelmed her. She could never detach herself from how gorgeous he was, and he became more handsome with age.

She put him out of her mind as she listened for the hounds. What was there about physical exhilaration, about the fluid beauty of foxhunting, that could open her soul? She searched the woods then glanced back at the people. In her own way, she loved them, even the ones who drove her crazy.

A lone howl alerted her—Ramey, the basso profundo of the pack. Not a fast hound but as steady as a rock, Ramey never bayed falsely. Closer came the magical voice. Then she heard Lily Pons, a funny little bitch with pop eyes who straggled behind but somehow managed to keep in the hunt. Lily had an uncanny ability to stay on the scent no matter how rough the terrain and to stick to a cooling scent until it warmed again.

Cig held up her hand for silence since the group had begun to gossip. They quieted.

Fattail himself burst into the clearing, stopped in his tracks right in front of Cig. He had the audacity, the sheer gall to bark right in the Master's face. If the field hadn't seen it they wouldn't have believed it. Then Fattail, flicking the mighty crimson plume for which he was named, trotted around the group, downshifting to a walk out the west side of the small meadow and back into the woods. Within seconds, the pack dashed into the field only to run around the horses who naturally began moving about a bit, thereby disturbing the scent. Everyone in the field turned his horse's nose and held his hat in the direction of Fattail's imperious exit so that when Carol first rode by on the right, then Jane on the left, at least they knew where the fox had gone. It was a rare sight indeed to see the entire field indicating the direction of a fox's path, but Fattail's display was so blatant, even the least observant couldn't miss it. Roger, followed by Agnes, emerged, appraised the situation and dove back into the woods, Cig hot on his heels.

They cantered through the trees, praying their knees would survive it, headed up a steep, rocky incline, and came out in Bob Maki's hay field, the hay bales in rows, a flat hay wagon standing between the rows. The sun glittered on the hay, squares of gold. The fox shot through the hay field, leaving the hounds and the field a torturous path to follow. Cig, impatient, did something she would chide a member for doing. She set her course straight for the other side of the field, soaring over the hay wagon.

At the fence line into the next field she cleared a coop, the field following behind her. She ran hell-for-leather through that field, down-hill most of it, taking a coop at the other fence line. Into the woods again but only for an instant because Fattail scooted through a huge tree trunk just to drive the hounds nuts and get a few stuck behind him. Then Fattail charged into a herd of sheep. That trick slowed the hounds for some time. Roger could have lifted them and brought them to the other side of the herd but Fattail, a genius at dumping hounds, had vanished. Roger let his hounds work while the field checked for a moment, grateful for the rest.

Ramey stopped and lifted his nose, then put it back to the ground. Caruso and Pavarotti, far in the front, began to whine. They lost the line.

"How does he do it!" Cig slapped her hand on her thigh.

Grace joined her as did Hunter and Laura.

"Mom, he's got some mojo working in this field." Hunter lifted his cap off his head and ran a hand through his pasted down curls. "He always disappears in the same place."

"Into thin air." Grace found need of her flask, full of Harvey's Hunting port, which she offered her sister who took a big swig and handed it back.

Then Cig pulled on her own flask, straight scotch, and offered it to Grace.

"God, no. I'd die."

"Wimp." Cig smiled.

"Mom?"

"Hunter, I'll avert my eyes since you aren't of age." Cig passed him the flask, and when he returned it, offered it to Laura. "A sip?"

Laura shook her head. "No."

"What I don't understand is he has no den here. If he went to ground—well, it's just too weird." Grace accepted a drink from Harleyetta's flask. It brought tears to Grace's eyes.

Cig spoke to the field. "Fattail ditched us again. Same time, same station."

"I can't believe that he barked in your face." Harleyetta, like the others, was astounded.

"What do you think he was saying?" Bill laughed.

"Fuck you," Binky offered.

"And then some." Cig laughed.

Carol, on her way to gather hounds still in the woods, just shook her head.

Cig called out to her, "If I live to be one hundred years old I swear I will find out *how* he does this."

"Better turn into a fox then," Carol called back.

"I bet other foxes don't even know," Florence Moeser added, her voice cracking a bit.

Cig, grateful that Florence had survived the chase, exhaled. She knew, too, that someday Florence would die hunting—and that's exactly how the eighty-four-year-old wanted it.

"Folks, let's hold up here for a minute."

A hound squealed back in the woods. It sounded like Streisand, hurt or scared.

Cig waited a moment but the yowling continued. Carol had ridden to the other side of the woods to gather hounds so she wouldn't be able to hear this one. Wanting to speed things along Cig noticed that Roger was checking on the other side of the sheep. Fat chance.

"Harleyetta, come with me. Grace, take the field—just in case." Cig singled out Harleyetta to make her feel good and because the woman had to have known she was often the butt of many jokes, both because of her intermittent drinking and the fact that she couldn't hold her horse. She was a loyal member of the club, though, and Cig liked her.

They rode into the thickly scented woods. The mist, heavier than before and odd for this time of the morning, nine thirty now, continued to roll up from the river. They spied Jane Fogelman, on foot, trying to overturn the huge old fallen tree trunk that Streisand refused to leave. Cig was glad Jane had found Streisand. The bitch put her head back and howled at the top of her considerable lungs.

"Jane, what's the problem?"

"I don't know. She won't leave here and she's just—well, look at her." Jane was at a loss to explain the hound's distress. "Bet Fattail ran through the trunk or stopped and left a little marker, you know." Jane, with a major effort, rolled the trunk a bit more. A bony hand, what was left of it, protruded through a rotted hole in the trunk. "Good God!" Jane involuntarily took a step back.

Cig dismounted, handing her reins to Harleyetta, whose eyes bugged out of her head. Without saying a word Cig knelt down and began tearing at the hole in the trunk. A skeleton was wedged in the fallen tree trunk. They stared.

"This huge old chestnut has been here for three hundred years at least. Look at the size of it." Jane kept blinking. "The body was in the trunk. Now who would do something like that? And why?"

"Why is obvious," Cig answered her. "To hide it."

Harleyetta handed the reins to Jane and carefully examined the bones, which had fallen apart over the decades. "He's been here for a long, long time. There's not a scrap of flesh, a bit of hair, nothing." She plucked out the skull; the big square teeth were still intact.

Jane patted Streisand to calm her down.

Cig took the skull from Harleyetta. A strange flash of recognition made her nearly drop it. There was something unnervingly familiar about that dead smile.

"Maybe he's a leftover from the War Between the States." Cig stared at the whitened bones, a faint shiver running over her body as she replaced the skull.

"Could be," Jane said. "But the Yankee gunboats didn't get this far upriver and there was nothing to come up here for anyway."

"Meanness. Never forget that." Harleyetta stood back up.

"Well, let's call the sheriff, and he can give this fellow, or what's left of him, a resting place with a stone on it." Cig held Gypsy while Harleyetta, with difficulty, remounted. A rustle behind some dogwoods diverted her attention for a moment. She thought she caught a glimpse of Fattail.

Then Cig, thanks to her height, easily swung into the saddle. "My God, what a day this has been—and it's not over yet." She half-laughed.

"Best run all season. Maybe ever." Jane took off her cap. She glanced again at the bones in the trunk, then mounted up. "I'm going back farther into the woods. We're still missing two hounds."

Streisand followed Cig and Harleyetta as they walked away.

"Guess you get used to seeing stuff like that, being a nurse."

Harleyetta shook her head. "Not quite like that. It's worse when you know them." Her lips clamped down as though she were fighting the words that threatened to tumble out of her own mouth.

"Speaking of knowing them, I don't know if I ever told you how much I appreciate all you did for Blackie when he came into the E.R. I know he was beyond help, but you tried everything to revive him. I'll always be in your debt, Harley. You've taken care of many of us since you've been down at the hospital."

"Oh, Cig, don't mention it. He died fast and happy. Even if I'd been at Grace's house I don't think I could have saved him, but you've got to try. That's—well—" She shook her head.

"Happy?"

"Uh—" Harleyetta stalled.

"What do you know that I don't?"

"Nothing." Her voice hit high C.

Cig, without knowing it, opened Pandora's box by her nonchalance. "Knowing Blackie, he'd probably just got laid and—"

Harley breathed a sigh of relief. "Here I've been carrying this around for a year and you knew all the time! I've got to hand it to you, Cig. You're something special. Most women couldn't have taken it."

Cig shrugged. Her breath caught in her throat. She wasn't sure she wanted to know whatever it was Harleyetta thought she knew. "Can't do anything about it when they're gone."

"Can't do anything about it when they're alive. Men."

Cig kept her voice as firm as she could. "How'd you know?"

"I put him on the gurney after we tried every procedure to resuscitate him. Helped undress him. His jockey shorts told the tale. I mean, I knew anyway. We all did. We didn't know if you knew what had been going on so everybody just clammed up. We talked to each other, of course. Can't stop that." She inhaled. "Well, he died in the saddle. Must have been hell for her to get his clothes on."

"Grace is a remarkable woman," Cig whispered.

"Oh, here, I've made you think about all this again, and you and Grace have made your peace. Blackie was just like that, you know. In his own way, he loved you."

"That's what he always said." Cig smiled reflexively. The mist felt clammy on her skin. A wound opened up in her stomach. The edge of the woods was ahead.

The field stood waiting.

"They'll never believe this. None of us will ever believe this day," Harleyetta said, voice filled with excitement.

Streisand bounded forward to join the pack.

Cig stared at her sister and wondered if she could keep from killing her.

Another yowl from the woods and a call from Jane drew Cig's attention away from Grace.

"Found it," was what her words sounded like, but then her voice faded away.

"Grace," Cig, relieved to have an excuse to be alone for a few moments to collect herself, called out, "I'm going back for a minute."

"Okay." Grace answered, unaware of what had transpired.

The hound's voice pierced the air. Cig turned Full Throttle back into the woods. "Harley, tell them what Jane found. I'll catch up to you if you move off."

She had to get through this hunt, get the horses back home and then think of how to kill Grace. Swiftly or a slow, wretched death?

She rode back to the trunk. The bony hand seemed to reach out for her. She shuddered now, uncontrollably. Within seconds she was enveloped in mist. She had no desire to be in the fog with an oddly familiar skeleton no matter how old it was.

"Poor bastard," she thought and then as quickly thought the phrase applied to herself as well.

She rode toward the cry of the hound, which suddenly stopped. She heard the sound of huge paws racing toward her. An enormous black and tan thundered past her. She'd never seen that hound before. Few people hunted black and tans in America. Some Irish hunts used them. She reined in Full Throttle, listened a moment as the footfall faded away. She started to turn then looked down past her left foot. Fattail looked right back up at her.

"You little shit."

He seemed to smile. Why not? There wasn't a thing she could do to him. With elegant insolence he walked in front of her.

PART II

7

∞

The mist thickened but Cig could see Fattail leading the way. She couldn't see much else. She thought she was heading toward the James River and in an easterly direction. When Fattail pranced out onto the old canal road she knew her sense of direction hadn't failed her. However, the silver fog made her think twice about cutting back up into the woods to try and rejoin her field. Common sense told her to stop and sit tight but she couldn't resist following the fox, who strolled along as though her pet.

She'd known Fattail for four years, as well as his mother and father and littermates. Born in a big den on George Lawrence's property, he had possessed a noticeable tail even as a cub.

Solon Deyhle and G-Mom taught her to learn the ways of the fox. If winter proved harsh she threw out dead chickens and rabbits for them. She'd put on her snowshoes or cross-country skis and visit each den in turn. When foxes bred, then taught their cubs to hunt, she was sure to keep her hounds far away from them.

During cubbing season, so-called because the fox cubs need to learn to hunt just as the hound puppies do, she noted who remained with the dens, who was missing and who moved on to form new dens.

As the fox preyed on rabbits and small game, so the larger predators preyed on him. Fattail survived his cubhood and quickly displayed that quirky intelligence for which foxes are famous, but he had something else, a kind of genius really.

She'd seen him once at the kennels by moonlight, on a muggy July night. He appeared to be studying the hounds. After hunting season she often glimpsed him over by George's cornfields where the pickings were rich.

Cig, like most American foxhunters, never wanted to kill the fox, most especially reds since they ran true. Grays ran in circles. The death of a red fox, a cause for lamentation, could only mean that the quarry had grown old or was sick.

She had witnessed amazing things in the wild. Only last year she came across two foxes, a male and a female, on the high field behind her own house. The male ran away, hoping to draw the pack after him. The vixen crouched in the pasture, hounds all around her, and not one hound found her. Her mate saved her and lost the hounds after a ten-minute chase.

Another time, she ran a red for forty minutes. She knew the fox, a vixen with forelegs that were white up to her elbows, a distinctive look-ing animal. The vixen ran to her den, which Cig expected since she was tiring, but instead of ducking in, the vixen lay down right on the lip of the den. She lowered her head and asked to die. The hounds killed her in seconds. When Roger called them off and examined the vixen, he dis-covered that she had shingles, an extremely painful disease, fatal for foxes. The vixen chose a swift death. There was a nobility in the animal's final moments on earth, a nobility denied fatally ill humans who were carted away to hospitals, sterile, clear tubes jammed in every orifice, drugs coursing down those tubes.

Cig hoped she could go down like the vixen when her time came. Blackie, the son-of-a-bitch, had had a good death. Roger, Wilco, over and out. A surge of fury welled up in her. She unconsciously squeezed Full Throttle, who broke into a trot. She relaxed. Fattail shot a look back over his shoulder.

Cig would have given anything to be a fly on the wall when Blackie died. Was he in the act with Grace? It was almost funny. She could just picture Grace, horrified, rolling the six-foot-four carcass off of her or hopping off if Blackie had decided to take his ease and lie back. Or perhaps she'd given him a blow job. Probably not. Not that Blackie didn't enjoy them but he was a grappler, he liked to get up close and personal, as ABC sportscasters used to say.

How could Grace do it? There were times when she had suspected, like at the Christmas party the year before Blackie died. Not that anything untoward occurred but Blackie's gift to Grace, a nineteenth-century stock pin, a fox head with ruby eyes, was extravagant. When she questioned him he replied, "Well, it just looked like Grace to me. Besides, you always bitch and moan that you have to do all the Christmas shopping." She wound up being proud of him for doing his own shopping. Then, too, he bought four new tires for her Wagoneer so she felt she got the better value. If he'd given Grace a more expensive present than he'd given her, she'd have known.

Did Will know? Did he care? The great thing about being a doctor was that a doctor can retreat into work. Since his work might mean life or death for someone, everyone rewarded him for his retreat.

But Grace. How many times had Cig dragged over to her sister's to cry when she had uncovered Blackie's latest infidelity? How many times had Grace told her he wasn't worth the tears? And Cig would say, "I know that but I love him." Grace's affairs, discreet ones, sometimes amused and distracted Cig, who lived vicariously. It never occurred to her that Grace's mischief would hit so close to home.

The more Blackie strayed the more she forgave him, at least on the surface. She sensed she had the admiration of the community for her stoicism. Admiration was some reward, surely, but it never got her what she wanted: a real partner. Hunter at seventeen was more emotionally responsible than his father was at fifty. Blackie felt that if he provided a high standard of living for his family then he was responsible, above reproach. The money made everything all right.

Cig came back to the present. She was lost. She had no idea where she was or how far she'd ridden as her mind churned over Blackie and Grace's betrayal. She checked Full Throttle. His flanks weren't tucked up so she supposed she hadn't been out too long. It was curious how time could collpase when you were in the grip of great, conflicting emotions.

In this case love and pure-D hate. She loved Blackie and she hated him. Same for Grace.

Fattail merrily moved along. His ears swept forward, his tail had a gay swag to it. Every now and then he'd look around to check on Cig.

She stopped for a moment. She heard music. So did Full Throttle. If Fattail heard it, he paid no mind, which was unusual.

How silly to be riding along the river, enveloped in this mantle of translucent silver, sinking into misery. She headed in the direction of the music to get her bearings.

The music grew louder. "Black Bottom," played by an orchestra, floated over the James River. The mist thinned for a moment. She thought she saw an old Rolls Royce and some other vintage cars. Light flickered within the house. She recognized it as Sherwood Forest. Her heart stopped in her chest. Sherwood Forest was the home, respectively, of William Henry Harrison, America's ninth president, and then John Tyler, the tenth. Sherwood Forest was in Princess Anne Hunt territory. That was at least ninety miles down river. She could see figures dancing. The music lifted her spirits. What a party. She headed for the house but the fog swirled around her. A theme party. She thought it would be fun to ride up. But—it couldn't be Sherwood Forest. There must be a house that resembled it. She racked her brain. Nothing remotely resembled Sherwood Forest, the longest private frame dwelling in the United States. How'd she get this far?

Fattail kept going. She could see only his tail now. She was afraid to turn back, afraid to stop, afraid to go forward.

The music died away. She heard nothing for a long time and then she heard voices off in the river, the slap of water against a hull but that died away, too.

Suddenly, a solitary figure, gaunt, armed, appeared on a slight promontory to her right, just on the river.

"Halt!"

She could see him clearly now. Some clown was dressed as a cavalry staff sergeant right down to the gold facing on his sleeves. His boots were worn. His eyes seemed to burn, as if with hunger. His uniform was in tatters.

"Who the hell are you?" Cig called out with all the command of a Master of Foxhounds.

"That's yours to answer, not mine. Are you friend or foe?"

"If this is some kind of costume party, your uniform is a mess."

His light brown mustache curled upwards. "Ma'am, I'd be most obliged if it were—any kind of party. But I am posted here and you cannot pass. The river is full of gunboats and the shore is full of spies. Who are you and why are you here?"

Cig decided she'd better play along with him. Perhaps he was a Civil War reenactor who'd gone off the deep end.

"I'm Pryor Chesterfield Deyhle. Blackwood is my married name."

"Kin to Brigadier General Reckless Deyhle?"

Fattail observed how this registered on Cig's face.

"Uh—yes."

"Come closer, ma'am. Let me look at you."

Not knowing why, fearing the man was a raving lunatic, she did in fact ride closer. After all, he had a rifle and she did not. "Spittin' image." He lowered his rifle. "Pardon me for seeming rude—but is this the fashion?" He indicated her hunting attire. "Is it a uniform of some sort?"

"Uh—kind of. Yes. What happened to yours?"

"I'm better off than most. I've got boots."

"I see. Is there a reenactment nearby?"

"A what?"

"A battle. From the War Between the States."

He cocked his head. "Miss Deyhle, the whole state of Virginia is a battlefield. The Yankee gunboats sail up and down the James at will now. They fired on Brandon, Shirley's tore to pieces, and they burned down the library at Westover. You'd best move on and get home."

She didn't know why she did it. She knew the man was out of his mind. She remembered the recitation of phrases for crazy she and her family had done in the truck that morning but none seemed to apply. He was crazy, but he seemed so sincere, so concerned for her welfare. She unsnapped her sandwich case and leaned over, handing him her sandwich.

"Thank you, ma'am, I can't. You won't have anything to eat."

"Please. I'll be home soon and I can find something."

He reached out and took the sandwich. "God bless you, Mistress Deyhle. God bless you and keep you safe in these terrible times. Pass on."

She rode away following Fattail, looking over her shoulder at the sergeant, already shrouded in a veil of silver threads.

She shivered uncontrollably. Tears came to her eyes. Maybe she was the one 'round the bend.

Again she heard sounds on the river and then nothing.

She stopped and dismounted. Her legs shook beneath her. Fattail tiptoed over and sat next to her. He looked up at her with pity in his eyes.

"Fattail, where have you led me? Is this the fox's revenge for being chased?" She leaned against Full Throttle's neck to steady herself, stifled a sob, then took the reins over his head and led him for a bit. She loosened his girth. He seemed grateful for the break.

For a moment she thought she saw poorly dressed men on the river in flat boats, one man at the rudder, the others on both sides of the prow, poles in hand. Each year people met on the James to compete in the bateaux races. Cig exhaled gratefully. Whoever the guy was in the Confederate uniform, it was coincidence that he knew Reckless Deyhle was her great-great-grandfather. Reckless had founded the Jefferson Hunt in 1888. Bizarre, but this day was turning into one she hoped never to repeat despite the fabulous runs of the morning.

She trudged on. Then she heard the hoarse cries of struggle, gunfire and the neighing of horses. She thought she even heard sabers clash. Quickly, she tightened Full Throttle's girth and hopped up.

The sounds were all around her. She heard nasal British accents and then American voices. Someone screamed, "Limey filth!" She smelled smoke, and the sulfur stung her eyes. Just as quickly the sounds died away. She trembled from head to toe. She wanted to go home. She'd check herself into the hospital. Why be proud? The mind can snap same as a bone. She'd had a terrible shock, after all.

The earth shook. Fattail scurried into the woods. She followed him. He stopped about fifty feet off the canal road under an enormous sycamore. Cig's heart rattled in her rib cage, her breathing became shallow and the ground moved underneath her. Full Throttle neighed. Cig wanted to hide, but where? She hoped the fog would swallow her. A curl in the mists opened for a moment and she saw, or thought she saw, a sea of British cavalry running hard but in formation, maybe a thousand of them. Frozen in terror, she watched. Could she have stumbled onto some movie shoot? Virginia was popular these days for locations especially because so much of the original architecture remained undisturbed. Shoot or not, the cavalry was frightening. After what she figured to be about twenty minutes the rumble died away. Sweat streamed down her face.

Fattail picked his way down to the canal road. As if in a trance Cig followed. She couldn't tell the time because of the mists. She never hunted with a wristwatch. The last thing she wanted to worry about when hunting was time. The hounds or Full Throttle told her when enough was enough.

After what seemed hours the mist began to lift. The first thing Cig noticed was the James River, sparkling and wide. She'd hunted here before. She *was* in Princess Anne territory, ten miles past Sherwood Forest more or less. She slumped in the saddle as the fear ebbed from her body. She had no idea how she could have come this far. It was impossible but here she was and Full Throttle wasn't heaving. As relief flooded over her she again checked for her bearings. Weston Manor should be visible on the other side of the river. She was certain the great estate was on the south side of the river's bend, far away given the great width of the river at this point. But Weston Manor was nowhere to be seen. Begun in 1700, it commanded one's attention.

Then she noticed the size of the virgin timber. She had no memory of the state or federal government preserving the forests this far down the James River although they certainly should have done so way back in the nineteenth century.

Fattail picked up a trot now. He determinedly pushed on, taking her to a slow, graceful curve in the James, where huge black walnuts marked the bend. When they rounded the curve a beautiful clearing greeted their eyes, emerald green, bounded by chestnut rail snake fencing. Framed by mighty chestnuts, a two-story brick home sat in the middle of a second pasture, which Cig could see about five hundred yards distant. A bluejay squawked overhead. A glitter crossed Fattail's eyes as the bluejay swooped down to tease the fox. He turned for a moment and stared up into Cig's eyes then ecstatically leaped into the air as the bluejay narrowly escaped being pinned between two clever red paws. Then Fattail rolled over like a cub, jumped up and ran at top speed into the sweet dense forest.

"Good-bye, you little devil," she called after him. "I'll figure out your disappearing act yet."

Happily she turned for the graceful house, praying that someone would be home and kind enough to give her a Coca-Cola. Three cats chased one another around the front door. Cig wearily got off Full Throttle. A wrought-iron hitching post conveniently by the door allowed her to tie the beautiful bay, something she would never have done without a halter if she hadn't been so weary. She noticed a half-stone, half-timber barn about one hundred yards from the main dwelling. As she had ridden in on the river side, her view had been obscured by the majestic trees but she could see now that a dirt river road widened and headed south and that another road came through the fields to the barn. There was also a simple dock on the river. The house didn't seem familiar, although the spot was vaguely so. She thought she knew every big house on the lower James. She was so tired and still vibrating with sorrow over the discovery of Grace and Blackie's affair; she didn't trust herself to know where she was.

She knocked on the door.

No one answered.

Cig walked around the back. A brick summer kitchen was behind the house, connected by an open walkway. A delicious aroma awakened her to the fact that she was about as hungry as the nutcase to whom she gave her sandwich. He seemed like such a good man. Mental illness takes many forms.

She walked to the kitchen. It was a true old-fashioned summer kitchen with a big brick oven, large enough to stand in. Bread slots curved along one side. Huge wrought-iron hooks hung from the ceiling and herbs dried overhead. An iron pot about as big as next week hung over the fire.

"These people are serious about authenticity." Cig smiled to herself as she beheld a pretty woman in a full skirt, maybe twenty-five or -six, bending over the pot.

"Excuse me, ma'am, but I'm lost."

The woman turned around, her deep green eyes widened, then she screamed, "Pryor!"

Cig felt terrible because she didn't recognize the woman who used her Christian name. Also, her greeting was unnerving.

Weeping, the woman threw her arms around Cig. "You don't know how we've worried." Then she held her out at arm's length. "The fashion?"

"Uh—"

"No matter, come, come. Your brother's clearing back acres. He'll be so happy to see you."

As if in a daze Cig followed the pretty woman who fairly skipped along she was so excited.

"You must tell me everything about London—once you've recovered from your journey, of course . . ." She lifted her voice. "There he is." She waved, jumping up and down with joy. "Tom, Tom, look who's here!"

Tom ducked out from under the heavy reins that rested behind his neck. The team of draft horses, two mighty bays with white feathers around their hooves, patiently stood as he left them. As soon as he caught sight of Cig he broke into a run.

"Praise be to God!" He flung himself on Cig who was nearly knocked over from the impact. When she collected herself and looked into this man's face it was as if she was staring at her male self. He kissed her and hugged her. She didn't want to be rude so she kissed him, too. "Praise God." Then he hugged and kissed the pretty woman who must have been his wife.

Pryor Chesterfield Deyhle Blackwood fainted dead away.

8

A warm flickering light filled Cig's eyes when she opened them. A heavy quilt covered her, and her boots had been pulled off. Burning cherry wood filled the room with a warm fragrance.

"Here." The pretty woman whom she had surprised in the summer kitchen helped her sit up and handed her hot cider.

"Thank you." A few gulps reminded her that she hadn't eaten in hours. "I'm sorry to trouble you."

"Don't you recognize me?" The green eyes beckoned.

"No." Cig closed her eyes for a second. "Your voice sounds familiar."

"A hot meal will enliven your wits." The young woman had a small pot warming in the fireplace. She ladled out some porridge into a smooth wooden bowl and cut off a large slice of moist cornbread, placing a big square of fresh home-churned butter next to it.

Cig stood up. Her knees shook and buckled under her.

"Pryor!" The woman quickly put her hands under Cig's armpits and with surprising strength hauled her to her feet. "Here, let me help you to the table." Alarm registered on her even features.

Cig felt like an overlarge toddler as she was assisted to a small, beautifully crafted table. She sank into a graceful, simple chair.

"Thank you."

The woman smiled, buttered the slice of cornbread. With trembling hands Cig managed to get the food into her mouth. She felt better.

"This is the most delicious cornbread and butter I've ever tasted."

"Should be. It's your mother's recipe."

"My mother's been dead for years." Cig blinked.

"See there, you remember your mother. A fine woman she was. You and Tom strongly take after her."

Cig ate, needing the sustenance to settle her nerves as much as her body.

"Hunger is the best spice." The woman brought her more food.

Cig wobbled up. "My horse."

The woman gently pushed her back into the finely made wooden chair. "He's in the stable getting acquainted with Helen, Castor, and Pollux. They have much to discuss."

"Thank you." Cig, relieved, reached for the bowl of porridge.

"Once you're yourself again you'll have to tell us where you bought such a handsome animal. That's the finest horse in Virginia, better than Governor Nicholson's or Daniel Boothrod's horses. And you know what popinjays they are."

Cig didn't recognize the governor's name. She let it pass. "I bred him myself."

"Ah—the Deyhle gift with horses. Tom is hoping to breed someday but there's so much to do, and we're shorthanded. Times are changing so, Pryor. Your father brought over two indentured servants and their term soon expires. Slaves are exorbitantly expensive and Tom says they're still heathens."

Cig blinked then chose to ignore what seemed like rant. "I apologize for the trouble I've caused you. I don't know what happened to me. I feel fine—honestly. I can sleep in the stable with Full Throttle. Wouldn't be the first time." She looked out the windows at the night, her smile revealing her dazzling teeth. "If you point me in the right direction I'll be off at first light."

"Off where?" The young woman asked, her brows knitting together.

"Home."

"This is home."

Cig's lower lip jutted out. "Please, I don't mean to be rude, but my home is upriver in Nelson County."

A flicker of bewilderment crossed the pretty face. "You're at Buckingham." As Cig didn't respond the young woman continued, "The land granted your mother's father in 1619. You're home at Buckingham."

"Buckingham?" Cig's mind spun like a kaleidoscope. Nothing held long enough for her to focus. Cig's mother carried Buckingham blood. "And what is your last name?"

"The same as yours." The young woman wanted to laugh. "Deyhle."

"What is your first name?"

The woman impulsively hugged Pryor. "Poor dear." She patted her on the back then released her. "Things will come back to you. In time. The familiar things will bring you home—really home. My name is Margaret and I married your twin brother June eighth, 1697."

The blood drained from Cig's face. "What year do you think it is?"

"The year of our Lord sixteen hundred and ninety-nine. November third, and just think, Pryor, it will soon be a new century. The eighteenth century. I can scarcely believe it."

Cig could scarcely believe it either. One of them was nutty as a fruitcake.

"1699—Margaret?" She half-whispered.

"Indeed." Margaret shook her head, the glossy curls spilling out from under her mobcap.

"It's 1995," Cig stated firmly.

Margaret appeared solemn for a moment then squeezed Pryor's arm. "You always were one for japes. If it were, what, 1995, I'd be dead and as you can see I am very much alive."

"Maybe I'm dead?" A cold claw of fear tore at Cig's entrails.

Margaret laughed as she thought Cig was joking. "Dead tired is what you are. The voyage from England alone would be enough to make me forget my name. And your ride fatigued you. You'll wake up tomorrow and all will be well."

"Where's Tom?"

"He and Bobby are feeding the stock."

"Margaret, I'll sleep in the stable with my horse."

"Nonsense," Margaret replied.

Cig wanted to shake Margaret to make her stop this charade. She counted to ten. Her limbs felt like lead. She meekly followed Margaret upstairs and crawled on the bed. "One more question. Are we rich?"

"Lord, no," Margaret roared.

"At least that's consistent," Cig wryly replied.

"You're home in your own bed now. Sweet dreams."

Cig, eyelids heavy, mumbled, "You don't have a telephone, do you?" She was asleep almost before she finished her sentence.

Margaret blew out the candle, stared at her sleeping sister-in-law then softly left the room, praying under her breath, "Thank you, Lord, for delivering our Pryor to us in this time of need."

9

A few embers glowed orange in the fireplace when Cig awoke an hour before dawn. She searched for the bathroom. There wasn't one. A bowl and pitcher of water stood on a three-legged, bird's-eye maple table in the corner of the room. A slender, polished toothpick was there, too, with a pewter mug.

She splashed water on her face, rinsed her mouth out with water, picked her teeth and remembered she had a folding toothbrush in her jacket's left pocket. She looked out the window, noticing that the hand-blown glass sported a few tiny bubbles. A light frost coated each blade of grass.

Tiptoeing down the stairs so as not to awaken Margaret, she carried her hunt coat and boots to the big room with a huge carved fireplace at one end. She pulled on her boots then tiptoed to the center hall of the house. She opened the back door at the end of the hall and stepped outside, the brisk temperature fully awakening her.

She noticed things she hadn't noticed yesterday when she was disoriented and exhausted. An outhouse was off to the side of the house by some thirty yards. A little dip near the woods revealed a springhouse solidly constructed of fieldstone. A corncrib stood next to the barn. A small granary was ten yards from the corncrib. Chicken coops dotted one edge of a small paddock. The cats patrolled the granary as well they should. Smaller brick buildings, the color of paprika, fanned out over the

handsome quad behind the big house. The barn anchored the near corner of the quad, roughly one hundred yards long by seventy wide.

Cig jogged to the outhouse. Once inside there were no amenities
other than a large bucket of water to clean oneself.

These people are around the bend, she thought to herself. It was one
thing to be authentic, another to be uncomfortable, and that cold water
tingled. She used an old towel to wipe her hands.

That finished she walked over to the barn, looking for telephone or
electrical wires swaying overhead. She knew the power company charged
ten dollars a buried foot. She hoped the Deyhles had buried their power
line and that she'd find some modern convenience inside.

Out of curiosity she investigated the outside of the barn. No fuse box
or circuit breaker revealed itself, no telltale black umbilical cord popped
out of the earth.

Could be inside, she thought, fighting back rising panic. Margaret
knew her name, which really unnerved her. She had no recollection of
reenactors using the Deyhle name. What she did know was that she had
to reach Hunter and Laura, who would be frantic.

Full Throttle joyously greeted her when she entered the barn. She
patted him and searched for grain, finding high-quality oats. She fed
Throttle, Helen, who looked like a warmblood, and Castor and Pollux,
the draft horses, as well.

She climbed up into the hayloft on a sturdy ladder to throw down the
hay, a delicious mixture of clover and timothy. The hay wasn't baled and
twined but rather stored loose in the cavernous, well-ventilated loft. This
was a safe method of age, ensuring against the combustion that could
occasionally happen with baled hay. Ladders were fastened to each side of
the loft so one could climb up to the two cupolas to clean them out. The
ladders were also useful for walking across the enormous beams to get
quickly from one end of the barn to the other. Peering closer at the
beams she could see they were handhewn tree trunks. The workmanship
was beautiful where the blade of the ax cut into the wood. The smaller
joists and beams were whipsawed, which meant two men, one on the
ground and one in a pit below, had held either end of a long saw as they
laboriously cut the slabs of wood perched over the pit. It was backbreak-

ing labor and few men knew how to do it anymore, or had the muscle power even to try.

The hayloft, carefully planned, allowed one to throw down hay directly into the horses' stalls, which were on one side of the barn, or to the cattle feeders on the other side. Sweet-smelling straw was also stored in the loft so when the horses were turned out and the stalls picked clean, one need only push straw from above, then go down and spread it around. The design spared the human back.

Labor was so terribly expensive that barns were rarely built to this scale anymore. So hay and straw were baled. You lifted the bales, tossing them over the edge of the hayloft. After cutting the twine you fed flakes of hay. The baled straw, twine removed, would then be strewn around the stall. As the leaf or stalk had been compacted in the baling process it took a little time to fluff up the straw. The hay bales grew heavier and heavier the more you tossed up or down.

Cig appreciated the wise design of this barn. Although Margaret had told her otherwise, she assumed the Deyhles were extravagantly wealthy to build something this huge, with handhewn beams yet.

She couldn't find phone wires anywhere. Perfectionists or not about recreating early Virginia, the Deyhles had to have a phone. She hoped it was tucked away in the barn somewhere.

No tractors, trucks, or manure spreaders appeared. She was stunned to think they ran this farm with draft horses. Wooden pitchforks and rakes hung neatly on the inside walls. Hay wagons and flat wagons sat side by side under an overhang and the peculiar odor of some kind of grease curled into her nostrils. Didn't smell like any petroleum product she used.

A saucy rooster sauntered outside, lifted his sleek russet head and let out a glorious cock-a-doodle-do, convinced that he and he alone had brought forth the dawn. She stuck her head out of the main barn door, painted blue, to behold the tip of the sun, deep red, breaking over the horizon. Within moments a path of molten red spread over the swift-moving James River.

Not a wisp of mist hung over the river this morning. The chill morning air would give way to another perfect October day.

Cig ducked back inside and saddled up Full Throttle. It seemed rude just to leave. Weird as her host and hostess might be they were kind people with a sweet directness which put her off-balance.

The satin lining of her hunting jacket felt smooth against her skin as she reached inside the interior pocket for the Smythe's leatherbound notebook she carried. She walked into the handsomely appointed tackroom to sit down and write a note. The brass saddle racks and bridle holders gleamed.

The flat saddles made her wonder if the Deyhles rode Saddlebreds although she had not seen any. The tackroom was paneled in golden oak. Uneven, heavy floorboards worn smooth completed the cozy feel of the place. She examined a long-shanked bit on one of the bridles. It was made of heavy steel; she did not recognize its origin. Cig could usually tell if steel was American, German, or English, the very best for bits. This bit was solid and in the wrong hands would be brutal, but then any bit in the wrong hands is brutal.

She let go of the bit as a jagged bolt of fear ripped into her. For a fleeting moment she could almost believe it was 1699.

A polished wooden trunk contained gorgeous blankets. She found a conté crayon, a hardened piece of rectangular graphite like artists use, on the lip of a standing desk like an old schoolteacher's. She placed her Smythe notebook on the slanting top, pulled out the small pencil from the spine and scribbled; tore out the page and hung it outside Throttle's stall where another bridle rack was placed for the convenience of tacking up in the stall.

Dear Mr. and Mrs. Deyhle,

Thank you for the hospitality. I couldn't find a phone so I'm heading for home. My family will be worried sick about me. My number is 540/279-4462. Please call me tonight so that I might properly thank you.

Yours truly,
Pryor Deyhle Blackwood, MFH

Normally Cig didn't attach Master of Foxhounds behind her name unless corresponding with other foxhunters but she thought it would help the Deyhles if they wanted to check her out before calling. All they needed to do was call the Master of Princess Anne, down the river, or Deep Run, upriver. Foxhunters are a good pipeline for information.

She then walked Full Throttle out to the massive mounting block, a huge, smooth, flat-topped river stone. She swung her right leg over, he twitched his ears, then they moved off as the three cats watched in fascination.

Cig trotted west on the winding river road. She passed the small dock that served Buckingham. She knew that nearby there was a two-lane paved highway, Route 5, which fed into Route 156. She vaguely remembered a gas station at the intersection. Anxious to call the kids, she urged Full Throttle into a brisker trot. They were both stiff from yesterday's wild ride but she'd be at the phone booth soon enough. The road didn't appear where it was supposed to, though; in fact, nothing familiar appeared except the James River, which conformed to her memory of it. Timber towered overhead. She'd never witnessed so much abundant wildlife. The great estates along the James were nowhere to be found. She knew this territory. She'd hunted this territory since childhood, plus she'd attended William and Mary, which was 150 miles from her home.

The James lapped against the shore. Unconsciously she squeezed Full Throttle and he broke into a canter. She slowed him down, tried to keep cool and trotted on. As the sun rose higher, she peered over the wide expanse of the river. She perceived a few cleared fields amid the thick woods but nothing else. Nothing. Not a stick.

The road continued. She slowed to a walk. It wouldn't do to push the horse or herself. She needed to think clearly, calmly, sensibly. A rustle to her right alerted her. She turned as a ten-point buck leaped out, saw her and Full Throttle, then leaped back into the forest. She heard him crashing away.

The road hugged the river. She peered down, hoping for a track, a hoofprint, anything to quell her fears. Baked hard as brick, the road yielded no comforts. Although the temperature couldn't have been over fifty degrees, sweat rolled down her back, under her armpits.

She scanned the river for sight of a boat, a skiff, a dingy, even a raft. Nothing.

As she rounded a bend, a wedge of mist, ground fog, curved across the road. Full Throttle snorted and stopped. She knew her horse well enough to trust his senses more than her own. A human form appeared, as startled to see her as she was to see him. He looked like an Indian, in ragged leather pants. The right side of his head was shaved clean, and a long knot of hair, braided, hung down the left side. She thought she saw a tomahawk in his belt, a knife in his right hand. That quickly he darted into the woods.

"Hey, hey, wait a minute. Please," she called out.

She again looked down at the road as the mist swirled around. Drops of blood dotted the dry, dusty surface. The mist lifted, and she rode forward. More blood. She shivered.

A crumpled figure lay to the side of the road. She hurried over. Cig had a strong stomach but it turned over.

An Indian, his neck half-severed, lay on his side. The killer had started to lift off his scalp at the forehead. His full head of hair was trimmed blunt at his shoulder. She must have startled the attacker just as he cut into the forehead. Full Throttle snorted and backed up. The odor of fresh blood upset him.

"Whoa boy, whoa boy." She stared at the corpse. A copper gorget protected his neck. His breeches, soft buttery leather, amazed her they were so beautiful. Blood seeped through his ripped deerskin shirt.

She had to call the sheriff and then her children. Why would anyone murder another human being like this?

She headed back down the James. If nothing else she knew where the Deyhles were and strange as they might be with their living history trip, surely they would summon a sheriff.

They cantered, brightly colored trees flying by, and a black bear scurried to get out of the way. Within twenty minutes she was back at the solid brick building.

Tom shot out the door. "Pryor, you had us worried to death."

"You have to call the sheriff—right now! A man has been killed. An Indian."

Margaret almost stumbled out of the house. Bobby and Marie, the indentured servants, frankly stared, mouths agape.

"You've got to call the sheriff!"

"Sheriffs are in England. We don't have them here," Tom evenly answered.

"Oh, for Chrissakes, drop the charade, will you? A man's been murdered up the road. You've got to call the police!"

"Margaret, stay here. Tell Bobby to load up the muskets—just in case. You know what to do." He dashed around to the back and reappeared mounted on Helen.

"Lead the way," he told her.

"Wait!" Margaret ran inside and returned. She handed up a flintlock pistol to Tom who stuck it in his belt.

She handed another to Cig who took it without grumbling. If it was the only weapon around, she was going to use it.

"Come on." She turned Full Throttle west on the river road.

The two rode in silence. As they reached the body, Tom dismounted.

He whistled. "This is a bloody harvest, all right."

"I saw the killer. For a second he appeared in the mist and then ran into the forest. He was going to scalp this man."

"They always do that. You know that."

"Not today they don't!"

"Pryor, you're not in possession of your senses," Tom firmly chided her. "This is a Tuscarora Iroquois."

"What are you talking about?" She was mad as hell now.

"The Iroquois and Manahoac peoples are west and north of the fall line for the most part, the Algonquin, east of it. Even though the savages have treaties between them this fellow"—he broke off and knelt down, rolled the corpse over on his back—"robbed him, too."

"How do you know that?"

Tom pointed to two cut thongs at the waistline on the Indian's leather breeches.

Cig squinted. The awful reality that this *was* another time was beginning to sink in. She pushed it back. "There has to be some authority. You've got to tell someone."

"I will. I'll tell our neighbors and I'll tell James Blair who has a brain in his head." Tom, a trace of bitterness in his voice, continued, "Won't do a bit of good to tell the governor or the House of Burgesses. They're too consumed with collecting taxes and sending them back to King William. The last time the Indians started slaughtering us, they wouldn't even raise a militia. Of course, that was a different governor so I'll hold my peace on this one. Still, the Crown wants our money but refuses to spend any to defend us."

She folded her hands over the pommel of her saddle. "What about the body?"

"Help me."

Cig dismounted and the two of them heaved the corpse over Tom's horse behind the saddle.

They walked back toward Buckingham.

She kept her mouth shut. Scanning each bend of the river for a landmark, anything, her despair deepened. She felt herself enveloped by time, as though a velvet glove was closing around her. All she wanted was a telephone. She regretted the times she had cursed Alexander Graham Bell for interrupting her life. She prayed there would be some logical explanation—that Tom Deyhle was suffering from schizophrenia or manic-depression or any psychological term she could fling at him. He seemed sane and sound although at this moment he was worried. Her teeth chattered. She clamped her jaws shut.

He noticed and said soothingly, "Don't worry, sister. It's been over twenty years since the last uprising. This is heathen killing heathen."

She turned to him with tears in her eyes. "That's not why I'm afraid."

"What then?" He smiled, his voice kind.

"I don't know where I am. I don't know what time it is. I'm not sure I know who I am."

He tilted his head back at the sky. "Eight o'clock about, you're on your way home, Pryor Deyhle. You know, I think the mind is like a child's toybox. Sometimes things are tossed inside and there's a jumble. It will all sort out."

"You really do not have a telephone?" The tears flowed.

"Sister, I never heard of such a thing." Love and impatience carried in his voice.

"Then what year is it? Truly, Tom, what year?"

"1699."

"Oh, God." She bit her lip until it bled. Otherwise she would have sobbed uncontrollably.

10

Drawing on reserves of self-control she scarcely knew she possessed, Cig continued to keep silent. Since the murdered Indian had riveted everyone's attention, she didn't have to say much. She tried to give no cause for alarm, because she figured this group of people wouldn't be different from any other group of people: they'd gossip.

If she acted too peculiar or disoriented she might find herself in a worse mess than she was already in.

Tom took the body to Shirley Plantation about eleven miles downriver. He quietly instructed Margaret to be vigilant—just in case.

Tom said the killer would probably head north or south toward the great swamps but not west over the fall line. Since an Indian in Jamestown was relatively uncommon he'd probably move through the woods to reach his destination.

Cig struggled to absorb what wasn't being said. The suppressed fear was palpable. Naturally, everyone's first concern was his own immediate safety. The next worry was that this killing could presage a war between the tribes with the colonists caught in the middle.

Tom wanted to get hold of Lionel deVries of Wessex Plantation and William Byrd, downriver. Both men were amassing fortunes by setting up trading posts with the Indians. Byrd rode into Carolina, specializing in coastal tribes, whereas deVries, apparently a bold soul, crossed the fall line, continuing even over the mountain range that people said was blue. He traded in the fertile Shenandoah Valley where few whites traveled.

Cig, as if in a daze, untacked Full Throttle, wiped him down and turned him out in the paddock closest to the barn. The two cows in the paddock paid no attention to him.

Margaret appeared, carrying two pails of milk. Cig took one from her.

"You've been buffeted about these last hours. Exhausted, hungry, and then this morning—well. . . . Not the homecoming you imagined, I fear."

"The truth is, I don't know where I am. Except geographically." Cig knew she wasn't making sense. She concentrated on not spilling the milk. Having a chore to do made her feel better.

"It must be terrible to lose your memory." Margaret sympathized.

"Memory? It's my mind I'm worried about," Cig blurted out. "There's got to be a telephone, a telegraph, hell, two tin cans on a string."

"String I have. As to the two other objects . . ." Margaret shook her head. "Do you recognize any of us?"

"Your voice sounds familiar but I can't place it."

"Tom?"

"Only that we look alike."

Margaret, genuinely sympathetic, said, "I am sorry, Pryor." She hesitated. "What about Castor and Pollux?"

"Don't recognize them either."

· "Ah, well, fretting will only make it worse. Patience . . ." Margaret left off her sentence as she opened the heavy oak door to the fieldstone springhouse. She placed the milk pails in the stone-lined trench through which the cool water flowed. Big, round wrought-iron circles bolted into the side of the springhouse provided tethers for the pails. Margaret lifted the pail onto a long wrought-iron S-hook, one end hooked onto the pail handle and the other through an iron circle.

"Beautiful stone work!" Cig exclaimed.

"William Henry Harrison, in his kindness, lent us two of his shipyard men. He has great plans for the Berkeley Hundred and the shipyards will no doubt provide him, in good time, with the money to build and build. It's his vice."

Margaret lifted up a white square chunk of butter as they left the springhouse, and the young woman carefully closed and bolted the door.

"Are you worried about thieves?" Cig wondered.

Margaret laughed. "I learned the hard way." She pointed to the cats. "We bolt the smokehouse, too. Of course, I think the raccoons and the fox have a lot to answer for, not to mention Highness, Nell Gwyn, and Little Smudge. She looks like a smudge, doesn't she?" Margaret pointed to the dark gray cat, her bright green eyes full of playfulness.

When they arrived back at the house, Margaret set out cold corn-bread and the butter while she ground coffee. "Our greatest luxury. I imagine you could drink it anytime you wanted to in London. I keep the coffee here and the tea next to it. The flour is in this crock and sugar here. I use honey more than sugar though. Your beehives are flourishing. You'll have to walk up to the clover meadows to see for yourself."

Cig gratefully ate the food placed before her. "Margaret, I appreciate your kindness. But I still can't believe it's 1699."

Margaret folded her hands in her lap. She had spent a restless night, worrying about the changes in her sister-in-law. Finally, she had reached the conclusion that Pryor, despite splendid good health, had suffered a mental affliction due to the rigors of her journey or perhaps some shock along the way that would reveal itself in time. No tainted blood ran in the Deyhle family or in the Buckinghams, for that matter, although the Buckinghams could be courageous as well as foolhardy. The knowledge that Pryor's disturbance was most likely temporary enabled Margaret to tolerate her peculiarities, although she didn't want anyone else to see Pryor until she had recovered her senses. She had always loved her husband's sister and was prepared to help her, nurse her back to reality and pray continuously for her restoration. She was well aware that her own experience was too limited for her to imagine all that Pryor might have seen and endured on her journey. Margaret had never known the horrors that drove people to cross an ocean, but her grandparents had told her enough about the Old World to make her quite happy she was in the new one.

"Actually, it's November four, 1699," Margaret quoted from the old-style calendar. The new, corrected calendar wouldn't be used until 1752.

Cig blinked. She vaguely remembered the calendar switch because she had read that presidents Jefferson and Madison could celebrate two birthdays if they wished, old style and new style.

"I . . . I . . ." Cig searched Margaret's face. If she really was in the last year of the seventeenth century, continuing to insist that she was from 1995 would make life harder for them both. Her main concern was not for herself but for Hunter and Laura. Were they safe? Would they manage without her? Grace, as their godmother, could provide for them but her heart broke each time she summoned their faces. "I remember names. Some names."

"Which ones?"

"Shirley Plantation. Williamsburg. Uh, Flowerdew Hundred." She rattled off some plantation names she could remember.

"So you heard about Williamsburg while you were in London? The ship carrying that news must have had wings."

"Uh—" Cig hated to sound stupid. "I'm a little confused. Isn't Williamsburg the capital?"

Margaret beamed. Now she knew Pryor's memory would return. "On paper." She laughed. "The Assembly passed an act to build the city where Middle Plantation now stands. An excellent location between the York and the James, I think. When the state building burned last year, the Assembly decided to move to a place less beset by contagion. But the Act only passed this June. You must have heard as you were packing to come home."

Cig ignored that. "So nothing is built yet?"

"Duke of Gloucester Street, a mile long, if you can imagine that, has been laid out. All other streets will be parallel to that. John Page sold two hundred eighty-three acres to the city. A most marvelous occasion for him." She appreciated foresight and profit.

"My God, we really are at the very beginning," Cig gasped.

Margaret tried to understand. "After London, we must look to you as the Indians look to us."

"Oh, no, nothing like that, Margaret. It's just—" She wiped her forehead then abruptly changed the subject. Her temples throbbed. "I'm not a lunatic even if I seem like one. I'm peaceful."

Margaret's response, spontaneous and warm, soothed Cig. "I think no such thing. This will pass. I feel strange that you don't know me for I look upon you as a sister . . . yet that, too, shall be set right. I know it."

"Okay." Cig weakly agreed.

Margaret asked, "Okay?"

"Ah—" Cig paused a moment. "It means 'yes' or everything's fine, good. Okay."

"The rage in London?"

"No—forget it."

11

∞

That night Margaret hauled buckets of water, which she poured into the huge cast-iron pot hanging in the winter kitchen attached to the back of the house. She thought a bath would lift Pryor's spirits, so the two worked together to prepare it.

A wooden tub shaped so a person could comfortably sit and stretch out her legs in it took up the center of the floor. Homemade soap from boiled pig's fat mixed with aromatic herbs, mostly lavender, made do for the body and the hair as well. Cig untied her one pigtail, which she wore at the nape of her neck. She shook out her hair and surveyed herself in the small but good-quality mirror.

"Margaret, every time I look there's more gray."

Margaret checked over the full, dark head. "Nonsense."

"Why don't you bathe first and I'll follow?" Cig offered.

"You go first, please."

"Do you ever take a bath with Tom?"

Scandalized, then amused, Margaret laughed. "Never. Gentlemen and ladies should enjoy separate toilettes. Besides, he slops water everywhere." After pouring the heated water into the tub she leaned over and tested it with her elbow. "Just right."

When Margaret had left, Cig stripped off her clothes and crawled into the tub. She stood straight up. It was a lot hotter than it looked. Little by little she scrunched down until she was up to her neck in deliciously warm water. As the temperature outside had skidded into the forties she appreciated the warmth. The big fire in the fireplace crackled and as the shadows danced around the kitchen, the pots loomed like a parasol of planets. The well-worn wood felt smooth and comfortable. Cig dozed off for a bit, only opening one eye when Margaret scooted back in to grab her dirty clothes.

"I don't have any clothes other than what you've got in your hands."

"Yes, you do. In your wardrobe. I haven't moved a thread." Margaret sat down on the stool next to the tub.

Margaret absentmindedly rummaged through Cig's vest and jacket pockets, natural enough if clothes are to be washed. She pulled out the dollars, the driver's license with Cig's photograph on it, two quarters and a dime and the little flashlight. Margaret stared at the driver's license. Her hands shook.

"It's you. It's the most perfect likeness I could imagine!" She read the dates of Cig's birth, 6/8/55, and the expiration of the license, 6/8/00. "I don't understand." Trembling, Margaret placed the driver's license beside her on the stool. Nell Gwyn jumped up and sat on it. No piece of paper, no matter how tiny, escapes the notice of a cat.

"I don't understand either, Margaret, but as you can plainly see that picture is of me and it's not a painting. It's a process called photography which was invented in the middle of the nineteenth century. And the license is so that I can drive a car. That's a machine that's like a coach in a way but runs on gasoline—you don't need horses. Automobiles, or cars as we call them, were invented around the beginning of the twentieth century. I truly am from the twentieth century. Look at the money."

"What money?"

"The paper—we use paper money."

Margaret's luminous eyes shone with fear and curiosity as she placed the folded-over bills in her left hand and opened them. The attire of Washington, Hamilton, and Andrew Jackson was close enough to what she herself knew that she intently studied their faces. "One dollar." She put the accent on the *lar*. The date on the dollar bill was 1992. Margaret stared at the date.

"Dollar. It's the money of the United States of America. We're a separate nation from England now—and we're huge. The country stretches from the Atlantic Ocean to the Pacific Ocean."

Margaret couldn't fathom that. She was still grappling with this strange physical evidence of another time, the photograph, and even if Pryor could have printed up the money—and beautiful it was, too, such high-quality engraving—she could not have created that—picture. "It's you. Truly with God as my witness, this is you." She read aloud the name, "Pryor Chesterfield Deyhle Blackwood."

"I'm widowed. I'm a Deyhle by birth. My husband died last year of a heart attack." Cig withheld the rest of that sorry tale.

"But you are Pryor Deyhle?" Margaret struggled to hang on to her own sanity.

"Yes, I am."

"And you are Tom's twin sister. You have to be. Look at you. Look at him."

"I—I don't know—we do look like twins, but Margaret, I have no memory of living—this life. I remember everything about my other life, including some stuff I'd like to forget."

"No one can have two lives."

"Then I'm crazy. There's no other explanation that I can think if— can you?"

"You've lost your memory but you're not without your faculties." Margaret ran her finger over the photograph. "It's smooth."

"Yes. Photography is a kind of miracle, I guess, I never thought about it before." She pointed to her breeches. "Look at the zipper in my pants."

"What?"

"Where the buttons would be in Tom's breeches."

"You mean these little teeth?"

"Yes. Now take the plastic tab and run it upwards."

Margaret clapped her hands together when she did just that. "Wonderful."

"That's a zipper. Some are made out of metal. That one is made out of plastic, which came into being, gee, I don't know, around World War Two."

Margaret blanched. "The world at war, what are you saying?"

"Oh, God, Margaret. We've had two of them. Millions upon millions of people killed. Fifty-five million in the second one alone."

"The whole world?"

"Yes, including places you don't know about because they haven't been settled yet."

"Wars." She shook her head. "That's why the Deyhles and the Woodsons came here."

"The Woodsons?"

"My maiden name. My grandparents ran from Cromwell's assassins just as did yours."

"Maybe the sickness is inside. It's in every time. My time has better weapons."

"We haven't had a war yet," Margaret stoutly said, "except for the Indians."

"You will. There's a real big one coming up in the 1770s."

"I'll be dead then."

"Will you?" Cig stuck her foot out of the tub. "Am I dead? How do you know you won't come back in another time? I'm here from another time and I don't know why, I don't know how, but I'm alive, you're alive and as you can see, those things in my pocket couldn't possibly be manufactured in 1699."

Tears ran down Margaret's creamy cheeks. "I don't know what to think."

"I don't either. But I swear to you by all that is holy that I truly come from the last gasp of the twentieth century."

"But you are Pryor Deyhle, *our Pryor*."

"I reckon I am but I don't know how. Maybe there *are* holes in time, Margaret. Maybe I fell through one and . . . here I am."

"What do you remember about that day?" Margaret wiped her tears.

"I was foxhunting and got lost in the fog. What was curious was that I had moments when I felt as though I was going back in time but I discounted them—it was too fantastic. And here's what's truly strange—a fox led me! I know this fox. I've hunted him for about four years now. Fattail."

"A big, big red with an enormous tail." Margaret gripped the side of the tub. "I know him," she gasped. "He's bold as Lucifer."

"Look at this." Cig picked up and turned on the flashlight.

Margaret leaned back then reached for it. She clicked it on and off, marveling at it. "Surely this is magic." Then she again stared at the license. "Pryor, you must feel," she searched for the words, "terrible pain and loneliness. You don't recognize me at all, do you?"

Cig shook her head. "But I trust you. In my time people don't really trust one another. Our lives are easier physically but in other ways we've only made things worse. It's difficult to explain because you trust so naturally. So trust me in this—I am from another time."

Margaret's lips quivered. "What happened to the Pryor I know, the sister I love? Where is she?"

Cig thought a long time. "I don't know but there are more things in heaven and earth than we can dream of." She quoted Shakespeare.

"You know the play?"

"Shakespeare is considered the greatest playwright that we ever produced." Cig smiled because they did know things in common. "Maybe I lived this life. Maybe I am the Pryor you know. After all, the soul *is* eternal. Somehow I slipped back to your time. I can't think of another reason, and maybe trying to find a reason will only make this more painful—you see, Margaret, I left two children behind."

"Merciful heaven." Margaret's hands flew to her face.

"A son, seventeen, and a daughter, fifteen." That did it. Cig's calm facade shattered, and her tears began dripping into the bathwater.

Margaret threw her arms around the sobbing woman, heedless of getting wet herself. "There, there, Pryor, God is merciful. He will not allow your children to suffer. Somehow all will be well. We must believe that. Truly we must or this burden will crush us both."

"I could give up the rest, I suppose. I could bear not to see my friends, but my children—that I cannot bear."

Margaret took her hands in a strong grip. "Trust in God. We must trust in His wisdom. Perhaps He sent you back to us as a gift. He will care for your children."

"I hope so." Cig cried until she couldn't see anymore and felt like throwing up. Finally she began to feel a little better.

Margaret looked at the dates on the license again. "Forty—but you're only twenty-eight, you and Tom."

"I'm forty."

"How is it that you look so young?"

"We have such good doctors, such excellent medical and dental care—unless one is terribly poor, that is. We get shots against diseases, diseases that kill you now. Some of them we've stopped entirely, or contained, like malaria."

"Malaria?"

"The sweating sickness—it's caused by the bite of a certain mosquito. Before we figured out how to eradicate it completely, a doctor called Walter Reed did that, we realized we could help people infected with it by dosing them with quinine. I don't know if you have quinine yet."

Margaret shook her head no, as she did not recognize the word *quinine*. Had Cig said Peruvian bark she would have had an inkling as to the medicine.

"Look at my teeth." Cig opened her mouth.

Margaret peered into Cig's mouth. "It's full of silver."

"Fillings. This way I won't lose teeth."

Margaret sat back down. "Pryor, we must not speak of this to anyone else."

"Because they'll lock me up?"

"No. You aren't harmful. And there are no lunatic asylums in Virginia unless you believe the whole colony to be one." A hint of sarcasm informed her tone. "People would say you suffered delusions—some would worry about tainted blood."

"Hereditary insanity." Cig exhaled slowly.

"Yes, your marriage plans would be compromised and in the future, when your children are grown, it could be whispered—tainted blood— and their chances would be compromised."

"Do I frighten you?"

"Yes and yet I *know* you. You may be this person here," she held up the driver's license, "but you are also my sister and I believe that God has brought you home—an earlier home. He has work for you to do." Her faith blazed from her. "And He will care for all those you love in," she paused but got it out, "1995. The Lord is my Shepherd; I shall not want."

"He maketh me to lie down in green pastures: He leadeth me beside the still waters."

"He restoreth my soul."

The two finished the Twenty-third Psalm in unison. "Surely goodness and mercy shall follow me all the days of my life: and I will dwell in the house of the Lord for ever."

12

Low clouds hid the sun. Cig didn't know what time it was when she arose. She missed her alarm clock, the one with the snooze button. She especially missed indoor plumbing as she dashed across the quad to the privy.

When she came back into the house she ducked out of the heavy woolen shift and rummaged around the huge wardrobe for something to wear. The dresses, some quite pretty, surprised her. She hadn't expected to find such beautiful clothing. She pulled out an old shirt, a pair of leather breeches, heavy cotton hose and a leather pullover shirt. The wearer of these clothes evidenced a practical streak.

Margaret's praying with her last night, her belief that this had to be for a purpose, helped Cig. She knew if she tried to figure out what had happened to her, if she tried to escape time, she would truly go mad. So she greeted the day with a small prayer.

"Dear God, thank you for this day, for my health and for the health of my children wherever they might be. Thank you for showing me your love through Margaret Deyhle. If you could help me back to my time I would be grateful. Amen."

Much as she wanted to head upriver on the James River road she knew dangers existed for which she was unprepared. The murdered Indian remained foremost in her mind.

She ventured out into the upstairs hallway, as wide as the center hall downstairs, with windows at both ends. Cig was impressed by the house. No one had money for frills but the ventilation and light were excellent, better than in many modern homes. The good furniture, which had to have been brought from England, shone with hand rubbings. Upstairs the beds, nightstands and chairs were fashioned from New World woods, maple mostly. The farm abounded in maples, walnuts, oaks, chestnuts, beeches, elms, dramatic sycamores, gums, and a variety of conifers. One large mirror, a prized possession given the expense of glass, hung in the upstairs hall. Her boots fit perfectly over the leather breeches while the worn lace of the pressed shirt spilled out from under the leather pullover. She hurried back downstairs, grabbed some cornbread and headed to the stable. She might as well earn her keep.

She fed the horses, the cattle, the chickens, and the one pig who followed her around oinking.

As Bobby and Marie made their way to the privy, Cig was glad she'd gotten there first.

The morning stayed cloudy and cool. Cig set out to explore the farm, what she knew of it. The clover fields, farther back from the river, were rich and a line of bee boxes marked one side. The tobacco fields rolled on and on. Tom had clearly put his faith in the crop, and well he should. Europe couldn't get enough of the weed.

Cig observed the chestnut rail snake fencing, how Tom took advantage of the roll of the land and the abundance of fresh water. Buckingham was a fine piece of Virginia, and the Deyhles were intelligent farmers.

A small apple orchard on higher ground lent a pleasing symmetry to the place. As she walked down the farm lane back to the barn she spied Tom and another man riding up from the south on the river road. The sun broke through the clouds, a shaft of golden light on the men. She stopped to admire the spray of diamond lights on the water. Tom's companion, seeing Cig, spurred his horse into a gallop, riding straight for her.

She thought to herself that she had to quickly find out who he was without appearing not to know. This plan was blasted the moment he came close.

He was at least six four, with hair so black it was blue, and a heavy beard already showing on his face, despite the fact that he'd undoubtedly been shaved that morning by a servant. A gleaming smile covered his face. He swept off his hunter green hat with its ostrich plume as he approached. Large soft leather boots, rolled over at the top, made him look the cavalier he was.

"Blackie, what are you doing here?" The blood ran out of her face.

"Mademoiselle?"

"You're alive!" she gasped, terrified yet thrilled to behold that familiar, handsome face.

"Alive? Alive, exuberant, overcome," he bowed in the saddle, "that divine Providence brought you safely home to me." He hesitated a moment. "Pryor, love, I'll answer to whatever you call me—Blackie?"

Cig's rib cage was bruised inside from her heart. Trust your heart, she thought to herself. Trust God. Whatever is going on, trust God.

He dismounted, swept her off the ground with one muscled arm and kissed her even though she took a step backward. He was not a man to be denied. His horse snorted. He held her so close she thought she'd suffocate. She remembered sweet, treacherous kisses and these tasted the same.

He kissed her again. "You deceived me." He playfully chided her, a glint of worry in his deep, dark eyes.

"Never."

"I have inquired at the harbor every day for the last two months. I wanted to be at the docks to greet my lady properly. How did you get here? No ship has come in from England."

"Oh," her mind raced, "I have my secrets."

Tom rode up. "You recognize Lionel! I knew you would."

Lionel put his strong arm around Cig, pulling her back toward the house, his horse obediently clopping after him. "Tom told me the journey was difficult, you need time to rest." He nuzzled her ear. "Not too long, I pray. I've waited too long as it is."

"She'll be her old self." Tom smiled reflexively. "A bit of a rest, and selfishly, a bit more time with us."

So many questions crowded into Cig's mind that she suffered an instant headache. She stayed silent.

Cig couldn't tear her eyes off the man, as like Blackie as spit. Same baritone voice, strong jaw, and from what she could quickly ascertain, same big ego.

Marie, Bobby's wife, a stout red-haired woman of vast energy, cooked a big breakfast while Margaret served. When Cig offered to help, Margaret told her to visit with Lionel and winked at her.

Cig felt giddy, disoriented. The safest bet was to avoid talking about herself. She encouraged Lionel to talk about himself, an easy task.

"What of the murdered Indian?"

"Bad blood, I should think." Lionel, despite refined table manners, ate his shirred eggs with obvious relish. "If you'd seen more than one savage I'd worry but this had the mark of hate, of revenge."

"I feel much assured," Margaret murmured as she passed around enticing cinnamon buns.

Lionel smiled at Margaret then at Cig. "If I find that savage I'll give him a thrashing before I hang him just for frightening you. In fact, I'll thrash any man who dares look at you cross-eyed."

"But what if he is cross-eyed?" The corner of Cig's mouth curled upward. This might even be fun, she thought to herself.

"Blessed man for he shall see God twice," Lionel replied.

They laughed, and Cig thought, that's not changed, that ready insouciant wit. Lionel held forth on tobacco prices, the need to pressure the Crown for lower taxes to be paid in tobacco or tobacco notes against the crop. He expressed an opinion on everything, and Cig appeared to drink it in, every syllable. Clearly, he was aggressive, rich, and accustomed to power. He was a man who got his way, and if he didn't get it, he'd find a way around the obstacle. Failing that, he'd smash whatever held him back.

After breakfast the two walked to Lionel's horse, a large-boned, 17-hand flaming chestnut. Tom and Margaret discreetly disappeared.

He put his hand on the flap of the saddle. "As soon as I attend to pressing matters I shall make a proper call upon a beautiful lady, an angel of light and laughter." Lionel bowed to her again, then paused.

"Lionel." Her heart pounding, she put her hand on his shoulder. She felt she knew him—yet. She wanted to warn him. "Do you believe we could have met before—or in another time?"

He studied her, his jet mustache setting off his tobacco-stained teeth. "There are those who believe such things—not good Englishmen, mind you. A curious concept. No. I don't believe it but," his eyes twinkled, "life can't be a veil of tears in those countries that hold such beliefs."

"Oh?"

"If life were terrible, why return?" He laughed. "Unless I could be *certain* I'd find you again."

His florid romanticism appealed to Cig more than she cared to admit. "Maybe we return because we have to solve a problem . . . or soothe a wound inflicted in an earlier life."

"Ah—continuous resurrection complete with thorns. Pryor," he kissed her cheek, "these matters are of no weight and therefore delicious to digest. The fanciful captures the mind like bright colors capture hummingbirds. I think we turn to other worlds and extravagant promises when this world bends our backs with pain or the infirmities of age." He drew his face closer to hers and whispered, "My beautiful Pryor is home!"

"Thank you, Lionel." She kissed him, a lingering kiss tasting of cinnamon and vanilla. Then he mounted up, returning south on the river road.

Dazed and dazzled, Cig followed his figure until he rounded a sweeping bend in the James. He turned, doffed his hat and then disappeared.

As Cig turned to go back to the stable she looked out over the James. Heraclitus said in 500 B.C., "You never step into the same river twice." She wondered.

Margaret caught up to her. "I knew you'd remember him."

"I don't," Cig continued as Margaret's expression shifted, "I can only tell you that Lionel deVries is John Blackwood to the teeth." She shivered. "My husband, Blackie."

Margaret was beyond shock. She neither believed nor disbelieved. "Then you should be happy indeed."

Cig gave her a withering glance. "You don't know what my marriage was like."

"Pryor, whatever that marriage was like, you need not repeat your tribulations, although all marriages share in some tribulation. Men are unreasonable creatures at times."

"Most times."

Margaret smiled. "Sometimes I think we live in different worlds but if you choose Lionel for your husband I wish you well."

"Do you like him?"

Margaret folded her arms over her bosom and stopped. "Pryor, what I think of the man matters not at all."

"That means you don't like him."

"I didn't say that."

"You didn't have to."

"He's a man who brooks no interference."

Cig clasped her hands behind her back, wistfully saying, "When I just saw Lionel I was—flying. I hoped for one ludicrous instant that Blackie had come back to me and he'd *learned* something."

"What about you learning something?"

Cig appreciated this shrewd remark. "I'm *trying*." She inhaled. "But I'm not sure what I'm supposed to learn."

"In God's time."

"God thinks in centuries!" Cig peevishly shot back.

"And so do you—now." Margaret, stifling a laugh, started back to the house.

13

A light frost made the grass crunch underfoot. The James River lapped little gray waves on the shores as low dark clouds brushed the treetops. The brilliant color of the leaves against the pewter sky provided the only cheer but the wind was fast ripping the leaves off the trees. Winter had arrived overnight.

Cig's spirits rose and fell in direct proportion to the sunshine. She'd taken over the animal chores and checking the bee boxes so that Tom could put in more hours in the back fields. He carried a huge flintlock, which he'd said he'd fire if there was trouble. A huge bell by the back door would call him if the house were threatened. A systematic, slow clap of the bell meant dinnertime. A rapid clanging meant fire, injury, marauders. Cig had little faith in Tom's flintlock but she declined to tell him.

"Pryor." Margaret called from the back door to wave her in. "Stew's ready."

Pryor wiped off her boots and stepped inside.

Margaret placed a bowl of lamb stew in front of her sister-in-law. "That money you showed me, the paper. I've been thinking, how much would that be in pounds?"

"Oh—twenty-five pounds," Cig guessed.

Margaret gasped, "Why would you carry so much money on your person?"

Cig laughed. "That's not enough to buy a good meal."

Scandalized, Margaret jabbed at her stew with a spoon. "Twenty-five pounds could buy you a strong man's labor for a year or one of the finest mares in the New World."

"Uh—I don't know how to explain what's happened to money. Inflation." This met with a blank stare. "Okay, think of it this way. One pound buys less and less because the price of things and labor keeps going up. Governments print more money and it isn't tied to anything—gold, for instance—it's just paper."

Margaret laughed. "No government that foolish could stay in power. The king would be toppled. Parliament would be swept away. You can't just *print* money."

"Ah, but they do—in my time, they do." Cig held up her hands in a gesture of supplication. "I don't have anything to do with it. I have no political power."

"What woman does unless she's the queen or mistress to the king?" Margaret continued poking at her stew. "But I cannot believe that men would be so foolish."

"Inflation is the least of it. We have something called the federal deficit. It's like running this farm on debt, literally. You are fueled by the debt and you work to service the debt so you never advance. That's how my government works. They don't have any money but they pretend that they do."

"Why would people allow this to happen?"

"I don't know. Lack of will?"

"That much hasn't changed." Margaret smiled for a moment. "Pryor, these things you tell me, they are so—so—"

"Outrageous?"

Margaret nodded her head. "—that they must be true."

"They're true all right. But for all the messes we've made, we've done a few things right. Just give me a minute to think of them." She reached for a warm apple crisp.

Margaret's fresh features underscored her natural openness. She probed a bit more. "The morning you rode away, you left us a note—with numbers."

"My phone number. In my time we have an instrument so we can talk over miles . . . continents even."

"Ah." Margaret sipped some tea. "Can you order supplies?"

"Sure. I was frantic for a telephone to call my children so they'd know I was all right. I couldn't believe you didn't have one but when Tom saw the dead Indian and said he'd ride over to Shirley to tell them, I think at that moment I *knew* this was 1699. Even if you all were reenactors you'd call—that's short for using a phone—in an emergency and you'd have let me call."

"Yes, I can see that. What's a reenactor? I hate to ask so many questions but I'm curious, and you use such strange words."

"I suppose I do sound funny—but our accents are surprisingly close. That's a comfort." She smiled sadly. "Much of what you know or do has been, maybe forgotten is the wrong word, superseded, replaced by something better and faster like the telephone." Margaret nodded that she comprehended and Cig continued, "Reenactors are people who—gee, how do I explain this?—people who become captivated by some era before they were born. They study everything and then try to live that way—almost like a living museum."

"Why, that's a lovely idea."

"It is, actually."

"I could be like Cleopatra." Margaret struck a pose.

"Watch out for snakes." Margaret laughed as Cig continued, "I'm the one that needs to ask questions—like why did Pryor go to London?"

"Your father wanted you to see civilization before you became a broodmare, as he put it."

"Why didn't he send Tom? I thought men were more valuable than women in this time."

Margaret refilled her teacup. "Value depends on what you want and need, does it not? Tom had no inclination to visit the Old World. You did, and you were the apple of your father's eye."

"What happened to him?"

Margaret cast down her eyes. "No memory?"

"None."

She sighed. "Charles Deyhle filled up a room. He'd argue with the governor or he'd tease James Blair, an important man and not a Toady to the Crown, although he can often be too serious. He'd take issue with Lionel and few men would dare. He had a way about him that even if you disagreed with him you liked him."

"He sounds wonderful."

"He was."

"But what happened?"

"After your mother died, which happened shortly after you left—"

Cig interrupted. "Had she been sick? What I'm trying to get at is, would I have left if I'd known she was ill?"

Margaret's left hand fluttered up as she set down her teacup with the right. "Oh, no. Elizabeth was robust. She walked to the springhouse and fell over dead. Bobby ran over to her, he was fixing the fence, but she was gone."

"At least she didn't suffer."

"God is merciful."

"But what happened to my fa—to Charles Deyhle?"

"Oh," Margaret stalled, "he was despondent as you would expect, yet he continued to work and conduct his business. He missed you but refused to write to you. He felt the news of your mother's unexpected death was dolorous enough and as you'd recently arrived in England he thought it foolish to call you back because of his own low spirits."

"So—" Cig pressed.

Margaret's face grew flushed. "He was found hanging from the willow tree that used to be by the bend in the river."

Cig was distressed. "I didn't mean to upset you, Margaret. I'm sorry I brought it up."

Margaret's voice rose, "You see, Pryor, he wouldn't have taken his own life. I don't believe it for a moment. Although he mourned your mother he wouldn't spurn life. 'The Lord giveth and the Lord taketh away.' Charles Deyhle would never hang himself."

"What does Tom think?"

"The same. He cut down the willow." Margaret added that fact.

"Who would want to murder—"

Margaret jumped in. "No one! Oh, he had his spats. What strong-willed man does not, but those disagreements evaporated in time. I can't think of anyone angry with him."

Cig, curiosity flooding now, said, "When was he last seen alive?"

"Sunset."

"When was he found?"

"Around nine. When he didn't come in for supper we searched for him. It was December, dark very early, and that compounded our difficulties." She stared out the window. "Tom found him when he went down to the river to hail John MacKinder." She added, "He's the ferryman and he happened to be coming up this way. When Tom saw his lantern he ran to shore to hail him and when John came closer they both saw your father."

"How awful." Cig imagined a swinging corpse on a cold December night. "You all have had your share of sorrow."

"Everyone does," Margaret stated.

"Forgive me for pressuring you."

The turn of phrase was unusual to Margaret but she understood. "You had to know sooner or later."

"Did you write—me?"

"Tom wrote that your father had been carried away by grief. He didn't mention the hanging. He instructed you to stay out the year as that had been your father's wish."

"And I've returned, in a manner of speaking," Cig ruefully said, "with no memory, wild stories, or so they must seem to you, and peculiar ways." She stood up to clear the table. "How did Charles Deyhle dispose of his property?"

Margaret picked up a wooden bowl. "You and Tom own everything in common. Should you marry, the two of you will divide the land in half as well as tools, livestock, furniture, if you wish. Or, if your husband can work with Tom, we will keep the land intact."

Cig halted. "Isn't that unusual?"

"No, not for your father. Your father hated lawyers and this way he ensured you and Tom would cooperate. You see, he was a lawyer." A wry smile played over her lips.

"I can't imagine marrying."

She paused for she didn't want to offend Pryor. "Your father swore you would never marry—he didn't mean that as an insult . . ." she paused, "he meant—"

Cig interrupted. "That I was too independent."

Margaret nodded.

"Lionel and Tom seem to think I'm going to marry."

"Lionel courts you vigorously. You respond yet slip from his grasp. He could have any woman in the colonies, you know."

"Then why does he want me?"

Margaret shrugged. "Because you're elusive—and because marriage would greatly increase his land holdings. If he marries you, he would own more land than anyone in Virginia."

"I see." Cig had hoped Lionel's ardor was only about her, foolish as that may have been. "Margaret, we have an expression in my time. The more things change, the more they stay the same."

14

∞

The wind howled that night as Cig curled up in a ball under the covers. The fire helped keep the room warm but the wind found its way through every crack. Now and then she could feel a little puff emanating from a crack under the window. Insulation was yet to come. She could bear that but she'd find herself craving Coca-Cola or a candy bar—especially Snickers. And potato chips. Indoor plumbing joined her list of lamented luxuries, but somehow that was easier to forego than Coke or the radio. Classical music helped her muck stalls.

If she set aside the niggling problem of nearly three hundred years, then everything appeared normal.

Whoever Pryor Deyhle was, she must be a good person. People genuinely cared for her.

Whenever she felt madness brushing her cheek, Cig told herself to hang on for Hunter and Laura. If there was a way back, she'd find it. Lately she told herself to hang on for Tom and Margaret.

Perhaps in the end it didn't matter how she got to this place. Perhaps she could do some good in this life. And reflect on that life she knew in 1995.

When crushed by loneliness, she could call up Hunter's face, Laura's smile, Woodrow's enormous bushy tail, Harleyetta's penciled eyebrows, and Binky's inept leer. She could recall Grace's lovely alto voice and had to fight the tears for as much as she hated her, she missed her.

The sound of their voices, the cadence of their footfalls, those tiny triumphs of individuality, how vivid they were in her memory. Margaret and Tom could never imagine these unborn people whom they would produce.

The future used to seem like a distant point, an X or Y coordinate on the graph of life, yet the future was all around her. It must have been all around her in 1995, but she couldn't taste it.

The past always seemed clear enough and now she knew that wasn't true either. She realized that when a generation passes they take with it their breath, their laughter, the colors of their lives like a flag of being. Reduced to dates, battles, economic forces, or even to the more personal, a birth date, a death date on a tombstone, their experiences flattened until half or totally forgotten.

The past was not at all what she had been taught: a chain of seemingly inevitable events. No, it was a multitudinous, simultaneous chaos of choices made or not made by each human being alive. Sometimes those choices were made for you and some you made for yourself. The exercise of will, compassion, intelligence, complacent brutality, the stench of fear, and the struggle for beauty: choices. Even the choices you didn't know you were making, like Tom's acceptance of a sovereign, would set the future. Or Margaret's choice to reach for whatever was good in any human being she happened to meet.

Cig wondered about her choice to accept surfaces, to go along, to ignore what she felt powerless to change . . . until she blocked it completely. What was she accepting that she didn't even know could be questioned, just as Tom accepted the idea of a king and queen? Choices. Brutus stabs Julius Caesar. Genghis Khan sweeps out of the East. Leonardo starts projects and rarely finishes. Elizabeth I beats back Philip II. The Germans, the English, the Russians, the Americans, all said they didn't know about Auschwitz until after the fact. Choices. Not just in knowing; in not knowing. Ignorance demands constant effort.

At the cusp of the eighteenth century, what incredible choices. And for her, on the cusp of the twenty-first, what choices.

Perhaps time wasn't linear at all but elliptical, and she truly had fallen through the loop. Perhaps everything was occurring at the same instant and the human mind needed to organize it into discrete cubes of time. The centuries were like railroad cars hitched to one another, pulled by the engine of fate or God.

Time as a lie. The thought intrigued and terrified her. Not just an illusion but an outright lie. Too many choices are too frightening. Perhaps we had to limit them or blow apart from sensory overload. Yes, she did come from another time, a cacophony of facts and little truth, an orgy of comfort yet no peace, a glut of pleasure yet no joy. What dreadful choices had people made since 1699? Or not made?

If nothing else, this fissure in her life, this slipping of a tectonic plate in the brain if not in time, helped her to know there was no golden age.

She uncurled in her bed. The last log in the fireplace glowed incandescent scarlet edged in gold. Dislocated and disoriented, she felt a gratitude welling in her. Perhaps she was lucky to be in this place with these people.

Perhaps God—or the gods—was wiser than she could know. Submission to a higher god's or goddess's will was freedom. Cig smiled. What would Margaret think of the notion of a female god? Was it twentieth-century feminism that produced the notion or was it an intimation from an even earlier time when goddesses made the world tremble and sing?

It didn't matter. What mattered was that she found sanctuary in the human heart. She'd found her family.

A thought did flash through her mind. Why couldn't this have happened to Grace? She fell asleep laughing and crying.

15

⟨∞⟩

The temperature plunged during the night, a stiff wind kicking up a fuss. The wind had slowed little by daybreak and it swept over the James, dumping on Buckingham its cargo of moisture.

"I'll ride with you this morning." Tom walked into the barn. "Do us both good." He smiled. His upper teeth were strong and straight, the lower ones were a little crooked. Tom was lucky, because he had no recourse to an orthodontist.

They quickly tacked up and Tom swung into the saddle, his coordination and timing a double of Cig's way of moving. "Monkey!" He laughed, pointing to her legs, her forward position in the saddle. Tom sat farther back on the horse's back, legs nearly straight and out in front of him and hands held high although the line to the bit was soft, much like the modern saddle seat.

"You ride your way and I'll ride mine but you'll be surprised at what I can do."

"All right," he said with no conviction.

"I love this time of year," Cig remarked as they rode west along the river.

"Taquitock."

"Pardon?"

"Taquitock. The Powhatans call the harvest and fall of the leaf taquitock. They celebrate five seasons. You remember—don't you? Winter is cohonk. They count their years by winters so you and I are coming into our twenty-eighth winter." His voice rose as if waiting for her to recall.

"It will come back to me."

"When we were little we had an old Indian friend and—" he broke off for a moment. "Well, I guess there are more important things to remember. You recognized Lionel. I didn't tell him everything, only that you'd been exhausted by your journey and weren't quite yourself."

"Thank you for protecting me."

He nodded, then pointed across the river, wide at this point. "See there where the Appomattox River flows into the James? Across from Eppington there?"

"Yes, but I thought the house was called Appomattox Manor, not Eppington."

"Francis Eppes likes to name things after himself, but I'm happy you remember him even if you've mixed up the name. Well, sister, right across there you can see how they've cleared more land. Francis is going to build another mansion as his daughter's wedding gift."

"Weston Manor. Of course, that's what I was searching for when I rode in but the mist was so thick." Then she stopped herself. There was no Weston Manor. Not yet.

"Weston Manor?"

"That's what Eppes will call it." Then seeing how this affected him she softly said, "I'll bet you a pound sterling."

The Deyhle sense of humor was in evidence. "Pryor, I don't have a pound to spare but if Francis Eppes names that Weston Manor I'll build you four new bee boxes."

"Better get out your saw, Tom." She felt in her breeches pocket for her money. She wanted to show Tom her money but then she put aside the idea. The concept of a person from another time would overwhelm his linear, logical mind. It overwhelmed hers.

They rode on. One lone poplar, straight as an arrow, lay by the side of the road up ahead.

"Now you'll see why this forward seat is special." She took Full Throttle at a slow canter toward the tree trunk and jumped over.

"Ha." Tom rode right after her and jumped the old way, leaning back, legs far forward. He had good hands and didn't interfere with Helen's mouth.

"All right." Her competitive blood warmed. She dismounted. "You hold my boy here. I'll show you."

She dragged some branches and placed them at the bottom of the poplar trunk to fill out the jump. Horses don't like airy jumps. Then she found some branches with fewer leaves on them. It took some doing as she had no axe but she managed to make a scruffy three-foot-nine jump, which usually was big enough to get most foxhunters' attention.

"You'll break your neck."

"I won't."

Once she swung back into the saddle she cantered in a large easy circle to relax Throttle. The bay never even looked sideways at the makeshift jump. If Cig wanted to jump this mess, why, he was only too glad to comply. He had a great Thoroughbred heart and sailed over with the fluidity of a natural athlete.

"See!" she triumphantly called from the other side. "I go with his motion instead of leaning back against it."

"And if he stops you're over his ears." Tom wanted more insurance than the forward seat offered.

"Well, if Helen stops you'll slide off her ass."

She circled, clearing it from the other direction.

"When there are fences, hedgerows, and ditches, this makes it so easy."

He swept his arm out indicating the land. "Few fences, no hedgerows, and nary a ditch in sight."

She considered this. Tom didn't need the forward seat. "Ah, well, I guess there aren't many man-made obstacles—but I'm sticking to the forward seat."

"Once you set your mind on something, I'm not going to dissuade you. Nobody ever could anyway." He chuckled. "Mother would try one argument and then another. You two were like banty roosters sometimes." He turned Helen to head back. "I said to her once, 'Mother, *agree* with her. It makes life so much easier, and when she comes around she'll think it's her idea.' And she said"—he imitated Elizabeth Deyhle's voice—" 'I can't agree with her when she's wrong!' "

The words piled up unsaid behind her teeth. She wanted to tell him that two hundred and ninety-five years separated her mother from Elizabeth Deyhle. If she screamed loud enough would they hear her in the twentieth century? Would God hear her? Instead she cleared her throat. "And you were a model of obedience?"

"When they were looking in my direction, I was." He smiled.

"Do you want me to marry Lionel deVries?" She caught him off-guard.

"Yes. He's a good match and will provide for you." He put his left hand on his waist, holding both reins in his right hand. "You are a prize. You can have your pick of the litter and he's the biggest and the strongest."

"Why am I a prize?"

For a moment he looked annoyed. Her memory lapses unnerved him. "Because women are so scarce, you know that."

"Ah. What if I don't want to marry?"

"Everyone wants to marry unless you're a convert to the Church of Rome. In which case, get thee to a nunnery."

"I don't know which is worse."

"Pryor, don't be obstinate." Tom couldn't imagine anyone choosing to remain single, a pitiable state. "This match benefits our family as well as his." His face reddened, he looked to the sky and then out to the river. "Anyway, 'Whoever sups with Lionel had better use a long spoon.' "

"I'd be supping with him and sleeping with him."

This made Tom laugh. "That you would."

"Are you afraid of him? I apologize for being so direct but I have to know. I'm desperately trying to remember but—" she shrugged.

"Afraid? I'm cautious. Always a prudent idea to be on good terms with your neighbor."

Cig pressed her lips together. "Did he ask Father for my hand?" She assumed this tradition was way older than the era she was in.

"Father never mentioned it."

"Did I go to London to get away from Lionel?"

"No. I don't think so."

"Tom, I don't want to be a burden, nor do I want to keep the Deyhles from material gain—"

"Thankful increase." He grinned broadly. "That's what Father called it."

"Yes, my father, too," she blurted out.

"He *was* your father, Pryor."

"I'm sorry. I, well, I get addled." She dropped her feet out of the stirrups to wiggle her toes. "I'm drawn to Lionel but something is holding me back. Can you understand that?"

"Yes."

"Did you harbor doubts about marrying Margaret?"

He shook his head and smiled. "Love at first sight. It took me a good year to convince her though—perhaps you ladies are more sensible in such matters. Now understand, Sister, I don't mean to push you toward Lionel, but the union of our families would ensure our prosperity, God willing." It didn't occur to Tom that Lionel was slippery enough to get the better of almost any deal.

"When will I see him again?"

"In a few days. We'll all be hunting at Shirley."

"I thought he had business to attend to."

"He'll be back. He's at the Falls with William Byrd. They have fifty armed men there. Lionel and William have bought up as much land as they can. Speculation is a vice with them."

Cig knew the Falls would eventually become the city of Richmond.

"We should buy land there, too."

He studied her for a moment, surprised at her suggestion. "Land speculation has ruined more men than drink."

"Made some men fabulously wealthy, too." Cig held up her hand as he was about to protest. "Think on it. No hurry." She exhaled through her nose. "I had another thought."

"Oh—" He shot her a scalding glance.

"Do you believe Lionel's idea about the murdered Indian, that it was bad blood?"

"Why?" A note of alarm rang in Tom's voice.

"I don't know. Do you believe him?"

"Yes. He trades with the tribes west of the fall line, and he knows them."

"I don't believe him."

"Why?" Tom's voice rose.

"I don't know. Just a feeling."

They rode in silence for a while, Tom struggling with thoughts he had formerly suppressed. "Pryor," he said at last, "don't tell Margaret."

She met his eyes then nodded her assent.

16

Frost, translucent, etched fanciful shapes on the windowpanes. Geometric perfection yielded to human imagination as Cig traced an eagle with her forefinger and then a Christmas tree. Without a clock she couldn't tell what time it was in the dead of night. She'd been awakened by a dream in which she was driving a midnight blue Porsche. She couldn't go back to sleep so she wrapped herself in blankets and stared out the window.

She was looking for Fattail. He had led her here. Perhaps he could lead her out. No sight of his saucy face but she did see a large black fox. She'd never seen one before but he came close to the house and in the shimmering moonlight she could plainly observe him.

She wondered if the black fox, the bear, the rabbit, all the animals living alongside of her, ever took notice of her other than to get out of the way. Did other animals perch motionless to watch the human animal? Were we worth watching or did we stink too much? Humans throw off a strong scent that no amount of perfume can disguise. Add tobacco and whiskey to that natural odor and the scent must be overwhelming.

Once, when she was fourteen and Grace was twelve, they'd dozed off under the big oak tree in the middle of the hay pasture. A rustling awoke them. It stopped just as she opened her eyes to behold a woodchuck staring right back at her. Both human and animal stayed still for a moment, each wondering what the other would do. Finally the woodchuck waddled off. As there was a light breeze, it blew their scent away. That was the closest Cig had ever come to a wild animal other than Fattail. She and her sister had laughed over it.

Even at twelve Grace showed signs of that beauty which would mature into a kind of perfection. She used to coach her older sister in how to conquer men.

"You talk to boys like you talk to me. You can't do that." Then Grace would demonstrate. "Make your voice go soft, and go like this, see?" She ended the sentence with a rising note, a form of asking a question.

"Gross."

"It works!" Grace would say. "And you have to lower your eyes and then raise them. They love that."

"I'm not doing it. It's fake," Cig would reply.

"It's not fake. You can't be honest with boys, Cig, they aren't honest with us. The whole thing is a big, fat, stupid game but you'd better learn how to play it or you lose," Grace would counsel.

As Cig pressed her fingertips to the cold pane of glass she wondered how her younger sister could be so wise in the ways of the world at such a young age. Grace wanted the upper hand and she got it. How was immaterial to her. Furthermore, she didn't fret over her charade. She had no desire to have her husband or any man really know who she was, really understand her. She used to say that Cig was the only person who understood her. Did she say that to throw Cig off the track or did Grace really believe it?

How could Grace have lied to her like that? The fact that Grace had slept with Blackie was painful enough but the lying hurt more. Not that Grace had outright lied, she never *said* anything, but she must have scrambled to cover up the affair. Had Cig ever come close to walking in on them? Had Grace burned letters or hidden telltale gifts? Were there love letters in the glove compartment of Grace's car, all those times Cig had ridden in it? How could she not have known? Then again, how *could* she have known? How many women suspect their sisters of sleeping with their husbands?

If Mother were alive, would I go to her? Cig thought. How could I tell her what happened? It would shock Mother as much as it shocked me. And she'd harpoon Grace. God, what a mess. Hell, what a mess without Mother.

Who could she tell and what good would it do? Number one, why burden others? Number two, why should they care? People liked her well enough but she couldn't imagine any of them wanting to be part of this sordid story. Then again, she never gave any of them a chance to show if they truly did care. She'd seen enough human blowflies feeding off the meat of dead romance to want to avoid telling anyone. The only person Cig confided in was Grace. The times she'd cried over Blackie's cheating in the beginning of the marriage . . . just thinking about crying in front of her sister made her want to spit. Once the tears had run dry her confessions were more in the nature of reporting bad weather. "Blackie's storming over Jennifer Garland, Blackie's raining sperm on Paula Biancouli," etc. Grace would tell her to keep on keeping on. It reached the point during the end of the marriage, those last five years, when Grace would ask, "Who's the latest?"

Grace was the latest.

"My God, how could I be so blind?"

Even the kids knew their father ran around. She certainly never told them. Hunter had cornered her one night in the library two years ago. He'd heard stories at school. Cig's heart had snagged in her throat. Whatever Blackie's faults, he did love his children, and no matter how much pain she'd swallowed over the years she didn't want to turn a vulnerable fifteen-year-old against his father. She picked her way through an emotional minefield, trying to explain that while husbands and wives can have rough times, the children come first. Hunter asked good questions, some that she had never thought of. "Does Dad have any other children?" was one zinger. Cig replied that she didn't know. Hunter cried because his father had hurt his mother. She held him and told him no matter what, she was fine and his father loved him. She beseeched him not to judge his father. When he himself was a man he would understand these temptations. Hunter cooled toward his father after that but as far as she knew he never confronted him. She reached a point where she surrendered trying to monitor that relationship, too. It was their relationship, not hers.

They'd have to settle it themselves. It seemed that the last decade, an agonizing lesson in not being able to control anybody or anything, had finally collapsed in on her like an old brick wall. Now she couldn't even control time.

Was Cig, the 1995 Cig, dead? Was she a bunch of disconnected molecules? Was she in heaven with Blackie posing as a cavalier? If she was dead then how could she feel? Or maybe when you died you got packed off to another time, a kind of purgatory. Your time zone depended on your life, reverse karma.

She couldn't be dead. Mother and Dad were dead. She wished Grace were dead in a savage burst of jealousy. If she wasn't dead she had to press on. If there was a God, she believed she would get back to Hunter and Laura. What if she got back but it was 2015? What if her children didn't know her? What if Grace had died and she hadn't had the pleasure of knocking her teeth down her throat? Oh, what if!

A movement at the edge of the woods caught her eye. The frost on the windowpanes distorted her vision. She shut one eye for a better look. A big animal, crouched like a bear, stood up. Cig held her breath. It wasn't an animal but a painted Indian. She threw off the blanket, ran downstairs and grabbed Tom's musket. She didn't know how to load one of these ancient things but she hoped the sight of it would scare off the intruder.

She flung open the back door, the blast of cold air stinging her eyes. She hurried outside in her bare feet. All she saw was his back disappearing into the woods.

Shaking, Cig sprinted back into the house. She shut and bolted the door, then bolted the front door. Tom hurried down the stairs, his nightshirt flapping.

"Indian!" Cig gasped.

Tom grabbed the musket from her hand, quickly poured in powder, rammed down the ball and they both unbolted the door and dashed outside.

"Margaret, stay inside!" Tom shouted.

Cig pointed in the direction in which she'd seen the figure. "Over there."

"Are you sure he was alone?"

"No. But I only saw one man."

"Did you get a good look at him?"

"Yes."

They stood in the heavy frost in their bare feet, their ears straining. A huge owl swept over their heads, swooped down as if to attack them and then passed over. It startled both of them.

"Let's get inside," Cig suggested.

They were chilled to the bone. Margaret had stirred up the fire while they were outside. "Did you see anything?"

Tom shook his head. He carefully hung the loaded musket on the wall. "Pryor, what did he look like?"

"His face was half red and half black and he wore a mantle of feathers. I'd guess he was middle-aged. I didn't see any weapons."

Tom sat down heavily. "A priest, I reckon."

"How do you know?"

Tom stared at her then Margaret spoke. "The priests of the Algonquin tribes paint their bodies half black and half red. They are as powerful as the Weroans, the chiefs. It's the priests who decide whether a tribe or indeed the whole confederation goes to war."

"But I thought all this was behind us."

Tom crossed his leg over his knee. "As far as the tribes here, yes, it is settled. The Powhatan, Accomac, Arrohattoc have withdrawn to lands west and south of here. We seem to be at peace with all the Algonquin peoples, but they are enemies of the Iroquois tribes, and the Sioux tribes could raid and push them back."

"What's to stop the three big tribes from making common cause against the whites?"

"The same thing that keeps France and England from making common cause against Spain," Tom answered.

"Is it still possible for small groups to raid us?"

"Yes," Tom replied, "it's possible."

"It's been almost twenty years since they've attacked here," Margaret added. "There's trouble upriver. I certainly wouldn't venture too far on the other side of the Falls."

"Then what's an Indian doing here?" Cig asked.

"Hungry, maybe, or just curious," Margaret answered. "They'll travel to Jamestown to trade occasionally. Maybe he was passing through."

"Priests don't usually travel alone." Tom stood up and stirred the fire.

Cig shivered again. "You'd think, given how big Virginia is, we could learn to get along."

"They can't get along with one another. Why should we get along with them?" Tom said.

Margaret handed her a piping cup of tea. "We're so different from one another I don't see how we can live together."

Cig wanted to argue, to convince Margaret that cultural divisions like European versus Indian, Christian versus Muslim, could be overcome. She wanted to brag that great progress had been made in her own century. Great progress had been made in the service of hypocrisy. Few people would say "redskin" or "nigger" or "infidel" but such verbal niceties didn't prevent them from killing one another should the occasion arise.

Cig swallowed hard at Margaret's straightforward assessment of the situation. Such honesty was rare—in Cig's time.

17

∞

A web spun by a black-and-yellow banana spider swayed in the early morning breeze. The dew hung on each perfect strand like diamonds. The huge spider sat perfectly still at the edge of her wide web. Banana spiders wait at the center or the edge of their webs. When an insect falls prey, they strike with blinding speed. Although usually gone by the frosts, occasionally one will survive a few days longer, to be revivified when temperatures rise.

Cig hadn't stopped to watch a banana spider in years. As a child she used to take twigs and lightly touch the fat abdomen of the spiders. Other times she'd tap the web to watch the spider rush to the side only to become furious that no lunch was forthcoming. Then the banana spider would sit in the web bending and unbending her legs until the web swung like a trampoline.

Cig and Margaret were walking to the family gravesite on a high hill overlooking the James. The sky, robin's egg blue, heightened the exploding color on earth: fiery orange oaks, poplars as yellow as tulips, maples scarlet orange, with dogwoods pure red.

"The end of Indian summer," Cig said, a basket of spring bulbs over one arm.

Margaret also carried a basket. "That's a good term for this time of year. The Indians have a story that their great god blew the southwest wind, which cleared the skies. The trees donned their most festive clothes to honor him. When he had exhaled all this wind then the god from the north would blow. Winter is sure to follow."

"Let's hope the southwestern god has a little breath left."

"Sometimes he can blow deep into November." Margaret hummed as she walked, swinging her basket in time. Puffs of dust attended each step.

They reached the crest of the hill. A large square surrounded by a two-and-a-half-foot wall of river stone marked the graveyard. A white gate, the top cut in a crescent, hung on huge iron hinges. Margaret opened the gate.

Two large stones, beautifully carved, marked the graves of Charles and Elizabeth Deyhle. Elizabeth's read:

Elizabeth Rinton Buckingham Deyhle, Beloved Mother, Cherished Wife, Born April 9, 1642, Died June 20, 1697.

Next to her rested Charles Richard Deyhle:

A Founder of the Fifth Crown, Born January 18, 1629, Died December 20, 1697.

She noticed the smaller marker.

Braxton Harburtson Deyhle, Born 1678, Died 1695.

"Who was Braxton?"

"Your brother."

"How did he die?"

"The sweating sickness." Margaret knelt down and began digging the small holes for the spring bulbs.

"Poor fellow. So young."

"And gifted. Had he lived your father would have sent him to Hannover to study music. Braxton wanted to go to Vienna but Charles said Hannover housed temptations enough."

"Why Hannover?"

"Your father had friends there who assured him there was a fine organ master."

Cig surveyed even smaller stones. "Babies?"

Margaret nodded.

"Where are Charles's parents buried?"

"In England. After the Restoration they returned to London to petition King Charles for help . . . help in the form of cannon and soldiers. Your grandmother's lungs gave way. Shortly thereafter your grandfather died in a duel. They say he grew intemperate after Priscilla's death. Someone bumped into him one night leaving Court and he drew his sword. Your grandfather was a fine swordsman but he had the misfortune to pick a fight with the king's blade."

"Who, or what, is 'the king's blade'?"

"The finest swordsman in the kingdom, the personal bodyguard of the king."

"Sometimes I think our lives are nothing but footprints leading to death." Cig placed a daffodil bulb in a hole. "I wonder how many carcasses I've left behind. How many lives have I lived—if indeed I've lived any of them fully? How many times have I known you and in what relation?"

"Since you can't answer those questions, why fret over them? Do what you can."

A flash of irritation prompted Cig. "Practical. Very practical."

"Yes," Margaret flashed back. "Wherever you are you might as well be useful."

"I am useful! I'm just lost, goddammit!"

"Don't take the Lord's name in vain."

"Don't be a Puritan."

Margaret squinted at Cig. "I am not, but you should take more care with your faith. Look . . ." she pointed to the darkening western sky, the clouds piling up.

Cig shielded her eyes. "Maybe they'll slip by. Anyway, we have another hour or so before they get here. That gives me another hour to bitch and moan." She made fun of herself. "Margaret, do I seem like the Pryor you knew?"

"More somber." Margaret brushed loose dirt off her apron. "But yes, you are the Pryor I knew."

"Can you tell me about myself? I know that sounds strange."

"Well, you would rather be outside than inside. You've never cared a fig for adornments. Both your mother and I would have to dress you for society. You are particularly stubborn about your hair." She reached over to pull Pryor's single braid. "You liked horses better than men and you were always laughing. You had, as your mother put it, 'a sunny nature.' "

Cig listened then slowly replied. "I used to be that way when I was younger. Laughing. Playing. I got away from it somehow."

"Worries."

"Huh?"

"We care too much for the world and it cares too little for us." Margaret smiled sweetly. "We worry what others think. We worry about money, the weather, and there are those for whom worrying about this world isn't enough woe. They're worrying about the next."

"Is Tom religious?"

"He cares not a fig for his immortal soul." Margaret felt the thin skin of the daffodil bulb. "Are you religious?"

"Don't look at me." Cig shrugged.

"Who else am I to look at?"

Cig laughed. "No, I'm not religious. I don't trust people who think they have answers about my spiritual life. It's even worse when God gets into politics."

"Why would He lower Himself? Kings and governments are transitory. God is eternal."

Cig rested on her haunches to sort out bulbs. "Margaret, I've got a lot to learn from you. I assumed you all would be primitive, I guess because your living conditions are primitive by the standards of my time. Actually, you're further along," she tapped her head, "than most of my friends." She sighed. "I live in an empty, cynical time."

"That's up to you." Margaret smoothed earth over a bulb.

"Huh?"

"Just because people around you are cynical doesn't mean you must follow suit."

Cig stood up to rest her knees and to consider what Margaret had just said to her. Margaret was right. She had no reply. Like most riders her knees hurt the older she got. "We need rose bushes." She pointed to where she'd place them.

"I know. I want some at the house, too."

"Can you buy them?"

"If I order a huge cargo from England. Tom would die—actually, I'd be the one to die. He hasn't the time for fripperies, as he puts it."

"What about cuttings?"

"Mrs. Boothrod grows handsome roses. I can't bring myself to ask the dragon for any."

"Will I meet her?"

"You will. At Shirley. Oh, I should tell you, their son, Abraham, is smitten with you. He's a bit younger."

"Am I smitten with him?"

"No, but you like him tremendously. I have high hopes for that young man."

"You sound like an old lady. How old are you?"

"Twenty-five. Not old. Not young."

"You'd be quite young in my time—the bloom of youth, and you do look very pretty."

"I do?"

"Yes, indeed."

Margaret perked up. "As long as I keep my teeth! I just hate when people's teeth fall out and their mouths shrink in."

"Use a toothbrush." Cig pulled her small portable one from her jacket pocket.

"Isn't that clever?"

"You use toothpaste and water. Baking soda does the trick, too."

"I use a toothpick."

"Use them both, although you don't have a toothbrush—well, if you study this I bet you can make one."

Margaret ran her thumb over the bristles. "What kind of animal hair is this?"

"It isn't. It's plastic. I'd try pig bristles. If they're too thick then use horse whiskers."

"I bet I could make one." Margaret stood up herself for a moment, the soft dirt sprinkling off her apron. "Pryor, if you don't recognize me, if you really are from another time, do you know what will happen to me, to Tom?"

"My sister has the earliest Deyhle Bibles and papers. I have the records after 1860. I don't know, although if I ever get back home—I mean back to that home—I will know because I'll get the papers from Grace. But you had to have lived a pretty long life and had children or I wouldn't be here. Are you worried?"

"No."

"Feeling sick?"

"No."

"Curious?"

"Being in a graveyard makes me think on mortality. And we lost Braxton, Elizabeth, and Charles so close to one another. Then we were afraid we'd lose you at sea. It was a terrible time. I thought it would never end."

"But it did."

"When I was a little girl I would cry when anything upset me. I had a little puppy, Roger Dodger. I can still see his silly face. One of the horses stepped on him and he died. I cried and I cried and I cried. And my mother said, 'Sorrow is how we learn to love. Your heart isn't breaking. It hurts because it's getting larger. The larger it gets the more love it holds.' You know, I've thought of that so often—when everyone died, when you hadn't come home to us after so many months."

"She's a wise woman. Is she still alive?"

"Oh, yes. She lives in Charleston with her second husband."

"Have I met her?"

"At the wedding. You two got on but then you are hard not to like."

"What a kind thing to say. I don't feel very likable." She knelt back down to push in the last of the bulbs. "I've been afraid to ask you questions about myself."

"I don't mind. Perhaps my answers will help you to remember. I find if I can call up a picture in my mind that I can remember the smallest items, the color of a snuffbox, say, or the pattern of lace on a fine shirt."

Cig stood up. "I'm afraid if I learn about this life that I will have lost *my* life, the life I know, and then I'll never see my children." Tears filled her eyes.

"Pryor, poor Pryor." Margaret wrapped her arms around her, hugging her tight. She offered Cig a handkerchief to blow her nose and continued. "I can't know how you feel and I must sound unconvincing but I do believe you are here for a reason and—and do you have a better answer?"

"No—I guess the world is crazy no matter what time you live in, or where."

"Were I to visit your time I imagine I'd be lost. Some things would be familiar, many strange and frightening. But people are the same, are they not?"

Cig nodded. "You put different clothes on them, that's all. There are fashions of ideas, too, but people are people. Some are crooked, some straight. Some are smart, most aren't." She laughed. "And I count myself in the latter group. Some are serious and some know how to laugh and most of us can't see any farther than the nose on our face."

"And neither will we for those storm clouds are flying across the sky." Margaret looked up at the roiling, black clouds, which seemed low enough to touch.

18

∞

Light frost hugged the ground, and the crisp air promised good scent at Shirley Plantation. Neighbors gathered from throughout the Tidewater. Many followed the hunt on foot. Elderly ladies and gentlemen and their servants traipsed to higher ground to better follow the hunt's progress. A few followed in carriages.

The barns, with their simple, handsome brick exteriors and graceful arches over the windows, were as Cig remembered them, which gave her some feeling of security.

As they approached the main gathering she asked Tom, "Where's the main house?"

"Where it's always been." Tom pointed to a serviceable but not distinguished brick building.

The lovely mansion Cig had known was yet to be built. She tried to remember the history of Shirley Plantation but all that came to mind was Edward Hill II's beating by Nathaniel Bacon. Bacon, rebelling against the governor of Jamestown and those who supported him, held the second owner of Shirley captive, along with his pregnant wife and their children. That rebellion in 1675 might have fomented far more trouble than it did had Bacon not perished from dysentery. Bacon's Rebellion and the prior great massacre of 1622 left their mark on the survivors.

Margaret discreetly pointed out Edward Hill III, who had been Bacon's captive as a child. Mounted on a stout seal brown gelding, Hill greeted his guests with enthusiasm. Intelligence shone from his face. He could not have known, Cig thought, that he would be remembered even into her time for his business acumen and wise use of his landholdings, or that his family would contribute to Virginia in each succeeding generation. Here he was, already third generation, no firsthand memory of the Old World, a new man in a New World.

" 'Pon my soul!" Daniel Boothrod waved his lace handkerchief at Cig, then tucked it in his sleeve.

"Who's that?" Cig whispered to Margaret.

"Daniel Boothrod, a most enthusiastic gentleman."

What a jolly popinjay he was, with a towering peruke, a kind of wig, a frock coat of deep burgundy, a burnt orange brocaded waistcoat and a white silk shirt, lace spilling from under his coat cuffs and at his throat.

Margaret giggled. "It's not prudent to wear a wig whilst hunting."

"Too hot," Tom offered. His hair was close cropped so that he could wear a wig when the occasion demanded it.

"Do you wear a wig, Tom?"

"As little as possible, you know that," he said. "I don't look half-bad though."

"You only look half-good." She jabbed at him with her hunting whip, the deer bone handle smooth in her hand, as Daniel strode over with his stiffly arrogant wife, even more festooned than her husband.

"A vision, a vision for these eyes." Daniel removed his hat with a flourish and bowed low from the waist. His wife's eyes narrowed to slits. Mrs. Boothrod inclined her head, which was a way of bidding them hello without curtsying since one curtsied only to superiors and equals. Her snub couldn't have been more plain. The Deyhles and her husband chose to ignore it and her.

"You flatter me, sir." Cig smiled at Daniel whom she instinctively liked.

"I greet your return with profound thanksgiving for many are the travails of travel, as St. Paul was wont to tell us . . . but then St. Paul might have fared better in those wretched countries had he been less aggressive in his zeal." He gulped a shallow little breath so he could continue in his florid manner. "And how did you find that queen of cities, London?"

"Bursting with commerce but rather dull, sir, since you were conspicuously absent." She struggled to think of not just what to say but how to say it.

Tremendously pleased with the compliment he bowed again, turning one foot out perpendicular to the other like a ballet dancer. This choreographed display of courtliness and a handsome calf finally proved too much for his madam. Her teal-colored hat dipping over one eye, she had to cock her head to gaze eye to eye with her husband. "Mr. Boothrod, we'll be adrift in the back of the riders if you don't come along." She smiled tightly at Cig. "My husband cherishes the notion that he has the best legs in the colony."

"The best calves, I'm sure." Cig couldn't resist.

"Ah, every man has a calf and an ass." Tom's cheeks blushed with glee.

"Oh, good, Tom, next you'll be asking to see my ass." Daniel guffawed.

"Really!" Mrs. Boothrod tapped the side of her riding skirt with her crop, the picture of righteous irritation. "Don't be an ass." Realizing what she had said, her small mouth opened like a tiny surprised bivalve.

"Christ rode an ass into Jerusalem . . . so I don't mind being one." Daniel glanced from his wife to the Deyhles then bowed again. "By your leave ladies, Tom."

"How did I do?" Cig whispered as Daniel propelled a sputtering Amelie Boothrod toward her horse.

"Splendid." Margaret praised her. "You handled the dragon like a St. George."

"A pain in the ass," Tom whispered. "I've got to get that word out of my mind." They all laughed.

"Daniel must be quite wealthy."

"Some years he is and some he isn't," Margaret replied.

"The same could be said for us all. We rise and fall on a tide of tobacco."

"Plant peanuts."

"What's that?"

"Ground nuts, I mean."

"Pryor, ground nuts are for animals." Tom grimaced at the thought of eating fodder.

"Put a crop in anyway," she insisted.

"Let's discuss this later."

The Deyhles rode over to their host. He leaned out of the saddle and warmly kissed Cig's hand. "Pryor Deyhle, I am so happy to see you, mademoiselle. If you're with us we'll run red foxes!"

"There are always red foxes at Shirley." She smiled, knowing there always would be, and she began to feel confident, for foxhunting was her element regardless of the century.

A throng of people rode over, all talking at once, all eager to greet Pryor. With Margaret and Tom's help she chatted, laughed, and got through it with few mistakes, although people thought her attire quite severe and a few were scandalized by her wearing breeches.

Lionel deVries joined the group. A small coterie swam around him currying for favor.

Lionel swept off his hat and bowed his head, beaming at the sight of her.

"Artemis herself."

"Flatterer." But she loved it. She felt that giddy sensation, the warm flush of confusion and attraction, and it was as though she was seeing him for the first time, seeing him as she had once before . . . in a time to come.

Lionel rode up beside her, reached for her hand and pressed it to his lips. "I have no need of invention in your presence. Simple descriptive powers will do." Then he touched his hat and said to Margaret, "You, of course, must be Hera."

Margaret's silvery laugh was infectious. "I hope I have a more faithful husband."

The gathering laughed although Amelie Boothrod's was forced but she did say, "Zeus was faithful for three hundred years. That means Daniel has two hundred and fifty remaining."

The group howled.

Daniel replied, "In your presence, my angel, two hundred and fifty years will be as the twinkling of an eye." He winked. "But how could I fall to a circus of vices after a feast of such virtue?" The men whistled while the ladies applauded. Amelie beamed, although she didn't believe a word of it. Somehow it didn't matter at the moment.

In this frontier, this fragile outpost of European ambition and culture, social gatherings were cherished. The dueling of the Boothrods enriched the celebratory atmosphere. People labored long and hard on their farms and at their trades. Sunlight, as precious as gold, guided their activities. Laughter, even more precious than gold, bound them together. If there were a shortage of foxes they would chase anything that ran, including one another.

The loneliness of the fierce New World struggle to survive could be dispelled by gossip, laughter and the chase.

Here among these people she felt the bonds of community, true communion. It surprised her for she thought she lived in a fairly tight-knit community. She began to realize that she was compressed, her life had been squeezed into artificial blocks of time. Everything had to fit. Harried by numbers, from the clock to her social security number to her credit cards to her mortgage, she had been lulled into believing life was finite; after all, numbers are. But experience isn't measurable and friendship can't be squeezed into fifteen-minute intervals of telephone exchanges. She'd fallen into the trap of her epoch: frantic activity just to keep one's head above water. She wanted out of that trap as much as she wanted to return to her children.

She began to dream—could she bring them here?

She felt oddly infused with light. She grasped a tiny truth for herself even as Lionel grasped her hand. She wasn't a number. She might mean nothing to her government other than a yearly tax payment, but the impersonality of large institutions could be resisted, could perhaps even be changed, if people like her declared, I'll live my life as I please. I'm not a silent victim. I might lose the battle for individual freedom but I'll surely lose if I don't fight.

She'd never in her forty years entertained the idea that she could affect her time or the future. Yet looking at these people who endured more than she ever had or probably ever would, she felt gratitude and courage. If they could build a new world, some of them carried here against their will, if they could work, love and live, what in the hell was the matter with her? She could do whatever she had to do and a lot of what she wanted to do. The choice was hers.

"Dearest lady, where did you get that horse?" One young man, long-faced and blond, grinned as he rode toward her, snapping her out of her reverie and causing Lionel to squeeze her hand even tighter.

"Abraham Boothrod, Daniel's son," Margaret said out of the corner of her mouth for she rode on Cig's near side.

"Mr. Boothrod—you've grown into such a handsome fellow!"

He glowed. Abraham was a young man in his father's shadow. "You do me a great honor to flatter me so."

The sound of the hunting horn cut off conversation as all eyes turned toward the hounds. Cig gasped, for moving around the side of a barn was a pack of black and tans, big-boned, handsome hounds. She'd always heard that black and tans were stubborn, hard to control. She'd expected a pack of English foxhounds, heavier than the American foxhounds she ran.

"Good hunting!" Abraham saluted her with his crop.

"Good hunting to you, sir." She returned the wish then asked Lionel, "Black and tans?"

"Aye, a new man from Ireland brought the whole pack over last year. The fellow has a gift with hounds. They're in fine voice and so is he." He dropped her hand at last.

She looked from the glistening pack to the other riders. Most rode in flat, saddle seat–type saddles. The stirrup irons were just that, irons, although she saw a handful of black men riding with wooden stirrups.

"Grooms?" Cig asked.

Tom nodded as Lionel was reluctantly called away by their host.

Margaret added, "Some are slaves. That fellow over there wearing the blue coat is a freeman."

"Slave trade is picking up." Tom rubbed his chin. "The more hands a man can put in his field the richer he'll become. Of course, you have to be rich to buy a slave in the first place."

Cig half-listened, overwhelmed by the spectacle and by Lionel's presence. She studied the other hunters who wore clothes comparable to her own. The coats, woven of sturdy fabric, were cut longer as were the waistcoats. Her waistcoat had contracted into a vest. All the men wore folded-over boots, which some were in the process of unfolding over their knees. Most of the ladies rode sidesaddle although a few did not. The women wore shorter boots and most wore skirts of practical fabrics, though a few wore silk, which they arranged on either side of their horses if riding astride. One young woman had wedged the ends of her skirt under her stirrup leathers. Most of the ladies looked comfortable in the saddle.

Except for Daniel Boothrod's attire, the predominate colors of the coats were dark blue, dark green, or black. The waistcoats were white silk or cotton, a few were canary or buff. The breeches were all buff-colored and the young Huntsman wore deerskin breeches, a French hunting horn over his left shoulder. His close-cropped hair was curly blond, and his thick eyebrows were blond with a tinge of red. His jaw was strong, his nose straight and his teeth unusually white. He was perhaps a lean five foot seven. His smile could melt a heart of stone. It haunted Cig. He was a gorgeous flash of lightning.

"Who's the Huntsman?" a mesmerized Cig asked.

"Patrick Devlin Fitzroy. He's the fellow who brought over the black and tans."

"Handsome," Cig said.

"Him?" Tom shrugged.

"You never think any man is handsome but yourself," Margaret teased him.

"As long as you think that, my love," he replied.

"What happened to Edward Hill's pack?" Cig correctly assumed a man of such property would keep a pack of fine hounds.

Tom frowned. "They rioted on deer."

"Well, if it's in the blood, forget it," Cig, at home in the hunt field, responded. A foxhound should never chase a deer.

Fitzroy blew the horn. The notes were deeper, rounder, than the straight, short hunting horns Cig knew, but the calls were identical. And the first sound of the horn always gave Cig goosebumps.

Fitzroy wore no cap or hat. The other riders wore broad-brimmed hats, which a few had pinned up to one side in cavalier fashion.

Tom, excited, edged up to the front of the field. Cig decided she'd stay back to watch people ride. Politeness overcame curiosity because they were watching her, too. Her habit was different enough to cause comment and her forward seat appeared precarious.

Fitzroy blew deep staccato notes, three times in succession to cast his hounds. Quiet in the saddle, he moved behind his obedient pack.

Cig noticed that Edward Hill's groom, the African, Marker, fanned out to the left of the pack, and a giant of a man whom she didn't know worked over on the right. Fitzroy worked like Roger with two whippers-in to keep the hounds in line.

As they moved away from the barns the country road opened up before them. There were fewer meadows than Cig remembered in this territory and fewer fences.

A lone, deep voice called. Others answered. No matter how many times Cig heard hounds find, it thrilled her. Full Throttle, accustomed to leading the field, complained about being stuck in the rear. "Behave yourself," she chastised him. He swept his ears back, snorted once, but obeyed.

They picked up a trot and then the cry, full, burst out of the hounds' throats like a canine Magnificat in C Major. Mrs. Boothrod, face flushed with excitement, rocked back and forth in her high-sided sidesaddle, her skirt draped over to one side. Abraham Boothrod sat straight up in his saddle, feet forward, heels down. His father's insistence on haute école showed, for the son was a much better rider than the father.

Although not a dressage rider, Cig recognized the very same dressage principles that had been drummed into people's heads throughout the centuries. The field of riders evidenced those principles. A good rider was a good rider no matter what discipline—or the century.

Within seconds the whole field exploded down the road, flat out. Cig forgot to stay behind. The pace was too good. She passed Margaret, loping along on Pollux, enjoying himself tremendously. From Pollux's point of view this beat plowing, she blew past Lionel deVries and his acolytes. He spurred his horse to keep up with her. One minion slid off his horse trying to keep up, too. Daniel Boothrod became a blur. He called out something but she couldn't hear him. She did hear Lionel though, drawing alongside her.

"No mortal rides like that! You are the goddess of the hunt."

"Lionel," she replied, exhilarated, "you *can* ride."

His hands followed the motion of his horse's head and neck. He fell in behind her. "I just want to keep my eyes on *you*."

She naturally took the lead. She didn't mean to be rude but no one appeared to be acting as Fieldmaster. She zipped right in Patrick Fitzroy's pocket, staying close in behind him and the hounds. He looked around in amazement then delight.

The hounds, longer-legged but much heavier than her hounds, couldn't cover ground as quickly as her pack. Still, they were wondrous hounds.

The pack, running tight, swerved left into a wood filled with massive black walnut trees. No one had cut trails so the riders picked their own way through. She glanced around to check on her field, as she thought of them, and discovered that Tom on Helen was behind Abraham Boothrod and behind him, riding hard, was Daniel. Many of the ladies in their velvet seats elected to go around the woods but they knew their hunting etiquette and were careful not to cross the line of the fox.

Margaret, keenly listening for the hounds, rode in the middle of the field. Many people were mounted on draft horses, draft crosses, or carriage horses, heavier-boned and slower than Full Throttle who among this crowd was an animal of surpassing beauty. But then Cig thought him beautiful even if he'd been among Olympic show jumpers. Throttle, all heart and a good brain, relished his position. He was in front. He knew his job: stay close to the hounds. Running at a slow controlled canter behind a draft horse, clods of dirt flying in his face, would never do.

With everyone crashing about in the thick woods Cig thought the black and tans would lift their heads or become distracted. Noses to the ground they pressed on, jumping obstacles, but as she feared, getting more entangled in underbrush than her own pack simply because they were so much bigger.

One hound twisted a leg in a vine and howled bloody murder. Cig, seeing the field slowed by the underbrush, pulled up, quickly dismounted, and freed the hound. He crashed about on his way. She swung back in the saddle as Tom, Abraham, and Lionel watched approvingly. Fitzroy, turning in his saddle as he rode on for he had to keep up with his pack, touched his whip handle to his brow in thanks.

"The fox will find a creek if there is one or he'll run over deer tracks," she said.

Tom pointed to his left. "There's usually a current of strong cold air along the run there." Cig recognized the word for creek.

"Follow me," she quietly said.

The field did as she told them because she was a natural leader—and they were having great sport.

Cig lifted her head, feeling the cold air on her cheeks. Tom knew this territory. She did, too, but it sure didn't look like this. There were forests where she knew miles of pasture. Once she hit the creek, though, she knew she wasn't far from the edge of Shirley Plantation as she knew it. They were heading northwest.

The hounds straggled out of the woods. She pursued, plunging into the creek, clambering up on the opposite bank. The field followed her. Soon they arrived at a huge pasture, one end marked by snake fencing.

The sidecar ladies, as Cig thought of them, were nowhere in sight. Cig raised her hand to halt the group. Lionel rode past her.

"Hold hard." Command drenched her voice.

Lionel halted, raised a bemused eyebrow and said, "Yes, your Highness."

Without missing a beat Cig shot back, "Better than your Lowness."

Abraham Boothrod guffawed and Margaret's jaw hung on her ample bosom.

Cig turned to the field. "If you follow me I promise you the hunt of your life."

Edward Hill, blood hot for the chase, held up his silver-headed crop. "We'll follow you to the gates of Hell!"

"You might have to." She called over her shoulder for the hounds, in full cry again, stretched out their longs legs, eating up the ground. A flock of extremely fat turkeys flew up out of the edge of the woods. A horse in the rear shied, the rider hitting the turf with a thud.

Cig soared over the snake fencing. Lionel, not to be outdone, followed suit although it wasn't easy for him. Tom and Abraham leaned way back in their saddles to clear the chestnut rails. The rest of the field ran around the fence, costing them time.

"Close up!" Cig instructed them.

The tail hounds, clearly in sight, held steady on the line. The pack worked efficiently. Cig reined in and slowed to a trot behind the last tail hound. He wasn't off course but something had caused him to slow down. He lifted his sensitive brown eyes to Cig then picked up speed.

She could see Fitzroy, relaxed in the saddle, horn to his lips, up ahead. The hounds slowed a moment, then opened again with one collective cry. They swept into a bit of woods only to turn and charge right back out of them.

Cig turned with them, galloping back in the direction from which they came. They wound up on the road where the sidecar ladies had been following. Without hesitating or slowing her pace Cig jumped the drainage ditch by the road, thundered by the ladies, one of whom—smart woman—had stood up in her stirrups, hat off, pointing in the direction of the fox.

"Gray or red?" Cig asked as she blasted by.

"Red!" came the resolute reply.

They know their foxes, Cig thought to herself.

She lost a few more riders as they attempted to negotiate the drainage ditch. Straight ahead squatted a stone fence, gate closed. She recognized neither the fence nor the gate but figured it must be the back entrance to a plantation with a lot of livestock.

She checked over her shoulder; her brother and Lionel kept close.

Daniel was falling behind. Abraham passed him. No horse in the field possessed Full Throttle's speed. In her excitement she didn't realize that this was the first time she'd thought of Tom as her brother.

"If you can't jump get the gate and close it when everyone is through," she bellowed at Tom.

"I'll clear the fence if I have to jump it myself."

She laughed as Throttle lifted off over the fieldstone fence. My God, he feels good, she thought.

Tom wrapped his hands in Helen's mane, squeezed with all his might and the mare launched herself over. Tom flopped back a little but stayed on. Lionel, bold and supple, never flinched, nor did his horse, a solid roan, hunting fit. Abraham made it over as well.

Daniel stopped, turned right and shouted to a groom to open the gate. This he did and the field barreled through, the thinning frost still heavy enough to hold down the dust. Daniel Boothrod stood in his stirrups to catch sight of the frontrunners.

Edward Hill, panting by his left side, called out, "Daniel, are my eyes deceiving me?"

"They've no fear!" Daniel replied.

"That's the way to live, by God." Edward enviously smiled.

" 'Pon my soul." Daniel laughed.

Cig pushed her little band along another verdant pasture. The hounds abruptly stopped their music.

A few confused yowls bespoke their frustration. Fitzroy blew on his big horn. The hounds gathered together then fanned out again.

Cig held up her arm. The field knew enough by now not to run past her. She shifted in her saddle to see who'd survived. More than she'd anticipated.

A tough bunch, she thought with pride.

Edward and Daniel came alongside of her, breathing hard, happy for the check.

Daniel, in particular, gasped. "Still as a statue, yes, still as a statue when you jump that animal. *Magnifique!*" He accented his French.

"Thank you. Gentlemen, if you sit still for a moment I'm willing to bet another red fox is going to burst out"—she pointed to a gentle grade by the meadow that rolled toward the forest stream—"right over there. I believe our first sprinter has gone to ground and passed the baton."

Before they could comment, sure enough the hounds gave tongue. The strike hound, a spectacular compact bitch with tremendous drive, moved toward the forest.

"Shall we?"

Lionel nodded, catching his breath. Abraham and Tom exchanged glances then fell in behind her. Daniel floated off to the right hoping for sight of the fox. Margaret remained in the middle of the group, her legs clamped to Pollux's broad sides.

Lionel rode eight strides back. He knew better, now, than to crowd Pryor.

They trotted along a thin slice of creek, the stones slick as patent leather. The hounds worked steadily, the terrain slowing them. Cig picked an easy spot to ford.

She motioned to Tom. "How far to the river? A mile?"

"Not even."

"Is it all wooded?"

"Most ways," Tom replied.

"If we could head straight out we'd reach Ranke's cornfield," Abraham added.

"Okay," she said and smiled as he shook his head at her peculiar speech. "Reynard has lots of choices."

Full Throttle carefully picked his way through the woods. Eventually they reached the cornfield. The hounds fanned out into the field, the corn swaying as they moved through, their voices rising and falling. Fitzroy rode with them, his whippers-in spreading out on the sides.

Cig reached a slight rise in the pasture along the cornfield. The group gathered on the hill. They waited about five minutes for the sidecar ladies to join them for they circled around the woods.

Edward asked her, "Have we cornered Reynard?"

Cig noticed his clear light eyes, kind eyes. "He's having as much sport with us as we are with him. When he's ready he'll shoot out of that cornfield like a hot cannonball unless he's got a den in there. Usually, though, a fox doesn't want to live where we traffic."

"I don't want to live where we traffic," Edward replied.

Daniel dabbed his forehead with his lace handkerchief. "Now, don't decry rude Jamestown." He mocked Edward's voice.

"*You* live there, Daniel." Edward jabbed at Daniel's paunch.

A sleek vixen, at a dogtrot, emerged from the end of the cornfield. With saucy eye she perused the humans and horses on the low hill. She considered them species of low degree.

Cig put her finger to her lips before the group could screech at the sight of the vixen. The silence created even more tension.

A few long minutes passed and then three hounds, hard on the scent, cleared the cornfield. Fitzroy followed, looking to Cig.

She removed her cap, pointing in the direction the vixen took. He smiled and pushed on, and a strange chill racked her body. By now the rest of the pack came out of the cornfield. Cig moved down the hill, falling in behind the pack.

The sweet smell of the ears hanging on the stalks to dry, fodder for winter, curled into her nostrils as she approached the bottom of the hill. The hounds picked up the scent and opened up. She squeezed Throttle but just as quickly pulled him up. The hounds lost the scent.

"By the saints!" She heard Fitzroy curse.

The sun was near the top of the sky; it must be close to eleven. The day warmed considerably, the scent rising with it.

Without thinking about it she rode over to Fitzroy much as she would to Roger Davis. He was even more handsome at close quarters, his blue eyes sparkling.

"Given the warmth the only hope is to cast by a creek."

He said nothing for a moment. "A Huntsman, are you, madam?"

"I'm sorry. Second nature." She blushed. She'd forgotten that she wasn't the master, this wasn't her Huntsman. She had no right to offer direction. "You've a beautiful pack and my enthusiasm for more sport made me forget my manners."

He nodded his head. "Patrick Devlin Fitzroy at your service, madam." His brogue had a lilt to it.

"Pryor Deyhle." She smiled. "It's the strangest thing, but I feel we've met before."

He smiled now. "I regret that we have not, but you ride like the Devil himself. Dress like him, too." He indicated her scarlet jacket.

She didn't know whether to laugh or be insulted. "You won't lose me in the woods this way."

"Ah, Virginia practicality. Not much forest in County Cork." His eyebrows pointed upward for a moment. "You are Tom Deyhle's twin, I gather?"

"I am."

"And where did you find such a horse? Not in the New World, I'll wager."

"Uh—" She lied, "A Barb I purchased in England."

"If ever I'm a rich man I'll send you back over the water to buy one for me."

As the field caught up to them and gathered round Cig said, "Thank you for this fine day. It was a pleasure to hunt with you, sir."

The others thanked Fitzroy as Lionel joined Cig. Abraham came along her other side, much to Lionel's irritation.

When they returned to Shirley a famished bunch, they rushed to the sumptuous hunt breakfast as their grooms and Edward Hill's servants rubbed down the horses, which, once cooled out, were rewarded with oats laced with a bit of bran and molasses made into a mash.

Ham biscuits, sausage gravy, hot cornbread, mountains of sweet butter, slabs of bacon, eggs, pancakes and waffles drenched in the thickest maple syrup or creamy clover honey, and orange rinds dazzled the guests for whom citrus was a rare delicacy.

As they ate, the hunt became fiercer, the fox bigger, and the stone wall loomed large as Hampton Court.

The ladies peppered Cig with questions about her riding habit. Margaret, at her elbow, said or whispered names, mentioned children and subtly nudged her in the right direction.

The men, swilling stout home brew as well as more refined spirits along with the biscuits, spoke of tobacco prices, the hopes of acquiring land farther upriver, and they picked over the issues before the Assembly.

The subject of the murdered Indian was thoroughly dissected with Lionel firmly expressing the opinion that if the Indians could benefit from trade, plunder would be less alluring.

The men also discussed the ladies. Abraham wanted to have a few moments with Tom. He wanted to ask about Pryor but Tom, in the center of the group and well-liked by all, couldn't be pried away. So Abraham pretended to be interested and peeked out from time to time to catch a glimpse of Pryor.

Fitzroy, irreverent, had the men laughing and he didn't mind being the butt of the jokes himself.

In time the gentlemen joined the ladies, which provoked more hilarity. Daniel Boothrod declared that what Virginia needed, apart from more good women like his wife, was more foxhunting and more dances. Abraham declared that they should invite the foxes to the balls at which point Fitzroy bowed to the ladies and purred, "But we have."

Lionel fumed inwardly. He wished he'd said that for Pryor laughed with delight. Willful and independent from birth, she was even more so since her return from England. He stared at her and felt that she had changed. She had always been reckless and wild but now she openly challenged him. Well, that would change when he married her.

19

A warm south wind fluttered over the pastures and lawn. If Cig closed her eyes it felt like spring. Before she could rise to carry her plate back to the table a servant, Welsh from the look of her, gently lifted it from her hands.

"Thank you."

"Anything more, m'um?" the young woman asked.

"No, thank you." As everyone was talking to everyone else, and she found herself alone, she chose the moment to gratefully slip away. She walked toward the stable, a magnet for her since she gravitated toward animals whenever she needed to think. Hearing the laughter of the grooms, she stopped then walked over to a black gum tree at the edge of the lawn.

She leaned against the textured bark, her eyes sweeping the buildings, noticing the efficient use of topography and materials. The laughter and conversation hummed in the near distance, the horses nickered to one another as the grooms hauled buckets of water, snapping each other with rags. An old man, his white beard patchy, his teeth long gone, dozed while seated on an upturned wooden bucket. Between his boots rested curry combs.

The squeal of children, dressed like tiny adults, made her smile as did the barking of the house dogs chasing the balls thrown for their benefit.

Cattle grazed on good pastures, chickens strutted and scratched, careful not to waken sleeping cats stuffed full of ham biscuits.

Shirley Plantation was quick with life, with plans for the future. The sweet smell of hay, roasting ears of corn and cleaned leather filled her with memories of parties at her parents' farm. Grace would rush about begging anyone and everyone to chase her. Cig usually did, invariably getting her starched dress dirty whereas Grace never seemed to attract so much as a speck of dust. If she shut her eyes the sounds were the same except no horns honked, no motors started and stopped, no big rubber tires crunched down the stone driveway and no radio played in the background. Her mother used to bring out the kitchen radio, putting it on a wide branch of the lowest tree. Extension cords snaked over the lawn. Apart from that, the energy, the gossip, the flirting and fighting, the dogs ecstatic with excitement—it was the same.

She closed her eyes as tears filled them. When she opened them she wanted to see Hunter and Laura. She didn't care what century. She wanted to hear their bickering and laughter.

And she missed Blackie.

The tears left wet trails down her cheeks for she desperately missed her sister, angry and wounded as she was.

She wondered who she was. Who thinks about their surroundings, about the minutiae of daily life? Ivory soap ads, Melissa Etheridge songs, baseball caps in every color and cowboy boots to match, faded Levis and crisp white T-shirts, the Messiah sung on Christmas Eve, water balloon fights on a sweltering August afternoon, a poem by William Butler Yeats, a painting by John Singer Sargent or Arthur Munnings, photographs of the family, hunting photographs by Marshall Hawkins, tedious State of the Union addresses by a droning president attempting to be forceful. All those things rushed before her, the primary colors of childhood mixed with the splatterdash of adolescence.

Never could she have imagined how much she was a part of her time. Because she lived on a farm she usually felt out of step, a throwback. She was happy with that. She often grumbled that her era was vulgar, crude, and violent. It was also relentlessly commercial. At least vulgarity could be fun. Commercialism was nothing but deadening.

But she wasn't a throwback. She was a creature of the last quarter of the twentieth century and she would surely be a denizen of the twenty-first, soon to be wired in by her computer to the globe, to inner space, to a new undertow of violence and revelation as interactive media unleashed people in all their sickness and their glory. As the world teetered on the cusp of two centuries, people craved safety, wanting to go backwards to some dream of a golden age, yet inevitably pushing on into God-knows-what—the ever-dangerous future.

She wiped her eyes, closing them more tightly. She could smell the gas from the pump, hear the clank of the gas cap as she set it on her trunk lid, vowing not to drive off and leave it there.

She opened her eyes. Shirley Plantation unfolded before her. She needed to find and hold to herself bits of life from this time. And she knew she would change because of this. The Pryor Deyhle of 1699, in ways she couldn't understand, by necessity, would have to be different from the woman of the twentieth century . . . even though her core remained pure, an integrity of the soul.

The soft linen of the good handkerchief Margaret lent her felt reassuring against her cheek. She inhaled sharply, squared her shoulders and pulled herself together.

A footfall behind her made her clear her throat, blink away the last of the tears.

"Mademoiselle." Lionel swept off his hat, the feathers waving in the slight breeze. He held his hat in his left hand as with his right he propped himself against the black gum. "Are you well?"

"Yes. A bit overcome." The strong but clean odor of perspiration reached her. He certainly smelled like Blackie minus the benefits of modern deodorants. "All the people . . . this place . . . I had forgotten so much . . ."

"Not me, I hope."

"You are etched on my mind."

"Rather your heart." He drew close. "You puzzle me . . . but then you always have."

"Lionel, if I were like every other woman you would be swiftly bored. Anyway, I puzzle myself." She smiled.

He laughed and reached for her hand. "Then we'll have a lifetime of finding answers, I should think." He brushed his lips across the back of her hand. "Again, mademoiselle, I ask for your hand."

The smoothness of him, the brimming self-confidence born of physical power and intelligence were the same as what she remembered. So was the ambition.

"Would you like my foot, too?"

"All of you! Head to toe," he roared, putting his arms around her. "You'll want for nothing, Pryor, nothing. If you want rubies from India you shall have them!"

She wrapped her arms around his waist and buried her face in his shirt. His waistcoat was unbuttoned due to the warmth. "Oh, Lionel, if you only knew how much I want to believe you."

He kissed her cheeks, felt the tears. "I pledge my heart, my wealth, my future."

She held on for dear life. "I need to settle my mind and my fears." She let go and looked him in the eye. "There are things going on inside of me which I don't understand." She brightened, smiled up at him. "Let's join the others."

He laughed as she slipped her arm through his. They walked back to the group. Out of the corner of her eye Cig knew Patrick Devlin Fitzroy was observing them intently.

20

Happily worn out from the hunting, the festivities, and the ride back home, Cig, Margaret, and Tom rested before the fire. Each cat had chosen a human lap, snuggling in the warmth, tail curled around her nose.

"Who is Patrick Fitzroy?" Cig asked, absentmindedly stroking Little Smudge.

"A damned Irishman."

"Tom," Margaret admonished.

"For an Irishman he's—" Tom held up one palm indicating the man was acceptable, "but he's poor."

"Well born though. The younger son of a great lord in the south, I hear."

"I don't believe that. The man's a blacksmith."

"That's a useful occupation," Cig commented.

"That's why I don't think he's high born," Tom said agreeably.

"You don't believe any Irishman is high born."

"Must you point out my failings, my love?" Tom stretched out his legs, greatly disturbing Nell Gwyn who slid off his lap. She wedged herself between his thigh and the high-backed chair.

"There's not enough time." Margaret smiled impishly.

Cig laughed.

"Two against one. All right, ladies, be cruel to me. Abandon me to your depredations." He laughed with them then softly said, "Remember how Braxton complained? How he'd run to Mother crying, 'Two against one,' and it usually was, poor fellow."

"God needed musicians."

"Ah, Sister, if only I hadn't made light of that. I criticized him for not studying medicine or law . . . even surveying."

Margaret soothed him. "He was a most forgiving young man . . . and he loved you. Don't dwell on it, Husband, there's nought you can do."

Cig changed the subject. "When all the men gathered to smoke, what did they say about the murdered Indian?"

Gingerly Tom tried to step around it. "Not much."

"All those men standing around—who had seen the body—Edward Hill, Daniel, Lionel, and no one said much? I don't believe it."

"Pryor, there's nothing to fret over."

"Then why don't you tell me what the other men thought?"

A flicker of irritation played over Tom's face. "You don't have to know everything. This is men's business."

"I think not." Anger flashed in Cig's eyes.

"Tom." Margaret lowered her voice. Tom knew that tone.

"All right then." He stood up before the fire while Nell remained in the chair. "Some think it was individual revenge. Others remember 1622—when the Indians attacked on Good Friday . . . almost as though they knew it was a day of suffering. All were slaughtered at Bermuda Hundred. Odd," he put his hand on the mantelpiece, "that rich land at the mouth of the Appomattox River—no one will go near it."

"1676," Margaret added, "more horrible killing."

Cig leveled her eyes at Tom. "Are the Indians gathering together? Do you think they're getting ready for war?"

"Hard to tell. William Byrd and Lionel deVries don't believe we're in danger. They report no preparations for war or movement of their peoples but I think the Indians could gather before even they would know."

"They can move farther west. There's enough land for all." Margaret innocently thought this seemed reasonable.

"But more of us will come here." Cig put her hands behind her head. "How long before they want to drive us back into the ocean?"

Both Tom and Margaret considered this disturbing thought. Cig wanted to tell them about the West, about the later, sorrowful Indian Wars, but even if Tom could have believed this for one instant, what good would such knowledge do?

"By that time I hope the Crown has sent us troops."

"I wouldn't rely on the King of England for one skinny minute." Cig used a common Southern phrase.

Tom guffawed. "You've the strangest way of speaking sometimes."

"Well, maybe when the door to my memory was shut the door to language opened."

"And what of the door to your heart?" shrewd Margaret murmured.

Cig declined a reply.

21

∞

A languor sweetened the end of a hunting day. No matter how exhausted they were from the ride and the chores that followed, a sweetness remained like the aftertaste of rich chocolate.

Cig curled up before the huge fireplace after Tom and Margaret retired to bed. She loved to stare in the fire as the flames changed colors from yellow to scarlet to deep red with a hint of blue or green around the edges. Their dance and crackle was hypnotic. All three cats curled around her. She dozed on and off.

The hunt astonished her. She wondered what else had passed down generation to generation. She remembered the first time she set foot on English soil, 1978. The damp familiarity of the place, the rich expressions, the attitudes were much like those of her own family yet they'd left during Cromwell's reign. She marveled at how persistent was culture, with language as the bedrock.

Each generation thinks everything started with its birth. In fact, we inherit all that went before. The automobile is a carriage without a horse, a telephone is a legless courier. What we've done over the centuries has been to change and accelerate the things we've always done. We travel from place to place faster. We get messages faster and faster. We want happiness faster. But underneath, little had changed.

Cig was not a contemplative person. It was her strength and her weakness. This bizarre time warp forced her inward. She kept coming back, like a hummingbird to an orange trumpet vine, to her children, Blackie, Grace, and herself. She existed in an emotional fog, no different from the fog she rode through to arrive at Buckingham. Slowly emerging from this interior mist was the ripe suspicion that she might be the architect of her own undoing. This disquieting thought would push its way forward and she'd push it right back.

She didn't drive Blackie into Grace's arms. As for Grace, what did Cig ever do to her other than the stuff all sisters do? Why would Grace want the only thing that Cig loved apart from Hunter, Laura, and fox-hunting?

What did she do to deserve this? Intellectually she knew that we build our own lives. Emotionally she didn't believe this mess was her doing, and then a little fishhook would snag in her brain, a little painful tug of memory, like the time she told Grace to marry the richest man she could find. She was nineteen and Grace, seventeen. She didn't remember what started the fight but she remembered yelling at Grace, "You couldn't think your way out of a paper bag so you'd better marry some rich jerk who thinks you're beautiful and who'll pay your bills." Okay, she was hitting below the belt, but that was a long time ago, more than twenty years.

She shifted in her chair. Smudge grumbled. "I'm not a perfect person." The cats twitched their ears but didn't bother to open their eyes as Cig spoke in a low voice to them. "But I can't see that I'm any worse than the next guy." A flush of self-righteousness seized her. "Dammit, I would never have betrayed Grace."

She relaxed. She felt justified. She really was right. That fishhook snagged again. What did *I* do? Then it occurred to her that maybe she really was here to find out.

22

～∞～

Marie's porcine face, shiny and scrubbed, exhibited a sheen of sweat even on such a cold day. She stood in the middle of the back pastures and called to Cig, "Mistress Deyhle, you've a visitor."

Cig, a heavy veil over her face as she tended her bee boxes, couldn't hear the servant. She stepped back, lifting her veil. The bees, more asleep than awake, stayed in their hives. "What?"

"I'll not be going near those bees, ma'am," Marie, hands on hips, complained.

"Oh God," Cig whispered to herself. She walked toward the rotund woman, unfastening the veil from one of Tom's floppy hats as she walked. "What is it, Marie?"

"I've told you a hundred times, Mistress D, I don't like the bees and the bees don't like me."

"I can't imagine why." Cig folded her arms across her chest. "Now, what was it you were yelling at me?"

"You've a visitor." Marie, relishing possessing information, was in no hurry to relinquish it.

Cig, alert to that, started walking down the lane without asking Marie who.

Marie, huffing and puffing, fell in just behind and beside her.

"You need exercise."

"I work hard enough."

"I know that, Marie, but consistent exercise is different from hard work. You ought not to be breathing so hard."

"I'm fat. Fat people breathe hard," Marie obstinately stated.

"Aren't you worried about your heart?"

"My heart?"

"Never mind." Cig realized no one in 1699 understood the connection between obesity and overtaxing the heart. Low-fat diets had yet to bedevil the human race. There was a certain wisdom to getting fat in winter in these times. Marie overdid it.

"Don't you want to know who's calling for you, ma'am?"

"Guess I'll find out when I get to the house."

"It's Patrick Fitzroy." She pronounced this with solemnity. "He's never called here before." This was said with significance dripping off every syllable.

"Ah—"

Frustrated, Marie exploded. "Well, don't you see, ma'am, he's here to call on you. Master Tom has no business with him."

"What makes you think you know my brother's business?" Cig sharply replied. Self-important tattlers rubbed her like sandpaper on a brush burn.

"I've been in service long enough to know what's about."

"You're implying that my brother doesn't like Fitzroy."

"If a man's a Papist let him find solace in Maryland."

"Marie, for heaven's sake," Cig growled, "religious wars are for the Old World not the New. If he's a Catholic he can worship in peace."

"That's just it. There is no Roman Church so if—" she measured her words, "he's any kind of Christian he needs to head to Maryland to worship."

"Church of England is good enough. If he has to sit through a service of interminable boredom, one service is as good or as bad as another."

"You haven't changed," Marie smugly said, folding her hands in her coat sleeves.

"Good. Someone's got to put you in your place."

"And it will be Lionel deVries putting you in yours, I should say." The large features broadened in a wicked smile.

"Don't bet on it, Marie." Cig saw Fitzroy leaning over the snake fence admiring Full Throttle. She hurried, leaving Marie to chew on the fat of their conversation.

"Mr. Fitzroy."

He nodded his head, smiling. "Mistress Deyhle."

"What can I do for you?" she automatically said.

"Ah—that is an offer, isn't it?" He mischieviously smiled.

She blushed. "A modern turn of phrase—in London."

"That center of bustle." He hopped over the fence in one easy motion. "May I have a bit of a chat with him?"

"Yes, but you'll have to have one with me, too." She climbed over and walked up to Throttle, whose ears were forward, eyes wide open with curiosity. "Throttle, this is Patrick Devlin Fitzroy. Mind your manners."

Fitzroy studied the animal. "The finest specimen I've seen in Virginia."

"Thank you. I hope you'll forgive my curiosity but Marie, ever the blabbermouth, says you're a Catholic. That makes you an exotic, I suppose?" Her eyes smiled although her lips stayed firm.

"Aye. We all find God in our own way."

"If we're lucky."

"I'm not a priest. Theology escapes me." His eyes ranged over Throttle. "If my faith troubles you—"

"It doesn't. Not a bit. Sure seems to get other people—you know."

"Indeed. That's why I'm here. Some people have their noses out of joint but it's still better than Ireland."

"Why?" Cig innocently asked.

He looked at her, puzzled. "Parliament passed an edict banning Roman Catholic bishops and clergy. A Catholic can attend mass but then as a result cannot inherit land. Nor can I buy property. I cannot bear arms or send my children to the Continent for a Catholic education. Harsh measures. Do you know so little of Ireland, ma'am?"

"No." She trusted him. She didn't know why. Spontaneously she confided, "I have no memory left. I feel like a blank sheet of paper."

"That might be an advantage." He half-smiled then said in his melodic voice, "I am sorry, Mistress Deyhle. I'm sure it causes you pain."

"It does. And please call me Pryor. Mistress Deyhle makes me feel like a schoolteacher."

"Thank you. You must call me Fitz." He held out his hand, palm upward, for Full Throttle to sniff. "Do you know when this happened?"

"Sometime within the last year. I haven't spoken of it. People will add on their own inaccuracies to my predicament, and I didn't want to embarrass my family."

"Yes." He understood perfectly. "You must be wondering what I'm doing here in this fine pasture."

"I am."

"I've never seen anyone ride like you. Strange as it is, your way of going has a flash about it, a boldness. I wanted to learn how you came by this method."

"Grabbed mane and sat down deep." She smiled, using a horseman's phrase.

"Did you learn from anyone in the colonies?"

"No."

"Indians?"

"No. I taught myself to ride," she lied, "and that's how it came out. Tom rides more conventionally. You're a fine rider yourself."

He smiled broadly. "The horse does all the work."

They laughed. "Would you like to come in for a hot drink?"

"No, no thank you. I was just—curious." He walked back to the barn, untied his horse and mounted. Cig stood by his left foot. "Please don't take me for a rude man, Pryor Deyhle, but I beseech you not to marry Lionel deVries."

Startled, she replied, "Why?"

"He'll toy with your affections."

She looked up at him, her deep brown eyes clear and honest. "But why would you care, Fitz?"

He stammered, "You're a bird whose wings should not be clipped. Forgive me. I have overstepped my bounds." He turned, squeezing his well-groomed horse into a canter.

"Patrick Devlin Fitzroy . . ." she called after him but he didn't turn back.

23

∞

Snowflakes twirled down but not much snow had collected on the ground. The wagon lurched and pitched over the road as the wheels crunched in and out of deep ruts. The sun peeping over the horizon cast long pink shadows on the barren trees. Tom, reins in his hand, grouchy, was half-asleep. Wrapped in blankets, Margaret slept behind him in the bed of the wagon. Cig marveled at her sister-in-law's ability to sleep in the midst of such discomfort.

Her skirt wound tightly around her ankles, Cig pulled a blanket tighter around her shoulders. She knew better than to strike up a conversation with Tom. Put out as he was by her insistence that they visit Wessex, he finally succumbed to her entreaties that she didn't remember the place. He would describe it in detail, she'd shake her head and reply, "But, Tom, what good does it do if I don't remember? You want me to marry Lionel, don't you?" He said yes to that. She urged, "Then I've got to see what I might be getting into."

However, what truly provoked him was the news that Patrick Devlin Fitzroy had paid a call on his sister. Tom, no fool, knew a hunting man would appeal to Pryor.

Margaret, wisely, had said nothing.

Well situated on the York River, almost directly across from Buckingham on the James, Wessex stood to profit handsomely by the creation of a city at the former Middle Plantation. In time the town would grow, nudging toward Wessex's southeastern borders. Land would shoot up in value. Lionel expected either he or his heirs would profit handsomely. If Pryor would marry Lionel it meant that both families would control thousands upon thousands of acres between the York and the James rivers. In order to head overland up to the Falls or down to Williamsburg or Jamestown one would have to traverse Deyhle or deVries land. If turnpikes worked on the Continent and in England, Lionel and Tom saw no reason why they wouldn't work here. Both were shrewd enough not to speak of this, of course.

Cig missed the sweet hills of Nelson County, the ancient allure of the Blue Ridge Mountains, but the ease of the Tidewater topography impressed her. The sandy soils drained well except for the few swamps. The flatter land made travel easier in any century. The temperature was milder, although this winter felt cold to her. Then she remembered that there was a period in the sixteenth and seventeenth centuries in which winters grew fierce. She tried to remember where she had read or heard that.

As Tom swayed from side to side, the reins slipped through his fingers. He, too, was asleep. Cig reached over, removing them from his gloved hands. Not that Castor and Pollux were going to run away but a light hand on the reins to a horse is what a good handshake is between people: a pledge, a reassurance.

She remembered Mark Twain's *A Connecticut Yankee in King Arthur's Court*. Not much of a fiction reader, she loved Twain. She reflected upon her situation, which was similar in that she, too, found herself in a different century. However, the hero in Twain's book busily applied nineteenth-century mechanical know-how to Arthur's problems, while she felt her knowledge was useless. She couldn't build an internal combustion engine. Even if she knew how to make a television or a computer, there'd be no use for them. She thought she could take a stab at indoor plumbing if she could get Tom and Bobby to dig a huge cistern on the hill behind the house, then lay pipe to both the house and the barn in a two-foot-deep trench below the frost line. It wouldn't be heated, but it would run just fine. However, the only materials available for pipes were lead or copper, both astronomically expensive. She'd bankrupt the family for convenience. She wondered if she could build a wood-burning stove. She'd need cast iron and a good foundry. That took care of that. She consoled herself with the thought that at least she knew where future profits rested: peanuts, the Falls, Williamsburg, and horses. As for tobacco, everyone in the colony understood that; Europe couldn't get enough of the stuff.

A sharp bump woke Tom. His eyes opened wide, he clenched his hands, no reins, then looked at his sister.

He grunted.

"That it for your conversational abilities?"

"I'm still laboring under your whim."

"It's not a whim. Would you want to marry without seeing your future home or your future relatives?"

"But you have."

"I don't remember, dammit. How many times do I have to tell you, I don't *remember*?" She felt heat rising in her cheeks.

"Pryor, I'll remember for you."

"Oh, thank you so much." She dripped sarcasm. "What the hell am I to you, a heifer to be sold to the highest bidder? Jesus, Tom, don't you care what happens to me?"

He turned to look her full in the face. "I don't want you alone in the world. And I don't want you poor."

"Well, I'll survive."

"Don't be so cocksure. Your mind is not settled." He caught himself. "You're coming along, though." He breathed deeply. "There comes a time in life when a woman can be preyed upon by a man. Her judgment falters if she's not married. Any base flatterer can turn her head."

"Not mine."

"You can't be sure of the future. None of us can."

"Well—people do change. Guess we have to." She half-agreed with him.

"For better or for worse." Tom reached over and took the reins so she could stuff her cold hands in her pockets. "Can you bend them?"

"I can but my joints ache." A little gust of wind made a snow devil whirl in the road. "Margaret and I could have made this journey. I could have made it by myself if you'd told me the way. I know why you're coming along."

"You do, do you?"

"You're worried about Indians. You don't really know why that man was killed in the road. You don't know why we've been seeing Indians in the woods. And I bet we aren't the only whites who've seen them either."

Margaret, awake, sat up in the back. "Tom, have other folk seen Indians?"

"Here and there."

"You should have told us." Margaret compressed her lips.

"To what purpose? Tongues start wagging and one Indian becomes one hundred. Better to wait and see." He changed the subject. "Since you don't remember, Pryor, Lionel's mother, the formidable Kate, possesses a sharp tongue, a sharp mind and no hesitation to use either. His father died years ago, when we were small, of bleeding lungs."

"Does she like me?"

"As much as she likes any woman," Margaret filled in.

"Oh." Cig was beginning to regret her insistence upon visiting Wessex.

"She lost four children, you see," Margaret said, "and I believe that compelled her to favor Lionel although she doesn't hesitate to criticize him."

"He's devoted to her, of course," Cig flatly stated—they always were under those circumstances.

"Yes, but he's not unaware of her tyrannies."

"Oh, brother," Cig exclaimed under her breath.

"What?" Tom asked.

"Just an idle expression." She sighed.

Two and a half hours later they entered cleared lands, which in spring would be planted in corn, tobacco, and oats. Hickories, walnuts, and chestnuts towered in the pastures beyond. Finally Wessex hove into view. The central portion was a red-brick four-over-four home executed in the latest style, the beginnings of what would later be termed Georgian. The windows set in white wood provided a pleasing contrast to the brick. Crisp black shutters, each held back by a wrought-iron scroll, gave the house a formal facade, as did the fan window over the large double doors. Gray smoke curled from two of the four symmetrical chimneys.

On both sides of the house in the back, perpendicular to it, ran rows, or ranges, of smaller brick houses; tiny dependencies housing servants, a foundry, salt storage, a carpentry shop, a wheelwright's shop, and other shops that Cig couldn't identify. Wessex, a hive of activity, astonished her. Most of the workers were English, a few were African, but what really knocked her back was the number of Indians on the property.

Margaret, noting her surprise, said, "They're here to do business with Lionel or to pay homage. They stay over in the dependencies or camp by the river. They've a fondness for copper like our fondness for gold. Lionel trades copper kettles and flat pieces cut into foot-square sheets. The finished items he imports from England, of course, but he has a mine somewhere up the river. A few people have gone there—"

"Escorted by soldiers," Tom interrupted.

"Why don't the Indians take it away from him?" Cig asked.

Tom smiled. "Because they don't know how to smelt the ore and Lionel does."

"They also bring him copper to work," Tom added, "from mines far north, where the Indians say there are lakes of fantastic size."

"The Great Lakes," Cig said.

"What?"

"That's what they're called."

"I've never heard that." Tom checked Castor and Pollux who were eager to reach their destination because it meant getting unhitched, rubbed down and fed in a luxurious Wessex stall.

"The Indian names are too difficult to pronounce," Cig replied, thinking fast. "It's easier to say great lakes." She stopped, staring at a young, tall Indian. "He looks like the Indian in the mists." Then she noticed another Indian, the right side of his head also shaved, the hair on the left side twisted in a long coil about four feet, with little bits of copper and brightly colored thread woven into the hair. "But then—"

"Powhatans."

"Why do they shave the right sides of their heads?"

"Easier to draw a bow that way. The priests have the whole head shaved with a lock running down the middle. Each tribe of the Algonquins has a slightly different way of dressing its hair or cutting its clothes. The Iroquois and Sioux confederations differ in dress more than the Algonquins."

"Some men are covered with tattoos of fanciful design. And what strikes me as odd is how quickly they have learned our language," Margaret said.

"Why is that odd?"

Margaret wrinkled her nose as a snowflake fell on it. "Not many of our people have learned their languages."

"Our grandfathers knew more than we do," Tom said. "Father used to say, 'If the Powhatans and the Appomatucks wanted to kill us they could easily have done so.' "

"Then what went wrong in 1622?"

"No one knows." Tom shrugged. "There was a great queen of the Appomatucks. While she lived all was well. Things soured after she died. I don't suppose anyone will ever know the truth."

"Maybe one of us did something wrong." Cig's heart raced. Much as she wanted to relax around the Indians she was afraid of them.

"I've thought of that myself," Tom mumbled.

Before Tom reined in Castor and Pollux, two wiry young men sprinted toward the wagon, reaching for the horses' bridles. Another man, a bit fat, dressed in livery, emerged from the house.

"Welcome, ladies." He bowed, reaching up to assist them.

"Good to see you, Samuel." Tom smiled as the butler led them up the stairs.

Lionel nearly knocked him over as he rushed through the door. "Pryor . . ." He bowed to Margaret then took Cig's hand, glancing over his shoulder. "Didn't mean to slight you, Tom."

"I'm glad you didn't greet my wife that rapturously, Lionel."

"Only because you married her first, Thomas," Lionel gallantly replied.

"Lionel, you could charm the birds out of the trees."

"I'm singing only to this swan." He smiled broadly at Cig as Samuel shut the door behind them.

Before Cig could admire the center hall, the rows of ancestral paintings, the luster of the rich, patterned floors, a commanding alto voice rang out. "Lionel, who is here? I demand to seem them this instant."

Samuel winked at Lionel, trotting ahead to pacify the lady of the manor.

"We're flying to you, Mother," Lionel called, then under his breath said to Cig, "Amuse her and ignore half of what she says. You know Mother."

They entered a room with mahogany wainscoting in a squared design halfway up the wall. Pale yellow silk moiré covered the rest of the wall up to an ornately carved ceiling, also in mahogany. Cig, unprepared for such splendor, gaped.

"What are you staring at, missy?" Kate demanded.

"I—I had forgotten how beautiful this room is," Cig stammered.

"Ha! When it's gilded then I'll have something to brag about. Lionel, you don't listen to me. I tell you to bring over a gilder from Paris. What does he do? He brings over more copper pots."

"Patience, Mother, patience." Lionel smiled at his mother, a tall woman by the standards of the day, and she was stretched to her full height standing in the middle of the room to receive her guests.

"Old women don't have patience!" she snapped.

"I don't see any old women in this room," Cig said, but not obsequiously. Cig had dealt with imperious dowagers all her life and knew the first rule is never let them bully you.

"You always were the prettiest liar, Pryor Deyhle." Kate grumbled but she was pleased despite herself. "Well, sit yourself down so I can hear more of your prattle. You, too, Tom and Margaret."

Samuel hovered at the doorway.

"Don't just stand there, Samuel, bring our guests refreshments. Hot."

"Would madam wish the spiced wine and some breads?"

"Madam would and quickly." She rapped the floor with her foot. Samuel disappeared.

"We missed you at Edward Hill's," Margaret said.

"Lionel spared me not a detail, to further accent my misery. My lumbago flared up and I languished here in a stupor of pain, I tell you, a veritable stupor. What does my fine son do but burst through the door to tell me that Mistress Deyhle rode like a centaur and nearly up on her horse's neck. And where did you learn that, young lady?"

"In London."

"Well, if it's the fashion soon every Tom, Dick, and Harry will be doing it. I heard also that you were most peculiarly dressed."

"Again, the new fashion."

"Fashion is for imbeciles!"

Cig fired back, "Then all is lost for you are the most fashionable lady in the colonies."

"Pshaw!" Kate frowned then smiled. "Oh, do tell that to Amelie Boothrod, how I would rejoice to see that painted face fall." She cocked her head to focus on Cig.

The motion made her look like a parrot. It was then that Cig realized the woman was blind in her left eye; a faint dot of white in the pupil gave evidence to that.

"Perhaps she uses all that paint because she regards herself as a work of art."

Kate exclaimed, "Well said, Pryor!"

Samuel arrived, flanked by two other liveried servants, bearing trays of cakes, spiced hot wine and sweetmeats. Lace napkins, neatly folded, were also on the trays.

"Lionel, don't just stand there. Get your mother some wine." She paused. "After our guests are served, of course." That meant for Samuel to step on it which he did.

Kate brought the cup to her lips but sniffed the enticing aroma before tasting the wine. "I've had better," she barked.

"Sorry, madam."

"You're too modest. This is the most delicious mulled wine I've ever imbibed," Cig responded.

"A bit of orange rind ground fine, my dear, very fine. Naturally, there is more to the recipe, which I refuse to divulge until you marry my son. Mind you, I don't relish the prospect of a useless daughter-in-law underfoot spoiling my routine, but he won't be happy until you are his bride. He speaks of love. Oh, Lionel, really," her voice dropped, "marriage has little to do with love and a great deal to do with stability."

"You loved my father."

"I learned to love him. I certainly didn't start out loving him. You young people are putting the cart before the horse. All this blather about love. If you're in love before you get married you surely won't be in love afterwards. Love is a slow flower and flourishes best upon the soil of respect. Cart before the horse, I'm telling you." She defiantly glanced around the room. The servants bowed their heads. Cig laughed outright. "Impudent! You always were impudent."

"Mistress deVries, perhaps love can be cultivated in many fashions," Margaret suggested.

"Are you now going to upset my digestion by informing me with soulful eyes that you cannot live without my son? That you love as no one has loved before?" She turned to Cig.

"Mother—"

"When I want your opinion, I'll ask for it."

"You never want to hear anyone's opinion but your own." Lionel laughed. His mother could drive him to distraction but he did love her.

"Simply because my opinion has not been hatched in a broody box of untrammeled emotion." She trained her one good eye on Margaret. Margaret, not comfortable under that searing gaze, nonetheless stood up for herself. "I confess, when I look at Tom I am, as you put it, all untrammeled emotion. My knees sometimes go weak."

"Ha, the beginning of rheumatism," the old woman shouted as Samuel discreetly handed her another glass of spiced wine. She noticed Tom smiling at his wife. "Oh, don't look at her with those cow eyes."

"She is my alpha and my omega," he declared.

"Lovesick puppies." She knocked back her wine with one hand while the other reached for a sweetmeat. Samuel quickly placed the tray under her hand as the other servant relieved her of her cup, returning it refilled. She swept her eye over them. "What is love?"

Cig replied, "Don't ask me."

"Love is what you make of it. Like a humor, some are choleric, some sanguine—"

She interrupted her son. "That's a tepid explanation."

"Love is a mystery. If we knew the answer then where would be the pleasure? The joy of a mystery is precisely in *not* knowing." Margaret's long eyelashes lowered.

Cig added, "Since love concerns the heart, how can the head comprehend it? You feel it—and that's what frightens me."

"Ah yes." The slender hand with one large diamond paused while bringing the glass to her lips. "Now that I do understand. Pryor, you've changed. London seasoned you. I've changed, too. I've gotten even older. I didn't think I would live this long. I'm bored. I've seen people marry. I've seen them have children. I've seen fortunes made and fortunes lost. The same old prattle wearies me: tobacco prices, land prices, the Crown plays chess with France—it's all the same. Only the cut of one's bodice changes." She sipped her wine this time. "But you, Pryor, you have changed. I find women suffocatingly boring, you know. Make no secret of it." She opened her mouth to say that for this instant she was not bored but decided that too great a compliment to bestow. Besides, the minute the remark escaped her lips she probably would be bored.

"Mother, you must be tired—"

"Not at all." She smiled wickedly at Lionel, delighted in his discomfort for he wanted to be rid of her. "Tell me, Pryor, what did you learn in London?"

"That we are not truly Englishmen, ma'am. They do not understand us. They cannot imagine life here in the New World. We are becoming a new people and in time we will be quite different—we will be Americans."

Shocked by this radical thought, Kate blinked then leaned forward, pointing at Cig. "How are we different? For I believe I am as good an Englishman as King William himself or the late Queen, God rest her soul."

"We have no limits. We will someday settle the Falls, Mrs. deVries."

She forgot that Mrs. wasn't a form of address. It was mistress, madam, mademoiselle, or the title of nobility, as in your Grace. "We will march ever westward. What do we care for the wars of the Continent? We have enough here to keep us happy forever. And someday we will build theaters and libraries and hospitals. In London their thinking is circumscribed by the boundaries of that small island. We are so enormous a land mass we have no boundaries, and it will affect how we think."

"That's extraordinary," Kate gasped. "I don't know what to think. I like being English."

"We have no choice, anyway." Lionel laughed, but he was intrigued by what Pryor said, intrigued and a bit worried. That kind of talk could create difficulties. "You are still a loyal subject of the king, no matter—"

Margaret quietly said, "We are all loyal subjects of the Crown, Lionel. Still, I can see how we will become different. What of those Indians we passed coming here? No one in London can imagine such men."

"Lionel, it seems you wish a bride with a brain."

"Well, Mother," he smoothly replied, "I learned it from you."

The corner of Kate's mouth turned upward. "Pryor, will you marry my son?"

"Mother—" He was exasperated.

"He is so handsome that a woman has to guard against him." Cig's voice was warm. "One is so dazzled by the cover one has not had time to read the book."

"What she's saying is . . ." Tom cleared his throat, "is that she loves Lionel but needs some time and—"

"I know perfectly well what she's saying." Kate cut him off.

"A union of our families is highly desirable. We would all profit from it," Cig said. "But I want more from my one little life than profit. I suppose I do want love. For me, that's a partner, a man who will share his life with me not just his resources. I don't want to be a broodmare or an ornament or a prize. I want to be a partner, a sister, a lover, a friend."

A smile played across Kate's lips then faded. "Dear Pryor, a woman can never be a man's partner. She must think for him and make him believe it was his idea. She must plan for the future whilst he is crowing and displaying his tail feathers to other shortsighted men. Men are children grown large, and I don't mind saying it in front of them." She waggled her forefinger at Lionel and Tom. "That is our destiny."

"And they take the credit for our labor." Cig flared for a moment forgetting herself.

The old woman shrugged. "What of it? What of the world? What matters is that we know what we have done."

Lionel studied his mother intently, surprised at this revelation. "Everyone in Virginia knows what you have done, Mother. Not even Father overshadowed you. You truly built Wessex."

She cocked her head staring at him. "Perhaps—not that I care a whit for the opinion of the rabble."

"Woman has her sphere, man has his." Tom spoke the prevailing attitude.

A pause redolent with the echoes of their conversation settled over them. Samuel returned with another tray, this one bearing hot tea along with cut-crystal decanters filled with rum and whiskey.

"Madam?"

As if pulled unwillingly from a reverie, Kate motioned for him to put the trays on a big sideboard. "You forgot the port."

"So I did." He hurried to fetch it.

Outside the snow swirled.

Margaret glanced out the window. Kate turned her head to see.

Samuel reappeared with the port, and Kate commanded, "Have Sybil and Dorcas ready rooms for our guests and bring out the whist table, will you?" She turned back to the Deyhles. "You're my captives."

Staying overnight or even for a week at a friend's house, common in these times of bad roads and bad weather, provided many a hostess with an excuse for an impromptu house party. Kate deVries set aside growling, deciding to have fun.

"Let me see to the horses before we start playing." Cig thanked her sorority sisters at William and Mary for teaching her both whist and bridge, a later variant.

"Done." Lionel smiled at her.

"You all retire to your rooms. If anyone wishes a bath or fresh clothing, tell the girls upstairs. I'll confer with the cook. Samuel will ring the bell when we're ready. Pryor, you'll start as my partner, of course."

"Delighted."

In about an hour Cig heard the small bell tinkling below. She'd fallen asleep on the featherbed, a fire roaring nearby in the fireplace. Margaret met her on the stairs. As they descended they observed the men coming in the front door.

"It will play itself out, Tom." Lionel handed Samuel his coat. When he saw the ladies his voice changed. "Mother never forgets a card."

"We know." Margaret laughed.

She didn't. Kate, peering fiercely at her hand, remembered everything. Because there were five of them everyone rotated playing and keeping score except for Kate who never relinquished her position.

She discussed everything—clocks, the needless expense of too many servants, the customs of the Indians, the foppishness of the House of Burgesses who ought to be shipped up to Massachusetts for punishment. "Let them live with the enemies of King Charles," she boomed as she smacked down a trump card. She held forth on the rebel Nathaniel Bacon, whom she had known and thought strange because his eyes bulged like poached eggs although he seemed intelligent enough.

She was winning and therefore happy. "Did I tell you? The last time I played whist, Amelie Boothrod had the effrontery to tell me why it's called whist." She imitated Amelie's singsong voice. " 'Whist means be silent and in order to play a good game one must be silent.' Ha, said she who never once held her tongue. I'd like to hold it. Indeed, I'd like to grasp it between my thumb and forefinger and yank it right out of her empty head. Oh, she sat there like a great rhubarb given the gift of speech."

Cig laughed until the tears came into her eyes, which only encouraged Kate to continue. Lionel, from time to time, would chide his mother to pay attention to her hand.

She pointed to the scorecard. "I'm winning. You're not." She had her son for a partner on this game. "Margaret, when you have sons teach them whist, in both respects."

They laughed. A gust of wind rattled the panes.

"Cohonk," Cig mentioned, the Indian name for fall.

"Their language is quite musical, I find." Kate smacked down a jack of diamonds. "Lionel, has anyone heard from the forts?"

She referred to the four English forts that had been built, after the massacre, on the Blackwater River, the Pamunkey River, the Rappahannock River and the Potomac. This feeble military presence gave the whites the illusion of security so the immigrants kept pouring in.

"Whatever made you think of that?"

"Cards. Remember that handsome lieutenant who played 'honors'— he had Francis Eppes's daughter swooning."

"All is well." Lionel's stomach grumbled. "Pardon."

"I've quite forgotten the time. I've won, so let's retire to dinner. Samuel. Samuel, you sloth! Where are you?"

"Here, madam." He glided into the room.

"Dinner must be ready by now."

He bowed. Tom helped Kate up from her chair as Lionel attended to Cig and Margaret.

Dinner brought forth another torrent of chat from Kate. Cig listened mesmerized as she recounted her childhood in the colony. She had been born in 1645, which made her fifty-four, old in this era but not ancient. Not that some people didn't reach eighty or ninety, a few did, but so many women died in childbirth and so many men in accidents or from diseases, that a vigorous older person was treasured.

"—and while I applaud James Blair's creation of his grammar school I ask what is taught and who is teaching it? When you see a schoolmaster counting on his fingers you must consider the consequences once he passes twenty."

Margaret laughed. "William and Mary will teach them their sums because all the pupils can add up everyone's fingers and toes."

This made them laugh.

"I prophesy that it will become a great school." Cig smiled.

"Well, I won't be here to see it." Kate's lower lip jutted out. "Lionel, did you learn anything at those schools in France?" Before he could answer she announced, "Violently expensive."

"It doesn't matter what I learned, I still can't keep up with you." He smiled, his mustache curling upwards ever so slightly.

"Oh la." She threw up her hands.

Another blast of wind created a downdraft in the chimney, a puff of scarlet embers swirling upwards then falling back into the flames.

"No more foxhunting for a time," Tom said.

"How I used to love to hunt." Kate smiled as Samuel placed some candied yams on her plate, her second helping.

"I think the fox represents happiness: tricky, bright, and just out of reach," Cig said.

This set them off on a lively discussion of happiness, which was finally ended with Margaret declaring, "I am happy right now."

24

A light rap on the door prodded Cig, sitting in front of the fire. She'd stretched her feet before the blaze, hoping to drive the last of the chill from her toes. Beautiful as Wessex was, she longed for twentieth-century insulation.

She opened the door.

Lionel, wrapped in a glossy bearskin, his nightshirt visible underneath, whispered, "May I come in? I thought I'd never get to see you alone."

She hesitated. "Come on." She quietly shut the door behind him.

He pulled up a chair next to hers. His feet were covered in beaded moccasins. "I don't know when I've seen Mother so jovial."

"She's a remarkable woman."

"As are you."

"Thank you."

His dark eyes reflected the fire. "She's right, as she so often is, you have changed. You're more philosophical." He smiled. "I hope that's the apt word."

"Don't you think time does that to each of us—makes us think about things we used to take for granted?"

"Yes and—"

She interrupted him before he could start getting romantic. "The Indians here—do you trust them?"

"With my life," he said with a swagger.

She wanted to reply, "You might have to," but remained silent. She must have seemed fragile enough to Lionel with her imperfect memory. Accusing a man of murder whom she'd only glimpsed would make her appear more unreliable, maybe even unbalanced. But she feared Lionel had bet too many lives on his faith in his trading companions.

"Do you think they're planning to attack us again?"

"No." He smiled, reaching for her hand.

His big hand wrapped around hers. "Lionel, you're here in a fit of desire or whatever. I apologize for not being the most romantic woman on earth but I am vexed," she recalled hearing that word, which carried more weight in this time, "by seeing the murdered man and by the Indians lurking about our place. We see them and then—they vanish."

"It's winter, Pryor, and a hard one. They're hunting and if they can't hunt they may be driven to steal. I know these people."

"And you also know something you're not telling me."

He squeezed her hand. "If I thought you were in danger I would sound a clear warning." He breathed in deeply. "The disaffection between the Algonquin people and the Sioux, especially the Monacans, is growing. What I hope to do is persuade the Assembly to form an alliance with the Algonquins."

"And if an Indian war erupted we would fight with the Algonquins." Cig instantly appreciated his thinking.

"Yes. The Assembly is so dazzled by ordnance they think we have little to fear. When I ask them how they intend to drag cannon into the wilderness I am met with stony silence. They believe we can fight European wars here. Impossible! We need allies among the natives. They counter with, 'Why risk a white life for a red one?' Now, my dear, you know what I'm thinking." He smirked. "Frederick Janss said we'll bring in more Africans and let them kill the Indians. When I mention that they would surely run away or turn and kill us he found me not a bit amusing."

"Stupid man."

"You've heard me say this before but it's folly to bring in slaves from

Africa. Far better to work with the Indians who know the New World than ship in captives who are as lost as if on the moon."

"Who are those Africans I saw when we arrived?"

"Xavier and Petrus, you don't remember them?"

"Well—no."

"Freemen."

"Oh." She felt the warmth from his hand. "If I were dead, who would you marry?"

This shocked him. "Don't say that, Pryor. It's bad luck."

"No, it isn't. I know you like me well enough but if I were a poor woman I'd be your mistress, not your wife."

He sighed, perturbed. "How would I know unless you were a poor woman? I only know you as you are and I love you. Why are you cruel to me?"

"Not cruel—careful."

"It's all a gamble, like whist. Better to sit at the table and take your chances with the cards than to stand aside and watch." He rose from his chair and bent over her, his hands on the arms of her chair, his face inches away from her own. "I love you."

The blood was pounding so hard in her temples Cig thought her head would burst. "You don't *know* me."

"I've known you all your life."

"But"—she fought to breathe—"there are things about me you don't know."

"There are things about me *you* don't know. I love you, that's what matters."

"I don't think you can love someone if you don't know her."

"You're wrong." He leaned down and kissed her. As she didn't resist he put his hands under her armpits, lifting her to her feet, then wrapped his arms around her.

He felt strong, smelling of tobacco smoke, leather, and sweat. His kiss tasted familiar. Cig wasn't swept off her feet although Lionel was trying. But she was lonely, adrift, and had lived without physical love for a long time. She kissed him in return, feeling that old heat flame up in her belly.

She whispered as they moved toward the bed. "This doesn't mean I'm going to marry you."

He nodded, tossing off the bearskin robe, pulling his nightshirt over his head, hoping that tonight would put an end to her stalling.

Later, as the candles sputtered and Lionel slept, Cig propped up on one elbow to study him. She'd not known Blackie this young. She figured Lionel to be thirty to thirty-two. Blackie would have looked like Lionel, except his mustache was a military one whereas Lionel's, a bit fuller, curved upward slightly and his hair was cut quite short—she wondered what he'd look like in a wig. She'd probably laugh.

It had felt good to make love with him, but she knew she would never surrender herself as she had done with her husband. Then she had been too young to know any different. Now she was old enough to take a man's measure. And while there was much of Blackie in Lionel, he was still a separate person.

Lionel probably told her the truth when he said he loved her. He didn't need to know her in order to love her. He had a program. She was to fit into that program. He would provide, protect, and honor her as his wife. Her inner life was as foreign to him as Mexico. More to the point, it had no value for him. Lionel was no different than millions of men. Tempting as it was to fall in line and relax in comfort, she wanted more. Many would say that was proof positive that she really was insane.

25

〰

"Samuel, don't stand there like a lump! Get the fur throws."

"We're fine," Margaret protested weakly.

"You'll freeze with only those blankets. Horatio, Horatio, are you deaf?"

"No, ma'am." The squat servant stuck his head around the corner.

"Did you hitch up the sleigh?"

"Yes, ma'am, I surely did."

"It's a good thing, Horatio, or I would have had you pull them back to Buckingham yourself."

He grimaced. "Miz Kate, you're . . ." He shuffled off, not finishing his sentence, his wide Saxon bulk out of place in this refined house.

"The sky is as blue as a robin's egg. You all have a safe journey. Samuel's packed a basket for you."

Impulsively Margaret threw her arms around Kate's neck. "How good you are."

"Me? Ha."

"Oh, Mistress deVries, we promise not to tell anyone." Cig kissed her cheek.

"See to it. Next thing you know I'll have riffraff lying about the place. Better to be thought a mean old woman than a kind one." She folded her arms across her chest and greatly resembled the sixteenth-century gentleman under whose portrait she stood. She noticed Pryor's interest. "You used to stare at him when you were little. My grandfather. He backed Essex, the wrong horse."

"Mother," Lionel opened the front door, shaking the snow off his boots, "can't you convince them to stay?"

She looked from him to Pryor. "I do wish you would. Give me the singular pleasure of trouncing you again at cards. Or we could throw the dice."

Tom shook his head. "Oh no, I'd sooner roll with Beelzebub."

"I'm not that lucky." She smiled.

"In your son, you are." Cig inclined her head.

"Ah . . ." Her hand fluttered to her breast. She thought a moment, pursed her lips then set aside that thought. Instead she said, "Much as I wish you to stay, and Lionel, of course, fervently desires it, this weather will not hold. I can feel it in my bones."

Kate and Cig kissed one another good-bye, Lionel lingering over Pryor, then walking her to the sleigh. He kissed her again as he lifted her beside Margaret who sat next to Tom.

"I miss you already."

"I'll see you soon, Lionel." She touched his cheek. "I had a wonderful time. Thank you."

He bowed low. "You honor me, mademoiselle. I shall see you at Francis Eppes's Christmas party."

"Do bring your mother."

He smiled wryly. "She'll vehemently complain of the fripperies of this world but she'll come along."

"Tell her she has to outshine Amelie Boothrod. We count on her for that."

He nodded that he would tell her just that. Tom picked up the reins and the sleigh slid easily through the snow.

As they moved away Cig marveled at the quiet. She could hear the runners slicing through the snow, the muffled hoofbeats of the horses, their rhythmic breathing, the breathing of Tom and Margaret.

Kate squinted from the windows. She observed Lionel watch the sleigh until it receded from sight. Then he turned and came into the house.

"She's become a lady, a force," Kate noted.

"Yes."

"She won't be easily led, Lionel. Let her come to you. Don't pester her."

His face reddened. "I'm not pestering her."

"You bull ahead. What you see as courting has the whiff of a military maneuver about it."

Hurt, he blurted out, "She accepted me into her bed last night."

"Don't be a fool," came the acid reply. "That doesn't mean you've won the lady. She's different, Lionel . . ." Her voice trailed off. "From another world."

26

Kate deVries was right. The weather didn't hold. By the time they'd reached Buckingham the sky looked like the backside of a skillet. The temperature, which had stayed at just below the freezing point, started slipping.

Cig unhitched the horses while Tom and Bobby brought down extra rations for the livestock in case a howler kept them from reaching the corn crib.

Marie had taken the precaution of stacking almost a cord of firewood by the south side of the summer kitchen. She'd also carried a lot of firewood into the main house as well as her own. Margaret could see she was exhausted and sent her to her quarters to rest.

No sooner had Cig come inside than the wind picked up. "Perfect timing."

"What?"

"An expression."

Tom ducked in the back door. "Ripped my breeches." He laughed, pointing to the tear running from the inside of his thigh to his knee.

"I don't think I can fix them. They're too worn."

"Aren't you glad they tore now and not halfway between Wessex and here?" Cig stated.

Later, as they sat around the fire, repairing tack and the old breeches, Cig thought of Lionel. It was as though a door had opened. Not love.

Not some rush of emotion but a letting go, a willingness to encounter new people and new experiences. She felt as if she had been swaddled in cotton. The cotton was unraveling.

Tom, also pleased with how the visit to Wessex had transpired, whistled as he worked.

"Was Kate deVries considered a beauty in her day?" Cig asked.

"Father thought she was." Tom deftly braided a torn rein. "She has pleasing features even now."

Cig reflected on how important proportion was to people of this time. Proportion along with teeth and complexion were usually mentioned in describing someone's appearance, male or female. Rarely were bosoms mentioned, they seemed to be taken for granted. Height was also mentioned but no one appeared obsessed by it as they were in her own century.

Without surgery or good dentistry, without the ability to straighten misshapen childhood limbs, this concern for regularity, uniformity, wasn't odd, she decided. It mirrored the unspoken concern for mental stability. Since people had few ways to correct defects, the hope was to prevent their occurrence in the first place. The intelligent selection of a mate was an attempt to provide for straight-legged, clear-eyed, intelligent, healthy children.

Slowly Cig was grasping the reality of this time. She couldn't help but judge by her own standards. After all, they were the only ones she had, but she was smart enough to know that the standards of this time were born of reality and she had best listen and learn.

The heaviness of the air made her sleepy. She blinked frequently to try and focus on her task. The awl and waxed thread took concentration or she could just as easily poke a hole in her hand.

Tom winced, then rubbed his knees.

"Ache?"

"Don't yours?"

Cig replied, "Everything hurts in this weather." She remembered the Motrin in her vest. "I have something that will help."

"Can't drink this early in the day." Tom smiled.

Cig got up and fished the small, white plastic bottle out from her canary vest hanging on a peg. She filled a glass with cider, giving it to Tom with two pills.

"Try these."

His lips curled upward.

"Tom, there are worse things than medicine."

"Such as?"

"The doctors."

"Yes—" He smiled and took the pills. "Odd shape."

"Easier to swallow." Cig handed him the glass.

"You first." He noticed she had pills in her hand.

She knocked them back. He gave her the cider. She gulped.

He imitated her.

About half an hour later Tom stood up and shook his legs. "Sister, what is that medicine?"

"Motrin. It's a new painkiller that's easy to buy . . ." she thought a moment, "in London."

He walked to her vest and pulled out the container. The words *Kalamazoo, MI,* and *USA* meant nothing to him, nor did the bar code and *EXP 12/96.* What fascinated him was the container. He unscrewed the cap a few times then put it back on listening to it click. He squeezed the firm plastic, which indented a bit then resumed its shape.

"I've never seen anything like this—it's the toughest hide I've ever touched. How can it be so white?"

Cig observed him as he slipped the small jar back in her vest pocket.

"What will they think of next?"

She breathed a sigh of relief.

27

The heavy snowfall continued as Cig and Margaret strung rope between the buildings so no one would be lost. Sweating, her legs aching from pushing through two feet of snow as well as falling into drifts, Cig stopped at the smokehouse, the last outbuilding.

"While we're here, want me to bring back a ham or something?"

Margaret shielded her eyes. "I can't even see the hand in front of my face." Her clumsy mittens made opening the frozen iron latch difficult.

"Here." Cig reached under the latch, giving it a rap.

Together they popped it up, the door swung open in the wind, knocking against the brick wall. They stepped inside.

Cig blinked the snow off her eyelashes, closing the door behind her. "Winter makes everything look beautiful but," her chest heaved, "what a lot of work. I'm ready to go to Florida."

"Why would you want to do that?"

"It's a beautiful place with palm trees, beaches, bright sunshine, and in my time, too many visitors. 'Course, I guess Spain still controls Florida in this time."

Margaret shook her head. "We shall yet collide with Spain."

"Actually, we don't. We go to war against the French in the next century."

Margaret laughed. "Good, I don't like them either. Do we win?"

"Yes." Cig laughed, too. "Sounds crazy, doesn't it?" Then she shrugged. "I wonder, if I die, will I go home?"

"Don't say such a thing."

Cig held up her hands in supplication. "Think about it. I'm from another time, a time later than this one. If I die maybe I'll go forward."

"What if you go backwards?" Margaret's lovely eyes opened wider.

"I never thought of that."

"You shouldn't be thinking of dying, no matter what. Life is a gift, Pryor, it will be snatched away soon enough."

"Yeah—well, I still wonder if it would work, my dying."

"You'll go to ground, that's where you'll go." Margaret's breath hung, a puff in the cold. "Are you that unhappy?"

"I'm neither happy nor unhappy. I'm beyond that." She put her gloved hands in her armpits. "I don't mean to sound ungrateful. You have been very kind to me. If it weren't for you I think I would have lost my mind or tried to kill myself." She reached up, lifting a cured ham off a hook. "Let's go back. The cold is creeping into my bones."

"Mine, too." Margaret pushed the door open. "Pryor, when the ham becomes too heavy, I'll carry it."

"All right. You go first and I'll stay right behind you." She grabbed the rope with her left hand, balancing the ham on her right shoulder with her right hand.

They stopped a few times to catch their breath. Cig held onto the ham. When they reached the summer kitchen she eagerly dropped it on the big table. Margaret shut the door behind them. A fire, embers flying upwards, roared in the huge fireplace.

Margaret removed her mittens and her heavy coat, standing with her back to the fire. "That feels good."

"Why don't you brick-in the walkway between here and the house? You could make it another room."

"Because I'm deathly afraid of fire and they always seem to start in the kitchens. I warm foods or make tea in the house kitchen but I like to do most of my cooking and baking here."

"Makes sense if you don't mind running back and forth." Cig, too, took off her coat and gloves. "Put me to work. I'm an indifferent cook but I take direction really well."

"You can knead the dough for our biscuits."

As Cig measured out flour, Margaret lifted a coil of sausage from a high hook. Highness opened one green eye. Nell, snoozing next to her, sniffed and did likewise. "Go back to sleep." Margaret laughed at them. Smudge brushed against her legs. "Beggar." She chopped up the sausage into little bits, grated a chunk of white cheese and mixed it into the batter Cig had made. "You know, you never told me what happened, exactly, on the day you rode through the fog. Tell me." The cool dough squeezed through her fingers as she listened, occasionally tossing tidbits to the cats.

"The way it started was odd. I was having one of the greatest days foxhunting I've ever had in my life. Toward the end of the chase a hound was howling in the woods. I put Grace in charge and rode into the woods with another lady, Harleyetta, who is a nurse." Cig paused. "In my time there are special schools to teach people to be nurses and doctors."

"That's a good idea," Margaret said.

"I wish you could see Harleyetta because she shaves her eyebrows and then pencils them in but she does it too low on her brow," she indicated where on the brow, "and if she's had too much to drink they wiggle. Anyway, in the woods we found the hound baying at a huge old tree trunk which had fallen on the ground. Here's the weird part. There was a skeleton in it."

"Oh no." Margaret's hands fluttered a moment, scattering some sausage bits to the cats' delight.

"The man, dead a long, long time and most likely murdered, had been stuffed in the tree trunk. Harleyetta thought the skeleton was much older than the War Between the States, which we first thought the most likely explanation. Don't worry about the war, that's another whole bag of beans. Took place in the 1860s. Anyway, Harleyetta said we wouldn't know just how old this skeleton was until we could get the bones to a forensics lab. That's a place where they can tell how long a body's been dead and the cause of death. It's very scientific—so on the way back to the field, with my sister in charge, remember—am I losing you?"

"No, no, it's just all these new ideas and another war, it's hard to keep up."

"I'm sorry. Anyway, Harleyetta was in the hospital when my husband was brought in, dead from a heart attack. Through a slight misunderstanding, she told me he was having an affair with my sister. She thought I knew but you see, I didn't at all, and it slipped out of her mouth as we rode back to the group."

Margaret's eyes widened, her face flushed. "A betrayal on two fronts, no wonder you were—distressed."

"I accompanied Harleyetta back to the group. My head was bursting so I returned to the woods to retrieve the hound. I needed to collect myself, you know what I mean? When I rode past the skull again it seemed that he was smiling at me."

Margaret shuddered. "They do grin."

"What was weird—I don't know, I felt like I knew something but I couldn't remember. Fattail, the big fox, trotted out. I followed him into the fog. The next thing I knew I was here."

"You've suffered a terrible shock."

"Sometimes I think I'm too stupid to feel it," Cig said honestly.

"The mind has wondrous ways to soothe itself." Then a flicker of a smile flashed across Margaret's pretty features. "It's a wise woman who doesn't inquire too closely into the business of her husband."

"I knew about his other affairs, most of them, and in time I did as you suggested. I pretended not to know. What would I gain by having it out with him? I tried that once early in my marriage and that son-of-a-bitch freely confessed it, said he'd never do it again and then turned right around and started up with another one!"

Margaret whistled. "The blackguard!"

"My sister was worse than he was. I confided in her. I trusted her." Cig stopped abruptly. "Do you have a sister?"

"She died of the pox. Just a little thing, and God only knows why I never contracted the contagion." Margaret placed the biscuits on a flat, thin iron sheet. "Pryor, can you forgive your sister?"

"I don't know."

"You won't return to your time until you can forgive her."

Cig put her hand on Margaret's shoulder. "Second sight?"

Margaret shook her head no. "Time means nothing when it comes to the human heart. That never changes. You must forgive Grace. God will judge, not man." She paused, weighing her words. "Pryor, did you know that the Indians bury their victims in trees?"

28

The periwinkle blue of the snow seduced Cig into a dreamy happiness as they flew along in the sleigh. She felt as if she were swooshing through a curtain of blue for the snow was coming down in undulating waves like a theatrical curtain.

The snow stung her face and bit her tongue when she opened her mouth to laugh. Cig didn't remember having this much fun in winter. Since Lionel's sleigh was expensive, the latest thing, painted a deep cherry red with gold pinstriping, Tom couldn't resist taking it out along the river road before returning it to Wessex.

Cig and Margaret, swathed in furs, screamed as they took a curve.

"Slow down."

"Live at a gallop, my love." Tom leaned over and kissed Margaret's rosy cheeks but reined in.

"Thank God you didn't try to hitch Full Throttle to this thing or we'd be in the next state by now," Cig said.

"State of what?"

"I meant colony," Cig replied to her brother. "I wish we had a sleigh like this."

"In good time, in good time." Tom's jaw stuck out. "Patience, hard work, and a bit of luck. Of course, a good marriage would help, sister."

She rolled her eyes.

Margaret spoke for her. "In good time—in good time."

Hearing his own words come right back at him, Tom could only nod in lukewarm agreement.

A lone figure rode toward them. Tom slowed the horses to a walk.

"Patrick Fitzroy," Cig called to him as they approached, "how is it you are riding in this blizzard?"

"What's a blizzard?" he asked.

"A snowstorm," she answered.

"Ah, another of your fashionable words." He paused. "I wanted to show you something."

Tom, quiet, watched as Fitzroy drew alongside the sleigh. "A beauty. Looks like Lionel deVries's sleigh."

"It is. I'm going to return it to him today."

"What did you want to show me?" Cig asked.

"If you'll be going back I'll show you at your barn. I've put a bit of leather in my mare's foot and I want you to see it."

"Why?" Tom didn't like Pryor's surge of energy around the Irishman.

"Keeps the snow from balling up in the foot. I'll have to shoe her more often, mind you, but that's a small price to pay, I should think."

Tom turned the sleigh around and Patrick trotted alongside, the snow crusting on his heavy blond eyebrows. He asked Tom, "Would you like me to go with you to Wessex? A bit of company makes every journey short."

"No, thank you." Tom smiled.

They chattered about the weather, the upcoming Eppes party, the odds and ends of daily life that inform every time and every group of people.

When they reached Buckingham, Tom pulled the sleigh up to the open barn doors. Patrick dismounted, leading his horse into the aisle. He offered to help Tom unhitch but Tom refused, saying he would be leaving soon.

"Let me see what brought you out here." Tom walked over to the mare. Fitzroy lifted her left foreleg, pointing out a supple piece of leather carefully cut to match the shape of her hoof. The shoe was nailed over it, creating a protective pad. This accomplished two important things in snow. It prevented the snow from balling up in the hoof and since neither horse nor rider could be certain of what was underneath the snow, it gave the animal some protection against stones and other sharp objects.

"Good work," Cig said, standing behind Tom.

"How long before the leather tears?" asked Tom, not one to be easily swayed.

"Depends on what she steps on, now doesn't it?" Fitzroy put down her hoof. "It ought to last until the next shoeing."

"Do you shoe every six weeks?" Cig asked.

"I let the horse tell me when but that's close enough."

"Do come inside for a hot drink. I've some sausage biscuits, as well," Margaret invited Patrick. "What about you, husband?"

"I'd best be on my way."

"Don't forget to give Kate deVries the basket. There's biscuits in there for you and jams for her. Do you think you'll be home tomorrow?"

"Depends on the weather, my love." He kissed her on the cheek.

"Safe journey," Cig called over her shoulder as she led Fitzroy's mare into Pollux's stall.

Tom made a point of asking, "Any messages for Lionel?"

"My regards, and I'll see him at the party." She turned to Fitzroy. "Let me untack her and put a blanket on. It only takes a minute. No point in her standing around all dressed up and nowhere to go."

"I'll do it."

"Done." Cig smiled as she slipped the bridle off the horse's head.

Tom lingered a moment then hopped back in the sleigh. "I hate to take this back." He laughed at himself.

" 'Tis a grand piece of work." Fitz ran his finger along the pinstriping. He looked up at Tom. "If you'd like to try the leather soles I'll put them on Helen. No charge. See how you like it."

"I'll think it over," Tom replied. "Appreciate the offer." He winked at Margaret, turned the sleigh and drove past the stable, easily climbing the low hill and soon disappearing in the snow as he headed toward Wessex.

•   •   •

Once inside, full of sausage biscuits and hot tea, Fitzroy removed a package wrapped in brown paper, tied with a string, from his outer coat hanging on a peg. From the other pocket he pulled out another package. The larger one he handed to Margaret, the smaller to Cig.

"Oh . . ." Margaret glowed when she unwrapped it to find a book with drawings of the latest fashions of the courts of Europe. The artist was reputed to be a lady of high standing. Naturally, this paragon didn't wish to use her name.

Cig's book was written in French, *Haute École*. It also contained drawings, of men on horseback performing dressage movements.

"What a lovely gift!" Cig exclaimed. "Thank you."

Margaret leaned over to see. "Mr. Fitzroy, you are a most observant gentleman." She laughed. "Imagine if you'd given Pryor my book and vice versa."

Reaching over and flipping the uncut pages in Margaret's book, Cig appreciated the comment. She got up to fetch a sharp knife, and began meticulously cutting the pages in her book then in Margaret's. "Patrick Fitzroy, you surprise me."

"Good—then you won't find me tedious."

She faltered for a moment then slowly replied, "I don't find you tedious. In fact, I find you the most interesting man I . . ." She couldn't find exactly what to say so she shrugged.

"Do you ever feel like a fish out of water now that you're back?"

"All the time," she answered him.

"I feel that way, too." He smiled at Margaret. "Everything is so strange, you see."

"I'm sure I would feel that way were I to travel to London or Dublin." Margaret mentioned Dublin since he was an Irishman.

"A beautiful lady such as yourself would fit in anywhere."

"I think so, too," Cig agreed. "Margaret has what some people call 'star quality'—she sparkles."

Blushing, Margaret laughed. "You'll turn my head."

"Star quality." Fitz considered the description. "I've never heard that before but it aptly describes the lady of the house."

"How did you come to be in Virginia, sir?" Margaret held her fashion book as though it were a precious jewel.

"You know of the troubles in Ireland."

"Indeed." She nodded her head.

He continued, half-smiling, "The English have made it very difficult to be Irish. And forgive me for I know you two are English."

"That doesn't mean we agree with all the king's policies," Margaret sagely commented but in a low voice. One had to be careful.

"Seeing how bleak was my future, I resigned my commission in the army for there was no hope of advancement and I should soon have been asked to take an oath that I could not in good conscience take. My older brother fervently embraced the Church of England, but then he will inherit all my father's estates. I can't say I blame him. I took what money I had left from my service, my father kindly paid for my passage to the New World, and here I shall stay. It was learn a trade or starve, for I hadn't enough money to become a planter. I love horses and I know a bit about the beasts—and here I am."

"Many's the man won't work with his hands," Margaret said. "They come here, charter in hand, discover what must be done and quickly turn tail. I admire you."

"Me, too," Cig chimed in.

"Ladies, now you flatter me. This is a new world and calls for new ways. I find I'm content to work so. Idleness breeds imaginary ills, I think. If I can put aside enough money I'm going to start breeding horses, blooded horses. I would like to start with that fine animal of yours." He looked to Cig.

"Well—I don't see why not." She smiled at him. She couldn't help but like him. He was a feeling man and a modest one. "It seems to me, Fitz, if you can breed a fine pack of foxhounds you'll be able to breed good horses."

"Thank you." He warmed to his subject. "I know I'll have to import some mares and one fine stallion but over time I hope to no longer rely upon Ireland or England. And," he leaned forward, excited, "I want to travel to each of the colonies to see what blooded horses they have there. That will take time—years, but I am hopeful."

"It's a wonderful idea," Cig said.

"I love a good horse race," Margaret dreamed out loud.

"The Lord willing, you shall have one." His blue eyes danced. "Ladies, I must take my leave. The day will be gone before I know it. Thank you for the repast and the lovely company. Lifts my heart."

"Thank you for my present." Margaret was thrilled with her book.

"I'll walk you to the barn," Cig said.

"No, no, stay inside and keep warm."

"I don't feel the cold when I'm around you." From any other woman's mouth the comment would have sounded flirtatious but from Cig it sounded like a statement of fact.

"Then I am honored."

They trudged through the blue light into the barn. Cig removed the blanket and Fitz threw his saddle up on the mare's back. Within minutes she was tacked up.

"She's a nice mare."

"Good bone. Not refined, mind you, but sturdy and willing. Temperament first in mares and women." He laughed.

"True enough. I'm glad you rode out here. I love the book. I'll read it before I next see you." She didn't comment on the fact that it was in French. She'd surmised that educated people were expected to read Latin and French. Fortunately, she could read both, at least enough to get by.

"Want a leg up?" she said.

"Are you thinking I'm that old and stiff?"

"No. Sometimes when I mount from the ground my left kneecap hurts."

"Well, your horse is a mite taller than my own, you see, so I can just swing up"—which he did—"and look the graceful fellow. I don't think I could be quite so light off the ground if I had far to go."

"That's good of you to say." She placed her hand on his boot calf much as she would do with Hunter, Laura, or one of her students. It was such a natural gesture she wasn't even aware of it. "I like your ideas, Fitz, and I like you."

"Then I'm a happy man."

She paused. "You know, I really am a fish out of water . . . some-

times I feel lost. Tom wants me to marry Lionel and Lionel beseiges me."
The words began spilling out. "It would be good for both houses, but I
can't find my way to him, and I'm not just saying that because of what
you said to me once. I don't belong here, but I'm trying, and Margaret
and Tom are so good to me. I must be a trial to them because I can't
remember people and what I do remember . . ." She stopped a moment, afraid she was going to cry.

He reached down, putting his hand on her shoulder. "A burden's
never so heavy when two carry it. You're not alone."

She removed his hand from her shoulder and kissed his palm. "Thank
you."

He placed his hand on her burning cheek. "You only have to ask. If
you need me I will fly to you." He lifted his hand, turned the mare
toward Jamestown and rode into the heavy snow.

When Cig returned to the house, Margaret was devouring her book.
She glanced up. "You like him best, don't you?"

Cig nodded. "Yes."

"There will be trouble."

"I know. I was a fool. Margaret," her voice pleaded for answers as she
blurted out, "I slept with Lionel when we visited Wessex."

Margaret placed a hand on both pages of the open book. "Ah, then
there *will* be trouble."

29

~

"I can't!" Cig complained.

"You'll learn."

"Margaret, I'm not doing this."

"Yes, you *are*," Margaret firmly ordered her. "It's rude to spurn the request of a gentleman and it's uncivilized not to dance. Now stand up."

"I hate this," Cig mumbled, wishing Tom would return from Wessex. At least then she might escape this lesson.

"Hate it silently." Margaret reached over and took Cig's hand and bowed, playing the gentleman's part. "Curtsy."

Cig wobbled down.

"I've seen eighty-year-old women curtsy with more grace than that. Now do as I do. See, put your right foot behind your left, just turn the toe in ever so slightly and there. Arms out at a pleasing angle, hands just so."

Cig observed the fluid movement of her graceful sister-in-law. Grumbling, she tried to imitate it.

Margaret lifted Pryor's hands with her own. "Up a bit, you don't want to give the impression of drooping, like a wilting flower. Better. Now again. Much better."

"Liar."

"How is it you never learned to curtsy?"

"I went to cotillions but it wasn't the same. No curtsy and the dances are different."

"Am I to gather from this that the social graces have eroded?"

"Eroded? Hell, Margaret, they were washed out into the Atlantic with the Industrial Revolution." Cig practiced a few more dips. "Never mind about the Industrial Revolution, but your children will live to see the beginning of it. And the queer thing is that Virginians believe they are the most civilized people in America if not on earth. Compared to you, though, we're a crude lot."

"Ah, well, there must be compensating gifts. God never closes one door but what He opens another."

"I haven't found it yet." Cig put her hands on her hips. "Will my curtsy pass muster?"

"No. Practice makes perfect."

"What else do I have to know for this Christmas ball?"

"Just follow me. If you can dance, your wits will save you in conversation, so don't worry about that. . . . Now, I've bowed to you and you've curtsied to me. Next I lead you onto the floor." Margaret lifted Cig's hand up high. They traipsed a few steps. "Pryor . . ." She motioned for her to back up.

"What am I doing over here?"

"Dancing."

"But you're over there."

"Of course. You're with the ladies and I'm with the gentlemen."

"You mean no gentleman is going to hold me in his arms?" Disappointment hung on every syllable.

"Certainly not!"

Cig racked her brain to remember when the sexes began dancing close. Was it the waltz? "Are we doing a minuet?"

"Yes. There are quite a few steps to learn. Part of one's standing in society depends on this. You must dance well."

"All right."

"Now I will turn left and you will turn right. Imagine that you've a lady in front of you and one behind, so you must keep in step or there will be a frightful collision, especially if it's Amelie Boothrod."

"She colors her hair. That reddish tint is a color not seen in nature."

Margaret laughed. "She swears she doesn't, not that I've brought it up to her, but Kate deVries has. Kate will say anything as I'm sure you gathered."

"Who knows how to color hair?"

"Wealthy ladies bring over indentured servants skilled in enhancing ladies' gifts or lack thereof. After a few years their term of service is up, they've a pocketful of money, and they set up shop . . . it's discreet, usually a millinery shop or a dressmaker's establishment. The hair coloring is done in the back. They'll also visit you in your home if your servants can be bribed into silence. There's no such thing as a hungry hairdresser."

Cig remarked, "Gossip, the fuel of life!"

"In Virginia, yes!"

"Have you ever noticed, when we talk it's gossip, when men do it's the 'news'?"

Margaret laughed. "Keep in step." She clapped her hands in rhythm. "Now turn right, come down the line, hold your hand up. Stop. Now nod to your partner."

"Would that be you? If you were a man, I mean?"

"Depends on the dance."

"What a wonderful way to be with men. One gets to exchange a few steps with everyone."

"And in front of everyone."

"Perfect." Cig smiled. "How am I doing?"

"Glide your feet along. Don't lift them."

"Ah." Cig half-slid, half-glided.

"Better. It's a bad sign for a lady to have a heavy foot and as you will slightly lift your skirts from time to time you don't want a big one either."

"Margaret, I'm not dainty, and neither are my feet. I tower over everyone but Lionel."

"Your feet are proportionate. Stop. Yes. Now come towards me, pass and then turn to face me as I do the same to you."

"This is the Virginia Reel."

"What?"

"This is a fancy version of the Virginia Reel. It's a dance we still do."

"Then you're not entirely uncivilized."

"Rudiments of elegance linger." Cig smiled.

"Lift your chin up, Pryor. You don't want to drop your head. Apart from being clumsy it makes one look old. Double chins will come soon enough."

"Perish the thought." Cig felt a sharp twinge of nervousness. This kind of dancing was a true performance and stage fright was creeping in even here in front of the massive fireplace. Grace would have been in her element. "Margaret, do I have to dance with any man who asks me?"

"Yes. I told you. It would be rude to refuse a gentleman."

The corner of Cig's mouth twitched upward. "What if he's not a gentleman?"

"You wouldn't be a lady to say so."

Cig bounced around a bit. "I suppose Lionel will pounce on me."

"Keep your head up. Up, up, up! Considering he shared your bed I guess he will. Up!"

"It is!"

"Now it is."

"You know, I look at Lionel and I see Blackie. I don't ever want to fall on my face again like that—in this life or the next."

"You'll fall on your face if you don't learn these steps."

"I'm not good at this."

"The music helps."

"Grace is the dancer."

"Well, Grace isn't dancing at the Christmas ball, *you* are. Come back to the middle," Margaret ordered her. "Begin again. With the curtsy. Good."

Cig watched as Margaret pointed her toe to coach her.

Margaret continued, "Don't point your toe like that, Pryor. That's what the gentleman will do. You point yours into the line. This way we are mirror images of one another."

"I get it." The symmetry of the dances was part of their appeal.

"Practice now."

They ran through the steps one more time. Cig held her hands in the time-out sign. Margaret kept dancing. "Time out . . . stop."

"Why didn't you say so in the first place?"

"I did." She made the T sign again. "That means stop in my time. We have a game called football, except it's not soccer—"

Merrily, Margaret imitated the sign. Cig stopped. "Pryor, I have no idea what you are talking about."

"Let me start again. There's a game in my time, I think it started in the late nineteenth century, it's violent but very addictive—that is, you can't stop once you've started. Teamwork is the key . . ." she noticed Margaret's bemused stare. "Anyway, when you need a break you do this."

"Why not stop completely?"

"No. It's a time-out." She raised her voice. "Time out. You go to the sidelines to talk to your coach. He helps you and you run back in again."

"That's cheating."

"No, Margaret, it's in the rules. Trust me. I am *serious* about football."

"I can see that."

"The ball is elliptical." Cig drew a football in the air with her finger.

"Shouldn't it be round?"

"No. This makes it harder because the ball flops around except when you throw a pass. Then it spirals."

"Pryor, this is a most peculiar game."

"Well," Cig's lower lip jutted out like Tom's when perturbed, "what sports do you like?"

"Horse racing, as you know." She thought a moment. "I think I should like court tennis if ever I visited London to see such a game, and fencing, I like that."

"What about track and field? You know, foot races, throwing the javelin, that stuff."

"I like foot races." Margaret put her hands on her hips. "Hunting, of course." She sat down. Cig sat next to her then rose to put another log on the fire. "Why did you not tell me straightaway about you and Lionel?"

"I couldn't say anything on the way back from Wessex. Tom would jump to conclusions."

"You had other opportunities."

"I forgot—really, I did. Or rather whenever I thought of it Tom would be around or Marie. Fortunately, she's rotund so you hear her coming." She smiled, lips together. "Is it a bad thing in this time to go to bed with a man if you're not married to him?"

"Not so bad. It's better than suffering from the green sickness."

"What's that?"

"You don't use that expression?" As Cig shook her head Margaret explained. "It's used to indicate that a lady needs time with a gentleman."

"Our expression is more crude . . . needs to get laid."

"Ah, I see what you mean." Margaret suggested, "If you're going to pace about bring us some apple cider."

Cig opened the back door, dashed to the summer kitchen and returned with an earthenware jug of cider. She poured two glasses and returned to Margaret.

"Thank you. Sit down, Pryor."

"Restless."

"Green sickness. A bad case." Margaret laughed.

"Maybe I didn't use my best judgment. He's so much like Blackie— oh, I don't know. But you say it isn't awful?"

Margaret quizzically looked at Pryor. "It's natural. It's better if you're wed but . . ." She shrugged.

Cig wished William and Mary had taught classes in real-life history. She knew dates, battles, and treaties, but nothing of the texture of life in other times. "Sex is natural, but things happened later—in the nineteenth century, I guess—and people began to regard it as sinful but necessary. I wonder if I'm putting this right. The opinion was, men desired sex. Women didn't."

"Absurd." Margaret couldn't believe it for she was a product of an earthy age.

"Yes. But since that time these ideas have infected us like a sickness. Some people rebel and become promiscuous. Others," she thought a moment, "suffer. Mostly people turn into hypocrites. They say they believe in abstinence or faithfulness to their partners but they don't practice it."

"That's true in any time. I think the first words spoken by man were, 'Not me.'"

Cig laughed. "You're right! You've made me feel better. You don't think I'm a whore."

Margaret frowned. "No one would ever use that word, Pryor. But Lionel is determined to marry you and you've given him hope."

"I know. I was stupid."

"No. Just a woman. He is a handsome man."

"Do you think he'll say anything to Tom?"

"No." Margaret was firm.

"Do whites marry Indians?"

"Yes. Not many do, but some."

"What about sex with servants?"

"Of course." Margaret finished her glass. "That will always happen. You use the word curiously. To me *sex* means male or female."

"It does for me, too, but *sex* can also mean the act of copulation." She ran her hand through her hair. "I'm not sure when that started. I know my grandmother never used the word that way—but then I'm not sure she ever discussed these matters."

"Let me dress your hair for the ball."

"What made you think of that?"

"You ran your hand through your hair."

"Is it that bad?"

"No, but you can't wear it braided like that. Not to a ball."

"Margaret, this is making me nervous."

She held out her glass for more cider. It had a kick to it. "All will be well. At Edward Hill's I carefully told a few ladies that you'd endured a temporary loss of memory. You needn't fear not recognizing people if Tom or I aren't beside you. They'll understand. After all, you do have your wits about you and people, quite healthy people, lose their memories sometimes."

Cig coolly appraised her. "I underestimated you."

30

Because of the snows the James was higher than usual, the current swift. Cig fixed her eyes on the dock on the south shore because if she looked down into the river she'd become seasick. She loved ferries and would take them across the Potomac, the Mississippi, wherever she found them. This ferry, not motor powered of course, proved how consistent the art of crossing a river was over the centuries. Burly John MacKinder, notable for his heavy beard and big red hands, gripped the tiller while punters stood on either side of the craft. Not that there'd be much punting at this depth but when they closed to shore the long poles would be dipped into the water and mud for a directional shove.

The distance between Buckingham and Eppington couldn't have been more than seven miles, but two of those miles were over water. John had crisscrossed the river throughout the day as people gathered for the Christmas ball given by Francis Eppes and his family.

The sunset melted over the waters, transforming them into a scarlet path. Margaret pulled her cloak closer around her shoulders. Tom chatted with the other men at the prow.

Cig's heart beat faster as they approached the dock. Parties excited her, even though she had been shy as a child. Her great-aunt had coached her on how to talk to people she didn't know. G-Mom had advised her at the tender age of six to look for special jewelry or the color of someone's shirt and to start from there. People love to talk about themselves,

G-Mom swore; the secret was to get them started. Cig's first conversational success was Binky West's mother, deep in the grape.

Cig smiled thinking of the skinny, middle-aged woman she had approached at a hunt club party. "Mrs. West, you have the prettiest pearls. I bet you know a lot about the ocean." This sent the blue-haired lady into fits of laughter; but she did talk about her pearls, how pearls are formed, the difference between white and black pearls and of course, freshwater pearls as well. By the time Mrs. West had exhausted her discourse on the secretions of the oyster, Cig knew that G-Mom had given her one of the keys to survival: the ability to talk to anyone. She tested her abilities on unwary adults after church, at school gatherings, at hunt club meetings, and best of all, at her parents' parties.

Adults would exclaim, "What unusual poise Cig has."

Well, she had to have something since Grace clearly had the beauty.

The ferry bumped into the dock, rocking the passengers off their feet. The men leaped off first, offering their hands to the ladies. This also afforded them the delicious opportunity of lifting the ladies onto the dock. Cig, too big for such gallantry, nonetheless had her hand held tightly by John MacKinder whom she liked on sight.

"Thank you, Mr. MacKinder," she said.

"Why, 'iffin I lacked the bark I'd swim ye across."

She squeezed his hand and then dropped it as they hurried to the two carriages sent for them from the big house.

"Where is John MacKinder from?" Cig whispered to Margaret.

"Highlands. Hardworking man. His wife is crippled now, poor thing. She lost the sensation in her legs then grew dizzy. After that she shriveled before your eyes. He's a good man. You've known him since childhood."

"Thanks, Margaret. What would I do without you?"

"Fall on your face." Margaret's hazel eyes twinkled.

Tom heard them laughing. "Margaret, I've never heard you laugh so much as since Pryor came home to us."

Edward Hill III's wife called out from the other carriage, "You see, Tom, Pryor's safe return heralds good fortune. Good fortune starts with laughter, I always say."

Tom doffed his hat to her. "Fine philosophy." Then he hopped into the carriage while the driver, a slender fellow, clucked to the matched pair.

A candle blazed in Eppington's every window. Lanterns hung along the drive created a festive air.

The house was a simple, long white clapboard structure with neat black shutters. White clapboard dependencies stood near the main house. Eppington made up in warmth and simplicity for what it lacked in grandeur. When the head servant opened the door, music and laughter flooded over the lawn.

A tall, lean Creole, Henry Jardin, the head servant, had been born in the West Indies. Clean-shaven, with skin the color of café-au-lait and soft green eyes, he was a breathtaking example of masculine beauty. He could remember names, protocol, and who was feuding with whom, which endeared him to Francis Eppes, whose memory was porous. He also served as secretary to the energetic man whose business interests encompassed both the Old World and the New.

"Henry, good to see you." Tom clapped him on the back.

Henry pointed the way to the table as servants took their wraps. He whispered to Cig, "You're a vision tonight."

Half the colony of Virginia turned out for the party. Children, dressed as miniature versions of their elders, raced and screamed throughout the rooms. The elderly were as animated as the children. Holly berries and big waxy magnolia leaves decorated the table and the rooms.

Cig marveled at how attractive people appear in massed candlelight. Having known only the harshness of electrical light, she was amazed at the emotional difference candlelight created.

Before she could study the surroundings more clearly she felt light pressure on her elbow.

"I'm so glad you're here." Patrick Fitzroy handed her rum punch in a handblown crystal glass.

Her heart gave a thump. "Fitz, I'm so glad you're here, too."

"May I escort you to the table, or shall I bring you a plate?"

"Let's see the table."

He offered her his arm and they made their way into the long room.

Moving through the crowd, people nodded, called out and held up their glasses in toast. Pryor recognized some of them from hunting but many were new faces to her. They bubbled for she was escorted by Patrick Fitzroy.

The massive table overflowed with turkey, capon, venison, bear, an entire suckling pig, succotash, sweet potatoes, white potatoes, cornbread, dark bread, mountains of sweet butter and jellies and jams, pickled corn as well as pies made from every fruit grown in the colony, a five-layered moist chocolate cake, and bread and rice puddings, Cig's favorite.

Servants carved the meats, releasing the rich aroma into the room.

Cig smiled at Fitz as he dutifully worked his way around the table. She pointed to the turkey, the venison, whatever suited her, and he put the food on a fine white-and-blue china plate. She felt silly but all she could do was smile.

He found her a seat, returning to fill his own plate. Daniel Boothrod paraded by, the buckles on his shoes gleaming.

" 'Pon my soul, the man is a Mercury, a veritable Mercury for I would have served you myself." The intricate lace on his sleeve swayed slightly when he spoke and the snowy white lace at his throat was handiwork of exquisite delicacy.

"Daniel." A shrill voice pierced the room.

Fitz concealed a grin. "Your angel, Daniel."

"Ah, yes, my bride, my bride," Daniel mumbled, then bowed to Cig and ambled in Amelie's direction with a singular lack of enthusiasm.

"Daniel, you know more about shipping than the rest of us." Francis Eppes spoke as Daniel passed. "I say it's time we had a proper shipyard in Virginia."

Soon half a dozen men gathered around Daniel as he discussed how to raise capital for such a venture, how much tonnage Virginia could be expected to send over to England, France, and whoever else wanted Virginia's crops.

Cig, overhearing, said, "It's exciting. I feel as though all things are possible."

Fitz smiled and started to say something but a bass voice interrupted.

"Pryor, you are radiant." Lionel bowed to her. "I told Samuel to inform me the moment you arrived but he was too slow and," he paused, "this huntsman is too fast."

"I would have found you but," she pointed to her plate, "I'm famished."

"As soon as you are ready, mademoiselle, I wish the honor of the first dance."

"I'm a terrible dancer," she blushed, "but I will try."

Lionel bowed again. Glaring at Fitzroy, he withdrew.

Really nervous now, Cig concentrated on watching the people.

The coats of the men, cream, sky blue, deep plum, rich navy, contrasted with their brocaded waistcoats. Accustomed to seeing men in drab clothing at formal occasions, Cig was entranced by this swirl of peacocks.

Another new sensation caught her ears, the rustle of women's skirts as they moved. The silk fabrics, like the men's clothing, abounded in luscious colors, each carefully chosen to complement the lady's complexion.

The visceral appeal of color, sound, and candlelight made Cig spontaneously smile despite her apprehensions. She no longer felt awkward in Pryor's ball gown, a warm melon with burgundy ribbons, cut low on the bodice.

The small orchestra took its place at the end of the main room. Ladies demurely waited, eyes bright. Men preened then plucked up the courage to ask for a dance.

She noticed Abraham Boothrod bowing to a petite blond woman then saw Lionel heading in her direction. His mother emerged from the next room.

"Not so fast."

Lionel slowed to accompany his mother to the side of the room.

"Well," she boomed, large pearls heaving on her bosom and pearl and diamond earrings dangling from her ears, "isn't anyone going to ask me to dance? I may be old but I'm still vertical."

Fitz touched Cig's elbow, stood up and gracefully bowed to Mrs. deVries. "Madam, may I?"

She curtsied smoothly. Cig could see she had an athlete's grace and thought she looked wonderful for her years.

As Fitz led Kate onto the polished floor, Lionel claimed Cig. She knew she would trip over her own feet, slam into the lady in front of her, turn right instead of left. Frozen with fear, she stuck in her seat.

"Mademoiselle?"

"I think you'll have to pull me up," she whispered.

Margaret noticed and joined them for a moment. "Come on."

Lionel held her hand tightly and half-led, half-pulled her onto the floor. "Your hair shines so."

"Thank you," she mumbled.

Margaret had dressed Cig's hair in the latest fashion as represented in her new book. She had trimmed it a bit just below shoulder length and curled it. Even Cig had to admit it was pretty.

She took her place as the music started. Stiff with fear, she found she nonetheless did remember the steps. Then again, she had Margaret behind her whispering to her, "Toe out, hand up. Right turn."

Fitz, opposite Kate, lifted her hand with a combination of brio and tenderness.

A little boy dashed through the line, his mother pursuing him. "Jacob!"

Jacob ignored her, careened into the dining room and grabbed a handful of cake, stuffing it into his mouth as he sought to escape his mother, a determined but slow lady.

As the dance ended a crash was heard in a distant room. Jacob bouncing off a wall, Cig assumed.

Lionel held onto her hand but Fitz, after escorting Kate back to a chair, walked up to Cig. He bowed. "This honor is mine."

Lionel smiled tightly, relinquishing Pryor to Fitzroy. He stalked back to his mother.

"Get that scowl off your face. She may dance with whomever she chooses. And you may dance with me."

"Of course." Lionel bowed to his mother.

Amelie Boothrod, seething with envy because Kate's pearls overshadowed her rather muddy sapphires, inclined her head in greeting. Kate did the same.

The dancers laughed out loud as the tempo increased, the steps growing intricate. Cig tripped but Abraham, holding her hand on that pass, held her up and laughed, too, not at her but for the sheer joy of dancing.

Francis Eppes, at the end of the dance, clapped and motioned for his servants to bring drinks to the musicians. "Well done, boys!" he shouted. The orchestra took a small bow. "When we step over the threshold of my daughter's new house I shall have you play again." He held up a glass to his young daughter and her husband. "To Weston Manor, my dear."

"Thank you, Poppa." She curtsied to her father.

Tom, amazed, looked at Cig.

"Bee boxes." Cig grinned.

"How's that?" Fitz, at her side, asked.

"A bet with my brother. I just won some new bee boxes."

Lionel joined them. "We're buzzing around you with or without bee boxes." Since a woman's vagina was referred to as a "honey pot," Lionel stayed just this side of a double entendre, relishing the raciness of his statement.

The music started again. Abraham Boothrod hurried over, bowing. "May I?"

"See ya, fellas," Cig called over her shoulder before she realized they might not get it. They did. The phrase wasn't in use but they understood her saucy intention. Fitz laughed. Lionel did not.

As she danced Cig glanced over at Fitz, partnering Margaret now. Tom partnered Kate. Cig thought Fitz reminded her of another man of Irish stock, a movie star before her time, Errol Flynn. Fitz was blonder, more rugged, but he possessed that same fluid movement, that erotic quality of Flynn.

Kate, her color high, was at the head of the ladies' line. She nodded, laughed, and hummed at the gentlemen she passed as they danced down the row. Afterwards, she repaired for a good drink, propelling Cig along with her.

"You seem happy, at last," Kate said as they moved over to a window. "It's snowing again."

"So it is. Did I seem unhappy before?"

"Your mind was far away."

Cig wanted to say, "Yes, it was. I miss my children, I miss my friends, and I miss being able to put Bach in the CD player whenever I want." Instead she said, "I've been considering the future." She smiled. "I think it weighted me down."

"Take the world as you find it, as I always say. The future will be here soon enough."

"Yes, I know that now."

Daniel Boothrod swanned by, lifted a devilish eyebrow but kept moving, a spring to his step. Since Amelie was dancing he was escaping her watchfulness. Ribbons fluttered where his silk pants met his silk hose, just below the knee.

"Pins, legs like pins."

Surprised, Cig responded, "He has good legs."

"Fillers." Kate snapped her mouth shut like a big turtle.

"No." Cig couldn't believe it. "What do the ladies do if, you know—?" She indicated bosoms.

"Push themselves up with mountains of gauze. Can't breathe. I always pick out the ones red in the face. A sure sign." She laughed. "Didn't your mother teach you such wiles?"

"My mother didn't have to."

Kate frankly stared at Cig's bosom. "Quite."

Then they both laughed. Kate spoke again. "I did not marry for love, Pryor, and as you know, my union was a good one. If one must engage in matrimony, it's far better to do so with a rich man than a poor one. Here in Virginia radical notions like marrying for love are current. Of course, we hear about such things in England, too. The world has never been the same since King Charles lost his head. And then the Civil War—my father used to tell me that when I was a child—it all went topsy-turvy. He was right. Not only did parliaments change and heads roll, but men and women changed. People became indulgent." She waved her hand. "You've heard me say all this before. I don't know why I'm saying it now—except that I wish you would marry my son and something tells me you will not."

Cig cast her eyes down then looked into Kate's slate gray eyes. "I don't want to marry anyone—not right now."

"I understand that. Lionel is impatient. Always was. Always will be. He doesn't heed my advice on this matter for I tell him to—" She made a motion with her hand meaning to slow down. "There he is now." She called out to him. "We were just talking about you."

"I'll take my chances anyway." He joined them.

"Daniel, Daniel . . ." Amelie called, stopping before them. "Have you seen my Daniel?"

"No, we haven't," Kate lied with glee.

Amelie walked on. "Daniel, Daniel . . ."

"I fully expect her to arrive at some function with her husband on a chain."

Fitzroy also entered the room. "Ladies. Pryor, may I have this dance?"

"Of course." She curtsied to Kate deVries and to Lionel, then walked to the dance floor.

Watching them dance Lionel vowed to his mother, "I'll thrash that pup."

"Leave him alone. Pryor has a unique allure about her, rather like the chaste Artemis, I should think."

"She is no chaste huntress." He smirked.

"You miss my point, Lionel."

"Which is?"

"She may grant her favors yet remain indifferent. It is her aloofness which attracts men to her."

"She doesn't seem aloof from Patrick Fitzroy." He glowered.

Kate observed them. "He entertains her. You don't."

Angry, he left her, striding into the dancing room. Apprehensive, she followed.

As the dance ended, Fitz lingered with Cig then escorted her back to where Tom and Margaret were visiting with the Hills.

Lionel stopped in front of Fitz. "Leave this lady in peace. She belongs to me."

"The hell I do." Cig flared up.

"You will marry me, and the sooner the better."

Kate drew next to Margaret. "Lionel—"

"Stay out of this, Mother."

"I believe the lady in question has her own mind, sir," Fitzroy curtly replied and brushed past Lionel who grabbed him by the left shoulder, twirling him around.

"I know this woman," Lionel sneered, implying the old use of the word, as in to know carnally.

Outraged, Fitz replied, "No gentleman would expose a lady. You don't *know* her at all."

"And you do, sir?" Lionel was in his face.

"I would know her heart."

"Ha!" Lionel pushed Fitz as the crowd, first hushed, spoke at once.

"Don't." Cig rushed between them but Lionel, with one sweep of his arm, knocked her back.

"Defend yourself!" Lionel barked.

"Not in this house!" Francis commanded.

"Outside then?" Lionel smiled at Fitz.

"Outside."

The two walked out the front door, each picking up his sword as he left. The revelers grabbed their cloaks, wraps and coats, rushing outside.

Cig turned to Margaret. "Is no one going to stop them?"

"No one can." Margaret threw her fur-lined cloak around her shoulders. Tom was already outside. Cig, wrapped in her heavy coat, followed.

"I will be your second, sir." Tom bowed his head to Fitz.

Lionel, too enraged to realize he'd lost Tom by insulting his twin sister, asked Daniel to be his second.

The seconds inspected the swords, each handing his back to the combatant by resting it over his forearm, hilt to the swordsman. The seconds took off the dress coats of the men, folding them over their arms and then stamped down the snow in a square as best they could.

"Are you ready?" Lionel asked.

"I am," Fitz replied.

With that Lionel launched at him. Fitz stepped back, the snow crunching underfoot as he parried. Within seconds both men were sweating, the falling snow melting on their faces. Fitz's dress shirt, open at the throat, revealed curly blond chest hair matted with sweat. On and on, Lionel, the bigger, heavier man, pressed at Fitz, trying to use his weight as an advantage. He slashed, angry at his inability to quickly skewer the nimbler man. He tore Fitz's shirt from left shoulder to waist. Fitz darted from side to side, thrusting when he could, parrying when he must.

The flakes fell heavier, the lights from the windows spilling golden shadows onto the snow. The snow packed down by the seconds allowed the men to move back and forth, but when either one strayed from the square he floundered in the two feet of heavy snow. Lionel pushed Fitz into a drift then lunged at him but Fitz rolled away, hair white. As he jumped back into the square the flakes fell from his hair and body, catching the light. Cig thought it looked like golden confetti.

The onlookers, breathing heavily, sent up clouds of steamy air.

Lionel closed on Fitz, locking swords at the hilt, then he pushed him away with his knee. Fitz went down and Lionel kicked at him but Fitz again rolled away. This time Lionel jumped after him, rolling on the ground with him. Fitz wriggled free. Lionel, slower, lumbered up, and Fitz hit him hard on the jaw with the hilt of his sword. Lionel rocked back and shook his head, blood running down his chin onto his shirt.

"You filthy Irish dog!" Lionel bellowed and slashed low with his sword, catching Fitz in the thigh.

Blood poured down his leg. Fitz backpedaled but his leg wobbled. Lionel aimed for his head but Fitz parried again. Then he got his leg under him, ignoring the screaming pain.

They battled for twenty more minutes, both caked in sweat and blood. Panting, Lionel stabbed at Fitz's chest but calling upon a reserve of energy, Fitz stepped aside then with lightning speed twirled his blade around Lionel's, whose grip was loosened. Fitz then grabbed Lionel's left hand in his own, moving in with one catlike leap while smashing the hilt of his sword against Lionel's right hand. Grunting, Lionel involuntarily opened his hand, sending his sword falling onto the ground. Fitz put his boot on it.

"Do you yield, sir?"

Daniel Boothrod and Tom both moved forward. Fitz swayed unsteadily but then so did Lionel.

Daniel put an end to the duel. He reached down, picking up Lionel's
sword as Fitz lifted his foot for him to do so.

"Honor is served. Enough." Daniel put his hand on Lionel's shoulder; his mother took his right hand even as she turned her blind eye
toward him. Shaking with fatigue, Lionel said, "You're a better man than
I gave you credit for, Fitzroy."

Fitz put his sword to his face in salute then crumpled into the snow.
A brilliant red circle quickly stained the pristine white.

Tom and Abraham Boothrod carried him into a whitewashed cabin
near the big house. A fire warmed the place. An elderly German man
rushed in and in broken English indicated they should place Fitzroy on
the bed. He quickly cut away the breeches.

"Not so bad," he said upon examining the wound.

Cig quietly opened the door, Margaret at her side. Margaret, without
being told, brought water over from a large jar by the fireplace.

"*Dank.*" The wizened fellow washed away the congealed blood.

Fitz tried to prop himself up on his elbows but collapsed.

Cig knelt by the bed, running her fingers through Fitz's curly hair.
"You'll be all right."

Sweat rolled down his face and chest. Tom propped him up while
Cig pulled his shirt over his head. Margaret took a clean rag and began
washing him.

Out of the corner of his eye Fitz watched Dr. Helmut Steinhauser
thread a needle. He dreaded being sewn up.

Margaret heated water over the fire. They'd need it to clean the
wound thoroughly.

Cig knelt down again and held Fitz's hand.

"He doesn't know you at all." His voice cracked.

31

∞

Fitz slept soundly, exhausted by the duel and the stitching. Tom, with a wretched Lionel, took the ferry to Buckingham.

Cig and Margaret stayed behind to watch over Fitz. Dr. Steinhauser, whom Cig learned was a surgeon from Bonn, requested that Fitz sleep undisturbed. He didn't even want Francis Eppes to carry him into the big house, for the commotion of guests, music, and servants would disturb the patient. A good night's rest would promote healing.

Fitz had suffered a painful wound but he was young and strong. A bit of care and he'd be up and about in no time. The doctor's chief fear was that the wound would become infected or Fitz would tear his stitches.

Cig promised that wouldn't happen if she had to tie him down.

The cottage was toasty. The ladies fed the fire. Finally tiring themselves, they used the furs and blankets Francis had brought for them to make a place to sleep on the floor.

Snuggled together in their shifts, their ball gowns neatly laid over a chair, Cig felt as if she were at a slumber party.

"Sleepovers are a big deal in my time for young girls. You stay up all night, eat junk food, gossip, and then fall asleep despite yourself."

"What's junk food?"

"Pretzels, potato chips, popcorn, ice cream, pizza, I mean the worst. All it does is make you fat."

"Do the mothers cook such foods—pizza?"

"Nah. You buy them in stores. We have supermarkets. You wouldn't believe it, Margaret, it's an emporium of food—as big as the Eppes's house."

"Like a market?"

"No. We have those, too—although not as many as we should. At a market everything is fresh. In a supermarket, in addition to fresh meat and vegetables, the stuff is frozen or canned or processed so as not to spoil."

"I can't believe that."

"If I could take you home with me, I'd show you."

A moan from Fitz got Cig out from under the covers. She checked on him then threw another log on the fire. "He's okay."

She hurried back under the covers. "I'd take him home, too, if I could. Back to my time, I mean." She whispered for her face was not six inches from Margaret's. "Buckingham is home in this time."

"Do you love him?"

"We click."

"What's that mean?"

"Uh, click. It's when two people get along easily. You and I click. Fitz and I click."

"I like that." Margaret's lids began to droop.

"You know, for the first time tonight I was glad I was in 1699. At least Grace wasn't at the party. When she's around the men trip over themselves waiting on her."

"But the man who is right for you wouldn't hover around Grace. What does it matter if all the others do?" Margaret made a dismissive motion with her hand.

Cig considered that remark and thought about it later as she fell asleep.

32

The next day Fitz was able to take the ferry across the James. Cig and Margaret insisted that he stay at Buckingham for a few days. He protested but finally gave in. Cig surrendered her bedroom. She'd sleep downstairs in front of the giant fireplace.

Tom, a gentleman, thanked Fitz again for defending his twin's honor. Cig caught up with him in the barn.

"I know you're disappointed in the turn of events. And you're disappointed in me." She put her hand on his shoulder. "Thank you for rising above it."

He sighed. "For you to marry Lionel—that would have been a glory. We would never want and never worry. But after what he said"—Tom shook his head—"never. Never."

"Did he say anything coming back?"

"He apologized. Said he lost his head. His mother apologized for him. Kate deVries is a hard woman to please but she likes you, she approved of the match. She's as melancholy as he is."

"Did you accept his apology?"

"I did. Fitz put everything to rights. If Fitz hadn't fought Lionel then I would have. It's over and done. Still, how could Lionel say that?"

"Because it's true. I did make love with him. I'd explain it to you but it's better that I don't."

"Explain? That's like explaining the sunshine or the stars. Better you were married, Pryor, but still, he had no right to sully you. A man protects any woman who has granted him favors. Even the savages do the same. It's a point of honor. I can't understand how he could lose his—" Frustrated, Tom couldn't find the word.

"Composure?"

"More."

"Well, whatever, he lost it."

"And he lost my respect and the respect of most everyone there. A gentleman just doesn't *do* that no matter what the provocation—even if a lady drew a sword on him." He thought of the most outrageous situation he could imagine.

"Yes, I understand." And she did. She felt quite sorry that this masculine code of honor had been reduced to tatters in her time. "And Tom, don't worry about our future. If you will listen to me, the Deyhles will prosper. We don't need Lionel."

He smirked. "Are you going to tell me to plant groundnuts again?"

"I am. I am also telling you to buy land around the Falls—now. I'm going to write these things down for you."

"What else?"

"Drain all stagnant water. If you can't drain it put oil on it. There will never be sweating sickness at Buckingham if you do as I say."

He folded his arms across his chest but he was listening. "What else?"

"Don't buy Africans. You will profit in the short term and suffer in the long term. Trust me, Tom, *trust* me."

"How do you come by this knowledge?"

"The same way I knew the Eppes's new house would be called Weston Manor."

A flash of fear crossed his face. "You have second sight—you've lost your memory but you gained second sight."

"Yes."

"Keep this to yourself, Pryor." He sagged against a stall door. The sudden turn of events had taken its toll on him. "Pryor, do you ever think you lost your memory because some memories felt like the rack, the pain was too great?"

"I've thought of that," her voice softened, "and I believe if that is so then the memory will flood back in—in time."

"I have a terrible memory. I never told you. I wish I could forget it." He covered his eyes with his hand then spoke. "I found our father hanging from the willow tree by the dock. John MacKinder and I found him. I try to wipe the picture from my mind but it comes back."

Cig put her arms around him. "I'm sorry, Tom."

"Why?" His teeth were clenched.

"He couldn't bear the pain inside."

"But he seemed hardy—Mother's death and Braxton's passing, those were hard, hard—but he never betrayed any misery. He went about his business. He had a good word for all. We knew he was suffering but I never saw a sign." Tears rolled down his cheeks. "I would have done something. I would have hidden the rope!"

"There's nothing you could have done. When someone makes up his mind to die, you can't prevent it. He was going to Mother and Braxton. He knew we were strong enough to live without him. He's happy now."

"You knew, didn't you?"

"I was forewarned. Perhaps that was one of the things that affected my mind. It doesn't matter now, anyway. I'm here. We're together. Buckingham will outlive us. Do as I advise: peanuts, the Falls, drain the swamps, no slaves, and I almost forgot, send your children to William and Mary. Make certain the girls get educated, too."

"The grammar school only teaches boys."

"Margaret can teach the girls. Someone can. Not just sewing and that stuff. History, literature, music, mathematics. Promise me, Brother."

"I promise."

"And I will write this down."

"Give it to Margaret. I'll lose it."

"Done." She held out her hand.

He shook it. "Done—one other thing. What of Fitzroy?"

"You might let him put leather on Castor and Pollux's hooves. He wants to prove his method works."

"That's not what I mean."

"Ah—I'll not spurn a man willing to die for me." She smiled. "Tom, I believe everything you do affects everyone else for all time. What you and I do now will affect someone's life in 1799 and 1899 and 1999."

"Sister, you startle me with these notions." He took a deep breath. "I give you my blessing."

Later that day she sat at the graceful desk, the large family Bible resting on the corner. She found a small, clean sheet of parchment pressed between the pages.

Picking up the quill and dipping it in the inkwell, she wrote down the list. She poured a bit of fine sand on it to dry, carefully curled the parchment and dumped the used sand in her hand.

She placed the list back in the Bible and tossed the sand in the fire. She told Margaret where she'd put the list.

She discovered she liked writing with a quill. It made everything seem so much more important.

33

⁓

"Our maternal ancestor, George Villiers, the first duke of Buckingham, was appointed Master of the Horse to James I in 1616." Tom chatted with Fitz, who sat on a chair, his leg propped up before him, his foot on a stool and three cats artfully draped around his body.

Cig and Margaret buzzed back and forth from the summer kitchen to the dinner table. Marie, normally a good worker, was so enchanted with Fitz's bravery and the romance of it that she lingered to stare at him.

Tom continued, "That's when we English began to study bloodlines and families instead of just looking at a stallion and a mare and saying, 'Try it.'"

"Crossing the Barb, that's the answer," Fitz, contented to discuss horses, said.

"Of course." Tom gesticulated. "But who can afford it? Half the great dukes of England can't import a stallion, and it must be a stallion for the Infidels won't part with a mare. We could never bring one here. It would cost a king's ransom."

"Then we'll have to capture a king." Fitz laughed.

"Marie, Marie, we could use a hand here," Margaret called to her.

"Yes, ma'am." The small but round woman reluctantly headed toward the kitchen.

•   •   •

Later, after dinner, Cig and Tom finished the outside chores. Fitz complained about being useless. When they gathered together before the fire they talked of the upcoming century.

"1700. It sounds important." Margaret giggled.

"How can a number sound important?" Tom teased her.

"Put a pound sign in front of it," Fitz suggested.

"Seventeen hundred pounds." Cig whistled. "Sounds good to me."

A chill ran down her spine, though, when she thought of the year 1700. They were poised on the cusp of one of the greatest centuries in European and American history. America would free herself from Britain. Napoleon would be born in Corsica. The French would devour themselves in a revolution whose horrible legacy would leave a stain for a hundred years to come. Slaves would revolt in Haiti. Mozart would live briefly. His music would prove eternal. Washington, Franklin, Jefferson, Madison, and Monroe would walk the earth as would Sheridan, Goldsmith, Congreve, and Gibbon. Choderlos de Laclos would scandalize all of Europe with *Les Liaisons Dangereuses*. Science would yield results so amazing that life would change beyond recognition. Three cheers for Isaac Newton!

She thought of those things, but what was closer to her heart was the knowledge that the foundation of equine grandeur was being laid on both sides of the Atlantic. The efforts of men and women in the colonies would produce Herod, Eclipse, and Matchem from which would eventually spring Man O' War, Citation, Whirlaway, Count Fleet, Sea Biscuit, and later Nashua, Swaps, Native Dancer, Northern Dancer, Alydar, Affirmed, Mr. Prospector, Secretariat, and so many other names that crowded into her head. There was Kalarama Rex for Saddlebreds along with Rex Peavine, King's Genius, Black Squirrel, Stonewall King, the perfection of Wing Commander, MyMy, Daydream, Skywatch, Imperator, Man on the Town, Harlem Globetrotter, Will Shriver, Belissima, and Valley View Supreme. The Standardbred trotters would go from Hambletonian to Greyhound to Dan Patch to Bret Hanover.

She studied the faces in the flickering firelight and knew they would play their part.

Maybe there is no pattern to history, she thought. Maybe we make it up to suit ourselves. Maybe we can't stand the fact that some of us are born into good times and some of us into bad and it's all chance. Some of us are gifted and some of us are dumb as a sack of hammers. But we each have a chance to do something.

Maybe I needed to come back to realize that. I must live every moment. It's my choice. Maybe someday, three hundred years later, someone will look back and find my name on a tombstone or in a family record and say, "She played her part, now I better play mine"—and so I will.

As she chatted and laughed she wanted to memorize each feature, each nuance of voice. She loved these people.

34

A slashing wind loaded with sleet stung Cig's face as she rode back from Jamestown toward Buckingham.

Fitz needed to get back to work. He was healing quickly and except for his stitches itching, he was strong enough to ride.

She'd grown close to him during the four days he had spent at Buckingham over Christmas. She loved the simple, warm way Christmas was celebrated—a useful gift, food, and much affection. If Fitz had been allowed, they would have traveled to Jamestown for communion. Apart from missing the sacrament, she thought it was the most wonderful holiday she'd ever spent because it was about cherishing one another.

She and Fitz talked incessantly of bloodlines. She knew the names of Cream Cheeks and a few other royal mares of Charles I. The Byerly Turk was in England but the Darley Arabian and the Goldolphin Barb were yet to come, so she didn't mention them, which, for her, was like not completing the trinity in prayer.

Charles had supported the great Tutbury Stud. After the king's beheading in 1649, Cromwell disbanded it. Fitz's knowledge of English bloodlines encompassed that history plus Irish bloodlines.

When not talking horses, they chattered about anything that came into their heads. She felt as if she'd known him all her life.

She even showed him the list she'd written for Margaret and Tom with groundnuts as the number one crop. He said the worst that could happen was that one would have a lot of fodder.

Fitz, at twenty-five, was mature. Most men of that age in 1699 were accustomed to responsibility, many to hardship.

Riding back she discovered she missed him already and couldn't wait to see him again.

She had hoped to push on faster but the swirl of sleet slowed her down. She was at last getting close to home and glad of it. The sandy roads were frozen. Full Throttle picked his way around the little ridges. Still, it was better than the frozen red clay of the Piedmont region.

She dreamed of toasty toes. She couldn't feel her toes anymore. Her fingers stiffly curled around the reins. She'd given Fitz her heavy scarf knitted by Margaret. He gave her his white tie, the forerunner of a stock tie. It was lovely silk but her neck was getting cold.

Out of the corner of her eye she saw movement in the trees. Full Throttle snorted. She lifted her head and flinched at the sleet lashing her face. She blinked through the gauze of bad weather. She did see something. She strained to hear a sound but the only noise was the rattle-tap of tiny ice bits hitting the ground.

She headed toward the movement and then something, instinct, pulled her up short. She could barely make out the forms but she could now see perhaps five or six men, running hard—Indians.

She squeezed Throttle and flat-out galloped, slipping and sliding as they ran toward Buckingham, not more than a mile up the road.

Throttle, in good shape, covered the treacherous ground in six minutes. No one was at the barn when she pounded up.

"Tom!" But the wind jammed the words back in her throat.

She trotted to the house and hollered. Margaret, scrubbing floors, opened the door. Marie, brush still in hand, came up behind Margaret. "Pryor, what is it?"

"Indians running in the woods about a mile from here. Heading this way. I couldn't make out much more than that. Where's Tom?"

"He's on the bee acres."

They'd taken to calling the clover fields in the back "the bee acres" ever since Cig had won the bet.

"Load the guns and stay here. Give me the pistols." Margaret grabbed the two flintlock pistols off the sideboard. She tossed the gunpowder bag to Cig who stuffed it in her pocket, sticking the guns in her belt. She turned, shouting over her shoulder, "Don't let anyone in this house until you know who it is."

"I'm going with you."

"The hell you are, Margaret. You stay right here or I'll beat your ass."

Cig galloped, the sleet thicker now, her throat raw with the effort. She reached the top of the small rise behind the barn. In the distance Tom, Bobby, and Hugh, a young man of perhaps fifteen working as a journeyman, sawed trunks and branches in the acres he'd been clearing for the last year.

"Tom!"

The men couldn't hear her until she was closer. Tom dropped his saw and ran to meet her.

"Tom," she gasped, "Indians! Running! Maybe five or six."

"Where?"

"About a mile down the road." She bent over in the saddle to catch her breath as Hugh grabbed the bridle to steady Throttle who was excited. She reached under her jacket and handed him a flintlock and the gunpowder bag. "I'm keeping the other one. They were in the woods. I couldn't see any more than that but they were running hard and coming this way." He loaded his pistol and passed the gunpowder back to Cig, who did the same.

"Where's Margaret?"

"In the house. I told her to load the muskets, stay put, and not let anyone in until she knew who it was."

"If they were in the woods they were trying to keep out of sight." Tom's brows knitted together. "Running hard." He squinted at the sky and tiny ice bits stuck to his eyelashes. "Damn, it's good cover."

"They running from something or to something?" Bobby gruffly asked.

"Hugh, take Throttle to the barn, then go to Margaret," Tom ordered the boy. "Keep the axe close by."

"I want to go with you."

"No. I want a man in the house. Just in case."

Being called a man thrilled Hugh. He promptly headed back to the barn after Cig dismounted.

"Follow me." Tom moved back toward the edge of the woods by the clover fields. As Pryor and Bobby approached the woods they moved more cautiously.

Tom whispered, "If they're heading west we might be able to hear them or see them. They won't come out on the river road."

"Do the trails go toward the Falls?"

"Aye," Bobby whispered back, "and far beyond."

They slipped into the woods, senses alert. As they neared the old Indian trail, Tom crouched, holding up his hand to halt . . . no sound but the sleet crashing into bare branches. He motioned for Cig to get behind a large walnut. He inched forward, Bobby behind him. Then they lay flat on the miserable ground with hollies for cover.

The clatter of the sleet intensified. Cig felt woozy until she realized she was holding her breath. They stayed motionless for what seemed a long time. Then a footfall riveted them. Tom pulled out his flintlock. She pulled hers. Bobby reached for his knife.

A figure ran by, his sides heaving, the stench of fear on him. Moments later five other Indians sped by, the fleetest closing on his quarry. He dropped to his knee, put an arrow in his quiver and fired in one graceful motion. She heard a muffled yell. The pursuers leaped forward. She heard what sounded like grunts and then nothing. Just the sleet.

Tom lay stock-still. Ten minutes later he got to his knees as did Bobby. Tom motioned with his head for her to follow. They moved along the trail, nearly white now as the sleet turned to snow.

Five hundred yards up the trail a figure lay in a heap. Tom cocked his flintlock, warily moving in. He reached the Indian before Cig did. He uncocked his pistol. An arrow had pierced the man's chest but that hadn't killed him. Two or three mighty blows to the head had crushed his skull. His scalp had been torn off his skull in haste.

Instinctively, Cig made the sign of the cross over his body. "May the Lord have mercy upon his soul."

A tight smile crossed Tom's lips. "He's with his spirits now wherever that is. Poor savage." He carefully inspected the body. "Another Tusca-rora."

"Like t'other one." Bobby spoke in his guttural way.

Tom reached down to pick up the dead Indian's long hunting knife. Cig almost blurted out, "Don't, in case of fingerprints."

He handed the knife to Cig. "You need this."

Cig bent down for a closer look, the fresh smell of blood curling into her nostrils. "He's middle-aged and strong."

"And rich." Tom opened the pouch tied to his belt. It was stuffed with roanoke, an Indian form of money made from shells.

"Whoever killed him didn't kill him for his money," Cig said.

"No time to get rid of him." Bobby thought out loud. "Figured the animals would get to him before anyone else did."

"How do Indians dispose of their own dead?" Cig felt her throat constrict with the question.

"They wrap the body in skins and woven mats and put it on a scaffold about twelve feet high. The women paint their faces black and cry and howl for a full day."

Bobby added, "When there's no flesh left on the body the relatives wrap the bones in a new mat and bury them in a big pit along with other bones."

"Don't they put bodies in trees?"

"I've heard that, yes—the body of a great enemy warrior. As a mark of respect."

"Still scalp him though," Bobby laconically said.

"Barbarians." Tom stood up after tying the money pouch to his belt.

She shivered involuntarily.

"Cold?" Bobby asked.

"A touch." She was thinking about the skeleton they'd found in the tree the day she passed through time. Whoever he was, he had been a great warrior.

"Let's drag him out of here." Bobby grabbed a leg. Tom grabbed the other one. Cig took turns spelling the men. After an hour they reached the clover fields. Cig walked to the barn and put a halter on Castor, bringing the big draft horse back. Tom and Bobby heaved the body over the pliable animal.

Cig went to get Margaret. She found Hugh, armed with an axe, with her. Margaret threw on her shawl and the three of them met the two men at the barn. Margaret didn't flinch at the sight of the man's bashed-in head. Like everyone of the time, she had seen plenty worse than that.

"Tuscarora," Tom informed his wife, then said to Bobby and Hugh, "Tie up his chin, arms and legs. Let's put him in the corncrib. In this weather he'll keep. If the weather lets up I'll ride to Wessex tomorrow to fetch Lionel. Hugh, you can ride to Shirley."

Marie ran into the barn and shrieked. Bobby put his arm around her. "They're up to no good! They stole three cows from Flowerdew Hundred last week. Next they'll come for us."

"You don't know if it was Indians did the thieving," Bobby said to calm her. "Many's the white man blamed his misdeeds on the red man."

"Something's not right. Miss Pryor found a murdered savage and now another one. They're planning something."

"I hope not, Marie, but we'll stay vigilant."

"They're bloodthirsty savages. They skin people alive! They boil them and eat them!" Marie bordered on the hysterical.

"Marie, we'll post a watch throughout the night," Cig forcefully said. "That's the best we can do under the circumstances."

Marie started crying. Bobby put his arm around her and walked her back to their cottage.

"I'll take the first watch," Hugh said.

"Good." Tom smiled. "Well, let's tie this fellow up before rigor mortis sets in."

35

Lionel deVries, arms crossed over his heavy coat, studied the corpse. The men gathered around him—Edward Hill, Ernest Shackleton, Daniel and Abraham Boothrod, William Byrd, and Tom—waited for him to speak. They had all set out for Buckingham as soon as word reached them and were assembled there by midmorning.

"It's Tanx, son of Blackpaws, chief of the Tuscaroras," Lionel finally said, using the English names for the Indians as opposed to the proper long Indian names. The English usually shortened the proper names into something they could pronounce. "He was a prudent man."

"Would Tanx have been the next chief?" Ernest asked.

"Yes."

"Who will succeed him?" Tom stood by the Indian's bound feet.

"I don't know. Chief Blackpaws has a younger son, Ortley, who is a hothead and wants to make war on the whites, which the chief fears as did Tanx." He again looked at the bashed-in head. "But old Blackpaws is smart. He can refuse to pass on his power to Ortley. It's not heredi-tary."

"Could this trigger a war among them?" Edward tugged at his gloves.

Lionel breathed out heavily. "Yes." He looked at Tom, Cig, and Bobby. "You saw the Indians chasing him. Who were they?"

"Monacans," Bobby said a bit loudly. They were a fierce tribe living west of the falls in Rassawek, where the James and the Rivanna rivers met.

Tom nodded in assent and everyone looked back to Lionel.

Lionel's jaw clenched. "It would have been better had his own people killed him. This means the Tuscarora and the Monacans will go to war or"—he carefully weighed his words—"that a faction of the Monacans are allied with Ortley and they, too, want to be rid of us."

The men started talking at once. Lionel held up his hands. "I'll take Tanx back to Chief Blackpaws. If the cold stays with us I can be there in two days."

If the trails thawed it would be slower going as well as increasingly unpleasant since the corpse would be draped over a pack mule.

"I'll go to the Nottoway and Meherrin to gather what intelligence I may," William Byrd said, mentioning two Iroquois tribes in northern Carolina.

"We should enjoin the planters and their families to repair to Jamestown," Daniel Boothrod said. He tapped the head of his ornate walking stick. "After all, savages swept out of nowhere in 1622 and made mischief again when I was a young man."

"There are more of us now, and William and I," Lionel nodded in Byrd's direction, "keep a presence at the Falls. They can't sweep down the James without our being forewarned."

"No, but they can sweep out of the forests or up from the swamps." Edward Hill absentmindedly thwacked a corncob in his hand.

"They can't slip through the chain of forts without us soon knowing," Lionel stated.

He referred to the English forts immediately below the fall line that separated the Tidewater from the Piedmont. These forts, in place for twenty-some years, provided peace of mind to those who didn't know that elaborate drills and red coats meant nothing to Indians.

"But will we know soon enough?" Daniel, deeply concerned, said.

"Only God has the answer to that." Lionel clasped his hands behind his back.

"God smiles upon those who are prepared. Remember the seven foolish and the seven wise virgins?" Tom counseled the men. "Not that any of you are virgins."

Everyone but Lionel laughed, the humor dispelling some of the tension.

"Gentlemen," Lionel moved toward the door to call together his men, including the four Indians, faithful to him. "I'll take Tanx to his father and discover what I can. I counsel you not to jump to conclusions and not to provoke those Indians who have been loyal to us."

"Loyal to us or loyal to you?" Daniel nailed him.

"To us." Lionel clamped his mouth down hard.

"You wouldn't be pitting one tribe against another for favorable trading to yourself, now would you?" Daniel, worried sick, didn't much care if he upset Lionel's applecart.

"My business is my business, sir." Lionel's nostrils flared. "But I'll be damned if I'd start an Indian war."

That said, he motioned for his men to carry out the body.

"Damned indeed," Daniel said under his breath.

As the other men filed out toward the house Lionel put his hand on Tom's forearm. "May I speak to Pryor?"

"I've no objection but the lady herself might." Tom was terse.

Lionel found Cig outside the summer kitchen chopping wood. "Pryor."

She stopped. She knew he'd come to identify the remains so she wasn't surprised to see him. "Hello."

"I apologize. I was an ass. I'm lucky he didn't run me through although I've some skill with a blade." He couldn't conceal his pride.

"It's over. Maybe we all learned something."

"I want to marry you. I'll make it up to you. Please forgive me." Humility did not come naturally to this brawny fellow.

She held out her hand to him. "I do forgive you. I should never have shared my bed with you. I was in the wrong. I know I told you I didn't want to get married but . . . maybe it's difficult to hear that when a woman is kissing you."

"I can learn to control my temper."

"You can do anything you want to do. Let time do his work on both of us." She changed the subject. "Did you know the murdered Indian?"

"Yes. He was a friend. There's trouble between the tribes and within the tribes."

"So we are in danger."

"Much depends on their councils after I take Tanx's body back to his father. And worry won't make it any better. Let me worry about it." He kissed her hand. "My mother won't speak to me until we are reconciled."

"That might be a benefit." She smiled.

He smiled back. "Don't cast me out for one mistake."

"Lionel, we aren't the right two people, if you'll allow me an old expression, or a new expression. As I said, time will take care of our problems."

Margaret emerged from the back door of the house, saw them and started to go inside.

Lionel bowed to her. "I am heartily sorry that I offended you."

"I've forgotten it already." Margaret nodded toward him. What she didn't say was that she was as happy as she had ever been in her life. She thought she was pregnant.

36

Nell Gwyn shot past Cig and Margaret, a squealing mouse clamped in her jaws.

"Good job, Nell," Cig congratulated the cat.

In short order, Little Smudge and Highness followed just in case Nell had a gabby moment and her prey managed to escape.

"Has anyone figured out how to get rid of mice?" Margaret's knitting needles of polished bone clicked together.

"No. We have traps, poisons and even high-frequency—that means really high-pitched—sound devices to trouble their sensitive little ears but the answer is no. The only solution to mice is cats, owls, and blacksnakes. I prefer cats myself."

Margaret concentrated on the new scarf she was knitting. "So do I."

"Wonder how long Tom will be gone?"

"Once those men start talking—could be days. Weeks even if Daniel Boothrod and James Blair fill their sails with wind."

"Does it irritate you that women don't go to these special meetings, you know, of the Assembly or whatever else is going on?"

"Not a bit. Every man must state his opinion, rebut the other man's opinion, fluff his feathers, sit down, stand up again. Then every other man must state his opinion on the man's opinion who has just spoken. Around and around until the noise is dizzying and everyone forgets what he said in the first place. I've better things to do with my time."

Cig laughed. "Yeah, that hasn't changed either." She glanced out the window, darkness enveloping the house. "He'll surely stay in James-town."

"They all will, I assure you. It provides them an excellent opportu-nity to escape female supervision."

"My mother used to say, 'Men, you can't live with them and you can't live without them.' "

"Every woman's mother says that." Margaret held the portion of the scarf away from her to check the pattern.

"Do you feel that way about Tom?"

"Your brother is a good man, but there are times when I could crown him." She made a slapping motion with her hand. "He asks for my judgment on matters and then he discounts what I say. If I am proven right he gets cross with me and says, 'Why didn't you make me listen?' If I am proved wrong—not often"—she impishly smiled again—"then he crows about the vast degree of his mental powers and the shrunken state of my own." She dropped a ball of yarn. Highness grabbed it. "I can live without him very well during the days. The nights—" She shook her head.

Cig rose to stir the fire and drop on another slow-burning walnut log. "After a time you forget about that."

Margaret shook her head in disbelief. "You forget until a man comes along to make you remember. I have often wondered what it is that makes one man so appealing and another, oh!" She threw up her hands in mock fright, which made Cig laugh. "Take two strong, good-looking fellows and one will attract you more than the other. Perhaps Cupid really does loose his arrows."

"It helps sometimes to be short-sighted." Cig laughed.

"Ha." She felt a tug on her ball of yarn. Highness wanted to play. "Probably Tom will come home tomorrow, half-exhausted, and an-nounce the resolution of the meeting, which you and I could have re-solved in ten minutes. If the news were dismal he'd be here now so all is well."

"I hope so. I'm anxious to know what Lionel and William Byrd found out from the tribes they visited."

"You know what makes me laugh? Why would the Indians tell the truth to any white man, Lionel or William? For all their theories and posturing, men can't see the nose on their faces."

They worked in silence, Cig pricking her fingers with the needle. She was sewing a torn seam on her riding shirt.

"Didn't your mother teach you to sew? Elizabeth Deyhle had a beautiful hand."

"My mother, Amy was her name, dutifully tried. I hated it. All I wanted to do was ride horses."

"That hasn't changed."

"No, but in my time horses are a luxury. I don't think they are but many people think so. We don't need them for transportation anymore. We have vehicles that carry us about and we can move at speeds you wouldn't believe. So what happens? These machines belch noxious fumes, our air is so filthy, it makes your eyes sting and sometimes it's hard to breathe in the big cities. And worse, you speed to your destination so fast you don't appreciate what's in between. The journey has lost its meaning. There is no unfolding. You get where you're going, plunging immediately into business. The whole tone of social intercourse . . ." Cig thought a moment. "Here with you and your time, social events, even business, are an orchestra of music." She remembered that the symphony was not yet in vogue or she would have used the word. "For me, for my time, it's one note. Lots of one notes. Does that make sense?"

"Oh, I understand perfectly. I can't imagine it though."

"All the juice has been squeezed from community life. Nothing's left but the rind."

"Did you know this before you came here?"

"Actually, I did, but I didn't know what it would be like to live differently. People aren't stupid, Margaret, but there are so many of us, our contacts are impersonal and even disembodied like the telephone I once told you about. We don't know what to do. We don't know how to come back together. The bonds that you take for granted are as foreign to me as if a Chinaman dropped into your midst. We're helpless."

"No one is ever helpless. Pray to God."

"God is bored with us. I can't blame Him."

"It can't be that desolate."

"But it is, and it's a seductive desolation because in place of cherished people, of common threads, of a tapestry woven by all, we get things, lots and lots of things. Cars and televisions and I know you don't know what those things are, so how about clothing, that you can imagine, and jewelry and toys. We're choking in things. We're drying up from the inside out."

"That's true in any time. Don't you think Mrs. Boothrod is choking on things? She knows no real love."

"Yes." Cig pondered that, then slowly responded. "But if she wanted to be part of this, this circle, she could. She could find warmth and love by stepping outside her door. In my time, millions of people don't even know their neighbors."

"I don't believe it!" Shocked, Margaret stopped her knitting. "You can't live without your neighbor."

"Tell me about it."

"I *am* telling you about it."

"Sorry, Margaret, it's an expression. I wish I could take you home, but I was thinking again that I wish I could bring my children here. I'd almost rather bring them here than go back. Funny. I"—her eyes misted over—"I would like them to feel this—" She put her hands up in mute expression.

"Love." Margaret put down the scarf and put her arm around Cig's shoulders. "Pryor, love is where you find it. That's been said long before I was born but it can't be that barren in your time. You feel barren. You've been wounded by your sister and your husband. If that had happened to me I would no doubt feel as you do but truly, sister, there is always love."

"I know," came the wobbly reply. "But individual love can't replace community love. I wish I could find a better way of putting it. Margaret, in my time very few people love you or even like you for yourself. They like you for what you can do for them. No one has any time to waste. Waste. The word itself tells you how we feel about passing the time with someone else."

"I would guess that if you talk to your friends they will talk to their friends. Mighty oaks from little acorns grow."

"Perhaps. More than perhaps. You're right. If people want things to change for the better then they do." She jabbed her finger. "I hate this."

"I'll do it."

"Margaret, I've got to learn sometimes." She sucked her finger. "You've been chirping like a bluebird these last few days. What's up?"

"Another expression—well, I haven't told Tom because I won't be sure until next month but," she paused, thrilled, "I think I'm with child."

"Hurrah!" Cig threw the shirt on the floor and hugged her.

"I'm hoping someday to hug you for the same reason."

"Well—you never know. Anything is possible."

"And soon." Margaret laughed, her eyes twinkling. "We will prevail upon Fitz to stay the night after the foxhunt. It will save the road to Jamestown. That man will wear it out from travel."

"You know, Margaret, if I ever get back to my home I'm going to miss you." Cig felt her chest tighten.

37

A hard frost, silvery in the pale dawn, cloaked the earth. Everyone at Buckingham had risen before dawn to prepare for the day's hunt. The ladies from surrounding plantations would be bringing food. Margaret had been cooking an enormous pot of ham and bean soup for two days. Cold meats, cheeses, and sweetcakes were wrapped in moist towels and placed in the summer kitchen. After the chase Margaret and Marie would quickly lay out the food for their famished guests. Much as Margaret wanted to participate she needed to supervise the hunt breakfast.

People arrived with the sun, some coming across the river on John MacKinder's ferry. Horses would be brought for them by friends on the north side of the James River.

Cig wore her hunting clothes, including the white silk stock tie that she'd borrowed from Fitz, and she'd hung the Indian knife in a leather sheath on her belt.

"It's going to be a good hunting day, Tom," she greeted him.

"Aye." He smiled.

The hunt was to serve two purposes. The first was to bring people back together to demonstrate that the Deyhles, the deVries, and Devlin Fitzroy had made their peace. The second purpose was to celebrate continued good fortune. Blackpaws had commanded his people to live in peace with the whites. His younger son was banished from the tribe.

William Byrd returned to report that the tribes south of the James

River intended to keep their promises. As for hotheads, it seemed that was a function of youth.

Dr. Steinhauser traveled to Jamestown to remove Fitz's stitches. Fitz was eager to hunt.

When he rode into the Buckingham quad with his black and tans, Cig couldn't restrain herself. She ran out of the barn to greet him.

He dismounted and kissed her.

"I am the luckiest man in Virginia. A beautiful lady, a fine horse, and a good pack of hounds."

"In that order?" She hugged him.

"In that order."

"I'll be with you in a minute." She started for the barn.

"I hope you are with me for my entire life." He smiled but his voice was serious.

She stepped back to him. "Patrick Fitzroy, just try to get rid of me." Then she kissed him again and ran to the barn while he remounted, wincing as he braced off his left leg.

Cig joined the crowd of people assembling.

"Lionel and Tom, ride with me," she called, as Lionel had just arrived with his mother.

The two men rode up to her. Kate deVries stayed back with Margaret to help her set the table, warm the soups and prepare the breakfast.

The black and tan hounds gathered around Fitz, looking for a command, their sweet brown eyes eager. He winked at Cig, blew his horn and moved off. She rode in his pocket with Tom and Lionel stayed just behind in hers.

The hounds thrashed about for fifteen minutes and then a huge hound lifted his head, gave a deep cry, and then, nose down, dashed after the scent. The others honored his cry.

The hounds veered sharply right into the woods at the curve of the river. Cig, without thinking, leaped over a fallen tree trunk to plunge into the woods. Some of the riders fell off at the sharp turn. Those still seated picked their way around the fallen tree. The hounds stopped in the woods, cast themselves and then picked up the scent. They swarmed past Cig then moved west again.

The hounds ran at a blazing pace while the field still wended its way through the woods and muck from the melting snows.

Once out of the woods on the other side, Cig halted to listen for the hounds.

"If the hounds doubled-back we should have seen our fox," she half mumbled.

"Unless he climbed a tree," Tom added.

"Or unless there's more than one fox," Lionel said.

"There is always that." Cig smiled at him.

"Damned strange." Tom noticed a fog developing on the river.

Cig, thinking nothing of it, airily replied, "Means the water temperature is higher than the air temperature."

The thick mist moved in quickly as they watched it curl around their horses' legs.

"Can't hunt in this," Daniel complained.

"True enough but a bad day hunting is still better than a good day at work." Cig tried to raise their spirits as everyone had looked forward to the day's sport.

In the distance she heard the hounds. "Tom, why don't you take everyone back and I'll fetch the Huntsman."

"He's coming closer," Tom said.

"He is, but you turn back and I'll be hard on your heels with the pack. I don't want people sitting in this fog. You can take a nasty chill."

Tom stubbornly stayed put.

"Tom."

"What if they find again?" He wanted to hunt.

"We'll kill ourselves stepping into a hole or a low tree branch. We can't take people into this." She appealed to Lionel. "Lionel, please take them back. I'll be right behind you. I would consider it a very great favor."

He couldn't refuse that. He nodded. "As you wish." Then he called to the field, "Follow me."

People, disappointed, turned back toward Buckingham.

Cig rode toward the sound of the horn and the hounds.

"Tom, you can be pigheaded."

"Runs in the family."

"Fitz!" No answer, so she rode forward. A hound streaked by her, then another. "Fitz!"

"Yes," he called back. Within seconds he was by her side. "Damned filthy fog."

"Could have been worse. Could have been a blank day."

The remaining hounds trotted out on the road.

That quickly, those hounds found scent, surging forward. Fitz blew the return call but they didn't obey, which infuriated him.

A bark, higher pitched than a hound's, captured Cig's attention. In the road in front of her sat Fattail. He had eluded the hounds, doubled-back, and insouciant as ever, called out his challenge.

"Fattail!" She cheered at the sight of him.

"He's huge," Fitz said admiringly.

"I've been chasing this fellow for years."

"I've seen him watching me in the fields," Tom said.

"Let's chase him some more, the fog be damned." Fitz blew on his horn. A few hounds could be heard returning but the others were either out of range or practicing selective hearing.

The merry fox stayed just ahead of the three humans so they could see him in the fog.

"Bold."

"Bold as brass." Cig laughed, thrilled to see the familiar beautiful face. She charged in front of Fitz, who didn't mind.

The sound of the few obedient hounds drew closer. Fattail picked up from a trot to a moderate run. Fitz began to canter. The fog thickened, swirling around him. Cig heard a strange twang, a gurgle following. She turned and looked behind but could see nothing.

A rustle in the forest along the river and an odd bird call like a woodpecker sounded innocent enough.

Fattail barked again—*Move it*. There was urgency in his voice.

Both Cig and Fitz heard hoofbeats behind them. Helen, riderless, shot past them.

"Damn, he must have fallen off. I'd better go back."

Fitz turned to see if he could find Tom. His face whitened. He shouted to Cig, "Run, run, as fast as you can."

She hestitated a moment. "What about Tom?"

"RUN!"

She spurred Throttle, charging into the silver shroud. She heard Fitz immediately behind her then heard him turn his horse. A loud shout followed, a battle cry.

She wanted to turn back but she feared his fury as much as she feared whoever was chasing them. She looked to Fattail who was running flat-out, his ears back against his head. Throttle's nostrils were wide open. He reached long with his forelegs straining for ground.

She heard another shout, a cry of pain.

She clutched for breath. Throttle shot forward like a jet. The hoof-beats came closer. She heard a whizzing sound and a *thunk*. She knew better than to look back. She was running for her life.

She put her hands far up on Throttle's outstretched neck, lying low on the saddle as another whizzing sound sped by her ears. She sat up slightly and felt a sharp pain slide across her back. She doubled down, putting her head alongside Throttle's neck, crouching as low in the saddle as she could.

Her throat was on fire. Tears filled her eyes from the wind and from stark terror. Another *thunk,* louder, made her wince. Fattail stayed immediately in front of her, flying.

She rode hard, veering right off the river road, following Fattail as he clambered up an embankment, then they were in the woods. She saw a post-and-rail fence before her. Throttle gathered himself, soaring over the fence, Fattail shooting under it.

She burst into the meadow as the mist lifted. There was her hunt field, patiently awaiting her, Grace in charge. Fighting back her sobs, she charged up to them as Hunter and Laura, seeing her distress, pulled away from the group to meet her.

Cig wanted to say something. She wanted to say that she loved them, that Fitz was right behind her. She pulled up, sliding off the saddle in exhaustion. She took a few steps and then fell facedown in the grass.

Grace turned from her conversation with Binky and saw her. "Good God!"

Dr. Bill Dominquez dismounted and ran over to Cig as Hunter and Laura were already bending over their mother. He knelt down and noticed a deep slash across the back of her jacket. Blood was seeping through.

"Oh, Mom!" Laura threw herself on her mother as Grace, also now on the ground, ran flat-out to help. The entire hunt field was hurrying to her.

Bill took her pulse as Hunter, ashen, tears splashing down his cheeks, asked, "Will she be okay?"

Fattail sat down, observed, then melted back into the October woods.

PART III

38

∞

What's worse, the antiseptic white of a hospital or the disinfectant odor? Cig focused on the harvest gold floral pattern of the drapes. The only color worse than institutional harvest gold was avocado.

Her back stung. A single IV line ran into her arm but no tube up her nose and as far as she could tell she was not sedated. A shuffle outside her room alerted her to a possible intrusion but whoever it was passed the room.

She sat up, slid her feet out from the covers and padded to the window. She parted the offending curtains and discovered it was blackest night with a thick frost. Satisfied, she walked back to bed. She was in her century. She wasn't sure how or what had happened but she determined to keep her mouth shut.

Wincing as she lay down on the bed, she curled over on her side and tried to sleep but the sound of Fitz's voice rang in her ears. Each time she closed her eyes she heard him bellow "RUN" and trembled to think of what had become of him. She prayed that he had galloped through time with her and she'd see him in the morning.

Not for a minute did she believe her sojourn with Tom and Margaret was a dream. It was too vivid. She flicked on a light above her bed then flicked it off for the sheer excitement of it. Tiny iridescent dots danced before her eyes. No wonder people at the end of the twentieth century were hateful. Their eyes hurt from the harsh light and they didn't even know it.

The sound of a telephone ringing down at the reception room, such a familiar sound yet now so alien, irritated her even more than the electric light.

Her right shoulder ached so she rolled on her stomach to avoid pressing her back against the bed. That didn't feel much better. She was restless and out of sorts.

The split second she had laid eyes on Hunter and Laura carried her through the raw misery gnawing at her entrails. She knew Fitz was dead despite her prayers. Not just because it was 1995 and he'd been dead for almost three hundred years. The cry of pain she'd heard behind her in the fog was the last sound he made.

"So this was the trade-off of the gods? In exchange for seeing my children again they get the man I love." A flash of bitterness opened her eyes again.

To never see Fitz's strong sensuous mouth, hear his lilting Irish voice—the visceral reality of him overwhelmed her. Gone, as were Margaret's kindness and Tom's ready laugh. Lionel DeVries's imposing presence had vanished before the Revolutionary War. Unless Abraham Boothrod lived to an advanced old age that sweet young man had aged and died before the colonies became independent as well. Time could be measured in nanoseconds, yet this was an exercise in futility for Chronos always won.

We will die. Time remains eternal.

Hot tears splashed on her pillow. She could hear the lap of the James on the riverbank and John MacKinder's deep baritone as he sang out, pushing into the current.

The door opened a crack. She wiped her eyes on the pillow lifting her head. As she was looking behind her, over her shoulder, she couldn't really see so she sat up.

"You're awake."

"Yes. How long have you been here?"

"I rode in the ambulance with you." Grace walked over and pulled up the small, uncomfortable chair by the night stand. She sat down and snapped on the bedside lamp. "You were out cold for over an hour. We thought you had a concussion but you didn't. That cut on your back is nasty. I'd sure as hell like to find whoever pulled that stunt." Her voice vibrated.

"We'll never find them," Cig matter-of-factly stated.

"What makes you say that?" Grace reached for Cig's hand. Cig pulled it away.

"Whoever cut me up has disappeared in the fog."

"That was weird wasn't it, that fog?" Grace was troubled by Cig's withdrawal.

"It's funny though. Sometimes you need the fog to see clearly. We trust our eyes too much and our instincts too little."

"Well, I'm not ready for Philosophy 101 at four in the morning, but I am glad you're all right. Bill Dominquez says you can go home Monday. The doctor on duty down in the E.R. said it looks like you were shot with some kind of arrow."

"Stone head?"

Grace's eyes widened. "How did you know?"

"A guess."

"Well, that's what Dr. Sonneshine said—a steel-tipped arrow would have made a more uniform trench. Sorry—" She wished she hadn't used that word *trench*.

"It's all right."

"Bet it hurts like hell."

"Starting to." Cig asked, "How are Hunter and Laura?"

"Fine now that they know you're okay. They drove the rig home, along with Harleyetta and Roberta, and took care of the horses, so don't worry about that. Then the kids brought some clothes for you. They stayed until eleven when I made them go home. Bill Dominquez and Dr. Sonneshine assured them that you were none the worse for wear, you just needed to sleep and so did they. After a ceremonial tussle they finally left."

"Thanks." Cig lapsed back on her pillow, a mistake. She winced then sat up again and plumped the pillow behind the small of her back.

"Here, let me help." Grace took the other pillow and put it under

Cig's knees. "Always makes me feel better. Can't do anything about your back but I can make you more comfortable in other places.

"Will came by while you were asleep. He said he'd drop by out at the farm later in the week."

"That was good of him."

"It was," Grace agreed.

Cig studied the perfect face before her, a slant of bright light across the porcelain skin, a flash of those big blue eyes. She had forgiven her at Margaret's bidding. But back here she would have to forgive her all over again. It was one thing to recall betrayal. Quite another to have the betrayer in your face. "Grace, do you love me?"

"Cig—of course I love you. You're my sister."

"Lots of sisters hate each other."

"I do love you. I'd love you even if you weren't my sister."

Cig turned the light a bit more toward Grace. "Did you think Blackie and I were well suited?"

"Now how many times over the years have we talked about that?" A hint of impatience crept into the modulated voice. "No. You two weren't the right two people. Maybe he wasn't the right person. I don't know."

Cig switched the subject.

"I'd like to pick up the Deyhle papers, the ones you have, on my way home."

"You can borrow whatever you want." Grace wondered about Cig's mental state. She had never been interested in such things before, and it was an abrupt request for a woman sitting up in a hospital bed.

"I'm acting weird? You're looking at me as if I'm weird."

"Someone near killed you. That would make me a little weird myself."

"Do me a favor." Cig felt exhausted. "Go home and gather up the Deyhle papers. I'll stop by and pick them up. And if I'm strange or spacey—don't worry about it."

Worried, Grace said, "All right."

Cig fell asleep. Grace put her hand on her sister's forehead. She felt feverish. Grace checked her watch then reported to the nurse on duty that she thought Cig's temperature was too high. The nurse came in, felt her forehead and said not to worry. She didn't think it could be more than a degree above normal. Let her sleep.

Harleyetta came to work at seven A.M., popped her head in the room and saw Grace, fully clothed, stretched out in the bed next to Cig. She threw a blanket over Grace then quietly shut the door as she left the room.

39

"Mom, are you sure you're okay?" Hunter anxiously asked as he kept his eyes on the road. The old Toyota truck rattled and bumped. He'd cut school to pick his mother up at the hospital, the only time she ever countenanced such behavior. He made Laura go to school though, and she vowed never to forgive or forget. Hunter figured she would forgive him fast enough if he double-dated with her and Parry Tetrick.

"A little shakey, honey." She stared out the window, trying to get some perspective.

"Does your back hurt?"

"Stings."

"Mom, I'll find out who did this. I'll kill the bastard." His knuckles were white on the steering wheel.

"Revenge is a waste of time. You won't find them. Sometimes people literally get away with murder. What's important is that I'm back. I mean I'm here, I'm healthy, and I'd just as soon forget the entire incident."

"I don't know if I could," he said honestly.

"You'll be amazed at what you can do in this life." She turned and smiled at him and thought she'd never seen a young man more beautiful than her son. "And I'm here to see you do it."

He swiveled to catch her eye for a second then looked back to the road. "Mom, are you keeping something from me? I mean are you sick or something?"

"Just at heart. I'm as healthy as Full Throttle."

"What do you mean at heart? Dad?"

Her hand fluttered then returned to the Jesus strap over the passenger window. They always called it the Jesus strap because you usually said "Jesus" if you had to use it to hang on. "Yes and no. I think I'm having my midlife crisis. It's like being an adolescent in reverse."

"Buy a Porsche like Uncle Will."

"If I had Uncle Will's money I just might." She inhaled. "If I'm a little out there these next few days or even weeks, cut me some slack, huh?"

"Yeah." He pulled into Grace's perfectly manicured driveway, stopping in front of the dark green door with a fan window above it and glass side panels as well. "You stay here, Mom, I'll go in and get the papers."

"Those old bound books are heavy as horseshoes. I'll help."

"No, Mom. You aren't lifting anything. I'll only be a minute." He slid out, shutting the door behind him, then asked through the window, "Think Aunt Grace will be awake?"

"Tiptoe in, just in case."

Hunter opened the front door. Grace had stacked the Deyhle papers in bankers' boxes each marked with the dates. He carried four boxes, stacking two on the floor of the little truck. Cig had to put her feet up on them. One box sat between them and she held one on her lap.

"You doing research?"

"I need to know where I've been, or we've been, before I know where I'm going. Make sense?"

"Kinda."

"Where'd you get that cool knife?" Hunter noticed the Indian knife in the small pile of Cig's riding gear. "And I don't remember a silk stock tie."

"Long story. I'll save it for a rainy day."

When Hunter drove up to the house and Woodrow and Peachpaws scampered out, Cig threw open the door, hopped out juggling the box, putting it back on the seat, and scooped up the rotund kitty, hugging the dog as she knelt down. "Woodrow, oh, Woodrow, you don't know how happy I am to see you."

Hunter laughed. "Mom, you'd think you'd been gone for years."

"Feels like it," she said simply, hugging the violently purring animal. She thought of Smudge, Nell Gwyn, and Highness, Margaret's cats. She thought of Margaret with a sadness so profound she thought she would perish from the pain. Margaret was dust.

She walked into the kitchen followed by her brood. Hunter toted in the bankers' boxes. A pink stack of phone messages festered on her hole-in-the-wall desk. Papers spilled out of the fax machine. Hunter placed the books on the table and picked up the fax papers.

Cig threw them back on the floor to her son's surprise. "I doubt there's one damn thing of significance."

"Guess not." He opened the refrigerator, taking out a Coke.

"Oh God." She leaped for the refrigerator grabbing a cold can. "You don't know how badly I've wanted one of these."

"No Coke in the hospital?"

"Pepsi." It was a white lie but how do you tell your son you've been on a jaunt of nearly three hundred years?

"I'm going to the stable."

"I'll come with you. I can pick stalls. I'm not helpless."

"No, no, you rest. You had a shock, Mom. It won't kill you to take it easy for one day."

"I'm not an invalid."

"Only mentally," he teased.

"All right, smartass." She sat down in the kitchen chair, marveling at how familiar yet miraculous the place seemed. Electric lights, a big oil-burning furnace to keep every room, well, almost every room, cozy. A refrigerator and a gas stove, the flame pulsating like a blue daisy when she got up to turn it on for the pleasure of seeing it.

She glanced out the window. Hunter headed for the barn. His shoulders had doubled in width, it seemed. His step was light and quick, energy dancing off his young body. Tears filled her eyes as she gave thanks for her son and daughter.

She returned her attention to the blue flame, filling the whistling teapot from the tap and putting it on the stove.

"It's magic," she said out loud.

Woodrow circled the table, changed direction for a moment, and then settled down on the table for a nap.

"Woodrow, is there such a creature as a twentieth-century cat or are cats eternal in a way I'm not?"

He blinked his deep green eyes as if to say, "Only a human would ask such a question."

"Think about it, Woodrow. Your ancestors, whom I met, had to worry about horses and cattle just as you do but they didn't have to hurry out of the way of trucks and cars. They certainly didn't watch television, which you do, and I've been meaning to talk to you about your assaulting the screen during football games. Most unseemly." Cig laughed and then suddenly grew somber. "Woodrow, I'm afraid my mind is slipping like a faulty jack under a car."

She joined him at the table to drink her tea. Returning here was easier than being cast backward into 1699 but she supposed it would naturally be easier to return to one's own time. If Fitz, Tom, and Margaret could join her they'd have a hell of an adjustment.

Fitz. She opened the bankers' boxes. She grabbed a red morrocabound book. 1800–1860. That was yesterday. With trembling hands she opened each volume to check the dates. She finally found the right one, which had been rebound at least once. The handwritten note in the cover, her great-grandmother's handwriting, said that the deeds and letters had been bound to preserve them.

The bulk of the letters were from Ruppert Deyhle to his mother. A thirty-year-old man in the Continental Army, he described Cornwallis's depradations from North Carolina to Virginia.

A bill of lading for one desk of the latest fashion, 1711, to Margaret deVries jolted her.

One other letter, with bits of the old wax seal still clinging to the envelope, was from Charles Deyhle to Ernest Shackelford, another lawyer, describing the disposition of his estate in the event of his death. Dated July 17, 1695, it bequeathed four thousand acres and all his per-

sonal effects to his wife for the duration of her life. Upon Elizabeth's
death or in the event that she predeceased him, the property would pass
to the twins, Thomas and Pryor, born 1671.

In desperation she lifted out the enormous family Bible, turning to
the birth and death entries written in a variety of strong cursive hands.
She scanned to find the names:

Thomas Deyhle, born February 6, 1671,
married Margaret Woodson May 12, 1697,
murdered by Monacans December 30, 1699.
One son, Thomas Deyhle II, born to Margaret
Deyhle deVries, September 2, 1700.

She found herself whispering thanks to God that Margaret's child by Tom
survived.

Pryor Deyhle, born February 6, 1671,
disappeared December 30, 1699.
Believed murdered by Indians. No issue.

Thomas Deyhle II, born September 2, 1700.
Died March 29, 1782.

Margaret Woodson Deyhle, born November 11,
1674. Widowed. Married Lionel deVries May
29, 1701. Died in childbirth April 12, 1715.

Cig gasped. "He got what he wanted! Oh Margaret, were you happy
with him?"

She studied the handwriting again. The entries for Tom's and Pryor's
deaths, and Tom II's birth were in Margaret's hand. Eight subsequent
births, some of the babies dying in infancy, were also in Margaret's hand.
Tom II's death date was written in a different hand.

"Poor Margaret, dead at forty."

Cig wiped her eyes and got up for a tissue, she was crying so hard.

She made another cup of tea to settle herself then sat down to read more. Lionel was shot in front of the House of Burgesses in 1717, so he survived Margaret by only two years. Thomas Deyhle II married Isabeau Venable. His first daughter was named Pryor; the second, Sophia, in honor of his wife's mother; and the son born much later was Ruppert.

Stuck inside the Bible at various favorite passages were lists filled with tobacco tonnages and prices . . . and peanut prices.

A folded piece of parchment wedged in First Corinthians read, "Today, April 12, 1715, our mother, Margaret Woodson Deyhle deVries passed from this earthly realm to another, better one. She caused no harm, and did a great deal of good. Industry, prudence, and kindness were her natural virtues. In her final moments her mind took flight and she imagined she was with her first beloved husband, my father, and his sister. This fancy gave her great happiness."

Signed this day by Thomas Deyhle II.

Cig put her head on her crossed arms and cried until she felt nauseated.

The back door swung open and Laura, home from school, surprised her mother. She raced over and put her arms around Cig. "Are you okay? Can I do anything?"

Cig lifted her head and patted Laura's hands. "Just love me and know that I love you."

40

A warm wind swept up from the Gulf, bathing the reds, oranges, yellows, and deep russets in a magnifying haze. Full Throttle, ears forward, trotted down the winding dirt road to the back acres. Cig posted without thinking about it.

"Are you sure you should be riding?" Roberta asked, the mascara on her eyes caked up. "You just got out of the hospital yesterday." Much as Roberta wanted her lesson and much as she needed it, she worried about Cig, who was unusually distant and preoccupied.

"Can you think of anything better to do than to ride on a day like this?"

"One or two."

"Ah, Roberta, the soul of romance."

"You don't know if that's what I was thinking"—Roberta loosened her reins when she observed Cig's gaze move in that direction—"but I wouldn't mind a little hot romance."

"Speak to my sister, she's the expert."

Roberta frowned. "When you're that pretty it's easy."

Cig twisted in the saddle. "You know something, Roberta, maybe it doesn't have anything to do with pretty. Maybe some women send off a scent and men pick it up."

"Maybe." Roberta wasn't buying it.

"You think it's all looks?"

"A lot of it. Men don't care about substance or intellect. It's an animal thing with them," said the lady who had a lot of substance but little else.

"It's an animal thing with us, too."

They trotted over to three big tree trunks lashed together to make a jump. Cig made Roberta go first.

"Talk to him, Roberta, he's got a mind, you know."

"Good boy, slow, slow." Roberta spoke to Reebok who flicked his ears back then carefully snapped his front legs up over the jump like the good boy he was.

"See. Now pat him on the neck. He deserves it. Wish I had twenty more like Reebok in the hunt field."

"It's good of you to ride with me today," Roberta said. "Are you sure you're up to it?"

"I needed to get out and he needs light exercise. He'd been run so damn hard that he was tucked up when I rejoined you all."

"Cig, what did happen out there?"

"I don't know—guess I never will."

Suddenly animated, the normally timid Roberta rejoined, "They say that a near-death experience crystallizes your direction and that people change after something like that."

"I don't know if I had a near-death experience, more like near-life."

"Billy Dominquez said that if the arrow had pierced you from the side instead of across your back it might well have hit your heart. Whoever shot at you was behind you but off to the side. I just can't imagine someone doing something like that. This is a sick society."

"Violence is part of life."

"When you're primitive. This is 1995. There's no reason for anyone to shoot anyone else. No reason."

"I suppose as long as A wants what B has, and B doesn't want to give it up or negotiate, there is reason enough."

"Whoever loosed that arrow at you had to be doing it purely for the thrill. They couldn't get anything by killing you."

Cig wanted to argue, to say the times had been different then. The struggle for sovereignty over America was just beginning in earnest. "You know what, I'm not sure I even care. I'm just glad to be here."

"You're a better woman than I'd be under the circumstances."

Cig shrugged, turned Throttle, and they cantered back to the barn.

"Mom, Harleyetta called," Laura told her as Cig and Roberta walked their horses into the clean center aisle.

"Give her the fixture time?"

"No, she said she wants to catch up with you. She said to call on the car phone," Laura said.

"Catch up with me? She saw me day before yesterday."

"Binky's on the warpath again, most likely," Roberta said, leading Reebok into the wash stall, not realizing the true meaning of the word *warpath*. Cig now knew what it meant.

"Sometimes I think Binky West is living proof that the Indian fucked the buffalo." Cig's hand flew to her mouth. "Sorry. I wasn't thinking."

"You should hear what Hunter calls him." Laura giggled at her mother's uncharacteristic blast.

"What's that?" Roberta called out from the wash stall.

"Antimatter," Laura replied.

"That's good. That's why your brother will be a star at William and Mary." Cig smiled.

Laura brushed down Throttle as Cig picked up the phone in the tackroom and dialed Harleyetta.

"Hi, Harley. Cig."

"Cig, how are you feeling?"

"Fine, thank you. Ready to hunt. How about you?"

"Always. Could I come by in a little bit?"

"Sure."

"Okay. See you later."

The phone clicked.

Cig filled the water buckets in each stall and then walked back up to the house. A contract came through on the fax machine, which was a bright sign. Although the sale was small, any commission was better than no commission. A *beep, beep* alerted her to the fact that another sheet of paper was coming through the machine. She glared as it slowly squeezed through the aperture like a white tongue. She yanked it out.

Cig—

    Staff meeting Tuesday. Don't forget you're in charge of breakfast. Hope you're feeling okay.

                                                  Max

"Goddamned fax. Goddamned Max." She crumpled the paper and threw it on the floor, which delighted Woodrow who skidded to attack it.

As the cat batted the paper around the kitchen, Harley clumped in through the mud room door.

"Cig."

"Keep walking. I'm in the kitchen."

The door flung open and Harleyetta, her eyebrows well drawn today, wide bronze arches, walked through it, her flats squeaking on the floor. "I'm so glad to see you starting to look like yourself again."

"Thank you. Coffee, tea, Coke, spirits?"

"Tea. I'm on the wagon."

As Cig fixed a pot of tea Harleyetta plopped at the table. "I am. Really. I know you don't believe me. Nobody does. But I am. I'm bloated. I say things I shouldn't say when I'm drinking. I fight with Binky, that worthless bucket of guts. I don't like me much. So I'm signing off." She made a cutting motion with her left hand and her bangle bracelets clanged.

"Good for you. It's a hard thing to do but you've taken the first step." Cig handed her the tea, put out a tin of shortbread and joined her.

"I'm here to apologize."

"AA?"

"Yes. I'm doing the twelve-step program and I'm here to make amends."

"Harley, you haven't done a thing to me or mine except sometimes you can't hold Gypsy in the hunt field."

"Maybe if I'm sober in the hunt field I'll be a better rider."

"Or worse." Cig jabbed at her with her spoon.

"That, too." Harleyetta grimaced. She was working up to something. "Cig, I want to apologize for blabbing to you about Blackie's condition when he came to the E.R. I had no right to do that and I'm sorry. Even though you knew about his carrying on, I had no right to intrude on something so private. I apologize for that. I apologize for sometimes not knowing my place."

Cig put her cup back in the saucer. "You didn't do anything wrong. Blackie wasn't famous for fidelity."

"You didn't need the details and I know that you knew but still."

"You want to hear something funny? I didn't know."

"Oh, God." Harley's face blanched. "What a stupid idiot I am! I just assumed—I mean, we all assumed. Oh, I could die."

Cig reached over and touched Harleyetta's elbow, feeling the nubby texture of her beige sweater. "You didn't do anything wrong. I think we're blind when we want to be and I was. Not your fault."

"You must have felt *awful*."

"Yeah, I did. If we hadn't been in the woods with that skeleton, I think I could have taken a pistol and peppered Grace full of ratshot." Cig reached for a rectangular piece of shortbread. "But I've had some time to reflect on the situation. They didn't take anything away from me—not really."

"We all kind of knew why Grace did it."

"Why?"

"He was a sexy man, and maybe it was one way not to be your little sister. Know what I mean?"

"No," said Cig, now intensely curious.

"Well, maybe I shouldn't say this."

"Say it."

"Umm—Grace has always been in your shadow."

"My shadow?" Cig exploded. "Sorry, I didn't mean to raise my voice."

"You did everything better than Grace."

"Grace is one of the most beautiful women God ever put on this earth. I am not. What score has she got to settle?"

"Beauty doesn't mean anything until you're old enough to control men. When she was little? She tagged along after you in school. All the teachers knew she was your little sister. She wasn't smart and she wasn't as good at sports. Well, I just think those things fester."

"I never once thought of that. It—" She caught herself. She was going to say, "It doesn't make sense," but given a minute to think about it, it did. "I love Grace."

"I don't know if I would," Harleyetta flatly stated. "I think when you got engaged to Blackie, she was one jealous sophomore at William and Mary. She had a crush on him."

"She did have a couple of muley moments at my shower but that was so long ago. Anyway, she married better than I did."

"No, she didn't. She married up, not necessarily better. Hell, Binky West is First Family of Virginia and a disgusting drunk but there are plenty of women who would grab him."

"What are they teaching you at Alcoholics Anonymous?" An amused tone crept into Cig's voice.

The bangles flew into the air again. "Nothing. This is my own work. I never talk to you, I mean, really talk to you, I haven't really talked to anyone."

"Guilty." Cig held up her hand. "Lots of us are guilty of that. It's not only you."

"Thank you for saying that." She threw her shoulders back, gearing up for the big subject. "I'm leaving Binky."

"I can't say I'm sorry."

"I can't either. It's dragged on for too long and now that the booze is seeping out of my system, I have no hope of deadening my nerve endings. I make enough as a nurse to live. He took my Harley as hostage, too. Can you imagine that? He'll hire the most vicious divorce lawyer in Charlottesville, and they'll play starve-the-wife. It's all about money."

"Old game."

Harley shrugged. "I don't care. I'm going to get healthy. He can piss in the wind."

"Probably will."

Woodrow zoomed by with a piece of fax paper between his teeth. "That cat is having a fit."

"He loves paper and those little green plastic rings from the milk gallons. You know when you open the gallon you have to twist off the bottom of the cap. His favorite."

Harleyetta eyed Woodrow who was now on his back, the paper between his front paws. "Simple pleasures. Oh, I forgot to tell you. While you were out there in the mists the sheriff removed that skeleton. They laid it out and his left rib cage was smashed in—like with a sledge-hammer. Some of the bones had been cut clean through. Weird, huh?"

"Means he faced his enemy."

Harleyetta considered that. "Had guts."

"Yes, he did. His name was Patrick Devlin Fitzroy."

"It was?" Harley was incredulous. "How do you know that?"

"Just do." Cig shrugged. "He was ambushed by Indians and he turned to fight them so his friend could escape. I hope he died fast, God bless him. Before the Revolution. 1700, almost."

Harley cocked her head. "You sound as if you were there."

Cig pushed the shortbread tin toward her. "Maybe I was."

"Well, I *believe* in past lives. I just can't figure out what I did wrong. It had to be a whopper, like being Lucretia Borgia. Otherwise, how did I end up with Binky in this life?"

41

People glibly made comments about past lives. Harleyetta, no doubt sincere, didn't ease Cig's worries. Not that she would confide in Harleyetta. That woman had enough on her mind.

As she defrosted the hamburger in the microwave, the green digital numbers counting down, Cig wondered if everybody ultimately knew everybody. *Maybe we're all recycled.*

The mud room door banged shut.

"Hamburgers or meat loaf?" Laura walked over as Cig removed the ground beef.

"Meat loaf if you'll help."

"Deal." Laura retrieved bread crumbs from the pantry as her mother fetched two eggs from the refrigerator, plus milk, and tomato paste. "Got an A on my history test."

"Good."

"I like history."

"You're always good at what you like"—Cig paused—"and pretty good at what you don't. It's one of your better traits. Naturally, I take all the credit for it."

"Sure, Mom. Know what else?"

"What?"

"Seth Eisen made a crack about me going to the dance with Parry. Said I should wear a tuxedo and get a buzz cut. What an asshole."

"Did you inform him of your opinion?"

"Yeah." Laura kneaded the ingredients into the ground beef as Cig poured them in. "Why are people that way?"

"Meanness married to stupidity, I guess."

"It's not like Seth is poor or anything."

"Being poor doesn't make someone stupid," Cig replied.

"Seth thinks he's so cool. Wears his baseball cap backwards." Laura watched Cig turn on the oven to warm as she kept squeezing the meat through her fingers. "He's pissed because he can't have either one of us."

"I think I'll cut up some olives." Cig reached for a jar inside the fridge door. She would have loved to sidestep this but she couldn't figure out how to do it without upsetting Laura or herself. A major row would do her in; she was still queasy inside, trying to get her feet under her.

"Hunter says that guys like Seth say sexist stuff because they think it's a guy thing. Like pushing around Paul Vrana."

"Why is that a guy thing?"

" 'Cause everybody thinks that Paul is gay."

"Seth is small potatoes compared to Paul's father who is understudying Jesse Helms." Cig sighed. "School's a real hotbed of bullshit." Thought a minute. "Well, why not? It's a reflection of what we are."

Laura washed her hands and clicked on the small kitchen TV. She flipped the channels. The image of a scantily clad buxom woman working out was replaced by a scene of body parts around a car bomb in an African country, which Laura wiped off with another click; the happy face of a shiny Shetland sheepdog begging for treats appeared.

"Ah yes, the pet food and Tampax channel." Cig recognized the number. She wiped her hands on a dish towel, then unplugged the TV.

"Mom—?"

She picked up the TV, walked to the mud room door, and threw it in the trash.

"Mom!"

"I've *had* it. I'm working in my kitchen and I don't want to be assaulted by troubles I can't *fix* or advertisements for things I don't *need*. The hell with it. The hell with the whole damn twentieth century." She kicked the trash can.

Laura, frozen to the spot, watched.

"And furthermore, I don't give a shit if the microwave helps, if the stereo lets me hear Joan Sutherland. It's not worth the anxiety. I've been home two days and I'm bombarded by requests, phone calls, and piles of dead people in a city street on the other side of the world. It's insane."

Laura, quick-witted, shot back, "Then you'd like this meat loaf seared over an open flame?"

Cig stared at her daughter. She felt as though she were seeing her for the first time not as her daughter but as a woman. She finally grinned. "Point taken."

Laura slipped the Pyrex pan into the oven. She'd garnished the meat loaf with strips of bacon. When she completed her task she sat down at the table. "What's Harleyetta want?"

"Leaving the Bink."

"Oh." Laura understood that such events were extremely painful but as she had not yet experienced anything close to it she could only listen. "Crisis, I guess, huh, Mom?"

"Or a real bad comedy act."

"You feel okay?"

"My back hurts."

Laura folded her hands together. "You think you're still shaken up or something?"

Cig shrugged. "It's my midlife crisis."

"You going to get another TV?"

"*No,* I'm not. Number one, I don't have the money. Number two, I really *have* had it. I feel like my head is full of noises. I want quiet. Think about it, baby, an advertisement is a form of assault."

Laura wrinkled her nose. "Yeah—but."

"But what?"

"I want to know what's going on in the world."

"Read a newspaper."

"I do, but if I watch the news I know right this single second."

"No, you don't. You see a carefully selected image that is fed to you like pablum. You don't know the source of the trouble, both sides of the story or a possible solution. If it can't be said in a minute, it's cut. That's more damaging than not seeing the image."

Laura leaned forward. "But everyone is seeing that image, Mom. I *am* missing something."

Cig thought about what Laura said. That wasn't easy to refute. "Why is it so important?"

"Well—well." Laura, resembling her Aunt Grace, gesticulated. "I want to know!"

"Let me think about it. Still doesn't change the fact that we don't have the money."

"You threw away a perfectly good television." Laura's jaw hardened.

"Since I paid for the damn thing I can throw it away if I want to."

"If I said that you would accuse me of being childish."

"Laura, are you spoiling for a fight?"

"No—I just think you're kinda weird. Even if you paid for the TV that doesn't mean it doesn't belong to Hunter and me too."

Hunter came in, sized up the situation, and started for the library.

"Hunter, Mom threw out the TV!"

"Broke?"

"No, Hunter, I had a fit and fell in it and threw the damned thing in the trash. If I'm not seeing mayhem and blood on the news someone is trying to sell me Depends for when my bladder goes!"

"Cool." He left the kitchen.

42

Hunter and Laura listened as their mother paced downstairs, occasionally banging a door. Sometimes they could hear objects flung into the trash cans liberally scattered throughout the house.

Under the guise of studying, never Laura's strong point, she had retreated to her brother's bedroom to use his encyclopedias.

"What's she doing?" Laura tiptoed to the doorway and listened.

"Cleaning." Hunter twirled his pencil between his index finger and his second finger. He was beginning to worry about his mother but was not ready to let Laura in on it.

Laura strained and heard a faint "Shit," from down below. "Maybe she's having a breakdown."

"Why now?" His face turned toward the open doorway. "I mean, wouldn't it have made more sense to have one when Dad died?"

"I don't think breakdowns are about sense," Laura observed. "It's harder for her than for us. She worries about the money."

"I worry about the money." Hunter's eyes flashed.

"Yeah, yeah, but she sees the bills. They're piled up on the kitchen desk. We don't go through them. Aunt Grace said Mom's been juggling bills since Dad died and she hasn't had a single month where she's been able to pay all of them. She pays a portion and then pays more the next month . . . and I think she's getting behind, big time. That's what Aunt Grace says, anyway."

"Aunt Grace has so much money you'd think she'd give Mom some." Neither Hunter nor Laura knew that Grace had been helping out.

"Would you give me your money?"

"Would you give me yours?" he countered.

"Would depend on the situation and if you were *good* to me."

"I'm always good to you." He closed his math book. "Where's Aunt Grace? She's usually around and Mom needs her now."

"So, you *do* think something's wrong with Mom?" Laura triumphantly asked, having led him to the confession.

"Uh—she's stressed to the max."

"She's been stressed to the max before. This is different. She never threw out a TV before. She looks lost, kind of."

Hunter pushed aside his math papers. "Don't women go through a change—you know?"

"She's not old enough for that."

"Oh."

Laura sat cross-legged on Hunter's bed. He returned to his math assignment. She pulled off her socks.

"Hey, no toenails on my bed."

"I'm not going to cut them. I'm thinking about painting them."

"Gawd." He wrinkled his nose.

"Personal adornment is a mark of civilization. I read that in *National Geographic*." She rubbed her toes.

"Laura, get a grip. Painting your toenails flamingo pink isn't a mark of civilization. Means you've lost it. Next comes the pierced nose. Great when you've got a cold."

"Ha ha." Laura rose and walked to the doorway, heard Cig thumping up the stairs, and hopped back on the bed, quickly opening her American history book.

Cig stuck her head in the doorway. "I can't believe you two are cooperating on your homework and the stereo is silent. To what do I attribute this?"

"Midterms." Laura smiled at her mother.

"It's not time for them, is it?"

"Yep." Hunter punched numbers into his calculator.

"Hunter, if you don't learn to do that in your head you'll never really understand the problem."

He clicked off the calculator. "Mom, do you have any idea how long it would take to solve these trig problems if I didn't have this?"

"Yes, I took solid geometry and trig, too, remember. Got an A as it just so happens."

"You got an A in everything."

"Laura, did I tell you that?"

"No, Aunt Grace did. She said you were disgusting. And you missed being valedictorian of the class by a point."

"Just as well. I hate giving speeches." Cig sighed, remembering how devastated she was when that total creep, the nerd of all time, George Atwell Rivers, was declared valedictorian. The same George Atwell Rivers who took one acid trip too many at Dartmouth and was now a holistic healer in Aspen.

"What were you doing down there?" Hunter inquired, feigned neutrality on his features.

"Housecleaning." She saw her children glance at one another. "I was. I'm reorganizing."

"Does that mean we have to move furniture?"

"If I say so," Cig pointedly answered her daughter.

"Aunt Grace could help." Laura wanted to get out of an evening of lifting sofas and chairs. "She has a good eye."

"I am sick of hearing about Grace, goddammit!"

Laura's head snapped back a tiny bit and Hunter's pencil stopped over the yellow legal pad. Both children held their breath for a moment.

Then Hunter smoothly said, "Mom, you have a fight with Aunt Grace or something?"

"Something." Cig's face reddened, knowing that she needed to confront her sister yet dreading it. She felt like a coward.

"I think sisters fight more than sisters and brothers."

Laura interjected, "You and Aunt Grace, uh, well, maybe it's like competing for territory. Men and women don't compete for the same territory."

Cig stared at Laura, the history book artfully opened on her lap.

"Have you been watching those goddamned talk shows with their two-bit psychologizing? Pure unadulterated crap."

"Mom, you're saying *goddamn* a lot." Hunter laid his pencil neatly across the top of the yellow paper.

"Oh, I am, am I? Am I living with an incipient member of the Moral Majority?"

"No." He pressed his lips together.

"You're kinda emotional." Laura jumped in where angels feared to tread.

Leave it to your kids to tell you the truth. She sagged against the doorjamb. "Yeah, I guess I am. I don't know what's the matter with me but I feel like Pandora's box."

"That's okay—with us. But out there"—Hunter gestured toward the window—"I don't think people will, uh, cut you a break. Everybody depends on you to stay . . ." He made a smooth motion with his hand, a horizontal line, which meant "even."

Cig dumped herself on the end of the bed. "I'm definitely not myself except I'm more myself than I ever was."

"Huh?" Laura threw her mother a pillow to lean against.

"Don't you keep a lot inside? You walk around day after day and you don't say what you're really thinking or feeling, it's just, 'Hi, how are you?' and 'See you at Goodling's Farm at seven thirty next Saturday.' You know what I mean?" They nodded in unison and she continued. "But I'm thinking all the time. I just shut my trap. On the surface everything's okay. But nobody really knows who I am or what I think."

"Maybe they do," Hunter said somberly.

"Oh God, I'm transparent." Cig flopped on the pillow.

"Nah." He waved his hand. "But hey, everybody knows everybody. Habits, favorite colors, you don't have to say what you're feeling. Lots of times people do know."

"Yeah, but lots of times they don't." Laura pushed her pillow down at the end of the bed, and lay on her stomach next to her mother, both women propped up on their elbows.

"Is it so important that people know how you feel?"

"Or what you feel, Hunter?" Cig reached over and squeezed his knee. "We're skimming the surface, and that's okay until something really goes wrong. Then you don't know who your friends are."

"Find out, though." Hunter swung his chair around and rested his feet on the side of the bed. "Look at the people who helped us out after Dad died and the ones who didn't do bugjuice."

"We aren't their responsibility."

"Mom, Uncle Will isn't on food stamps." The right half of Laura's mouth lifted in scorn.

"No, but like I said, we aren't his responsibility."

Hunter didn't accept this. "We're a family, Uncle Will's part of it. He should pitch in."

Cig stiffened then forced herself to relax. "Grace helps me but Will doesn't know. So don't you dare tell. I probably shouldn't have even told you." Cig was sorely tempted to tell her children about what her sister had done. They might have understood, but what was to be gained by besmirching their father's memory and clouding their love for their aunt?—only sympathy for her, and she didn't need sympathy that badly. Maybe when they were older she'd tell them. No reason to spoil things for them right now. By the time they could handle it, she might well have forgotten. The thought amused her. Alzheimer's or radiant forgiveness?

"Hey, Mom, about this feeling thing . . . this mean you're going to, you know, emote all over the place?"

"I don't know. I'm going through a sea change."

"What's that mean?" He scratched his ear.

"I'm not sure except I'll be, uh, I'll be profoundly changed from the inside. Might not show on the outside."

"Throwing away the television shows on the outside."

"Laura, quit harping on the goddamned television."

"See, Mom, there you go again. Another goddamn," Laura chided.

Cig dropped her legs over the side of the bed and bounced up. "You're right. My conversational ability has hit the skids. I'm going to bed. I suggest you two do the same. Hey, before I forget it, we've got to start practicing for the Oak Ridge Fox Hunt Club's hunter pace."

"Piece of cake." Hunter snapped his fingers because it was anything but.

"Okay, lights out. Tomorrow will be a long day." Cig kissed them both on the cheek. She couldn't have known how long a day it would be.

Not taking her own advice, Cig sat in bed with the first family Bible. When she was lost in time she had wanted to come back here so badly that the early days were like water balloons filling with grief.

Now here, she missed Fitz, Margaret, and Tom almost as much as she had formerly missed her children.

She remembered when she and Margaret had recited the Twenty-third Psalm together. She drew comfort from that. She turned to the Psalms. When she reached the page for the Twenty-third a thin cut strip of parchment marked the place. It read:

1. Groundnuts
2. Land at the Falls
3. Drain swamps, pour oil on standing water
4. No Africans
5. Educate girls
6. Breed horses

Number six had been added later, the handwriting at an angle.

She sucked in her breath. It sure looked like her handwriting.

43

"My brother got ten thousand dollars an acre for his land on Garth Road and I'm not budging unless I get ten, too." Harmon Nestle stuck out his chin, not easy to do since it receded.

Cig smiled. "It's always nice to make a profit. The only real difference between your tract of land and your brother's is his lake." She wondered how many times she had pointed this out.

"Don't care."

"Well"—she forced the fatigue and disgust out of her voice because he'd received yet another very good offer on his raw land—"I'll take this contract back to the buyer and try to be creative."

"Not having anyone say my brother's smarter than I am." Harmon hit the nail on the head.

"No one's saying anything like that." Cig lied through her teeth.

He pointed his bony finger at her. "People think I'm stupid, that's why they offer me less."

"Harmon, Mr. and Mrs. Fincastle hail from Teaneck, New Jersey. They don't even know your brother and they think you own a nice piece of land out there on Route 810."

"Yankees got more money than this contract shows. You go back home and get me some." He slyly smiled.

"Yeah, well, Yankees taught me the value of money by keeping it all to themselves." She agreed with him, which elicited a chuckle from the bilious old man.

"My grandfather fought with your great-great-grandfather. He was just a boy at the end of the war, you know, PopPop Nestle. Said Reckless Deyhle was the bravest man he ever saw. Jumped right over a twelve-pound cannon once, and those Minnesota boys was just firing away. Kinda wish I'd been there."

She almost said, "Maybe you were." Instead she gathered up the documents. "You know, Harmon, you missed your calling when you didn't stay in the army. Daddy used to say that with your military bearing, you would scare the bejesus out of buck privates."

"Ha!" Harmon recalled his youth. "I 'member one time in Arnhem. . . . Oh, Cig, the Jerries was on the other side of that bridge and it was a pretty thing, real old, too, and they were so close I could see their features, real clear. We knew they was gonna blow the bridge the minute we set foot on it and I called out to this little wispy corporal from Tennessee. 'Get on up there in that house,' I said, 'and keep those buggers busy. I'm gonna go under that bridge and find the charge.' Well, that boy was a sharpshooter. He kept them hopping, a real square dance. Got the charge, too. I can still feel that cold water getting higher and higher and me trying to hang on to the belly of that old bridge. I was too busy to get scared." He put his hands behind his head.

"Reckless would have been happy with a soldier like you."

"You think?" His busy eyebrows curled upwards.

"I think." She stood up and he did, also.

As he walked her to the door, he glanced up at the ceiling. "Denby tears my ass with boredom. Know what I mean? I gotta get the same amount he did. Just once."

"Harmon, I'll do what I can."

Driving down the dusty lane she rolled up the windows of the truck and turned on the radio. The country music station boomed back at her.

"I'll write the reverse country song," she said out loud. "I'll make a goddamned fortune and be out of this mess. The lyrics will be: Got back my car. Got back my dog. Got back my house. Got back my wife." She laughed then pressed down on the pedal and felt the rumble underneath. Bad as the twentieth century might be, it sure was good to be hauling ass down a country road in a big dually truck.

She could see dust in the opposite direction. A stop sign at the Walnut Hill Baptist Church slowed her. She stopped as Binky West rolled to the sign on Harleyetta's confiscated orange motorcycle. She drove across the road and rolled down her window.

"Hey, Bink."

"Harleyetta been spilling her guts out to you?" he snarled.

"Said she was making some big changes."

"I'll cut her off without a cent!" He turned up the gas, but kept the motorcycle in neutral.

"Now, Binky, give this some time. You two might work something out."

In a falsetto voice he imitated his wife. " 'You drink too much. You don't pay enough attention to me but you pay too much attention to'— fill in the blank. 'You got to have some goal in life.' " He switched back to his voice. "I do have a goal in life. To be rid of that nagging bitch."

"Ah, come on Binky. You're wrought up. Don't be talking like that. She didn't say anything hateful."

"You women stick together." He glared at her because he wanted total agreement.

"It's not that. I think maybe time apart will help you both."

"She can drag her fat butt to Siberia and that still won't be far enough. We're not getting back together. Ever. And she's not getting one penny of my money. All she ever wanted anyway."

"That's not true." Cig's voice hardened.

"She sure spent enough of it."

"On what? She never blew your money on jewelry or clothing, and hell, she gets up and goes to work everyday and she doesn't have to do that. She could have just sat around the pool, know what I mean?"

He was so mad he revved his motor then shouted above it with his whiskey breath. "And I'm sucking off my trust fund! I know what you all say behind my back. Binky West couldn't get arrested. I'm good enough to pay my hunt club dues."

"Binky, you know, people say you're a real asshole but I don't listen to everything I hear. Now cut the crap, calm down and go home."

"Don't you tell me what to do. You couldn't keep your own man in line. Don't start with me."

"Adios, Motherfucker." Furious, she pulled the clutch back into drive and left him in a cloud at the stop sign. She didn't look back, but she heard him lay rubber as he tore out after her.

Binky roared up alongside the truck. He shook his fist at her then whizzed out in front of her. A sharp turn lay up ahead—a stone wall on the belly of the curve, a ditch on the other side.

Binky hit that curve at sixty miles an hour, the gravel spinning out from the hind tire. The bike swerved to the right. He turned hard left, causing the Harley to plunge into the ditch. The front wheel stuck in the ditch, the bike nosed straight up, and Binky flew like a trapeze artist. With a flop he landed in high grass and thistles.

Cig squealed to a stop, ripped open her door and vaulted the ditch. Binky, wobbling to his feet, fell down.

He got up again, saw the Master of the Hunt, and complained, "Damn mare refused the fence!"

The fact that he was drunk, loose as a goose, probably saved him. Cig put him in the truck and carried him to the hospital. She'd seen too much of that hospital.

The admitting physician found no broken bones but kept Binky overnight to sleep it off.

By the time Cig got home she'd calmed herself enough to walk into the tackroom and call the Fincastles. They were surprisingly accommodating, but then ten thousand an acre compared to the prices where they lived must have appeared a modest sum. They wanted to talk it over and they'd get back to her. She suggested that they meet Harmon's price but ask him to hold paper on a small second mortgage, the difference between the two prices.

She hung up the phone as Grace walked into the barn.

"Cig?"

"In the tackroom."

"Where is everybody?"

"The kids must have taken people out on a trail ride. I'm home an hour late because Binky West wrecked Harley's bike. I took him to the hospital. He's okay." She paused. "What are you doing here?"

"Came to see you—and Kodiak."

"You've seen me."

"You're acting like a hardboot. What's the matter?"

"I don't know where Kodiak is. He's not in his stall."

"Maybe Laura took him out." Grace ran her fingers through her hair. "I told her I didn't know if I'd get out here today." She paused. "Want me to help you muck stalls? You probably should take it easy."

"The kids will do it. I've got to call Harmon about my suggestion to the Fincastles. I'm trying to make this deal work. You'll have to excuse me."

"I'll make myself useful."

Cig bit her lip. She wanted to take on Grace when *she* was calling the shots. Having her sister come over unannounced—not that she needed to announce herself, she never did—put her off balance. She knew she was fishing for excuses. It didn't matter when she took out after Grace. It mattered that she did it. Pain and anger boiled inside her.

"Come up to the house."

"Okay." Grace tagged along thinking that Cig was a touch strange.

Once inside, Cig, reviving her courage, said, "I know you had an affair with Blackie and that he most likely died in the saddle, as they say."

A long scratchy silence followed.

Grace pressed her lips together. To her credit she replied, "It's true."

"It doesn't hurt me that he betrayed me. I'd gotten used to that. What hurts is that *you* betrayed me!"

"I didn't think of it that way." Grace's eyes moistened.

"Don't try to wriggle out of this." Cig pushed Grace into the living room. "Now sit down and shut up." Grace did as she was told. "Did you think I wouldn't care? Did you think I wouldn't find out? Did you think at all?"

Grace folded her hands on her lap, a curiously restrained gesture. "I don't what to say."

"That's convenient," came the sulfuric reply.

Suddenly Grace blazed. "I never loved you less."

"Oh balls."

"You didn't want him anymore."

"That didn't mean you could sleep with him." She rubbed her temples with her forefingers. "Did you love him?"

"No. He was great fun but I didn't love him."

"Did he love you?"

"I'm not sure Blackie loved anybody. You just shared his body for awhile." She paused, her lower lip trembling. "He loved his children. He did do that."

"So long as he didn't have to care for them. All this crap about equal child care is just that." She socked a sofa pillow, putting it behind her back. "As men go, he was responsible, I guess. I don't think they love children as we do. At bottom, they really don't. They can give their children up long before we can."

"He loved them differently."

"You certainly are defending him."

"No. Men love differently."

"Well, goddamned plenty of them can sure walk away from their kids."

"Those aren't real men. Those are guys who dumped their sperm somewhere. The point is, he was responsible. He paid the bills, even if he did get overextended. He didn't drink to excess, take drugs, or gamble. His weakness was women."

"Then why in God's name did you have an affair with him?"

Grace blubbered. "I don't know. It was so innocent in a way?"

"Innocent?" Cig bellowed.

Her voice rose to a thin pitch. "It was."

"Stop crying—if you don't I will knock your block off! You make me sick. You stab me in the back but you're the one sobbing your little traitor's heart out."

"It didn't mean anything. It was fun. You wouldn't understand. My God, Cig, you've been a faithful wife—ruthlessly faithful."

"Just what the hell is that supposed to mean?"

"You played the hardworking wife who endured infidelities, who stood by her man. You lapped up the respect it brought you."

"I'm supposed to fuck around like you?"

"A little experience never hurt." An edge crept into Grace's wavering voice.

"Well, I guess I just had to live through you."

Grace flared. "You're perfect. Pluperfect. I think Mom and Dad took away your allowance once. Everyone had you on a pedestal." She imitated a newscaster. "Pryor Chesterfield Deyhle, the child who can do no wrong. Straight As. Superior athlete. Always home by curfew. Gag me."

"Listen here, beauty queen—"

"Don't call me that!"

"You've traded on your looks since you were in kindergarten, you superficial shit."

"I traded on my looks because they're all I have. I am not a rocket scientist. With your brain, you could have done anything. So what did you do? You married John Blackwood. Your grades went to hell in college the minute you met him. You gave up."

"I did not give up. And I didn't always make straight As in high school."

"You made them enough times for Mom to wave your report card under my nose and ask why wasn't I more like my sister."

"What do you mean I gave up?"

"You could have been somebody."

"So could you. You didn't have to marry a meal ticket and move back home. I thought you would take New York by storm."

"No one takes New York by storm. It takes years to be discovered overnight and what would I be discovered at—having good manners at a party? Jeez, Cig, get real. I have no talent. I can't see much beyond tomorrow. Will was a good bet. He's still a good bet. I didn't know the price would be this high."

"So you add excitement to this dreary life of yours by seducing *my* husband?"

"Yes. Is that what you want me to say? Yes, yes, YES!"

"Revenge?"

"No. I really don't think so."

Cig calmed down. "A reasonable person would not sleep with her sister's husband. It's too close to home, forgive the old saw."

"Cig, you didn't want him anymore. Be honest."

"I wanted him. I didn't love him anymore. I couldn't trust him. I can't love someone I can't trust."

Grace burst into tears again. "And now you'll never trust me."

"Not around a man, no, I won't trust you. Of course, what have you got to worry about? I'm not going out with anyone. I probably never will."

"Everyone recently widowed says that."

"Thank you, Psychology 101." She threw a pillow at Grace's head who ducked. "What are you, some kind of nymphomaniac?"

"No. I like men. I don't sleep with every one of them."

"Grace, has it ever occurred to you that actions have consequences?"

"Yes—usually after the fact. I never have learned, 'Look before you leap,'" she ruefully confessed. "You know when Blackie and I started flirting, only flirting mind you, I didn't think it would lead anywhere. And when it did, I don't know, I didn't worry about it. Like I said, it seemed so innocent."

"You knew you were anything but innocent. You tell me everything. You lied about this."

"I didn't lie. I—withheld the truth."

"Liar."

"Oh, have it your way, Cig. You're always right! What would you have had me do—rush up and blab, 'Cig, Blackie and I kind of tumbled into it. Hope you don't mind. Really, it doesn't mean a thing.'"

"You could have stopped after the first time."

"I suppose I could—but I didn't. And Blackie had enough for everyone. You weren't cheated."

"That's the biggest bunch of bullshit I've ever heard in my entire life! Because he has enough energy to have sex with me, it's okay? What are we, stuffed olives? He just went around jamming in the pimento?"

"How do I know what he thought?"

"Did he say he loved you?"

Grace stalled. "He did but it wasn't romantic."

"I am going to throw up. Better. I'll throw up and rub your face in it."

Woodrow jumped off the bed upstairs. They could hear him.

"You've got to put that cat on a diet."

"Jesus, fuck my husband, lie to me, come into my house and complain that my cat is too fat. You're a real piece of work. The coup de grace."

"Touché." Grace put her head in her hands. "What we were doing didn't seem so awful at the time. I told you that. I didn't feel like I was sticking a knife in your back. Now, well, now I don't feel so good."

"Good. If I'm going to be miserable I'd like you to be positively rotten."

Grace lifted her head. "I don't think we're the first sisters to share a man."

"Great. You want to go on Oprah Winfrey with other siblings?"

"Thought you threw out your TV."

"How'd you know?"

"Laura called. She wanted to know if you should see a therapist."

"Because I threw away a goddamned television set?" Cig snorted.

"She also said you said *goddamned* a lot."

"Oh, for Christ's sake." Cig rose and rooted around in the big rosewood box on the coffee table. She fetched a pack of Lucky Strike unfiltered cigarettes.

"You gave those up!"

"I'm reviving the habit." She walked into the kitchen, lit the little white tobacco stick off the gas stove, clicked off the flame and leaned against the stove, inhaling that first soothing hit of nicotine. "God bless the Indians who first cultivated this weed."

"Thank God our family made its fortune in peanuts." Grace sniffed, having followed her into the kitchen. "I'd feel guilty if we'd made money in tobacco. 'Course we lost everything in 1865 so I guess it doesn't matter."

"We started out in tobacco like everyone else in the seventeenth century."

"How do you know?"

"I'm reading the Dehyle papers."

"I don't remember anything about tobacco."

"Doesn't matter."

"You know, it's bad for your lungs, it's bad for the kids' lungs, and you look like a 1940s movie star in drag."

"Tough. I need this cigarette. And since when have you become a health fascist?"

Grace barked, "I suppose I need to feel morally superior about something."

"That's a riveting insight."

"Oh, shut up, Cig, and sit down. Just don't blow that garbage in my face."

Cig circled her sister, ducked down, putting her face right in front of Grace's, letting out a mouthful of blue smoke. "Love you, baby Sis."

Grace coughed, put her hand to her throat, and sputtered, "You're such a bully. You always were a bully."

Cig hit the chair with a grunt. "I was bigger than the boys until tenth grade."

"You're still bigger than half of them. That's why you married Blackie. He was taller than you."

"I did not."

"Did so. You swore you'd never marry a man shorter than you were."

"I did not." Cig leaned back in her chair and put her boots on the table, which also disgusted Grace.

"You most certainly did. We were in your bedroom. It was your senior year in high school and John Root asked you to the prom. You said you wouldn't go with him because he was shorter than you."

"That's not why I didn't go with him. Georgette DeRosa broke up with him that weekend and he asked me as a second choice. I wasn't going to be his reserve date."

Grace twirled her fingers. "I don't remember it that way."

"Of course not. You don't remember the Ten Commandments either."

Grace clenched her fists. "You're so clever. You rarely let slip an opportunity to make me feel stupid."

"Yeah, well, you rarely let slip an opportunity to make me feel clumsy and plain."

"That is just not true."

"Grace, get real."

"When we were in high school the female model was petite and terminally cute. Every family sitcom had Miss Adorable in it. I'm smaller than you. Is that my fault? You grew into a statuesque woman. You're very good looking. I think Harleyetta West has had a crush on you for years." A gleeful glint of malice shone in Grace's eyes.

Cig laughed. She couldn't help it. She wanted to hate Grace, but that emotion fluctuated with the sheer enjoyment of her sister's company.

"Grace, Harleyetta does not have a crush on me and if she did she'd be barking up the wrong tree. I've got enough on my hands right now. In fact"—a flash of delicious malice crossed her face—"you probably slept with Blackie because of unresolved sexual conflicts over me."

Grace's mouth dropped open. "You have been watching those talk shows."

They both laughed so hard that Cig almost fell off her chair, the anger dissipating in the ritual of their relationship, the give and take of sisters.

Grace continued, "Lesbian incest. Oh I love it—but I didn't sleep with Blackie because of some unresolved sexual conflict. He just hit me that way."

"You went to bed with Frances Atkins though."

"How did you know that!"

"I'm not entirely stupid. You were spending too much time at the Kappa Kappa Gamma house way back when."

"Well . . ." Grace's voice trailed off. "I'm going to be dead a long time so I can't see denying myself any pleasure."

"Obviously. No wonder you're encouraging my daughter to have a jolly old time." Cig took a deep drag and rolled her eyes heavenward. "What'd you think?"

"About what?"

"About Frances Atkins."

"Oh, she was fabulous."

"She was drop-dead gorgeous, that's for sure."

"No one even had a clue. I mean if Frances thought anyone suspected for a single second she would have detonated. How'd you know?"

"I'm your sister. I *know* you."

"Then," Grace replied triumphantly, "you did know about Blackie and me."

"Did not."

"Did, too!"

Cig stubbed out the Lucky. "Okay, maybe I felt something, but that's not something you want to feel. I'm not immune to tension or hot looks. But you two covered your tracks, and since he screwed around all the time I'd stopped worrying about the latest. I didn't think it would be you, but you're right. If I had thought about it, if I had wanted to know, I'd have known."

"Feeling is knowing."

"Not in America it isn't. Everything has to be spoken before it's considered real. Spoken, hell, it's got to be shouted, advertised, picked over, and analyzed until there isn't a drop of surprise or originality left. Analysis is paralysis."

"Don't get cultural. I don't need a lecture. This is you and me. And I say feeling is knowing."

Cig threw up her hands. "You win. You're right."

"Jeez, you make me work hard."

"Tell me. Did you love him?"

"Not as much as I love you."

"It's not the same. We're blood. So you did love him? Tell me the rock-bottom truth."

Grace nodded, her eyes watery. "He liked champagne or trouble, whichever came first. He was irresistible." Cig nodded so Grace went on. "I knew he'd get tired of me eventually, and I sometimes think part of his attraction for me was the thrill of playing with fire. It's one thing to sleep with women other than your wife. It's another to sleep with your wife's sister. I knew all that—and I didn't care."

Cig again rubbed her temples. She stopped and was quiet for a bit. "He didn't give a damn about the rules. That was what made him so sexy, but it's what made living with him hell. I could never be with a man like that again no matter how exciting he was; but as a young woman, well—" She shrugged.

Grace sighed. "I should have known better but . . ." She trailed off then got a second wind. "I figured I'd get away with it or you'd overlook it. I never meant to hurt you. I wouldn't hurt you for the world."

"You did though." Cig sat up straight. "And you know what, Grace? It doesn't matter. People are tangled up with one another because of blood, love, money, wars. We can't unhook ourselves. We've got lessons to learn and we learn them on one another. I suppose everybody rips somebody even if they don't mean to do it. And I suppose my lesson is to let it go."

Grace pondered this. "You're talking Christian forgiveness."

"Call it what you like. If we don't learn to do it, I think we shrivel up into these little crisps of remembered wrongs, people hanging on to their tragedies, their angers, because it's all they have. Or they drink, take drugs, blot it out. I don't want to live that way. You hurt me. You *know* you hurt me. Nothing much we can do about it now. Done is done."

Grace stared at her sister. "Cig, you're a good woman, but I don't think I would have expected you to—"

"I had to grow up sometime, Grace—and so do you."

"What *happened* to you in the woods on Saturday?" Grace knew Cig as well as Cig knew Grace.

"If I told you, you'd never believe me. You'd have me committed."

"Try me."

She dragged deeply on her cigarette. She wanted to unburden herself but she was afraid. She finally decided that given what she and her sister had been through, if she couldn't talk to her she couldn't talk to anybody. "Got lost in the fog. I mean, I didn't know my butt from a banana. Fattail stayed right in front of me."

"That devil," Grace said, interrupting.

"He's a familiar to Pan, I swear it. Every now and then something would loom out of the fog. Like a party at Paynie Tyler's house."

"Down in Tidewater?" Grace's eyes widened.

"Except the cars were from the 1920s. And then I passed a Confederate sentry and, well, it sounds stark raving mad, but I rode back in time. All the way back to 1699. I can't tell you anything other than that, and that I believe I really was there. So put me away." She threw up her hands.

Grace's eyebrows knitted together. "That's not looney enough to warrant incarceration. Odd, yes, but not completely nuts. Movie stars write books about past lives and grow even richer."

"They're *supposed* to be nuts." Cig paused. "I learned a lot."

"Obviously. It doesn't matter if you were really there or not, does it? What matters is that something happened inside, something good."

"That's the truth." Cig reached for her sister's impeccably manicured hand. "Cut the crap. Leave Will . . . or make it work. You're traveling in circles, and time runs out faster than we can ever realize. Do the decent thing and set him free if you aren't going to love him. He can't be happy, not really."

"He doesn't even notice." Grace airily dismissed that thought.

"He does, too. Men aren't as stupid as women like to think. They just go about these problems differently."

"They retreat into work. They get ever so logical and controlling."

"So?" Cig arched an eyebrow. "He's not happy. You're not happy. You don't talk to one another."

"Can't."

"Won't."

"He's a block of wood."

"That's how he protects himself, and he learned it before he married you. If you can't talk to him or he won't talk to you then release him. You are never going to be happy living as you're living. Taking that risk with Blackie ought to have told you that. So either work it out with Will or set him free."

"I'm scared." Grace started to cry.

"Oh hell, Grace, what do you have to lose?"

Her head jerked up. "My house. My car. My social standing. I put in good time for that shit."

"That's what it is. Shit. You sold yourself cheap."

"I don't know if I've got the guts."

"You do."

"Men get vengeful when a woman leaves. If I could get him to leave I'd get a better deal. I could put a detective on him. Maybe he's fooling around." Grace was suddenly hopeful.

"Just go. Don't do that. We're talking about the inside of your life and you're hanging on to the outside. The outside isn't making you happy."

Grace wiped her eyes. "I'm a superficial slut, you know." She half-laughed. "Hell, I'll have to give up my membership at the country club."

"No, you won't. That'll be a negotiating point in the divorce. Grace, stop stalling. You know what I'm talking about."

"You want to know something really bizarre?" Grace's eyes filled again. "And it's ironic that you would mention Frances. I think I loved her, Cig. She couldn't give me social standing. She couldn't solve my problems and say, 'Honey, don't you worry about a thing.' You know, like men do. She could only give me herself. It frightened me so bad, I mean, just think about it."

"Doesn't frighten me."

"It's not the lesbian part of it." Grace raised her voice. "It's being with someone and not making a deal. Life with men is a deal."

"It doesn't have to be. That's how we were raised but it doesn't have to be that way. You know—I'll cook, honey, and you take out the garbage. We're raised to look at men as cash cows, beasts of burden."

"Yeah, I guess we are."

"Frances could only be what she was, a person in love with you. At least, I guess she was in love with you."

"Yeah. But her fear of being found out would have shot that relationship down in flames eventually. And I don't think Mother would have thrown me a bouquet either. So I was scared, too. God, I've been *stupid*." Grace got up and grabbed the Kleenex box off the shelf over the desk and rejoined Cig. "I really did sell myself short."

"We both did. I didn't think I had a right to happiness. Oh, I did when I first got married, but then when things went wrong I figured I was being punished for something. I deserved pain. It would make me a better person. I don't think it did. It shut me down is what it did."

"We both shut down, didn't we?" Grace blew her nose. "I was the party girl, you were the virtuous wife, but neither one of us was true." She stopped herself and blurted out, "You know, Cig, sex is like a drug, just like cocaine and bourbon."

"I'll have to try it sometime," Cig dryly replied.

"It's not worth it. I would give anything to feel love and lust instead of lust and a vague pull of attraction."

"You did for Blackie."

"Up to a point, but I saw what he did to you. I knew his pattern. I wasn't going to really let myself go. Kinda like a canter instead of a flat-out go-for-broke run. I want that feeling I have when we're on a scorching scent and I drop the reins on Kodiak. Oh, fly like the wind." Her eyes shone. "I feel so alive. I want to feel that with another human being."

"You have to give up the golden calf first."

Grace, like a drunk suddenly sober, folded her hands together. "I know. Now that it's out in the open I can't hide it anymore."

"Well, I can't either."

Wistfully Grace asked, "Do you think there's someone out there, someone *real*?"

"Yes—you. You're the real person. Once you get square with yourself you'll find someone else who's solid."

"If Will throws me out can I stay here?"

"Of course, you can."

"That is, if Harleyetta doesn't take the spare bedroom first." Grace grinned.

"She'll wind up with one of her AA buddies. And that's probably a good idea, too. Just think, you only have to deal with divorce, she's got to deal with divorce and alcoholism."

"I never thought of that." Grace paused. "But I've been so self-centered I haven't thought about what other people are going through. I kinda hate myself."

"Don't."

They sat, looking out the window together as the kids came back with the boarders from the trail ride.

"Cig, do you really believe you rode back in time?"

"Yeah, I do."

"What was it like?"

"That's a long story for a winter's night, but I'll tell you one thing."

"What's that?"

"I think for the most part they were better people than we are. There was a lot of love in those long-ago hearts."

44

As Cig accompanied Grace back down to the stable, she noticed Harleyetta's black Saab turbo pulling into the driveway. After parking next to Roberta's car, Harleyetta got out and walked into the barn. Cig flinched. She was in no mood to deal with Harley's marital problems. Glacial fatigue was setting in after all that drama with Grace.

Laura called from the center aisle, "Aunt Grace, Kodiak just threw a shoe. You better come have a look."

Harleyetta, bent over Kodiak's left hind hoof, grunted when Grace and Cig arrived. She put the hoof down.

"Hi," Grace said.

"Hi." A cool tone crept into Harleyetta's voice. "How you doing, Cig?" She warmed.

"Worn out but okay."

Grace bent over, picked up the hoof. "Hey," she admonished Kodiak, who thought it would be sweet revenge to lean on his mistress. He twisted his big head, looked her up and down then looked away.

"He's got your number, Aunt Grace." Laura giggled.

"My number is I pay his grocery bill. Isn't that right, you big brute?"

Kodiak sighed, not looking back again. Humans could be so very rude sometimes.

"It's not too bad, but a little hoof wall did come off." Laura handed Grace the shoe, twisted like an iron pretzel.

"How could he do this to me, right before the hunter pace?"

"Sheer meanness." Cig leaned against the wall.

Roberta moseyed over. Not that she had much to suggest as Roberta was a novice, not a horsewoman, but she was curious. "Will he be lame?"

"No." Grace put the hoof down. "I just want to get a shoe on that as soon as possible because I can't miss any practice time and neither can he," she said to Laura as Hunter walked into the barn from the other direction. "Call Nick Nichols, do you mind?"

"No."

"Ask him if he'll make a special trip. He's the best, and I don't want anyone else fooling around with Kodiak."

"Already did." Hunter joined them.

"You should have left a note on the board." Laura pouted.

"Chill out. I just did it. Like two seconds ago before I threw hay out to the field boarders. I was coming in to tell you."

"Oh."

"Thank you, Hunter. Will Nick be coming on out?"

"Oh, sure." Hunter climbed the ladder to the hayloft.

"Don't throw down hay yet. I want to brush out Go To in his stall. He'll be a pig."

Hunter hunkered down, peering over the edge of the hayloft. "Only for you will I alter my schedule, run with military precision. And if you'll lend me ten dollar." He emphasized the singular, *dollar.*

Instantly suspicious, Laura growled, "You spent your money already?"

Cig jumped in, too. "Hunter, this better be good."

"I lost my physics book and had to buy a new one, no kidding."

"Bullshit, Hunter. You took out Beryl Smith for lunch, I heard about it." Laura spoiled for a fight. She needed money, too, and she was mad he'd gotten extra from their mother.

"I didn't take her out. I went over to the No Name Café for one whole minute after school, and she was there. I really did lose my physics book. Go look in the truck. There's a brand new book. I thought you liked Beryl Smith?"

"Bow-head," came the tart reply.

Grace held up her hand as if asking a question. "What in the world is a bow-head?"

Hunter slid down the ladder, his heels on the outside.

Laura explained. "A girl, usually blond, who wears bows at the back of her head. Prep you to death. Of course at Christmas they wear red-and-green bows. Just Hunter's type."

"Jealous." Hunter sailed by, picked up a bucket and filled it with water. "I know they're not yours, you like jockettes."

"I like girls with brains."

"That's quite enough." Cig glared. She wasn't ready for lesbian banter.

Harleyetta and Roberta observed this exchange with fascination.

Grace patted Kodiak on the rear, took him out of the crossties, and led him back to his stall.

Harleyetta followed as Roberta returned to Reebok, whose mind was concentrating solely on the fact that it was close to feeding time.

"So who are you doing the hunter pace with?" Harleyetta asked Grace.

"Agnes Clark and Carol Easter."

"Good team." Harleyetta sucked on a piece of straw. "Binky and I were going out with Bill Dominquez but now I don't know if Binky will do it. He's being a prime grade one asshole. Well, I'll see if Jack Eicher will ride in it if he can get off work."

"Guess you heard Binky wrecked your Harley," Grace bluntly replied.

"I heard. I can't remember what I ever saw in him. There must have been something good about him. What was it?"

"The blind lust of youth. I mean, when you fall in love your brains fall out your underpants. Ask David Wheeler."

Harleyetta stopped then said, "Did his brains fall out of his pants?"

"No," Grace replied. "See if he wants to do the hunter pace with you—or try Jim Craig. He's always good company."

"That's an idea." Harleyetta took Kodiak's halter and lead shank as Grace handed it to her from inside the stall.

"I'm going with my gruesome twosome." Cig pointed to her off-spring.

"Gruesome? You're the one who threw the television into the trash," Laura came back at her.

"Laura." Grace shot her a stare.

"Well, she did."

"Next to go will be the goddamned fax machine," Cig said.

"Three cheers for you." Harleyetta shifted her weight, then asked, "Think I could board Gypsy out here?"

"You sure can." Hunter stepped forward. "Stall board or field board?"

"Field board. I don't think I can swing stall board on a nurse's salary."

"Oh, soak that son-of-a-bitch for all he's worth," Grace advised as Roberta peeped through the bars of her stall.

"You getting divorced, Harley?" Roberta asked.

"Yes, and I don't care who knows it. The way everyone talks in this town they'll have me pregnant by four different men by nightfall."

"I'm sorry," Roberta sympathized as Cig took a bridle off a tack hook to clean.

"Over the divorce or the gossip?" Grace closed the stall door behind her.

Hunter and Laura watched. They were learning how petty divorce could get.

"Neither. If they're talking about me they're giving someone else a rest. Like you, for instance." Harleyetta winged one straight at Grace.

"I never said I walked on water." Grace sniffed. "But at least I was sober when I committed my sins."

"And close to home, too, Grace." Harleyetta's voice had an edge.

Roberta, frozen in delight, watched.

"Shut up, Harleyetta," Grace warned.

"Give it a rest, you two," Cig wearily said.

"Why should I shut up? Grace has flounced around like Miss Mother Superior since I was in grade school. So my father loved Harleys. We weren't white trash, and you weren't Grace of Monaco."

"If you weren't white trash you gave a passing good imitation," Grace growled through her teeth.

"You and Will were kind enough to accept Binky's money for the children's wing at the hospital. You take the money and then make fun of me behind my back."

"It was never your money, Harley. The Wests have been working on that fortune since the earth was cooling. I think Binky married you to get even with his father, who wanted him to marry a—a bow-head."

The others watched, dumbfounded.

"Well, I'm taking your advice. Some of that West fortune will be mine. Now that you put it in those terms I really will fight for it, but you can take your arrogance and shove it up your butt. I was in the E.R. the night they brought Blackie in. Besides which—the whole town knew."

"Will you shut the hell up!" The chords stood out on Grace's neck because she was sure that Harleyetta had forgotten about Hunter and Laura.

She had.

Cig, however, had not. "Harley," she reached out and tapped Harleyetta on the back, "you might want to have this discussion somewhere else."

"Discussion! This is character assassination," Grace snapped.

"You don't have enough character to assassinate, Grace."

"Harley, have you forgotten that Hunter and Laura are here? There's no call for them to hear this." Roberta, trying to help Cig, tugged on Harleyetta's sleeve.

Harleyetta blinked for a minute. The message wasn't filtering through her anger.

"We knew Harleyetta was in the emergency room," Laura said, amazed at this flameout between her aunt and Harleyetta.

"And that's quite enough." Grace sounded like a Sunday school teacher who found out the kids had peashooters.

If she'd not said that, in such a grating tone, Hunter and Laura might have let it go, figuring it was a personality clash between two people who never did cotton to one another.

"Aunt Grace, what do you mean?" Laura's eyes looked deep into those of the woman who could have been her older double.

"Nothing. I'm going home."

"Forget it, Laura," her mother advised, her heart racing even though she was almost too tired to stand up.

Laura fired back, "What are you worried about?"

"I'm not worried, you are," came the unconvincing reply.

"Coward." Harleyetta spit out the word.

"Ladies, this serves no useful purpose. Maybe we should all count to ten and make an apology." Roberta squeezed between them.

"And let her sit in judgment of me? She was probably loaded when Blackie came into the E.R."

Harleyetta lunged for Grace, who sidestepped her as Cig, feeling a surge of adrenaline, grabbed her. "I have never, ever been drunk on the job."

"That's not what I heard." Grace mocked her in a singsong voice.

"You slept with your sister's husband and you think you can sit in judgment on me? ON ME!" Harleyetta took a swing at Grace, now bone white.

Cig, heart sinking fast, literally pulled a shrieking Harleyetta out of the barn. She pushed her into her Saab, shutting the door. Harleyetta slumped over the wheel for a moment then turned on the ignition and squealed out of there.

Hunter and Laura, dumbfounded, looked at Grace, who exploded in tears, collapsing on a hay bale, her head in her hands.

"Guess it's true," Hunter muttered to Laura.

Laura, shocked at her idol's downfall, said, "Aunt Grace, Aunt Grace, tell me the truth!"

45

The fire crackled as Laura sobbed on her mother's shoulder. They sat on the sofa. Hunter sat on the other side of his mother.

"She's horrible. I never want to see her again."

"You'll see her at the hunter pace." Cig patted Laura on the back.

"How can she show her face in public after what she's done?"

"Honey, everyone's known about it but us."

"That means they're all laughing at us."

"No, they're not. Most people have the sense to know it's no laughing matter. The only people who would laugh at a situation like this are hateful, spiteful shitheads."

"Well put, Mom." Hunter fought the lump in his throat. He swallowed. "Does everyone go through stuff like this?"

Cig nodded. "Same meat. Different gravy."

"Then I'm never going to bed with anyone. Not even Parry. Not if it ends like this." Laura wrapped her arms around her mother's neck.

"I didn't mean that everyone goes through something exactly like this, only that terrible things do happen. You deal with it."

"Dad didn't deal with anything," Hunter said.

"His way was to be a playboy, for lack of a better word. I'm not sure it solved anything, but it made him feel better. Hey, I'm not saying everyone learns how to handle pain or hardship, your father wasn't alone in escaping or trying to escape. A lot of folks start sucking on that bottle like Binky, or jam themselves full of drugs like Elvis."

Laura leaned against the pillow on the armrest. "Mom, why did Dad whore around? Do all men whore around? Is that the right word?"

"It'll do." Cig noticed how drawn Laura's features were, giving her a flash forward to Laura as an old woman. "I don't know why. He needed conquests. Some people, men and women, are like that."

"He had you." Hunter's jaw clamped shut.

She sighed. "We can analyze this and pull it apart. We can talk about it until the cows come home but it won't change anything. It doesn't matter anymore why your dad slept with every pretty woman he could lay his hands on. It doesn't even matter that he had a fling with Aunt Grace. He had his reasons and maybe he didn't even know them. I hope they made him happy."

"Mom, how can you say that?" Laura was amazed.

"Because there's so little real happiness in life, I can't see what good it does for me to begrudge him what he may have found."

"What about you, Mom?" Hunter's cheeks filled with color. "He was happy at your expense."

Cig cocked her head and considered that. "Conventional wisdom says yes. I'm not so sure."

"He was screwing around and you were home feeling miserable." Hunter sat up straight.

"How could I be miserable when I had you?" She reached over and touched his cheek. He fought back the tears. "You two were my happiness, and I don't mean that you're responsible for making me happy. I loved watching you grow up and I'll love watching you all my life."

Laura flung herself at her mother again, crying all over her shirt one more time. "Oh Mom, I love you."

Hunter didn't say anything. He nodded yes.

"Now look. Learn from my mistakes and your father's mistakes. It is true when you marry someone you take vows. You vow to forsake all others. You vow until death do you part. You vow in sickness and in health, for richer for poorer. Most everyone standing in front of the altar taking those vows means them but life plays tricks on you, tests you. If you hurt someone you pray they forgive you. If they hurt you, you forgive them."

"Did you forgive Dad?" Laura wanted to know.

"Not until, uh, yesterday."

"Why didn't you just punch his lights out?"

"Hunter, your father was six four."

"Coulda used a frying pan," Hunter replied.

"What good would it have done?"

"You would have hurt him on the outside as much as he was hurting you on the inside."

"Know something? That doesn't compute. Inside pain and outside pain have nothing in common." She took his hand. "Your father and I didn't make a good marriage. I was part of the marriage, too. I wasn't a pure victim. Maybe I drove him away or maybe I should have stood up to him long before I did. But I didn't. I kept to myself and I never asked for help. Don't make that mistake. If you feel terrible or you don't understand something, come to me or go to a friend. A true friend will listen and not tell you what you want to hear."

"I thought Aunt Grace was your true friend." Laura frowned.

"In her fashion—she was—is."

"I don't believe it." Laura crossed her arms over her chest. "I wouldn't forgive her and I wouldn't forgive Dad either. I mean, if Parry slept with someone else I'd never speak to her again."

"Thought you hadn't slept with her," Hunter noted.

"I haven't—I mean, if I did."

"Don't," Cig bluntly said.

"You can't tell me what to do. I'm an adult now."

"Oh God." Cig sighed. All animals needed to force the young to go out on their own. For humans, having a teenager fueled that process. You wanted to get rid of them even though you loved them.

"I am!"

"Laura, this isn't about you. It's about the fact that Mom's been stomped first by Dad and then by Aunt Grace." Hunter punctured her balloon.

"Don't pull that on me. You're not Mr. Mature. I know you carry condoms in your wallet."

He lunged for her across Cig's chest. She elbowed him even as she placed her hand on Laura's head.

"Enough!"

"He does—"

"You shut up. I mean it. Your brother's sex life is his own business."

"You're telling me not to sleep with Parry. My sex life is public. Oh great."

Count to ten, Cig told herself. "Laura, we've endured three hairy days. If you want to sleep with Parry, you will. I can't say that I understand this passion but we'll all work it out. Just please, go slow, calm down, and give me a break. All I need right now is for Lucinda Tetrick to roar through my front door and tell me my daughter has seduced her innocent flower."

"Huh?"

She reached for Laura's hand. "The Tetricks are not liberal people. When a family like that has a gay child they'll have to believe it's because someone *made* her that way."

"If Hunter gets Beryl pregnant it won't be a pretty picture. Her mother will buy an Uzi."

"Then be glad I carry condoms."

"You aren't helping," Cig warned.

The phone rang. Laura sprang up to get it.

"Sit down," Cig commanded. She rose, picked up the receiver and put it down. Before she could return to the sofa it rang again. "Goddammit to hell." Cig yanked the cord right out of the wall. "I can't stand it. Does anyone live in peace and quiet anymore?!"

The children, too shocked to reply, stared at Cig. A whole new side to Mom was being exposed.

"What are you two looking at?" Cig shouted.

"Mom, do you need medicine or something? A tranq?"

"No, I do not! I've been through hell and high water. I'm not jumping to other people's timetables. I don't want to hear ringing, beeping, clanging, honking, or whining!" She pointed her finger at them.

"I think I'll study." Laura rose.

"You have never wanted to study a day in your life. You don't want to hear what I have to say."

Prudently, Laura sat back down.

Cig plopped in a wing chair across from the sofa. "Listen to me. I am tired. I am—disoriented. My back hurts. I've gone fifteen rounds with my sister. Harleyetta blew up in the aisle and Grace melted her tires going home—because—and I know my sister—she's afraid Harley will tell Will and she's having a hard time facing you two."

Hunter's mouth dropped open.

"Days of Our Lives." Laura shook her head. "I hope Harleyetta does spill the beans. I hope Aunt Grace's nipples shrivel up and fall off."

"Laura." A soft reprimand was in Cig's fading voice.

"You know what's really weird?" Hunter hunched his shoulders.

"What?" Cig replied.

"I feel older than Aunt Grace."

"In many ways you are."

"You two are too easy on her," Laura said.

"Laura, the terrible thing about revenge is the time it takes. Leave her to heaven. Anyway, she's still my sister and I love her. It's hard sometimes but I love her."

Laura studied her mother then asked one more time, "But why did Dad do it? Why?"

Cig shrugged. "Karma?"

46

A light rain rattled on the fall leaves. Cig, reading, put aside the Deyhle chronicles to get out of bed and open the window.

She stuck her head out and a fine mist covered her face. The night, so inky she couldn't really see clouds, closed around her. She shut the window, thinking that three hundred summers, three hundred winters, lay buried in that night.

Peachpaws snoozed on the end of the bed. Woodrow lifted his head from his paws as he snuggled in the comforter.

Sliding back into the clean cotton sheets, Cig quickly found the warm spot where she'd been before.

"Woodrow, read with me."

He trilled, rolled over and showed lots of striped tummy.

She returned to the part where the family was divided on whether or not to stay loyal to the Crown. This decision, once made, committed the fortunes of the Deyhles to that of the rebels. Had the colonies lost the war, the men might have been hung as traitors. As it was, even though she hadn't gotten that far, she knew some of the men were killed at the Battle of Saratoga.

She recalled Margaret's face when she first told her America was an independent nation. Now she was reading about Margaret's grandsons fighting for that independence.

She wondered, for an instant, if Lionel had sent some of his Indians to kill Fitz, and they'd made a mistake. But he couldn't have known about the fog. She dismissed the idea.

She wondered, too, why he had been shot in front of the House of Burgesses. As no details were forthcoming in the family Bible or letters of the next generation she figured one deep winter day she'd drive down to William and Mary, invade the stacks of the library's history section and see if she could find out.

Did he fool around with another man's wife?

Did he cross someone in a business deal?

Was he late on a debt?

As there were few random acts of violence in those days, she knew there had to be a reason, however flimsy.

Her attention drifted back to the present. Laura's pain hurt her because she felt helpless. Nothing she could do would restore her daughter's innocence, faith and love for her deceased father and her beloved aunt.

Perhaps it was just as well that a mother couldn't totally protect her children from the ways of the world. They had to learn to survive and be self-sufficient emotionally as well as physically.

She dropped back on her pillow. She didn't remember life being this hard when she was their age. It certainly got harder later. Her father, not a cold man but a removed one, once said when she was red-eyed from crying over another of Blackie's infidelities, "You made your bed, now you must lie in it."

And so she did. The only life Cig could change was her own. If she had learned one thing from Margaret, Tom and Fitz, it was to celebrate life; the details of one's inconveniences and miseries were irrelevant.

She could see Margaret sliding the long peel under the bread, the bricks warm to the touch, the smell of the sweet burning hardwood mingled with the scent of fresh dough. She imagined the light in Tom's dark brown eyes, his broad shoulders and his bull-headedness sometimes, but most of all she remembered Fitz, the taste of his kiss. If she closed her eyes she could smell him. He was as close as a heartbeat. And he died trying to save her.

Cig buried her head in her pillow to muffle the sobs. There'd been enough emotion today. Laura and Hunter didn't need to hear her.

Woodrow, upset because Cig was upset, got up and licked her face. He reached out, patting her hair, purring loudly, offering his services. She wiped her eyes and rubbed his head. Gravely, he crawled up on her chest and rested his furry head under her chin, which only made her cry more. Love comes on four feet.

She felt the rumble of his purr throughout her body and then like a stiff wind clearing away a low-pressure system, she felt suddenly clear, crystal clear.

"My fears are petty," she whispered to Woodrow. "I'm afraid that our memories, our lives, our emotions, will be forgotten like Tom, Margaret, Fitz—even Lionel." She kissed his head as he crawled closer to her face. "Time erases nothing. Only the names change. We're all riding shotgun on history."

47

The Fincastles accepted the price hike on Harmon's place, if he would carry a small second mortgage. What seemed like a thousand phone calls later Cig iced down the deal.

A deluge had washed out the promise of tomorrow's hunting. With the memory of her disappearance so fresh, Cig was secretly relieved.

Max whipped up the sales staff with video management tapes. The flat voices, flat color, and droning emphasis on sell, sell, sell might have encouraged some staff, but Cig thought the tapes were about as innovative as Max and equally as repulsive.

She dreamed of those early plantations in the Tidewater. You carved out your acreage, your home, your life. A man like Max would have been sent packing.

After the staff meeting, she walked back to her office, picked up the multiple listing book to study when Jane rapped on the door. "Do you believe?"

Cig motioned for her to come in and shut the door. "He's maniacal. Too many elbows under the basket when he played center for UVA."

"Nothing sadder than an old jock trading on his name."

"Unless it's a young one."

"M-m-m. Hey, what do you get when you cross a Jehovah's Witness with an atheist?"

"I don't know." Cig sat on the edge of her desk.

"A person who knocks on your door for no apparent reason." Jane laughed.

At that moment Harmon Nestle knocked on the door, which made them both jump. Jane opened it, winked at Cig and left.

"Got my price." He shifted his chaw of tobacco into his other cheek.

"You sure did." Cig slid the papers over to him. He flourished a leaky ballpoint pen and signed.

"There."

"Congratulations, Harmon." She smiled.

He smiled back, pushed his hands in his pockets. "Know what I'm going to do with the money?"

"No."

"I'm buying a place in Naples, Florida, and when winter gets hateful they'll see my tail feathers around here. And you know what else?" Her rapt attention egged him on. "I am not inviting that smartass son-of-a-bitch brother of mine, no matter what. I don't give a damn if we have three ice storms like we did a few winters ago. He can freeze his ass. Not inviting Binky neither."

"Oh." Cig leaned forward as Binky and Harmon had been friends since Binky was a child, calling him "Uncle Harmon." Harmon was in his thirties at that time.

"Not right the way he's doing Harleyetta. She's working to improve herself and he hates her for it. He's clutching on to that bottle like it was momma's titty."

"Maybe he'll snap out of it."

"Damn fool will drink hisself to death. I made a big decision t'other day. Don't know why, just did. I don't want no one around me who ain't doin'. No drunks. No bums. No troublemakers. I heard all their stories, and they don't add up. Just made up my mind."

"Sounds good to me."

"Well, thanks, Cig. You did a good job." He held out his hand again, she shook it and he left.

She gathered up her papers and the phone rang.

"Hello."

"Will found out." Grace was sobbing.

"Oh shit."

"Did you tell him?"

"No, I'd never do that and you know it."

"Someone did." Grace's sobs downgraded to sniffles.

"Sit tight, you'll find out."

Later that evening, it was Cig who found out who spilled the beans: Laura. No matter how much Cig remonstrated with her, Laura was adamant that since Grace had hurt her mother, she was perfectly within her rights to give her a little of her own back. Hunter thought he'd seen and heard everything the last few days, but this knocked him over.

"You went to his office?" He repeated what he'd been told.

"Yep."

"Laura, honey, this doesn't solve anything." Cig was distraught.

Laura's eyes blazed. "It made me feel good."

"But honey, you felt good at someone else's expense."

"So did she!" Laura slammed her hand on the kitchen table where they were sitting.

"How are you going to face her?" Hunter rubbed his chin.

"Her? How can she face us? Hunter, whose side are you on?"

"Ours. I just . . ." His voice trailed off.

"You'll see her Saturday at the hunter pace," Cig reminded them both.

"If she dares show her face." Laura crossed her arms over her chest.

"Wonder if Harleyetta and Binky will be there, too? Everyone's losing their marbles. Maybe there's something in the water." Hunter couldn't understand the collapse of adult civility he'd been witnessing.

"Laura, pick up that phone, call your Aunt Grace and apologize for what you did."

"Never!"

"I'll call her then." Cig walked to the phone.

"Mom, don't. Don't."

"Jesus Christ, Laura, this kind of thing keeps the ball rolling. We can't change the past. Let's try to live a little better in the present."

"I'll never forgive her."

"Never say *never*," Hunter said.

"You shouldn't forgive her either," Laura shouted at her mother.

"Oh, honey, what good does it do to carry around all that anger? I'm too tired. In the long run it would hurt me more than it would hurt her."

"That's bullshit." Laura stomped up to her room.

Calling after her, Cig shouted, "You'll find out when you have to find out, I guess." Cig picked up the phone. It was dead. She remembered she had torn the cord out of the wall. She laughed. It was too absurd. She laughed until she cried. Hunter put his arms around her as she stood there, the phone still in her left hand.

"Mom, everything is a mess, isn't it?"

"I'm telling myself that destruction leads to construction." She hung up the phone then wiped her eyes.

"Mom, we can't live without a phone."

"The one in the barn works."

"How do I know you won't rip that one out like the others?"

She hugged him back hard then held him at arm's length. "There's always hope, Hunter."

"Huh?"

"Maybe I'll die of typhoid fever."

His face paled. "Don't say that."

"I'm sorry, honey. I guess we're still recovering from one death. We don't need two. I'm making fun of myself. I'm rebelling against the twentieth century."

"Is that part of your midlife crisis? I mean, am I going to act like this when I turn forty?"

"How do I know what you'll do? Nobody knows. I think midlife is an opportunity to make a grand fool out of yourself."

"You're succeeding, Mom." A smile crossed his lips.

She exhaled through her nostrils then laughed. "Finally—at something. Tell you one thing, son. I have learned one important lesson if nothing else."

"Yeah?"

"If you find yourself in a hole—stop digging."

48

A rattled Grace met Cig at the country club. A small stone room, used only occasionally for small parties, provided them with privacy.

"I'm so glad you called me." Grace started sniveling.

"I had to call from the barn. I ripped the phones out at the house."

Grace's eyebrows raised. "Cig, what's happening to you?" She paused. "What's happening to me?"

"You first."

Grace lingered over the decision to go first, then plunged in. "I don't want to hurt Will. He's devastated." Tears brimmed in her eyes. "I never thought he felt that much for me. Oh"—she exhaled violently—"the truth is, I never thought about anyone but *me*."

"Can you try to work it out with him?"

"If we can both stop crying. I almost brought him along but he asked Bill Dominquez to come over. He said he needs to talk to another man. Cig, I've been blind. He does love me."

"Women need to feel loved and men need to feel needed."

"Mom used to say that." Grace removed a Belgian handkerchief from her Botega Veneta purse.

"Make him feel needed again. Talk to him. If you want this marriage to work—it will."

"How can I live with him? How can I face him every day after what I've done—and him *knowing*?"

"That's love."

Grace buried her face in her hands. "I'm so ashamed."

"You're ashamed and vain."

"What do you mean?"

"It's your vanity that doesn't want to face Will. If you commit yourself to him you've got to surrender your vanity because he's seen the worst. You know, Grace, loving's pretty easy. It's letting someone love you that's hard."

Grace bawled some more. "I'm glad Mom's not alive. I couldn't face her either."

"She may not be alive but I bet she's here."

"Oh—" Grace cried harder.

"Come on, Sis."

Blowing her nose, Grace swallowed hard. "I do want my marriage to work."

Cig opened her hands, palms upward. "Then do it."

Grace squared her shoulders. "I will. God, I just hope I don't cry all the time. I can't stand it."

Cig shrugged.

Grace continued. "What about you? You're smashing TVs, tearing out telephones."

"I didn't smash the TV. I threw it out."

"Yes." Grace's voice was expectant.

"I hate this century. I hate the constant intrusions on my privacy. I want to go back to something *real*. A simple life."

"There's no simple life." Grace really did understand her sister's frustrations. She felt them herself sometimes although she'd never consciously expressed it in such a fashion. "Cig, no one has a simple life. All those Dehyles, Chesterfields, and Buckinghams who fought in World War I and the War Between the States and all those other wars—their lives weren't simple."

"They didn't have TV and telephones," Cig growled.

"No. And they didn't have laser surgery and vitamins either."

"Medical stuff. We traded quiet and understanding for knee surgery."

"What do you want to do, live like the Amish?"

"It's not a bad idea."

"It's not a good one—they don't foxhunt."

"Grace," Cig exploded, "I'm wrung out!"

"So am I—for different reasons. You told me I couldn't escape—well, number one sister, neither can you."

"I don't know if I can take one more day at Cartwell and McShane. I'll plunge us into poverty if I quit but I feel like I'll lose what's left of my mind if I stay."

"What would you like to do—if money weren't an object?"

"Work hard at the stable. Make it a real show barn. I love horses. It's the only thing I do well. Grace, I am just not cut out for business, at least, not the real estate business. Neither one of us was raised to seriously think about a career—I'm lost."

Grace pondered that. "I guess we weren't. We weren't discouraged from it but we weren't encouraged either. There was always going to be some man to take care of us."

"Yeah, and mine died—I had no idea how strung out he was."

"I know. I know."

"Grace, I have to work. But I'm unprepared. I don't like the way men do business—at least Max. Maybe other men are better."

"It's the difference between selling and another profession. Will doesn't think like that."

Cig fought back the tears. "I don't know what to do. I think the grief filled me up, you know, but now that it's passing I can look at my life. I'm totally lost."

They sat in silence.

"I'm going to get a cup of coffee. Want one? I'm parched." Grace stood up. "I'll be right back."

Returning in ten minutes with two cups of coffee, Grace handed one to Cig.

"Thanks."

"I called Will. I asked him to forgive me. He said he did. He said he was in this marriage, too, and he needed to get out of his bubble, as he put it. Said Bill helped him see his part in this."

"That's good news."

"Bill's still there with him."

"That's what friends are for."

"Boy, you sure don't know it until you need them. You'd be my friend even if you weren't my sister."

"Yeah, I think so, too. You're the expressive one. I'm the quiet one. We've got a good balance. When we were kids I let you do the talking."

"Well, I let you do the thinking." Grace stirred in the cream. "I love that color." She indicated the rich tan of coffee with cream. "Do you think you could feed yourself and get the kids through college if you had your hunter barn?"

"No way. The mortgage is taking me down. You know that."

"Cig, there are different kinds of responsibility. I asked Will. He agrees with me for all the right reasons. I can never pay up emotionally . . . but I can pay up. We're going to pay off your mortgage."

"What!" Cig had to put down her coffee cup or she would have spilled it.

"My reparations."

"I can't let you do that. I can't let *Will* do that."

"It's my money, too, remember? Sure, he's the doctor but who runs the house, writes the checks, organizes the social calendar, the wife stuff— ever think about what a man would have to pay if he hired for that labor?"

"No."

"Plenty. We're married. The money is our money. We're paying off your mortgage."

"No."

"Cig, wasn't it you who just said to me that loving someone is easier than letting them love you?" When Cig nodded Grace saluted her with her coffee cup. "Prepare to be loved."

"Love isn't money."

"Sometimes it is."

"I need to think about this."

"No, you don't. Abandon yourself to it. Just let it go and kick up your heels and—" She stopped. "Oh, Cig." She put down her cup, wrapping her arms around Cig's broad, heaving shoulders. She hadn't seen her sister cry like that since Blackie died.

49

∞

At seven thirty, the contestants had assembled at the huge 358-year-old white oak tree for which Oak Ridge was named. The temperature hovered at a crisp forty-five degrees, although by nine it would climb to the mid-fifties for sure.

The high-pressure system created startling blue skies and air so clean it was a pleasure to breathe. The fall colors radiated at their peak.

Grace, Harleyetta, and Binky were not speaking to one another. Laura seethed at the sight of her aunt. Grace attempted to speak to her, but Laura made a big show of turning her back and walking away. Everyone noticed, but they were too polite to act as though they had. Cig grabbed Laura by the scruff of the neck, marched her to the trailer tackroom and read her the riot act. Laura was smart enough to wring a concession from her, which was that Parry could spend the night. Cig promised to really get to know Parry, and Laura promised obedience.

The low buzz at the trailers when everyone was tacking up was proof enough that everyone was sharing the scoop, commenting on the scene.

Contestants lined up at a pine picnic table where they received their square white numbers, which they tied around their waists. David Wheeler returned with Jefferson Hunt contestants' numbers. The organizers were frantic. There were so many people. Contestants would arrive throughout the morning, since teams would go out at five-minute intervals as they were ready. Cig liked to ride a pace before the course was torn up. It meant she couldn't follow other hoofprints if she got lost, but she felt it was worth the risk.

Harleyetta and Binky shared a trailer and the truck. Unless one shot the other with a .38, they would have to continue to share until settlement, which would take six months if they were lucky. In the state of Virginia one could get a divorce in six months if no children were involved. There were no provisions about adults acting like children.

Binky, nervous about the situation and the competition, backed Whiskey off the trailer. Harleyetta watched.

"You could help me, Binky. You know Gypsy gets hyper if she's left alone on the trailer."

"Hey, you want to live without me, you can figure out your own goddamned way to get Gypsy off. I'm changing the locks in the barn and house, you bitch. You can live somewhere else if I'm not good enough for you."

"According to the law, that's my place, too, and I can do whatever I like."

"You sure can, and you can fuck yourself, too." He flashed his standard, stay-pressed smile as Gypsy pitched a fit in the trailer.

"You impotent toad!" she screamed.

"Impotent! How the hell would you know, Harleyetta? You never gave me a hard-on in your life." He pushed her onto the ground. Gypsy thought this was an excellent opportunity to dash off, which she did after realizing Harleyetta had unsnapped her tie in the trailer.

"Hunter!" Cig called to her son who immediately mounted up, taking off after Gypsy. His first task was to head her away from the road, Route 653. He'd try to grab the reins later.

Grace peeled off to help her nephew, which irritated Laura, who started to go as well.

"Laura, you stay right here with me."

"Mom!"

This lament instantly changed to gratitude as Laura and the rest of the early contestants witnessed Harleyetta rising to her feet and with one powerful kick of her booted foot laying into Binky's parts. He doubled over with a moan.

"I'd kick you in the balls if you had any." Harley dusted off her hands, turned her back on him and walked away.

That was her second mistake because once he had staggered to his feet he ran after her, laid both his hands on her shoulders and threw her hard to the ground, tumbling on top of her.

"I'll fix you right now, you walleyed—" He wrapped his hands around her throat, choking her.

Harleyetta, no wimp, couldn't get a knee up, couldn't roll him over. She was losing oxygen fast.

Cig unfurled her hunting whip, cracking it over Binky's head. It sounded like gunfire. He was so obsessed he paid no mind. She twirled the long thong with the green cracker end behind her then flicked it out, catching Binky hard on the side of the face. A big red welt appeared with a twinge of blood. He released his grip, and that fast Harleyetta rolled away, gasping, fighting for breath.

From the other side of his horse van David Wheeler emerged to tackle Binky, scrambling after Harley again. Slight though Binky was, his adrenaline level shot over the sun. Bill Dominquez gave David an assist tackle.

Roberta, appalled, hurried over to Harleyetta, whose throat showed a nifty set of fingerprints.

Hunter and Grace returned with Gypsy, stopping at the havoc. Neither one knew what to do with the horse or the humans.

"Binky, you are invited to leave," Cig commanded him.

"You goddamned women stick together. You even stick by your slut of a sister." He sniggered. "You know the *Lusitania* went down in eighteen minutes. Grace can do it in five."

"How would you know, Binky?" Grace coolly remarked.

"Because Blackie bragged you could suck the taillights off a Chevy. Said you had more suction than a jet engine."

No one said a word, but everyone looked at Cig then to Grace and back to Cig again.

Hunter dismounted, handing his reins to Grace, calmly walked up to Binky and then pasted him away with one right cross. Binky crumpled like a used Dixie cup. Then, just as calmly, Hunter returned to Tabasco, taking the reins from an amazed Grace.

David Wheeler, disgusted with Binky, took his hunting flask out of his pocket and poured the booze onto Binky's face. "Always said this whiskey wasn't fit to pour on a dog."

Binky blinked, licked his lips, opened his eyes. "Am I dead?"

"Only from the neck up," Grace told him.

He propped up on his elbows. "You know what's wrong with all of you? You take everything too seriously." He licked as much whiskey off his face as his tongue could reach. He was in his element. "So I give my soon-to-be-ex-wife-but-not-soon-enough a little push. Big deal. So I lose my temper. She loses hers. Big fucking deal. You all pretend like no one has any emotions, it's wrong to have them."

Harleyetta, voice hoarse, throat hurting, said, "It's not the having them, it's the showing them."

"Same difference," he grumbled, and unsteadily swayed to his feet. "I gave you some good times, Harley, gave you some rocks for your fingers, too."

"Binky, go home and get a grip on yourself. This is neither the time nor the place for this kind of thing." Cig kept her whip unfurled.

He squinted up at her. "You'll just take Harley's part."

"No, I won't just take Harley's part"—Cig's voice was even—"but we've got a hunter pace to ride. You're not helping our club."

He wiped his hands on his jacket flaps. "Jesus, Cig, there's more fornication, drinking, and carrying on in this hunt club than anywhere else in the country."

"Must be why we like it so much," David flatly said.

Binky reached inside his own coat pocket, pulled out a flask and took a long pull. "Hunter, you were right to hit me. No hard feelings."

"No hard feelings," Hunter said. The glances of the group subtly shifted to the boy, who became a man in their eyes.

"What about you, Grace?" He offered her his flask.

Grace waved it off. "I'm not overfond of being called a slut." She looked at the group. The pit dropped out of her stomach. She knew she had to do this. "But since you brought it up, I'll answer the charge. I was wrong, dead wrong. I publicly apologize. I hope you all will forgive me and help Cig, Hunter, Laura, Will, and me through this rough time."

"Takes two to tango." Cig defended her sister, which further astonished the club members who thought they'd seen and heard everything. Nothing like this had ever happened at a hunter pace.

Tears sprang to Grace's eyes. No one knew what to do until Cig spoke again. "God only knows what the rest of today will bring." That made people laugh. "Come on, teams, let's get ready."

50

By now the spectators spilled down the country lane onto the cut hay fields. Every hillock was dotted with clumps of people, many with binoculars. One hundred or more were inside the oval of the Oak Ridge racetrack, which was part of the course.

The hunter pace was divided into two divisions, optimum time, which was the time it would take to complete the course if hunting, and fastest time. Teams ran over obstacles such as one might encounter in the hunt field. Teams of riders selected which division in which to compete. Fastest time meant riders would go flat-out, usually over a shortened course. Most teams picked optimum time because members had to think a bit more while on the course. It was more challenging than running hard. Horses must negotiate stone walls, coops, post and rails, drop fences, water, and in-and-outs; usually one obstacle forced a team member to dismount, open a gate, let the others pass, then close the gate and mount up again. The bigger hunts might even put jump judges at the various obstacles.

The Oak Ridge hunter pace, held at the Oak Ridge Estate near the town of Shipman, had been steadily growing in popularity. Hundreds of people turned out. The weather was perfection and this contest was a preliminary to the granddaddy of hunter paces, the Orange County hunter pace near the Plains, Virginia. Teams from Pennsylvania, Maryland, North Carolina, Tennessee, Kentucky, and of course, Virginia, waited patiently for the starter to set them off, at five-minute intervals.

Grace, Agnes, and Carol were the first team to leave in the optimum time division. Cig, Hunter, and Laura followed at eight. Harleyetta, Bill, and David soon followed.

Cig figured the optimum time ought to be somewhere between one hour and one hour two minutes for the eight-mile course. She always gave her team time for mistakes.

People did pitch headfirst over jumps, the turf in front of the jumps could get mucky, and more than one horse refused to go through the swift running stream. A horse could throw a fit when threading through a herd of cattle. Sometimes the tension of competition unraveled even seasoned hunters. Like humans, some could take it and some couldn't.

Halfway through the course, as the Blackwood family trotted up a hill, they stopped for a moment to enjoy the panoramic view. The Blue Ridge Mountains lay west of them, rolling hills of golden oats lay to the east.

"My God, have you ever seen anything so beautiful?" Cig exclaimed.

"Remember what Dad used to say?" Hunter smiled as he sniffed the odor of rich earth and turning leaves. "All foxhunters go to hell because we've had our heaven on earth."

"Hey, there's the flag over there." Laura, the navigator of the group, had been checking her map. "Come on, gang."

They headed toward the red flag. Cig led, setting the pace, a brisk trot, and keeping time. Laura, in the middle position, kept charge of the maps and direction—she had a terrific sense of direction—and Hunter brought up the rear. He also kept a lookout to see if anyone was gaining on them. He was the anchor.

A triple combination lay dead ahead. The first jump was a tiger trap, one stride to a coop in a fence line, and then a solid railroad tie jump in yet another fence line. If you hit the first jump right the other two were a snap. Get your distance wrong and you could wind up stuck between jumps, trying to figure out how to get your horse up and over.

One, two, three, Full Throttle arched over with ease. He could pick his distances better than Cig, and she had the sense to stay out of his way. As soon as they were on the other side of the triple they moved into dense woods, single file.

"I reckon about a mile of this. How are we doing for time, Mom?"

"So far so good, but all these offshoot trails are confusing."

"I'll tell you when to turn," Laura confidently said.

Cig fought back her nervousness when a patch of ground fog rising off the fast-running Rucker's Run floated over the path. Once through that they were at the end of the woods and burst out into a big hay field.

"Okay, let's gallop to the top," she called back.

The three let their horses go, thundered up the hill where a copse of hardwoods burst into flames of orange, yellow, and red.

In the far distance they could see another team, too far away to identify their hunt colors, struggling with an in-and-out. Beyond that a crowd waited at the finish line.

Cig checked her watch. "I think we'd better keep up a trot here just in case there's a screw-up ahead. I mean, those guys could be at that in-and-out for days, you know what I mean?"

They turned hard right at the bottom of the field onto a rutted wagon lane, cleared a ditch and a bank jump, not often seen in these parts.

Heading for home, they easily threaded the in-and-out as the team that had been struggling far ahead of them crossed the finish line.

The finish involved circling the beautiful race track, jumping a small run-off ditch, then thundering along oat fields into hay meadows over the final obstacle, which was a thirty-six-foot-long coop in an old fence line. This was one of the reasons such a big crowd was gathered at the spot. It always provided moments some competitors would like to forget and no spectator ever would as the teams paced their horses to hit that long jump at exactly the same time. The finish line was fifty yards beyond the jump.

Cig checked her watch. If they stayed on pace they'd finish in one hour, one minute, and fifteen seconds.

They cantered across the hay fields checking their horses to keep them abreast. Laura adjusted her horse's stride about six strides from the coop. In a horizontal line they cleared the obstacle as one. The crowd hurrahed. As they crossed the finish line, Cig checked her watch. One hour, one minute, and sixteen seconds.

They patted one another on the back and accepted the cheers and calls from the crowd, many of whom they knew. Life may be chaos but this is perfect, Cig thought to herself.

Back at the trailer they checked the horses' legs, took off the tack and threw sweat sheets over their horses.

"How'd you do?" Cig asked as Grace came to the trailer.

"One hour two minutes flat."

Roaring around the race track was a team from Rose Tree Hunt in York County, Pennsylvania. The lead rider caught Cig's eye. There was something oddly familiar about him even at that distance. He plunged across the run-off ditch, his big gray snorting then shooting off. He called, laughing to his teammates, all men, as they synched up for the long coop. When they cleared the coop they doffed their silk toppers to the crowd, which applauded the elegant gesture.

"Fitz," Cig whispered.

"What, Mom?" Hunter watched the Rose Tree team.

"Nothing." Her face paled.

"Are you all right?" Grace noticed.

"Yes." Cig felt dizzy.

The handsome fellow, about forty, his red-golden curls shining in the October light, walked his gray over to his trailer, a green-and-gold rig. The lapels of his scarlet tailcoat bore the seal brown collar with gold piping of Rose Tree. He was laughing and joking with his teammates.

"Who is that?" Cig nodded in the direction of the man who looked like Fitz.

"I don't know," Grace replied.

"Carol," Cig called to Grace's teammate, "you know everyone. Who is that fellow with the blond curly hair?"

"Alex Maher. Widowed two years ago. Really a tragic thing. His wife and daughter were killed in a car wreck. A drunken driver ran a stoplight. Poor man, he nearly died himself of grief."

"Does he have—anyone?"

"Not that I know of, but then I'm not up on the Pennsylvania news. Would you like to meet him?"

"I expect I will," Cig half-whispered. Out of the corner of her eye she saw sauntering across the long coop a big red fox. Fattail.

Appearing to enjoy the tributes paid to him by the cheering crowd, he stared straight at Cig, sat down, and waited a moment, while flicking his tail. Then, as if satisfied, he got up, casually walking along the fence line before melting into the woods. Cig could have sworn he winked.

ABOUT THE AUTHOR

RITA MAE BROWN is Master of the Foxhounds at the Oak Ridge Fox Hunt Club in Nelson County, Virginia. She is the bestselling author of *Rubyfruit Jungle, In Her Day, Six of One, Southern Discomfort, Sudden Death, High Hearts, Bingo, Starting from Scratch: A Different Kind of Writers' Manual, Venus Envy,* and *Dolley: A Novel of Dolley Madison in Love and War.* She is the co-author, along with her cat, Sneaky Pie, of four Mrs. Murphy mysteries, including *Wish You Were Here, Rest in Pieces, Murder at Monticello,* and *Pay Dirt.* An Emmy-nominated screenwriter and a poet, she lives in Nelson County, Virginia.